Eternal Guardians Bundle

ALSO BY ELISABETH NAUGHTON

Eternal Guardians
(paranormal romance)
MARKED
ENTWINED
TEMPTED
ENRAPTURED
ENSLAVED
BOUND
TWISTED
RAVAGED
AWAKENED
UNCHAINED

Firebrand Series
(paranormal romance)
BOUND TO SEDUCTION
SLAVE TO PASSION
POSSESSED BY DESIRE

Against All Odds Series
(romantic suspense)
WAIT FOR ME
HOLD ON TO ME
MELT FOR ME

Aegis Series
(romantic suspense)
FIRST EXPOSURE
SINFUL SURRENDER
EXTREME MEASURES
LETHAL CONSEQUENCES
FATAL PURSUIT

Deadly Secrets Series

(romantic suspense)

REPRESSED

GONE

Stolen Series

(romantic suspense)

STOLEN FURY

STOLEN HEAT

STOLEN SEDUCTION

STOLEN CHANCES

Eternal Guardians Bundle

3 Stories by

Elisabeth Naughton

Ravaged
Unchained
Hunted

1001 Dark Nights

EVIL EYE
CONCEPTS

Eternal Guardians Bundle: 3 Stories by Elisabeth Naughton
ISBN: 978-1-948050-45-6

Published by Evil Eye Concepts, Incorporated

TABLE OF CONTENTS

ONE THOUSAND AND ONE DARK NIGHTS

Once upon a time, in the future…

I was a student fascinated with stories and learning. I studied philosophy, poetry, history, the occult, and the art and science of love and magic. I had a vast library at my father's home and collected thousands of volumes of fantastic tales.

I learned all about ancient races and bygone times. About myths and legends and dreams of all people through the millennium. And the more I read the stronger my imagination grew until I discovered that I was able to travel into the stories... to actually become part of them.

I wish I could say that I listened to my teacher and respected my gift, as I ought to have. If I had, I would not be telling you this tale now.
But I was foolhardy and confused, showing off with bravery.

One afternoon, curious about the myth of the Arabian Nights, I traveled back to ancient Persia to see for myself if it was true that every day Shahryar (Persian: شهریار, "king") married a new virgin, and then sent yesterday's wife to be beheaded. It was written and I had read, that by the time he met Scheherazade, the vizier's daughter, he'd killed one thousand women.

Something went wrong with my efforts. I arrived in the midst of the story and somehow exchanged places with Scheherazade – a phenomena that had never occurred before and that still to this day, I cannot explain.

Now I am trapped in that ancient past. I have taken on Scheherazade's life and the only way I can protect myself and stay alive is to do what she did to protect herself and stay alive.

Every night the King calls for me and listens as I spin tales. And when the evening ends and dawn breaks, I stop at a point that leaves him breathless and yearning for more. And so the King spares my life for one more day, so that he might hear the rest of my dark tale.

As soon as I finish a story... I begin a new one... like the one that you, dear reader, have before you now.

RAVAGED

An Eternal Guardians Novella

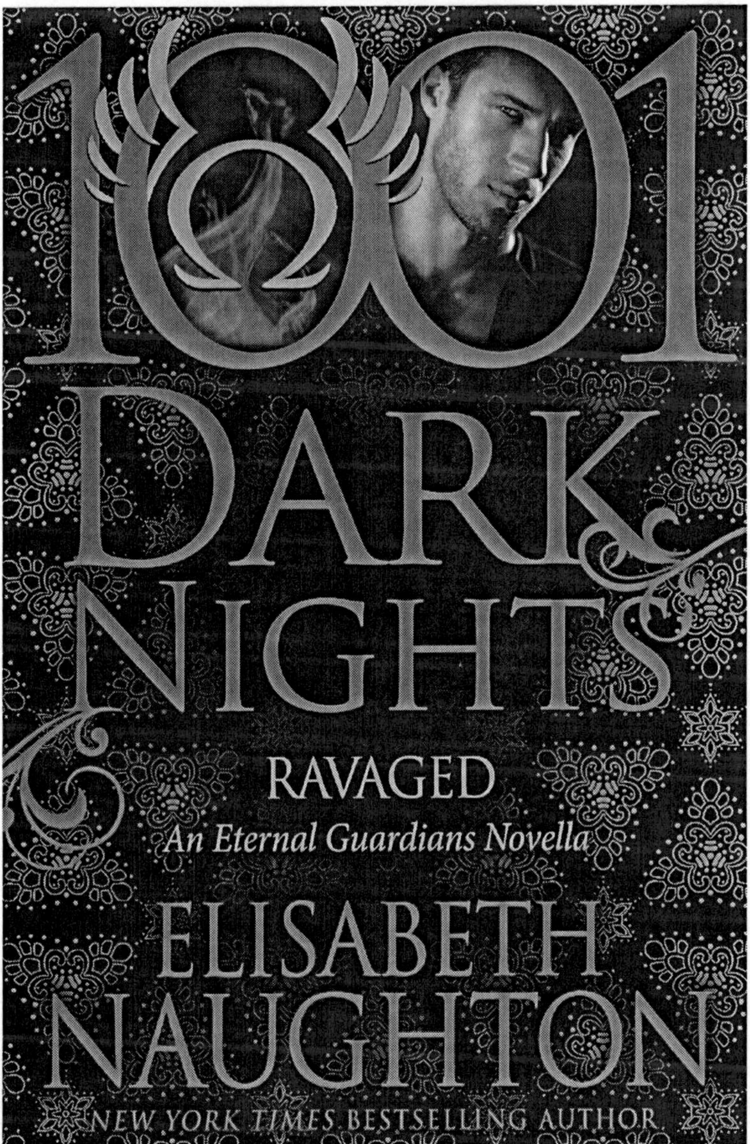

“There will be killing till the score is paid.”

— Homer, *The Odyssey*

CHAPTER ONE

Time was irrelevant on Olympus. Something Daphne was grateful for today.

The sun set low on the horizon behind the shimmering white marble of Zeus's palace as she lifted the magical bow and arrow all Sirens wielded, pulled the string back for the umpteenth time, and zeroed in on her target a hundred yards away. Holding her breath, she released the string. A sting echoed in her finger, and she jerked her hand back and winced as the arrow flew through the air toward the trunk of a tree carved into the face of the god of the Underworld.

A *thwack* echoed across the space. The arrow grazed Hades's right earlobe.

Daphne frowned. She'd been at this for three hours and still couldn't hit the stupid god anywhere deadly, let alone between the eyes where she was supposed to tag him.

"Better." Sappheire, Athena's right-hand Siren and the leader of Zeus's female warrior army, nodded at Daphne's side. "You keep practicing and you'll get there."

Daphne wasn't so sure. All Sirens went through rigorous training in a variety of different areas—combat, seduction, warfare, strategy—and she'd passed each section with high marks from her trainers. But she couldn't take her final Siren vows until she conquered the marksmanship exam. And at the moment, her aim wasn't even close to one-hundred percent, which was why she was out here now, on the training field behind Siren headquarters, working on her shot long after the other recruits had retired to the mess hall for dinner. So far she'd failed the test three times. Until she could hit a target repeatedly dead center—without injuring herself—she was SOL. Which meant her dream of being a full-fledged Siren kept hovering in the distance, just out of reach.

"That's a nice thought," she said, lowering her bow and shaking out her hand. "I'm not sure how realistic it is, though."

"Persistence will pay off." Sappheire's luxuriously sleek mane—a mixture of blonde and chestnut and ginger locks—swayed as she turned Daphne's way, and those brilliant blue eyes for which she was named sparkled. "If this is your calling, it'll happen. Just don't give up."

Dressed in form-fitting black pants, a tight, black, low-cut tank that showed off her cleavage and muscular arms, and kick-ass stiletto boots that elongated her legs, Sappheire pressed the button at the end of her bow, shrinking the weapon down to a six-inch metal bar. She'd lost the leather breastplate and arm guards she usually wore in the field, but she still looked as menacing as any warrior. And not for the first time, Daphne was glad this Siren had taken a liking to her instead of harassing her as she did some of the other recruits.

Slipping the weapon into her boot, Sappheire added, "Athena's been watching you."

Watching her fail? Daphne winced. She wasn't sure she needed to know that, not when she already felt like a major loser.

Daphne shrank her own weapon. She was dressed the same as Sappheire—tight black pants, fitted black tank, crazy high boots it had taken her years to learn to walk in—but where Sappheire wore the outfit with confidence and grace, Daphne still felt awkward in the take-notice-of-me-now getup. "Well, if nothing else, I'm sure she's entertained."

"Perhaps." Sappheire peered back toward the white painted building of Siren headquarters, less stately and ornate than the structures on Olympus, but still intimidating. "I think you're being summoned."

Daphne's gaze followed as she slid her bow into her boot, then focused on two figures standing on the back porch of the building. One she knew on first glance. The goddess Athena and head of the Siren Order flicked her curly chestnut locks over her shoulder and waved her hand in a come-this-way move. She was striking and gorgeous and every bit the goddess Daphne had imagined her to be as a child. But it was the other figure that made Daphne's pulse skip. The seven-foot tall, dark-haired god at Athena's side, commanding all with just his stately presence.

Zeus.

"Don't stand there dumbfounded, girl." Sappheire nudged Daphne toward the building. "The last thing you want to do is keep the king of the gods waiting. Go already."

Right. The king of the gods...

Swallowing hard, Daphne put one foot in front of the other and headed for the building. Behind her, the sun dipped below Zeus's palace until the sky above was nothing but a warm pink glow, but she didn't even notice. She was suddenly too scared that Athena and Zeus had finally figured out she wasn't Siren material and were going to kick her out of the Order.

She stopped at the bottom of the steps and looked up at the gods. Steeled herself for the inevitable. "My king." She bowed, then nodded toward his companion. "My lady Athena. You called for me?"

Zeus, every bit as handsome and muscular and intimidating as always, rested his enormous hands on his hips and peered down at her. "She's not been altered."

"No," Athena replied. "This one did not require any special enhancements."

Heat rushed to Daphne's cheeks as Zeus's gaze rolled over her breasts, slid down her waist to the flare of her hips, then followed the line of her legs to her feet. She wondered if he remembered her. Doubted that he did. Though Zeus occasionally came to the training fields, he rarely paid her any attention. In fact, she'd bet he didn't even remember meeting her as a child.

Slowly, as if he could see through her clothing to her nakedness beneath, he raked his eyes back up her body until every inch of her skin was hot and trembling. "This is even her natural hair color?"

"Yes," Athena answered. "She was born with the dark mahogany locks. No makeover necessary."

"Hm...." The king of the gods moved down the three stone steps and circled Daphne. Her pulse shot into the stratosphere and her stomach caved in as he examined her from every angle. "Curvy. I like that. Nice ass, small waist." He stopped in front of her and stared at her tits, desire flaring hot in his black as sin eyes. "And these. Enticing."

Daphne kept her arms at her sides. Didn't flinch. Didn't show any response. But her nerves kicked up even higher. It was normal for her to react to an attractive male. All nymphs did. But this wasn't a male she was even the least bit interested in, and not for the first time she cursed her overly sexual lineage.

"Ahem." Athena cleared her throat. "The matter at hand?"

Scowling, Zeus turned to look up at the goddess. "Seduction training?"

"Completed," Athena answered. "She received high marks from her instructor."

Zeus looked back at Daphne, and once again, his lusty gaze scalded her body. "I'm sure she did. She's a purebred Naiad. The spitting image of her mother."

So he did remember her. Images of her mother and the day Daphne had lost her filled Daphne's mind and tugged at the heart she kept carefully closed off.

"Marksmanship has proven to be a limitation for her." Athena moved to stand at Zeus's side and crossed her arms over her chest in a clearly perturbed manner. "If you'd rather see some of the others—"

"No." Zeus held up a hand but didn't once look away from Daphne. "This one will do. Tell me, female, have you taken a new name since being on Olympus?"

They were finally talking to her. Daphne had no idea what was going on, but so far it didn't sound as if they were going to kick her out of the training class. And as much as she hated the mention of her mother, especially in combination with Zeus's lusty looks, she knew the probability of the god-king propositioning her was slim. She wasn't her mother, even if she did resemble her. And Sirens, thanks to Athena, were the only females that were off limits to Zeus. "No, my king. I go by my given name, Daphne."

"Ah, named after the nymph who was rescued from my son Apollo's unwanted advances and changed into a laurel tree. Tell me, Daphne, do you wish to become a laurel tree like your namesake?"

"No, my king."

"I should hope not. Your skills would be extremely wasted in tree form." He clasped his hands behind his back and eyed her carefully. "Sappheire has had nothing but good things to say about you, and so far your training scores have been stellar. Aside from marksmanship, that is."

"I'm improving," Daphne said quickly. "I'm working very hard. If you just give me a little more time—"

"Relax." Zeus held up a hand. "What we need from you does not involve marksmanship."

Daphne's gaze darted between Zeus and Athena. "What you need from me?"

Athena shot a frustrated look at Zeus, but he didn't bother to glance her way. "We're in need of a Siren with your talents for a special mission. Are you interested?"

She had no idea what kind of mission they were talking about, but something in her gut said never to say no to the king of the gods. "Yes, of course."

"She's too naïve," Athena mumbled.

"That's exactly why we're going to use her." Zeus's eyes flashed. "You've heard of the rogue Argonaut loose in the human realm? The one they call Ari?"

Daphne's mind skipped over snippets of gossip she'd heard from her Siren sisters. "We all have. He's a monster."

"Yes, he is." Zeus's jaw clenched. "A very dangerous monster that needs to be stopped. Unfortunately, our conventional attempts at dealing with him have not worked. Which is where you come in. We want to send you in undercover for the Order."

Daphne stared at the god's face for several seconds, sure she had to have heard him wrong. "Me? But I-I'm not even a Siren yet. I haven't taken my final vows. I'm—"

"You are a nymph. A voluptuous, alluring nymph, like your mother. Aristokles has but one weakness: sexy, vulnerable nymphs. You will pretend to be in jeopardy, let him take you back to his lair, and when he least expects it, kill him."

Daphne's heart beat hard, and her hands grew sweaty. This was a suicide mission. She'd heard horror stories about the crazed Argonaut and what he liked to do to Sirens. "But...my king...he tortures and kills Sirens. I'll not make it past—"

"You are not a full Siren yet," Athena cut in. "You have not been inducted, you do not bear the marking, and because of your nymph heritage, your body was never altered. He will not sense that you are a Siren, because you are not one...yet."

"If you succeed in this mission, however," Zeus added, "you will be inducted immediately upon your return. Regardless of your marksmanship scores."

Daphne's pulse roared in her head. This was her chance to belong. To finally be one of them. Her stomach swirled with excitement and apprehension. "Wh-what would I need to do?"

"Kill him, of course," Zeus answered. "But before you do that, I need confirmation of something. I suspect the Argonaut has a very special marking on his body. Not the Argonaut markings on his forearms. This is different. Before he's terminated, I need you to search his entire body and either prove or disprove the appearance of the marking."

"What kind of marking?" Daphne asked.

Zeus glanced toward Athena. A silent look passed between the two gods before Zeus refocused on Daphne. "We're not sure. But the marking disappears at the time of death, so you cannot kill him and then look for it. You must find it while he is alive."

So all she had to do was get close enough to the mass-murdering psycho to check every inch of his skin for some unknown marking. Yeah. That sounded easy.

Not.

"I-I'm not sure how I would do that," Daphne said hesitantly.

"This is where your nymph background comes in handy." Zeus lifted his brows in a "duh, it's easy" move. "Use your seduction skills. Charm him. Get him to drop his guard. Earn his trust so he least suspects your mission."

Daphne's eyes widened. "You don't mean—"

"Yes, you'll have to fuck him," Athena said. "Probably several times." An irritated expression crossed the goddess's face. "You sailed through seduction training, Daphne. This shouldn't be that difficult for you."

Unease rippled through Daphne. She'd only been twenty when she'd been plucked from her foster home and brought to Olympus to train with the Sirens. Barely old enough to come into her sexuality, and the males she'd fooled around with as a teenager didn't count. Yes, she'd made it through seduction training easily, but only because she'd had an amazing instructor, a minor god who hadn't forced her. One who'd taken plenty of time to teach her about her own body and the powers of sex. That didn't mean she had any real experience seducing males—she'd been here for seven years, for crying out loud. And she had zero experience with savages like the psycho Argonaut Aristokles.

"We need an answer," Zeus said. "Either you are with us—"

"Or you are without us," Athena finished.

Daphne's gaze slid from one god to the other. She knew what they were saying. Either she did this and became a full-fledged Siren, or she didn't and was banished from the Order forever.

"Well?" Zeus asked.

Daphne bit her lip and nodded. Then prayed she made it through this alive. "I'll do it."

CHAPTER TWO

"This is as good a place as any." Sappheire nodded toward the log resting along the edge of a small stream in the mountains of the Snoqualmie National Forest.

"Here?" Shivering in the cool, damp air, Daphne crossed her arms over her belly and rubbed her biceps to stimulate blood flow. There was nothing but trees and moss and a scattering of snow in the dark forest of Northern Washington for as far as she could see. Nothing to indicate anyone besides them was even in the area. "Are you sure?"

"His hunting patterns indicate he'll come through this region soon." Sappheire looked toward the redheaded Siren at her side. "Rhebekah, take her jacket."

Without a word, Rhebekah stepped forward, tugged the jacket from Daphne's shoulders, and pushed her to sit on the log.

Grunting, Daphne reached for the wood beneath her to keep from falling over. Her stomach swirled with apprehension as she looked up at Sappheire, waiting for some kind of reassurance—any kind of reassurance—from her mentor. But just as she'd done while they were preparing Daphne for this mission and while they'd traveled to this location, Sappheire refused to look at her or offer any words of advice.

That apprehension turned to a wave of fear. Did the Siren know something Daphne didn't? Had Zeus lied? Was this really—she swallowed hard—a suicide mission after all?

Daphne's mind spun with possibilities, but she couldn't come up with a legitimate reason for Zeus to have lied. He clearly wanted the Argonaut dead. Ari had been wreaking havoc on Sirens for years. Regardless of Zeus's connection to her mother, she had to make this work. But Zeus's order that Daphne find a mark on the Argonaut's body—a vague mark which he hadn't bothered to explain—sent another wave of worry rushing over her.

Stealing her nerves, Daphne looked from Sappheire to Rhebekah and back again, focusing on what came next, not what she had to do down the line. "But why would he be here? There are no Sirens in this area. Except for, well, us. He doesn't know we're here. He certainly didn't know we were coming."

Sappheire nodded toward Rhebekah. "It's time for us to leave."

"Wait." Daphne pushed quickly to her feet. "How will I know where to find him?"

"You'll not find him," Rhebekah answered. "He'll find you."

Before Daphne could protest again, the Sirens disappeared, flashing back to Olympus without her.

In the silence, Daphne shivered and lowered herself back to the log. As she wasn't a full-fledged Siren, she couldn't flash after them, which meant from here on out, she was on her own.

Glancing around the forest, she tried not to freak out. Dusk was quickly moving to dark. In a matter of minutes it would be pitch black, not even a moon to guide her.

She wrapped her arms around her waist and rubbed her bare skin in the hopes of scrubbing away the fear. The dress Athena had made her wear was flimsy and white, with tiny cap sleeves and a hem that barely hit mid-thigh. The matching shoes were nothing but ballet slippers. She knew the outfit was meant to be alluring, but no female in her right mind—nymph or not—would be caught out in the cold in this getup. And right now she was more worried about freezing to death than what any crazed Argonaut was doing out here in these woods.

Don't think about Aristokles. Think about what you need to do next.

She rubbed her arms again. Tried to think clearly. She had no coat, no blanket, nothing to stay warm, and no idea how long she'd be here. It could take hours for the psycho Argonaut to venture her way—*if* he was really out here. In the meantime, she needed to find shelter and a way to stay warm. Needed—

A howl echoed somewhere through the trees. She jerked in that direction, her heart rate shooting up even higher, sending blood pulsing through her veins.

Okay, maybe cold wasn't her biggest problem right now. Her Siren sisters hadn't just left her without a coat, they'd left her without a weapon to defend herself.

A twig cracked off to her right. Lurching to her feet, she scanned the ground and spotted a downed branch, as long and thick as a baseball bat. Grasping it in both hands, she swiveled toward the sound and slowly backed up, her hands shaking.

Long seconds passed. Finally, a rabbit jumped out of the brush, spotted her with big brown eyes, and quickly scurried away.

Daphne released a heavy breath and dropped the branch to the ground. She was flipping out for no reason. If that didn't prove she needed to pull it together, nothing did. She was a Siren, for crying out loud. Not a wimpy female.

Or...she would be. As soon as this mission was over.

A shiver rushed down her spine, dragging her awareness back to the cold once more.

Shelter. That's what she needed to focus on. Not some stupid, irrational fear that wasn't doing anything but making her nuts.

She straightened her spine and glanced around the forest again. The ground rose steadily to the north. Through the trees she could see what looked to be some kind of rock outcropping. Deciding that was her best bet, she headed in that direction. If she could find a cave, she could at least get out of the elements and decide what to do next.

The air grew progressively colder the closer she drew to the rocks. Rubbing her hands vigorously against the bare skin of her arms, she tried to keep her teeth from chattering as she picked her way around stones and branches and roots sticking out of the ground that bruised her feet in the silly shoes. Just as she moved past a boulder the size of a car, a growl echoed in the steadily darkening forest, drawing her feet to a sharp stop.

The hair on her nape stood straight. Her heart rate shot into the triple digits. Slowly, she turned in the direction she'd just come and stared in horror at the creature moving out from behind the rocks to stand in her path.

It was at least seven feet tall. A mixture of goat and lion and dog and human, with the body of a man, sharp teeth, horns, and glowing green eyes like something straight out of a nightmare.

A daemon. One of the Underworld's monsters. She stumbled

backward.

"Nymph." The daemon drew in a deep whiff and growled. "Now this is a treat. What is a nymph doing out in these woods all alone?"

Daphne's mouth fell open, but words wouldn't come.

Before she could think of an answer—before she could think of something to *do*—another daemon stepped out from behind the boulder and growled. "The nymph is mine."

Fear shot Daphne's heart straight into her throat. The first daemon turned to the second and roared a menacing, aggressive response. The second bared his fangs and lurched for the first. Bones and fists and claws clashed as the two tore into each other.

Daphne swiveled and ran. Made it ten feet into the trees before another daemon jumped out from behind an old growth Douglas fir, right in her path. She skidded to a stop. Tried to lurch out of the way. He roared, reached out with claws as sharp as knives, and caught her across the side and abdomen, sending her flying into the brush.

A burn like the heat of a thousand suns lanced her side. She smacked into a tree, then dropped to the ground with a thud. Pain spiraled through every inch of her body, but she knew she had to get up. Had to run. She clawed at the dirt and tried to stand, but the wound in her side gushed blood, twisting her to the ground in a cry of agony.

The daemon growled and advanced. With the forest spinning around her, Daphne looked for something—anything—close to use as a weapon. Her vision came and went. But through descending darkness, she spotted a rock the size of her fist with sharp edges.

She dug her fingers into the ground, used every ounce of strength she had left to crawl in that direction. Another roar echoed at her back. She whimpered through the pain and tried to move faster, but it was as if she were crawling through mud. Just when she was sure she would never get there, her hand closed around the rock. She tugged it close, then rolled to her back and stared in horror at the sight before her.

A man—no, not a man, she realized—an Argonaut, battled back not one, but all three advancing daemons. His shoulders were broad, his arms muscled, his waist tapered to strong legs. And he moved like a seasoned warrior, swinging the blade in his hand like a ninja swings nunchucks. She watched in disbelief as his blade sank deep, he pulled it free, then swung out and decapitated the first daemon before moving to the second and third. In a matter of seconds, the fight was over, as if the daemons were paper dolls rather than living, menacing monsters.

The Argonaut turned Daphne's way. Daphne's vision flickered, but one look was all it took to send her scrambling backward in a haze of pain. A nose that had been broken more than once. Puckered scars that covered the left side of his jaw, ran down his neck, and disappeared under the collar of his long-sleeved T-shirt. And mismatched eyes—one a brilliant blue, the other a deep green—blazing and focused directly on her as if she were the next threat.

The Argonaut kicked the daemon's body out of his way and marched toward her. Blood and some kind of vile green goo covered his clothing, and that wild, fevered look in his mismatched eyes told her he was no friend, not to her.

It was him. The crazy Argonaut.

Aristokles.

Fear caused her to jerk back, but her head hit something sharp, stopping her momentum. Pain shot across her scalp, and she cried out, but the sound gurgled in her throat. He knelt beside her and reached one bloody, dirt-streaked hand her way.

She gripped the rock tightly, but before she could lift it to protect herself, everything went black.

* * *

Ari carried the injured female into the living area of his home high in the mountains and laid her on the couch.

"Holy Hera," Silas said, grabbing a blanket from the back of a chair and laying it over her limp body. "She's a nymph. What in Hades was a nymph doing out in the wilds unprotected?"

"I don't know." Ari moved back as Silas knelt close and worked on the female. In his old life, Silas had tended to the sick and injured of his village. Now he tended to Ari, which Ari knew was the most thankless job on the planet. "I didn't seal the wounds. If it was an archdaemon who did this, I didn't want to make things worse."

"Smart." An archdaemon's claws held a dangerous poison that could prompt infection. Silas peeled the female's torn dress back over her ribs so he could see her wounds. "But the chances she was attacked by an archdaemon are slim. I'm gonna need rags and hydrogen peroxide from the kitchen."

It took several seconds for Ari to realize Silas was talking to him. Tearing his gaze away from the female, Ari turned out of the living room with its high-beamed ceiling, roaring fireplace, and leather furnishings and headed for the kitchen. He was still covered in blood and slime from his battle with those daemons, tracking mud through the house Silas worked hard to keep clean, but couldn't think about anything other than the nymph lying half dead in the other room.

Silas was right. There was no reason for a nymph to be alone in those woods. She'd clearly been running. From who though, he didn't know. Before he could stop it, Ari's mind tumbled back dozens of years to another nymph he'd found alone and injured in the wild. To a moment that had cursed his existence for all eternity.

His vision darkened, and a flood of emotions that would only mess with his control threatened to overwhelm him. But he slowly beat them back. This was the reason he chose to isolate himself. Because he was unpredictable. Because he'd been cursed by the gods. Because some days, he was as much a monster as the daemons he'd sworn to destroy.

"Ari! The rags! She's bleeding, man!"

The sound of Silas's voice penetrated Ari's consciousness. He grabbed the items Silas had asked for then moved back into the living room. After handing Silas the materials, he stepped away again and watched as Silas cleaned the wounds then held his hands over the female and used his sensing gift to search for infection.

Long seconds passed. Finally, Silas eased back on his heels and lowered his hands to his thighs. "It wasn't an archdaemon. You can seal these now."

When Ari didn't make a move forward, Silas turned to face him. "I can't do this part myself. You know that. It has to be you."

The claw marks across Silas's face seemed to dance in the firelight as he stared at Ari, waiting for a response.

Scowling, Silas pushed to his feet. He was tall—over six feet—with broad shoulders and sandy blond hair in need of a trim, but he was no match for Ari. Thanks to his link to the ancient Greek gods, Ari was taller, more muscular, bigger everywhere. And he was never intimidated.

Except now. Right now, Ari wished he was anywhere but in this room, not only near a nymph but being forced to touch one.

"She'll die if you don't do something," Silas said. "You know this."

Still Ari didn't move. Didn't trust himself near a nymph. Nymphs were as dangerous to him as Sirens. Nymphs left him just as unbalanced and reminded him of a life he'd left behind without a second look.

"You brought her here," Silas said, stepping forward. "You could have left her in the woods to die, but you didn't. She's just a female, Ari. Show her the same mercy you showed me."

Just a female... She was. Ari had used his gift to heal dozens of females *and* males over his years. This female was no different.

History tried to hold him back, but that damn duty inside pushed him forward. Silas stepped to the side as Ari moved toward the couch and looked down. The nymph's head was tipped his way on the throw pillow, long, dark lashes feathering her alabaster skin, her dirty hair falling over her bruised shoulder and the remnants of her bloody dress. But even injured and unconscious, Ari could tell that she was attractive. Alluring. A nymph created to torment any male who crossed her path.

A heat he hadn't felt in years stirred low in his belly. One he didn't like and definitely didn't want. The fastest way to get rid of her was to heal her. Then forget he'd ever stumbled across the female in the first place.

He lowered to his knee and avoided looking at her face or the swell of her breasts pushing against the thin, once-white fabric, and focused on the red, bleeding wounds. Laying his hands over the gashes, he focused his strength until heat and energy radiated from his palms, permeating the skin beneath and knitting the wounds back together.

The nymph didn't even stir, even though it was a process he knew caused intense pain. She laid still, her eyes closed, her body deep in sleep. Soft. Vulnerable. Minutes later, Ari lifted his hands and pushed to his feet, intent on getting as far from her as possible.

He stepped back from the couch, turned so he didn't have to look at her longer than necessary, and moved for the archway that led to his wing of rooms. "As soon as she's alert and able to travel, I want her gone."

"Ari." Silas sighed. "Maybe she's—"

"As soon as she's able," Ari repeated, not waiting to hear Silas's protest. He knew what Silas was thinking. That a female in the house might do him some good. But Ari knew only bad could ever come from this situation. "I'll not have her here disrupting my schedule. Not a minute longer, Silas. Get rid of her. That's an order."

He disappeared through the doorway, but at his back he heard Silas mutter, "Maybe a little disruption's what you need, dipshit."

CHAPTER THREE

Daphne blinked several times and tried to make sense of her surroundings. She definitely wasn't on Olympus.

Slowly, she pushed up on her arm, wincing at the sting in her side. A soft bed lay below her. An eerie gray light shone through the window across the room. Sitting back in the pillows, she glanced around the bedroom with its dark furnishings and high-beamed ceiling and tried to figure out where the heck she was.

Her memories were a foggy mess. She remembered talking with Athena and Zeus. Remembered being in the woods with Sappheire. Remembered those daemons showing up. Remembered running and being struck in the side. Remembered...

Her eyes grew wide as her mind flashed back to the warrior she'd seen battling those daemons. To his mismatched eyes. His wild look. And the way he'd focused on her as if she were his next victim.

Throwing back the covers, she pulled up the long shirt she was wearing and checked her side. Four thin, red lines crossed her skin from her hip to just beneath her breast.

Confusion tugged her brows together. She brushed her fingers over the sealed wounds that should have killed her and tried to remember what had happened but couldn't. Tried to figure out how long she'd been out of it but drew a complete blank.

Her gaze drifted to the bed beneath her, the floor, then finally to the window. Cringing at the pain in her side, she pushed to her feet. Her breath caught as she pulled back the curtain and gazed out at the snowy forest and acres of mountains that disappeared in a dark gray sky.

No other houses. No other signs of life. Just miles and miles of wilderness and snow as far as the eye could see.

Her heart pounded as she let go of the curtain and turned to look around the room again. The walls were made of logs. Dark, scuffed hardwood floors ran beneath her bare feet. The sleigh bed she'd been sleeping in was old but more than comforting.

Think, Daphne.

Her hands shook as she pressed them to her cheeks. The crazed Argonaut had obviously brought her here, wherever *here* was. He must have sensed she was a nymph. Zeus had said he had a weakness for nymphs, and that meant she was over her first hurdle—finding him and not getting killed. She wasn't sure how he'd healed her, but just the fact he'd bothered meant she was halfway to her goal. And that meant all she had to do next was make nice and…and seduce the psycho so she could complete the second half of her mission.

Feeling lightheaded, she lowered to the bed so her legs didn't go out from under her. Squeezing her shaking hands into fists against the comforter, she drew a deep breath then let it out. She could do this. She'd trained with the best, after all. And when it was done, she'd finally be a Siren. He was a monster, right? Just because he'd saved her from a horde of daemons didn't mean anything. It just meant Zeus was right and that his brain turned to mush near a nymph.

That she could use to her advantage. Rising again, she stepped toward the door only to realize she was wearing nothing but a male's white button-down shirt. The tails hit at her knees, and the sleeves were so long, they'd been rolled up several times to her wrists.

He'd changed her clothes. He'd seen her naked. Her stomach swirled with that realization.

That's not exactly a bad thing considering your mission.

Straightening her spine, she pulled the door open, then peered down a long, dark hallway. Sconces lit the passageway on both sides. Her stomach continued to toss and roll, but she moved as quietly as possible through the corridor. Doors opened on both sides of her, but she didn't look to see where they led. Her focus remained fixed on the light ahead and what she had to do next.

The hallway opened to a balcony that overlooked an enormous great room with more antique furnishings set near a giant stone fireplace that rose to the ceiling. Drawing to a stop at the railing, Daphne glanced over the empty space and tried not to be completely awed by the three-story windows that looked out over a wide deck and across a snowy valley. A frozen river meandered far below, and though she couldn't be sure, she had a feeling those black dots down there weren't people but elk or deer wandering across the frigid earth.

Her gaze drifted up and around. The enormous lodge-style structure seemed to be tucked into the side of a mountain and built on the edge of a cliff. The perfect place to wait and watch. If anyone tried to attack this place, they'd be spotted long before they could even mount an offense.

And that meant if things went bad for her, she wasn't getting out of here unseen.

Pushing down the unease, she headed for the curved staircase. Escaping was five steps down the line. After she completed her mission. When he was dead. Until then, she had other things to focus on.

A twinge in her side made her stop near the bottom step and draw another deep breath. She pressed her hand against the wounds and fought back the wave of nausea that seemed to want to pull her under.

So, okay, maybe she wasn't totally ready for seduction just yet. Her body was still clearly healing from that daemon attack. But she could find her target and at least see what was up. Flirt a little. Play the damsel in distress. And start this plan in motion.

Determination firmly in place, she wandered from one massive room to the next. An enormous kitchen opened to a dining area that led to an office and another set of curved stairs. Still finding no sign of him, she headed down the steps and slowed when she heard voices.

"Your first mistake was accepting my challenge," a deep male voice said. "Your second was turning your back on me."

A *thwack* echoed, then another male said, "You've been practicing."

"Damn right I've been practicing," the first responded. "I'm tired of getting my ass handed to me."

A chuckle echoed up the stairs.

Daphne stopped midway down the steps where she could see into the gigantic room below. This one wasn't furnished like the rooms above. It was wide and open, with dumbbells and weight-lifting equipment along one whole side. Tall windows looked out over another deck and the sweeping valley view, but what held her attention were the two males in the middle of the room, both dressed in nothing but low-riding, dark pants, both carved and muscular, both circling around each other with reddened fists and bruised faces.

The first she didn't recognize. He was tall and broad, with sandy blond hair, sharp blue eyes, and a series of scars across his face. But the second she knew in an instant. Dark hair, legs the size of tree trunks, the unique Greek lettering etched into his forearms, and a wild look across his features that said he'd locked on yet another target.

A trickle of blood ran from Aristokles's temple down his scarred cheek and neck, but he didn't seem to notice. A wicked grin curved his mouth as he continued to circle the other male. "It's about time. You've been getting soft doing all that housework."

Aristokles lunged forward, but the other male ducked out of the way, swiveled to avoid being nailed by the Argonaut's fist, then rolled across the floor. Popping to his feet, he kicked Aristokles's legs out from under him.

The Argonaut went down with a grunt, but before the male could pounce, Aristokles did a backward roll and jerked back to standing. "You've really been practicing. I guess it's time I stopped going easy on you and—"

As if he sensed her, the Argonaut's gaze darted toward the stairs and focused on Daphne. And in those mismatched eyes, interest immediately flared.

Daphne's first instinct was to shrink back into the logs behind her, but unfortunately she didn't possess the power of camouflage. Her second was to run, but her legs wouldn't let her. Because as the Argonaut's heated gaze washed over her, her traitorous body was already responding—her nipples pebbling beneath the thin cotton shirt, her belly warming and sending waves of heat straight between her legs, her skin craving a dangerous touch she shouldn't want.

Her breaths grew shallow, her head, light. But this was more than just responding to an attractive male. This was instant arousal with just one look. Arousal on a scale she'd never experienced before, not even with a god.

The male Aristokles had been sparing slammed his fist into the Argonaut's stomach. Aristokles pulled his gaze from Daphne, grunted, then wrapped his arms around his belly and doubled over.

The other male stood upright and turned toward the stairs with a surprised expression. "Ah, you're awake. We expected you'd sleep at least another day."

We. Daphne had no idea who he was or what that meant, and she wanted to ask, but her gaze darted right back to the Argonaut. Aristokles shot the male a hard look, then stood upright and crossed to the far side of the room. After swiping a towel over his face, he reached for a shirt from a bench near the wall, tugged it on, and muttered, "You know what to do."

The second male looked Aristokles's way, but the Argonaut didn't meet his gaze. Didn't even turn to look at Daphne again. Just disappeared through a doorway on the far side of the room and was gone.

The heat in Daphne's belly slowly cooled, and a shiver rushed down her spine.

"Sorry about that." The male turned toward her and grimaced. "He lacks basic social skills."

His words seemed to snap her out of the trance she'd fallen into. Daphne cleared her throat and gripped the banister at her side. "I..." No, that wasn't how she wanted to start this. She needed to play it cool. Whoever this guy was, hopefully he could help her. "Where am I?"

The male crossed to the bench and pulled on his own T-shirt. "Stonehill Hold. Don't worry. You're safe here. No daemons can get to us. And if they did"—he nodded toward the door Aristokles had exited through—"he'd sense them."

Sense them. Right. Argonauts could do that. One of their many awesome hunting skills, ironically bestowed on them by the very god who wanted Aristokles dead.

Remembering she needed to play the damsel in distress, Daphne brushed the hair out of her eyes. "Stonehill Hold? I've never heard of it."

"Not many have." He moved to the base of the stairs and looked up at her five steps above. "How do you feel?"

"Fine," she answered hesitantly. "Tired." When his gaze dropped to her side, she remembered her wounds. "Sore."

"I'm sure you are."

Daphne couldn't help but notice the angled scars that ran across his features. A series of thin, white lines that stretched from one cheek, across his nose, to the opposite jaw. Claw marks, she realized.

She wanted to ask about them but decided now wasn't the time. Instead, she tried to figure out who he was. He wasn't an Argonaut like Aristokles. She would have picked up on that. As an otherworldly creature, she had the power to sense a being's race, and she already knew he wasn't a god or a nymph like her. But to be here with the psycho Argonaut and not be intimidated meant he had to be someone important.

Her eyes widened when his lineage finally registered. "You're a half breed."

He moved up the steps toward her. "We prefer the term Misos."

Misos. The race of half-human, half-Argolean beings. Argolea was the realm established for the descendants of the ancient Greek heroes, a utopia of sorts, one Daphne had studied during her time with the Sirens. But many Argoleans didn't remain there. They often traveled back and forth between the human realm and their own, and whether they'd intended to or not, they'd created an entirely new race. The Misos. Because of their link to Argolea and the heroes, each Misos was born with a special gift, and their lifespans were longer than those of mortal beings, but they weren't immortal in any sense of the word. As far as Daphne knew, they weren't even that special.

"I..." Words faltered on her tongue. If anyone knew what it was like to face a daemon, surely he would. Half breeds had been hunted by daemons for years simply because they were different, and to daemons that meant weak. "I didn't mean any disrespect."

"Don't worry. Where you come from, I'm sure Misos are few and far between."

That was true. He was the first Misos she'd ever met. But that didn't mean she condoned stereotypes. In the otherworldy universe, nymphs were considered less than the other races, interested only in sex. She hated that perception. It was part of the reason she'd worked so hard to become the best Siren she could be.

Even if she wasn't all that great.

That's why you're here. To fix that point.

He stepped past her and motioned for her to follow. "I'm sure you have a million questions. I'm starving though. We'll talk while I cook."

Daphne couldn't seem to stop herself from glancing toward the doorway where Aristokles had disappeared. "What about him?"

"Ignore him. He's being moody."

She had no idea what the male meant, but she wasn't sure she was *with it* enough to go exploring on her own just yet. She followed the Misos back up the stairs and into the massive kitchen.

"Have a seat." He nodded toward the hand-carved barstools near the counter. "I'll get you something to drink. I remember being extremely thirsty when I first awoke."

Daphne's mouth was suddenly bone dry. As she pulled out a chair and sat, she licked her lips, thankful someone seemed to know what she needed because right now, she had absolutely no clue.

He handed her a glass of clear liquid. "Drink."

Daphne drained the entire glass, then lowered it to the counter and swiped the back of her hand over her mouth. "I didn't realize how thirsty I was. Thank you..."

"Silas."

"Thank you, Silas. I'm Daphne."

He opened the refrigerator and pulled out lettuce and other salad fixings. "How is it you came to be out here in the wilds all by yourself, Daphne?"

She'd known the question would be asked, she just hadn't expected it to be asked by anyone but her target. Either way, she needed to relay the same story Zeus had suggested because it might trigger a useful reaction in the crazed Argonaut. "I was... escaping."

"From?" Silas reached for a tomato.

She thought about lying. She didn't know this male. He could be Aristokles's henchmen or even his slave. But he didn't act like either. His shoulders were relaxed, and there was a look of contentment across his scarred features as he worked. And when she thought back to what she'd seen of the two sparring downstairs, it was clear he wasn't afraid of the Argonaut.

She suddenly didn't want to lie. It wasn't in her nature to lie anyway. But she couldn't tell the truth either. She figured a half-truth was her best bet. "There's a god who wants something from me. I was in the wilds because of him."

"Running from him?"

Daphne definitely wanted to run from Zeus. His lecherous gaze put her at instant unease, and she hated the way he kept referencing her mother. In a way, accepting this assignment was running from him, wasn't it? "You could say that."

He sliced through another tomato. "If it was a god, I'm guessing you came through a portal."

"I did."

"Which explains the dress you were wearing when Ari found you."

Ari... Her body warmed just thinking of the Argonaut. He'd been the one who'd found her. Rescued her from those daemons. Brought her here and stripped her of her shredded garments.

Arousal stirred in her belly all over again, but as her gaze drifted to the knife in Silas's hand, it cooled. He sliced through the flesh of the tomato. Juice spurted across the cutting board, instantly reminding her of that daemon's claws slashing through her skin.

"Thank you," she said softly, "for taking care of me."

"You're welcome. But I didn't do much aside from make sure you were comfortable. Ari's the one you should thank. Without his healing gift, you'd be dead."

Daphne stared at the Misos's scarred profile, unsure she'd heard him right. The Argonaut. He was implying that the Argonaut hadn't just rescued her from those daemons, but healed her as well.

That went against everything she knew of the monster.

Silas glanced up. "I take it from your reaction you didn't expect that."

"I..." Heck no, she hadn't expected that. "I recognized the markings on his forearms. He's a warrior, not a healer."

Silas looked down at his vegetables. "He is. But Ari also has a healing gift. One he doesn't often use. Only when the situation is dire."

What situation would the crazed Argonaut consider dire? Daphne's gaze swept back over Silas's scars. "He saved you as well?"

Silas nodded.

"Why?"

A smile pulled at the corner of Silas's lips. "Because it's in his nature to help those in need."

Daphne's brow wrinkled. "I'm not sure I understand."

Silas moved the diced tomatoes to a salad bowl. "The Argonauts are duty-bound to protect the human world. My people are part of that world."

"Yes, but...if he lives here instead of in Argolea, he no longer serves with the Argonauts."

Silas looked up again, only this time when his eyes met hers, they narrowed. The knife in his hand hovered above the cutting board. "Now that, I know, you did *not* pick up from the markings on his forearms."

Oh Hades. A quick shot of fear rushed down Daphne's spine.

Think...quickly.

"I..." Her mind spun. "No, I-I didn't. But in my circle, I've heard whispers of a rogue Argonaut. One with mismatched eyes who no longer serves with his Order. I just assumed—"

"Naturally, you assumed the worst." Silas's jaw clenched as he went back to slicing. "Not everything those gods you surround yourself with say is true. Ari might not serve with the Argonauts anymore, but that doesn't mean his duty is any less."

An odd tingle spread across Daphne's nape. She'd offended the Misos. Her memory skipped back to the laughter she'd heard from the lower level. The two were friends. She opened her mouth. Closed it. Wasn't sure just what to say.

After several awkward seconds of silence, Silas said, "My village was attacked by daemons. We lived in a remote area high in the mountains. Kept to ourselves; were a peaceful community. We thought we were safe. Turns out we weren't. A daemon horde attacked us in the night. The raid was bloody and vicious, and before we could defend ourselves, it was all but over."

"I..." Daphne didn't know what to say. She knew what it was like to lose her entire village, too. "I'm sorry."

"Nothing to be sorry about. It happened." He moved all the salad fixings to a bowl, cleaned off the cutting board, then stepped toward the refrigerator again and pulled out a casserole dish covered in tinfoil. "I made peace with it a long time ago. Ari found us after. He'd been patrolling the area as he often does. He tried to heal as many as he could, but in the end, I was the only one who survived."

A humming sounded in Daphne's brain. Everything she'd been told about the Argonaut seemed at sudden odds with what she'd just learned. She wasn't sure what to believe. All she knew for certain was that the Argonaut could have killed her. He could have left her for dead in those woods. But he hadn't. He'd saved her, brought her here, and healed her. And though she wanted to chalk that up to his weakness for nymphs, she was starting to wonder if that was true. Because he'd done the same for Silas.

Her gaze drifted toward the open door. She had no idea where the Argonaut was or what he was doing, but her mind skipped back over that moment in the woods. After he'd killed those daemons. When he'd stalked toward her, knelt at her side, and reached for her. She'd been too afraid to listen then, but now two words echoed in her mind. Two words she hadn't realized he'd whispered until right this very second.

CHAPTER FOUR

Daphne wandered through the halls of Stonehill Hold late in the evening while Aristokles's words continued to ping around in her mind. It was late, well past midnight, but she couldn't sleep.

You're safe...

Had she ever felt safe? Maybe as a child with her parents, but they'd been gone so long she barely remembered what safety felt like. She'd never truly felt safe with her foster family, even though they'd been nice. She'd been too afraid something bad was lurking around the corner. And she'd certainly never felt safe on Olympus. Even with all her years of training, she still worried daily that someone would see she didn't have what it took and kick her out. Every day she struggled just to fit in. And every day she knew she really didn't.

Hating where her thoughts were heading, she ran her fingers over the spines of a series of books in the library. Tomes from all over the world filled the shelves, covering topics from gods to history to woodworking. Daphne had always loved books. As she glanced over the titles in front of her, she couldn't help but see the irony.

Books separated man from the animals. Learning kept him from becoming a savage. And the savage Zeus wanted her to kill was obviously very well read.

Turning on a sigh, her gaze drifting over the fireplace, the comfy seating area, and the table near the window holding a globe. After dinner, Silas had given her a tour, explaining that Stonehill Hold had been nothing but ruins when Aristokles had found it over fifty years ago. Silas was the one who'd pestered the Argonaut into rebuilding the fortress. Silas was probably the one who'd collected all these books.

She froze when she realized she wasn't alone, and her heart rate shot up. Seated in a high-backed chair in the corner of the room, a book in his lap, the Argonaut she'd just been thinking of watched her with wild, mismatched eyes.

Warmth gathered in her belly. A warmth that was both unwelcome and painfully arousing. He didn't speak, only continued to stare at her from the shadows, and with every passing second, her adrenaline surged higher and that warmth trickled lower, awakening places she wasn't willing to think about just yet.

Say something. Anything.

"I-I didn't realize anyone was here."

Aristokles didn't move a muscle, didn't look away, still didn't speak. And his face was so shadowed, she couldn't read his expression. All she could see were his eyes, fixed only on her.

Nerves bounced all over in her belly, and she pulled her gaze from his, glanced around the room, and tried to sound nonchalant when she said, "This is a fabulous library. I'm always so tempted by books. I hope you don't mind if I borrow a few. I'm not used to the quiet here." She wrinkled her nose. "Kinda hard to sleep."

When he still didn't answer, she fought back a wave of unease. "I'm sure you're used to being here. I mean, why wouldn't you be? This is your house, after all. It's a great house. Just a little big for me. And cold. You must like the cold though. I mean, to have a house way out here in the mountains, you'd have to, right?"

Oh gods, she was babbling. She'd spent years on Olympus training herself *not* to babble like she used to do as a child.

He didn't answer. Didn't move. Pressing her lips together, she twisted her arms behind her back and clasped her hands. One quick look toward the dark corner told her he was still staring only at her.

Sweat broke out along her spine. His hand resting on the arm of the chair was so big, she knew it could crush her skull in a matter of seconds. But even as fear churned in her belly, she held on to the fact that he'd saved her life. If he wanted her dead, she'd already be there. That meant he wanted her for something else.

Seduction. She needed to be a seductive, alluring nymph, not a rambling fool. *You trained for this, idiot.*

Right. She had. This was the easy part.

Straightening her shoulders, she unclasped her hands from her back and cocked her hip. The movement accentuated her breasts, which she knew were her best feature. Flipping her hair over her shoulder, she rested her hand at her waist and looked right at the Argonaut as she licked her lips in a move she knew would draw his attention right to her mouth.

"But enough about me." Lowering her voice to a throaty whisper, she added, "Is there anything here that tempts you?"

For a heartbeat, the Argonaut didn't move. Then very slowly, he unfolded himself out of the chair and rose to his full height.

Her pulse pounded. Arousal stirred low in her belly. He crossed the room and stopped mere inches from her, the scents of fresh pine and citrus wafting around her. Scents, she suddenly realized, she'd smelled before.

When he'd rescued her in the woods? She wasn't sure. And right now she couldn't think. Because this close, he was bigger than she'd first thought. Broader across the shoulders, more muscular everywhere, so tall she had to tip her head back to look up at his face. And hot. His body heat sizzled across the distance between them, seeping into her skin until that arousal slinked lower and her thighs trembled.

She didn't fight the arousal this time. Told herself it was because her arousal would produce pheromones that would draw him in. And drawing him in meant she could finish this job, maybe tonight. But something in the back of her consciousness knew that was a lie. She wasn't fighting it because he excited her. Because a wicked place inside her wanted to know what it would feel like to be devoured by a savage like him.

He stepped forward, and though Daphne wanted nothing more than to feel his skin brush hers, she moved back. Two steps were all she had until her butt hit the bookshelf behind her. The Argonaut lifted both large hands, and her stomach caved in, waiting for his touch, wondering where he would start. But instead of his skin grazing hers, he rested his hands on the shelf near her head, boxing her in.

His mismatched gaze skipped over her features. Heat surrounded her as he leaned in, jacking her arousal up even higher, making her forget the Sirens, her reason for being here, even her own name.

Her body instinctively swayed toward him. Her eyelids lowered. She lifted her head toward his, her lips trembling in pure anticipation.

He stopped millimeters from her lips and whispered, "Can't sleep, huh?"

His warm, minty breath brushed her sensitive skin. Her mouth watered, desperate for a taste. Without even realizing it, she eased even closer. "No. I'm not the least bit tired. I think I may need help with that."

"Help, huh?"

His words were a throaty purr, his massive legs so close they skimmed her own, making her sex ache. It was all she could do to keep from reaching him, but Sappheire's voice—something she didn't expect—whispered that he needed to make the first big move so she knew she could completely draw him in.

She didn't want to think about Sappheire right now. Didn't want to think about the Sirens or her mission. She just wanted to be taken. By this savage? Oh yes... She didn't even care what he'd done anymore.

He leaned toward her ear, his warm breath fanning her neck, sending tingles straight down her spine. His lips just barely brushed her lobe, and her eyes slid closed. "Here's your help, little nymph," he whispered. "Lock yourself in your room where it's safe because if I see you out here again, I won't be held responsible for my actions. I'm unpredictable. And not in any way you want a male to be."

A tremor ran down Daphne's spine, dimming her arousal. Cool air washed over her as the Argonaut drew back. Slowly, she opened her eyes, but the instant she looked up, she knew the Argonaut wasn't the least bit turned on like her. His jaw was hard, his eyes icy and cold. And when she heard the wood crack behind her where he still gripped the shelf, she realized what she'd missed thanks to her stupid excitement.

He was every bit the savage Athena had claimed him to be. His eyes were wild. His skin flushed. And it wasn't just arousal dragging him to the edge of control. It was something else. Something she knew instinctively she should be afraid of.

"I'm no hero, nymph. Don't invade my space again."

He let go of the shelf, turned, and exited the room without another word.

Daphne sagged back into the bookshelf and drew in a shaky breath. But fear didn't come. Because as soon as she was alone, she realized what she'd missed moments before.

He hadn't been icy until just the last moment. When she'd

obviously tried to seduce him. Before that, when he'd been watching her and she'd been her silly, rambling self, his expression had been one of noticeable interest, just as it had been when he'd looked at her downstairs in his gym.

He was attracted to her. Very attracted. He just wasn't attracted when she used her Siren skills. That meant straight up seduction wasn't going to work. She needed to finesse the situation, make him trust her. She just wasn't sure how to go about doing that.

She pushed away from the bookshelf and remembered Silas. Silas could help her. She'd talk to the half breed and figure out the best way to get close to Aristokles.

Then she'd finish the job she'd come to do. And forget about the sexy savage who made her body ache.

* * *

Ari found Silas in the lowest level of the hold, a dark, windowless room carved out of the cliff that they used for storage.

Dressed in jeans and a long-sleeved T-shirt, Silas stood on the far side of the room, making notes on the clipboard in his hand as he checked supplies on the shelves that lined the walls. "We're almost out of wine," he said without turning, obviously hearing Ari's footsteps. "You drink too much of it, you know. I'm pretty sure I replenished that stock two months ago."

Ari wasn't in the mood to talk about his drinking habits. He wasn't in the mood for anything except getting that nymph far, far away. Resting his hands on his hips, he glared toward the Misos. "If she's well enough to wander around the hold, she's well enough to leave."

Silas made another mark on his paper. "I thought you'd appreciate having something prettier to look at than me."

"How pretty she is has nothing to do with this."

"Ah." A mischievous smile curled Silas's lips. "So you did notice."

Ari's frustration shot up. Yes the nymph was pretty, but his opinion would be the same if she were Aphrodite beautiful or Medusa ugly. Stonehill Hold was his one and only refuge, and he wasn't about to be bullied by a nymph in his own home.

"I want her gone," he said. "I'll be back by nightfall tomorrow.

When I return, she'd better not be here."

"Daphne."

"What?"

Silas turned to face him. "Her name's Daphne, not she. And what you want and need are two very different things, Argonaut."

Ari's jaw clenched. "Don't pretend to know what I need. I'm no good for any female, especially that one, and we both know it." He stomped back up the steps, refusing to give in even an inch. "Tomorrow, Silas. No excuses."

"What you need," Silas muttered, "is a two-by-four to the head." Then louder, "Get some wine while you're out. It does wonders for your personality."

Ari ignored the smartass comments and moved back to the main level where he headed for his rooms. The entire west wing of the hold was his domain. An office complete with desk and chair he'd carved by hand opened to a bedroom suite filled with a bed, side tables, and a sitting area flanked by a wide stone fireplace. Crossing toward the closet on the far side of his room, he pulled out a backpack and set it on the bed.

His gaze slid over the empty wine bottle on the nightstand. Scowling, he looked down at his pack and checked the supplies he kept inside for his patrols. So he drank to fall asleep. Big deal. A lot of people did that. A lot of *normal* people did that, and he was way past normal. Normal people didn't have to deal with his curse. Normal people didn't have the blackout episodes he did. *Normal* people didn't have random flashes of the horrible things they'd done while in the midst of one of those episodes.

Needed a woman? No way. Sure, he had desires just like the next guy, and he had no problem fulfilling those desires when he was out on his scouting trips. There were always willing females if you knew where to look. But the last thing he needed was one infiltrating his personal space.

More frustrated than before, he snapped the top of his pack, pulled on a jacket, then slung the straps over his shoulders. Screw Silas and his opinions. Ari didn't need anything but himself. He'd been getting along just fine alone for dozens of years.

He headed for the door and the frozen wilderness beyond. And hoped he ran into another pack of daemons. A good bloodletting would take his mind off that nymph. But something told him it wouldn't be enough to make him forget that she now had a name.

* * *

Daphne hadn't slept well. Her dreams were a mixture of Ari and the Sirens and her long-destroyed village.

She climbed out of bed and yawned as she dressed in the sweats and T-shirt Silas had given her after dinner. The clothing was huge. She had to roll the pants down at the waist several times just so they stayed up, and the light-blue T-shirt wasn't much better—hanging like a dress almost all the way to her knees. After tucking it in as best she could, she fluffed her hair and told herself she could still make this work. She'd aced her strategy training. She simply had to think outside the box where Aristokles was concerned.

She turned out of her room and moved barefoot through the hall. When she reached the kitchen on the lower level, she found Silas filling a backpack on the table with supplies—water, bandages, gloves.

She approached slowly, not sure what he was doing. "I hope you're not running away."

Silas glanced up and smiled, his hair damp around the collar from a shower, his light-blue eyes sparkling, making her almost forget about the scars on his face. "Good morning. Sleep well?"

"Fine," Daphne lied as she pulled a chair out at the table and sat. "Are you going somewhere?"

Silas shoved a bag of granola into his pack. "Supply run. We're low on several things."

Panic clawed at her chest. "How long will you be gone?"

"Three, maybe four days. I'm supposed to take you with me."

Shit. She couldn't let that happen. "Um—"

"I don't think you're well enough to leave, though."

Daphne's gaze shot to his. The male's blue eyes sharpened when he added, "And call me selfish, but I think you can do some good here while you finish healing."

She didn't know what he meant but as he pushed his pack to the end of the table, pulled out a chair, and sat across from her, she found herself hanging on his every word. "Ari left on a scouting trip. He'll be back later tonight. He'll likely be ticked you're still here, but he can just deal with it. He *needs* to deal with it."

"Why?"

"Ari thinks it's better for everyone if he isolates himself."

"Why does he believe that?" she asked, playing dumb.

"Because he's bullheaded," Silas answered. "But I fear this self-imposed isolation of his is slowly catching up with him."

"You care about him." The realization hit before she could stop the words from spilling from her lips.

"Of course I do." Sighing, Silas shook his head and leaned back in his chair. "It's more than the fact he saved my life. I'd heard rumors about the crazed Argonaut just as you, but I quickly realized he's not what everyone says he is."

"And what is he?"

Silas didn't immediately answer, and in the silence, Daphne thought back over everything she knew of Aristokles. The stories she'd heard from Zeus and Athena contradicted with what Silas had told her last night. And after spending a few minutes with Ari in the library, she didn't know who to believe.

"You know the story of the Argonauts, right? How each are given a soul mate?"

Daphne remembered a story her mother had once told her. "Hera cursed them. Because of Zeus's affection for his son Heracles. She was jealous that Zeus had created a realm for Heracles's descendants, and she cursed him and all the Argonauts with a soul mate." She frowned. "I never understood how that could be a curse though."

"It's a curse because the soul mate in the equation is the worst possible match for that particular Argonaut. The person he's forever drawn to but who will torment his existence. Some Argonauts never find their other half. Some do. Ari found his, fifty-odd years ago, in the human realm while on patrol with his Order. She was a nymph, like you. Young and beautiful. And she was running from Zeus."

Silas leaned forward to rest his forearms on the table. "Olympians can't cross into Argolea. It was the one safeguard Zeus put in place, to protect the Argonauts from Hera's wrath. But that safeguard turned out to be a source of frustration for Zeus. See, Ari took the nymph to Argolea. He tended her wounds, gave her a place to live, and eventually they fell in love. But when Zeus discovered Ari had stolen his prize, he was livid. Since he couldn't cross into Argolea himself, he sent his Sirens to get her back. There was a confrontation. In the struggle, Ari's soul mate was killed."

It was the same story Daphne had heard from the Sirens. With one minor change: in the telling she'd heard, the nymph hadn't loved Ari. He'd recognized her as his soul mate, kidnapped her, and she'd been trying to escape his clutches when the Sirens arrived to rescue her.

"Ari lost it then," Silas went on. "The death of a soul mate is like losing half of who you are. He withdrew from the Argonauts, went into isolation in the human realm, struggled to deal with his grief. Months passed, but he couldn't find the strength to return home. His son Cerek wouldn't give up on him, though. Cerek tracked him down, tried to bring him back, but Ari refused to go. When it became clear to Ari that Cerek was never going to give up on him, he faked his death. You saw those scars on his neck?"

Daphne remembered the scars she'd seen up close last night in the library. "Yes."

"They cover the whole left side of his body."

"From what?"

"A fire. One he set on purpose. His son thinks he's dead. Most everyone does."

Everyone but Zeus and Athena and the Sirens. Daphne tried to imagine the scene but couldn't. Tried to imagine what it would take to isolate one's self so dramatically, but came up blank. Even in her darkest moments, she'd never wanted to be alone, which was why she'd jumped at the chance to become a Siren when she'd been chosen.

"It wasn't until after all this that Ari started having his episodes," Silas said.

"Episodes?" Daphne looked back at the male across from her.

"Spans of time where he completely blacks out. He's not aware of what he's doing while in these episodes, but he has flashes of them afterward, and of the things he's done while in them. From what we've been able to discern, the episodes are usually triggered when he senses Sirens close by."

Daphne's head was suddenly spinning. Zeus and Athena had implied he killed Sirens in his crazed need for revenge, but if that were the case, he would have started killing them as soon as his soul mate died. What Silas was describing made it sound like Ari's "episodes" began after he'd left the Argonauts. Months after his soul mate was already gone.

That didn't sound like revenge at all. It sounded like...a curse.

Daphne opened her mouth to ask more, but before should get the words out Silas went on.

"For a while, he kept himself locked in this hold. Thought if he isolated himself, he could stop the episodes. But his duty was too strong. The need to protect is engrained in his Argonaut DNA. He now runs his own missions, hunting daemons and safeguarding the people he swore to defend ages ago. But any time he has a blackout, it weighs heavily on him. Thankfully, they're few and far between these days."

Daphne's brow wrinkled again. Zeus had made it sound like Ari's attacks were stepping up, not lessening.

Silas shook his head. "Things changed a few months ago, though, when one of Ari's friends called asking for his help. Nick is one of the few people from Ari's old life who knows Ari's still alive. I was hesitant about Ari traveling to Mexico. Offered to go with him but he wouldn't let me. You see, he hasn't had an episode in quite a while, and I was worried about how he would react. Turns out Ari didn't encounter any Sirens on his trip, but something did happen there. When he came back, he was different. Sullen. Moody. No longer laughing and lighthearted as he'd been when we were renovating this place." He looked up and around again. "He's never said exactly what occurred, but I think seeing his old friend made him realize what's missing in his life—friendship, family...love."

Daphne's head grew light. Did she have those things? Definitely not love. She'd never known a male deep enough to fall in love. And with her parents gone, she had no family left. She had friends, though, didn't she? Her Siren sisters were her friends. But even as she tried to convince herself of that fact, she knew it was a lie. The way Sappheire had left her in the woods without a single word of comfort or encouragement proved she wasn't a true friend in any sense of the word.

"He reacts to you in a way I haven't seen him react to anyone else," Silas said. "He's nervous around you. Not in a dangerous way, but in an interested one. I'm not trying to set you up, just to be clear.

That's not my goal. I simply think your being here is good for him. It forces him to see that he can be around others and not flip out. And he needs that. He needs to see he isn't the monster everyone believes him to be."

Daphne stared down at the table, taking in all this new information, trying to process it, trying to fit it into what she'd been sent here to do. He still killed Sirens. That fact was irrefutable, and she couldn't ignore it. But if he didn't know he was doing it, if he really was cursed in some way, then that made a huge difference to her.

She needed to spend more time with him. Needed to figure out if Zeus or Silas was correct. Then she'd know how to proceed.

"I don't want you to think he's dangerous," Silas said. "He can be a grouchy pain in the ass sometimes, but he's never had an episode while he's been in the hold, and as I said, the only ones at risk when he does are Sirens, which you are clearly not." A half smile curled his lips then faded. "But yes, I'd like you to stay. If you're amenable to the idea. At least until I return."

She was. But not for the reasons he wanted.

Knowing she couldn't agree too quickly, Daphne bit her lip. She still needed to play the damsel-in-distress role. No matter what she decided to do about the Argonaut in the end, she couldn't let her cover slip. "He won't want me here. Especially if you're gone. He pretty much told me last night to get lost."

"I know." Mischief filled Silas's light-blue eyes. "That's why I have an idea. The question is simply whether or not you're brave enough to go through with it."

CHAPTER FIVE

Daphne wasn't sure about Silas's so-called plan. He wanted her to take the damsel-in-distress façade one step further and insist Ari teach her self-defense. She had to admit it wasn't the worst idea out there, but she wasn't a hundred percent sure she could pull it off. Sure, she sucked at marksmanship, but she knew full well how to take care of herself.

Like you did with those daemons?

She scowled at a book on the shelf in Ari's library. Told herself no one stood a chance alone against a horde of daemons—especially unarmed and wearing those stupid shoes Athena had given her. But even as she tried to justify it to herself, a little voice in the back of her head whispered, *You're not Siren material, and you know it.*

Shaking off the voice, she wandered through the library, looking at books and trinkets on the shelves. Silas had started a fire before he'd left, and even though the room was warm and cozy, she couldn't seem to relax. Reading didn't sound the least appealing, she didn't feel like tackling a puzzle, and she was too keyed up to sleep. Nerves humming, she wandered from room to room, wondering when Ari was going to return. Wondering how he'd react when she proposed her little "you teach me to fight and I'll agree to leave you alone" plan.

She stopped outside the wing that led to his suite of rooms. Drew a deep breath. Knew she shouldn't invade his privacy but wanted to know what he kept locked behind this door. To her surprise, the handle turned with ease.

A hallway led to a wide-open bedroom suite complete with a simple bed, another fireplace already burning thanks to Silas, a sitting area, closet, and a door partway open to a bathroom. The room was sparse, nothing hanging on the walls, only two pillows and a plain white blanket on the bed. No pictures or trinkets or anything that personalized it as his. She moved to the closet, flipped on the light, and eyed the scattering of clothes hanging on the rack. All rugged. All made for being in the elements. All boring colors and way too functional fabrics.

Turning out of the closet, she looked over the room again and couldn't help but feel a twinge of sadness for how boring his life must be. Silas had said he kept himself closed off from people. This room was a reflection of him—simple, empty, lonely.

An image of her room back on Olympus filled her mind. White walls, white furnishings, white bedspread and pillows. No pictures on her walls either. The only thing of personal value in her room was the stack of books she'd collected.

Telling herself she wasn't anything like the crazy Argonaut, she headed back for the hallway that led to the door. The last thing she needed was for him to find her snooping in his space. But just before she got to the hall, she noticed another door she hadn't spotted in the shadows when she'd first entered.

She pushed that door open and stepped inside. Darkness surrounded her. Feeling along the wall, she found the switch and flipped it on. Light flooded the room from above. She let her eyes adjust, then scanned the space. A scuffed wooden desk took up the middle space. A couch sat across the room. Shelves stuffed with books lined three whole walls. But her attention landed and held on the fourth wall, on the giant world map stretching from one corner to the other.

Her brow lowered as she stepped closer and looked at the tiny red flags stuck in various locations across the earth. They were scattered all over Europe, Asia, North and South America, even the Arctic. But it was the symbol on each flag that made her eyes widen and her stomach draw up tight. A bow and arrow cut by the Greek symbol for sigma.

"What in Hades are you doing in here?"

Ari's voice boomed at her back, but Daphne didn't turn to look, didn't move, couldn't take her eyes off the map.

"You're supposed to be gone." He moved back to the door, mumbled, "Skata," then yelled, "Silas!"

Daphne's gaze swept over the map, both disbelief and dread swirling in her belly to form a hard, tight knot. "You're tracking Sirens."

"Where the fuck is Silas?" he demanded.

She couldn't believe it. Silas had made her think Aristokles didn't hunt Sirens on purpose, but this map proved otherwise.

She whirled on him, no longer caring if he was upset she'd invaded his space. He was wearing jeans and a sweatshirt, his face flushed from the cold outside, his dark hair mussed, his bare feet insanely sexy against the hardwood floor, but she ignored the way he looked and focused on the facts. "Why are you tracking Sirens?"

His gaze narrowed. "How do you know what I'm tracking?"

She pointed toward the map. "Because I'm not stupid. I know the Siren symbol. You are hunting them."

A steely look crossed his features as he stepped slowly back into the room. "What do you know about anything I do?"

"I know—" Her mouth snapped closed when she realized she was about to give everything away. "I've heard stories. About an Argonaut who hunts Sirens. It's you, isn't it?"

He glanced toward the map with all its little red flags, then back at her. But he didn't say a word.

"Answer the question," she demanded.

He still didn't speak. Just stared at her with hard, narrowed eyes. And she knew instinctively that he wasn't going to answer, but she needed the truth once and for all.

Crossing her arms over her chest, she glared at him, no longer caring how this impacted Silas's silly plan or what Zeus wanted. "Silas is gone. He left to get supplies. Why are you tracking Sirens?"

"Stupid half breed," Ari muttered. He glanced toward the map. Still didn't seem to want to answer, but after several long seconds said, "Not that it's any of your business, but this is for avoidance, not tracking."

"Avoidance of what?" she asked skeptically.

"Sirens. I have a personal distaste for their Order. I started mapping their movements years ago so I could stay well out of their way. That's why I picked the Snoqualmie National Forest as my home base." He pinned her with an annoyed look. "Happy now?"

No, Daphne wasn't happy. She glanced back at the map. There

was only one Siren flag in the Pacific Northwest, south of their location, but still close enough to Stonehill Hold where he could get to the location quickly if he wanted. "What happened to those Sirens?" She looked back at him and pointed toward the map. "The ones marked there in Washington?"

He scrubbed a hand over his forehead. "I'm not going to get rid of you, am I?"

"Not until you answer my questions."

He dropped his hand to his side. "I'm going to fucking kill Silas."

When she only continued to glare at him, he scowled. "I don't know why you care but there was only one Siren in that location, and I never personally ran into her. She, luckily, was too interested in a different Argonaut to taunt me."

Sirens didn't taunt. They lured. But Daphne didn't bother to explain the difference because she knew it would be lost on him.

She looked back at the map, taking in the flags all over Europe, following the intricate lines he'd created of the Sirens' movements, thinking of the hours and months and years it must have taken to compile this information. But her awe drew to a shuttering stop when her gaze landed on a collection of flags marking a location in Northern Greece.

"What is this?" She stepped toward the map, her eyes growing wide. "Why are all these flags grouped together in the Pindus Mountains?"

"What are you looking at now?" he muttered.

Fabric rustled, indicating he'd moved further in the room, but she didn't care how close he was. The pressure pushing on her chest was all she could focus on. "Here." She pointed. "Marking this tiny village."

"Because Sirens were there. Just like every other mark."

"I get that," she said calmly when all she really wanted to do was scream. "But why so many? And what does the black flag in the middle mean?" Her gaze skipped over the rest of the map. There were only a few other black flags on the map, randomly scattered over the continents, but if there was a pattern to their marks, she couldn't see it.

"Black means they wiped it out."

Everything inside Daphne went cold. "Wiped what out?"

"The entire village."

Daphne's heart felt as if it skipped a beat, then picked up speed until it was a whir in her ears. Her hands grew sweaty. Her legs swayed. He couldn't be right. The map blurred in front of her eyes, but somehow, she found her voice and asked, "H-how?"

"Gods, you're curious." His feet shuffled. "If I tell you, will you go?"

"Yes! What happened?"

Panic was rising in her voice. She could hear it herself. Several minutes of silence ticked by, but she didn't turn to look at Ari. Couldn't because she was too afraid of what she'd see. Truth? Lies? She wasn't sure which she wanted at the moment.

"It was like twenty years ago," he said at her back. "Zeus has always had a thing for nymphs, and this village was made up of nothing but nymphs. There was a female there he wanted. Simple thing. Wasn't interested in Olympus or the gods. But you know Zeus. He always gets what he wants. He pursued her, but she repeatedly turned down his advances. When he grew aggressive, she threatened to call the Argonauts in to protect her."

"Argonauts aren't sworn to protect nymphs."

"They're sworn to protect the human realm from otherworldy threats. Zeus can be a definite threat. Anyway, Zeus didn't like the ultimatum. He backed off, let her think she'd won. When enough time had passed and she'd let down her guard, he sent his Sirens to teach her a lesson."

No. *No, no, no, no, no.* It couldn't be true.

"I heard they burned the village, top to bottom," Ari said. "When they were done, there was nothing—and no one—left. Nice girls those Sirens, huh? Now you know why I avoid them."

The room spun around Daphne. It couldn't be true. It couldn't be.

"You seem shocked by this," Ari said. "Sirens have killed hundreds of thousands over the years. Anyone Zeus wants gone. What does one little village in the middle of nowhere matter to you?"

The map blurred. Flames flared in Daphne's memory, cries for help echoed in her ears. Hot, burning tears threatened, followed by a wave of pain she thought she'd put behind her long ago.

"I..." Pushing away from the desk, she bolted for the door, rushing past him, needing space, needing to think, needing to figure this out before the memories swept her under and devoured her. "Get out of my way."

* * *

Ari was cold, wet, and more than a little frustrated. He'd spent the last twelve hours tracking a horde of daemons across two ridges before losing them in the snow. All he wanted was a hot shower, food, and a few good hours of sleep—in that order—so he hadn't been happy when he'd stumbled into his rooms and found the nymph who was supposed to be long gone invading his space.

Only now, food and sleep were the last things on his mind. Now all he could think about was the way she'd bolted out of this room as if she'd just relived a nightmare.

He looked at the map again, eyed the flags marking the location where that village used to be, then pictured Daphne's sickened face. And finally put two and two together.

"Skata."

He turned out of his room before he thought better of it. Was on the stairs before he even realized where he was heading. And pushed her bedroom door open before he could stop himself.

The room was empty.

For a fleeting moment, he thought maybe she'd left, then realized there was nowhere in this wilderness for her to go. He turned out of the bedroom and headed back for the staircase. Halfway down, he caught a flicker of movement through the tall, arching windows across the great room and stopped.

She was out on the deck. He watched her hair blow in the wind for several moments and told himself she wasn't his concern. He could go back to his rooms. Forget about the nymph. Forget everything but sleep. The sooner the nymph was out of his life the better. But that stupid duty inside him wouldn't let him walk away like he wanted.

He crossed the great room and pulled open one side of the double glass doors. The nymph stood at the railing looking out over the dark valley, snow already collecting in her thick locks. Her feet were bare, and dressed in nothing but the T-shirt and baggy sweats she had to have gotten from Silas, she was already shivering, though he doubted she even noticed.

"Come inside," he said.

She didn't move. Thinking she might not have heard him, he stepped out into the snow, the cold immediately penetrating his own bare feet. "Come inside before you freeze to death."

For a long moment she didn't answer. Then softly, so softly he barely heard her, she said, "Were you there?"

She was talking about the village. *Her* village.

Skata. *This is not your concern. You don't have to answer.* "No."

"It was the middle of June. So hot I could barely breathe. I asked my mother if I could run to the creek to cool off. She didn't want to let me go, but I persisted. Finally, she agreed, but only if I took Argus with me."

Dammit, he'd been right. Though he wanted nothing more than to run now as she had then, his feet wouldn't let him. "Argus was your dog?"

She nodded as she continued to stare out at the darkness. "I lost track of time. When I realized how late it was, we ran back as fast as we could. I knew my mother was going to be so mad that I'd stayed late." Her eyes drifted closed, and pain etched her features. "I heard the screams first. By the time I cleared the trees, everything was in flames. I was seven."

Ari knew what it was like to lose everything—your hopes, your dreams, your future. And as much as he wanted to stay indifferent to the nymph, now he couldn't. "I'm sorry."

It was a feeble thing to say. His Argonaut brothers had all told him they were sorry when his soul mate had died, and it hadn't changed a thing. He watched as she stared out at the black swirling storm. Her face was as stony as the rocks in the cliff below them. Except for the tears that slid down her cheeks in silence.

"And you're sure it was Sirens?" she asked quietly.

"Yes."

"But you weren't there. You can't know for certain."

Her protest didn't surprise him. As a nymph, she'd probably been taught that the Sirens kept the gods' peace. Denial was the hardest hurdle to clear. He knew that better than most. "There was one survivor, besides you. A boy. Eton, I think was his name. He was gathering firewood at the time of the attack. He saw what happened from the ridgeline and ran. After, he sought refuge in a Misos colony in Eastern Europe. He confirmed it was Sirens."

"I knew him." Daphne's eyes slid closed. "He was a few years older than me."

She stood still several long minutes, the wind whipping her hair, snow collecting on her dark locks, her clothes, her face, her arms and legs. And as much as Ari knew she needed this time to deal with her grief, the inch of snow that had collected near her ankles since she'd come out here told him it was time he got her inside. "Daphne—"

Abruptly, she turned back for the hold. "I have to go."

Thankful she was heading back in, Ari moved into the great room and shut the door at his back. But instead of heading for the stairs and the solitude of her room as he expected, she rushed for the entry to the hold.

She shoved her feet into the first pair of boots she found, then reached for the massive door handle. It took only two seconds to realize what she was doing.

Ari slapped his hand against the hard wood before she could pull the door open.

"You're not leaving like this."

"Get out of my way." She pushed his hand away from the door and yanked. "You wanted me gone, so consider me gone."

Cold air swept into the hold. But before she could get two steps outside, he captured her around the waist, pulled her back against him, then shoved the door closed with his foot. "I said you're not leaving."

She dug her fingers into his forearms and struggled against his grip. "Let me go!"

She was a strong little thing. Stronger than he expected. Twisting her around, he pushed her back against the wall and closed in at her front, bracing his arms on the walls near her head so she was trapped with nowhere to go. "Running after them won't do any good."

"How would you know?" She pushed at his arms but he held them still. "You don't know anything about where I'm going."

"No, I know everything about where you're going. I've been where you are right now. I've wanted them dead for what they did. But I also know there is no such thing as revenge against Zeus's army. The Sirens are too many."

Her struggle slowed. She looked up at him and glared, and in her heated look he knew that he was the closest target for her pain. But as their eyes met, the glare slipped away and was replaced with a sea of emotion. And he noticed for the first time that her eyes were a deep, emerald green. As green, he guessed, as the woods around her lost village. And completely and utterly mesmerizing.

"My mother's name was Eleni." Tears filled her gemlike eyes, and she blinked rapidly to hold them back. "I saw Zeus in our village days before it happened, talking with her, but I never put it together. I didn't know she was the reason..."

Her voice trailed off as tears overtook her. She lifted her hands to her face, her slim shoulders shaking with her sobs. And before Ari realized it, she leaned into him and rested her forehead against his chest.

For a moment, he stood stone-still. Didn't know what to say. Didn't know what to do. But when warm wetness seeped through his shirt and penetrated his skin, that duty took over, and he closed his arms around her, holding her while she cried.

She was small, the top of her head barely reaching his shoulder, soft and curvy, fitting perfectly against him. He didn't know a lot about comfort, had never been good at accepting or giving it, but he held her any way as she worked through her emotions. And though he told himself he was just being supportive, that there was nothing sexual about the situation, he couldn't stop his body from reacting to her.

His blood warmed. Tingles rushed across his skin wherever they touched. She smelled like vanilla, her scent rising in the air to make him lightheaded, and her damp hair was silky soft wherever it grazed his flesh. He forced himself to remain still, but the longer he held her, the more he had to fight the urge to slide his hands up and down her spine, back and over the curves pressed into him. And the more he tried to fight that, the more all he could think about was tangling his hands in her curly mass of hair, tipping her head back, and claiming her mouth with his own.

She shivered against him, and the movement snapped his brain back to the moment. In a rush, he realized the wetness pressed against him wasn't just from her tears. Her T-shirt and sweats were soaked from standing on the deck in the storm.

"You're cold." He drew back enough so he could lift her into his arms. The enormous boots on her feet slid right off to clomp against the floor. "You need dry clothes."

She didn't fight him when he carried her into the great room and headed for the stairs. Just sniffled and swiped her arm across her nose. "I don't have any other clothes. These were the only ones Silas gave me."

Ari stopped at the bottom of the steps. Skata. She was right. That dress she'd been wearing when he'd brought her here was nothing but rags now.

He moved for the hallway that led to his rooms before he thought better of it. She didn't say anything as he carried her in, set her on the bed, then pulled a blanket from the foot and wrapped it around her shoulders. "I'll find you something dry."

Still she didn't answer. Just clutched the blanket around her and stared off into space, her damp hair hanging around her face, her bare feet dangling above the hardwood floor.

She looked wrecked. As wrecked as he felt most days. Telling himself it wasn't the same, he moved into the closet and stared at the shirts hanging from the rack.

But he didn't see them. Suddenly, all he could see was the way she'd looked pinned against the bookshelf in his library last night. The way her breasts had lifted with her shallow breaths. The way her leg had trembled against his when he'd moved in close. The way her lips had parted and she'd lifted her mouth to taste him, an offering he'd been too afraid to accept.

His blood warmed all over again, and arousal flickered through his belly then rushed into his groin. It was wrong, so very wrong considering how vulnerable she was at the moment, but he wanted her. Wanted her spread naked before him. Wanted her writhing in pleasure. Wanted to feel her close around him as he slid into her from behind. She was a nymph built for sex, and he was a virile warrior who'd been locked away for far too long. It was basic biology that he should want her this much. But a little voice in the back of his head whispered now—right now—part of that wanting had very little to do with sex and everything to do with the fact wanting, craving, *taking* could make both of their pain and memories disappear. If only for a little while.

Skata. He blinked several times when he realized he was trying to justify it all to himself. Aside from the fact he hadn't been the least bit civil to her since she'd arrived, he'd just told her the truth about her village. She was in the next room falling apart *because of him*. There was no way in this world or the next that she'd ever want him again. And that was assuming she'd even been interested in the first place.

Disgusted with himself, he chose a long-sleeved henley he knew would be way too big for her and hide her trim little body from view, then headed for the bedroom. After she was dry and dressed, he'd shuffle her off to her own room and forget this night ever happened. And tell himself it was a good thing he'd come to his senses before it was too late.

Plan in place, Ari stepped back into his bedroom, then stilled. The wet shirt and sweats she'd been wearing lay in a heap on the hardwood floor. Blood pounded in his ears as his gaze skipped to the right, where she sat cross-legged on the sheepskin rug in front of the fireplace, the blanket wrapped tightly around her, her faraway gaze staring into the flames.

Naked. She's naked beneath that blanket.

Blood rushed into his cock, making him hard in an instant. But he fought back the arousal and told himself to hold it together a few more minutes as he walked toward her.

He held the shirt out. "I found you something dry to wear."

"Does it ever go away?" She didn't turn to him. Didn't reach for the garment. Didn't even look up. Just continued to stare into the flickering flames. "I thought it did. I thought I was past it. But knowing all of this...it's sharper than before."

She was talking about pain. The pain of loss, the pain of heartbreak. The pain of betrayal. He knew all three intimately.

He didn't answer. Didn't move. Focused only on keeping his emotions trapped behind the wall he'd erected to stay semi-sane. But the hitch in her voice hit him hard, right in the center of his chest.

Unable to walk away like he knew he should, he laid the shirt over the arm of a side chair and sank to the floor next to her. "It gets easier."

"Silas told me it's been fifty years. It's not easier for you."

Ari rested his elbows on his updrawn knees and stared into the fire, irritated Silas had told her about his past, thankful at the same time because it meant he didn't have to talk about it now. He thought about those fifty years as he watched a flame dance over the log and wished he had sage advice for her, but knew he really didn't. "If you're lucky, you learn to live with it. And you don't let it define you."

"But yours defines you."

"My situation is different."

Daphne continued to stare into the flames. "What was her name?"

Ironically, it was no longer pain that consumed Ari when he thought of his soul mate. It was emptiness. Emptiness for a life he'd never have again. "Penelopei."

Daphne was silent several seconds. Then softly, she said, "'Duty crumbles to ashes in the fires of love.' My father said that once. He wasn't a nymph. Just a human. Caught between two worlds. He left his job, his responsibilities, everything for my mother." She shook her head. "I don't know anything about that kind of love. Not like them. Not like you."

Ari held back a huff. "I don't know much about love either. Penelopei sure as heck didn't love me."

Daphne finally turned his way, her soft green eyes no longer tormented by the past, but filled with a thousand questions. Questions that made his belly tingle. "But she was your soul mate. Silas said—"

Gods, she was gorgeous. More gorgeous than she probably knew. And he had no right being anywhere near her. He looked back at the fire so he didn't do something stupid. Like grab her and never let go. "Silas likes to romanticize the entire thing. I think it makes him feel better about choosing to stay here with me."

She stared at him, eyes wide and curious, waiting for more. And though he didn't look at her, though he knew he shouldn't go on, that he had no reason to tell her any of this, for the first time in forever he found himself wanting someone to know the truth.

"Silas told you I found her on one of my missions in the human realm, didn't he?"

She nodded.

"And that she was injured?"

"Yes."

"When I came across her, her dress was ripped to the thigh, her leg scraped and bleeding. She begged me to help her. Told me Zeus had been chasing her. That she was trying to get away. I believed her. Took her back to Argolea, knowing she'd be safe from him there, and tended her wounds. Penelopei was..." He watched a flame devour a branch and couldn't help but see the similarity in the way Penelopei had devoured him. "She was like wildfire, consuming everything in her path. When she wanted something, she didn't let consequences influence her desires."

Disgust rushed through him when he remembered how he'd dropped everything for the female, even his duty. How he'd so easily walked away from his family. He shook his head. "As thanks for saving her, she seduced me. It was then I realized she was my soul mate. This may sound silly but sex is a powerful medium. Every Argonaut in the history of Argonauts has found his soul mate that way. What I should have keyed into, though, was the fact a soul mate is a curse, not a blessing."

"You're talking to a nymph," Daphne said softly. "I know how powerful sex can be. I've seen it firsthand. Zeus's desire for it destroyed my village."

And Ari's desire had destroyed not only his life, but his son's as well.

Guilt crept in. A guilt he'd tried so long to ignore, but it was there. It was always there, hovering in the background, telling him there was no way he could ever make up for the pain he'd caused his son because of his blinding desire for Penelopei. For a soul mate who'd never truly seen him as anything other than a pit stop.

"Penelopei quickly grew bored of me and life in Argolea," he went on, "and when Zeus's Sirens showed up to take her back to the god, she was more than willing to go. To her it was all a game. Jumping from one male's bed to the next."

He sounded bitter. And maybe part of him still was. Because thanks to Penelopei, his whole world had shifted. Not because he'd loved her and lost her but because a stupid curse had made him crave a manipulative and shallow female.

"When the Sirens arrived at my home outside the capitol city of Tiyrns," he went on, "I wasn't willing to let her go. I was blinded by the soul mate connection and convinced if I could just get her to stay, everything would work out. A standoff resulted. The Argonauts came to my aid. But she didn't want to stay and struggled against my hold. The Sirens thought I was going to harm her. Before any of us could stop it, a battle broke out. In the chaos, Penelopei was killed."

And there was the crux of the rest of his guilt. Knowing that because he hadn't been able to control his desire, not only had he abandoned his son, but a female had died. "It wasn't my blade that struck her," he finished, "but I killed her just the same. If I'd let her go, she'd still be alive."

"Maybe." Daphne looked back at the fire. "If I hadn't gone to the creek that day, maybe my parents would still be alive too. Then again, maybe not. We'll both never know. And maybe that's the point. Maybe we're not meant to know. When I was a child, my mother told me that life was a series of events that make zero sense at the time, but which come together to reveal a greater good in the end. I forgot that until just now. Maybe what happened to you stopped Penelopei from tormenting another male. Maybe Zeus's fascination with her—and you—stopped him from ruining another family's life, like he ruined mine. Maybe everything happens for a reason."

He turned to look at her, at her profile set against the flickering flames. There was strength inside her. A strength he wasn't sure she knew was there. There was also simplicity. Something he craved in his confusing, fucked up, crazy world. "Are you saying you believe in some unseen Fates pushing us around like pawns on a chessboard?"

"I don't know." She shrugged. "I just know that if someone had told me a week ago I'd be sitting here like this with you, I would have laughed and said they were insane. Everything's changed in a short amount of time, and not by my doing. There has to be a reason for it."

He glanced back at the fire. He didn't believe in reasons. He didn't believe in the Fates. Where were the Fates when his world fell apart? Where were they when he started having blackouts and went nuts? No, he believed in what he could see and touch. And right now, what he could see and touch was way too close and much too vulnerable, especially when his arousal was still up and his own vulnerability hovered on the edge. "Be careful. People call me insane, and they're not far off the mark."

"Those people don't know you. I'd say you're way more sane than I am."

He huffed. "You haven't seen me at my finest."

"Yes, actually, I have." She leaned close and kissed his cheek.

Her lips were soft and sweet and gone way too fast. And though he knew he shouldn't, he turned to look at her. "Why did you do that?"

"To say thank you for stopping me from going after Zeus and his Sirens. I wouldn't have gotten very far in the snow without a coat. You saved my life, Argonaut. Again."

Their eyes held. Heat and electricity crackled in the air, warming his skin all over, sending a rush of heat straight to his belly. He didn't know if she felt the charge the way he did, but as the firelight danced over her smooth features and she continued to hold his gaze, her eyes slowly darkened and a warm flush grew in her cheeks, telling him she was feeling something. Something dangerous. Something wicked. Something he might not be ready for.

"Don't worry," she said softly. "I'm not going to seduce you to extend my thanks."

A wave of disappointment washed over him even though he knew he had no right. But then she leaned close once more, and he sucked in a breath, afraid to move, afraid to hope, afraid to do anything but go stone-still.

Her luscious mouth stopped millimeters from his own, more sweet and hot and tempting than any mouth had ever been. And in a husky whisper, she said, "I can't, because you've already seduced me."

CHAPTER SIX

Daphne knew she was playing with fire, but she no longer cared. Before Ari could push her away, she pressed her lips to his.

He tensed against her mouth. Every muscle in his body went rigid. And though she tried to keep it back, doubt rushed in. Doubt that she'd misread the look in his eyes. That he wasn't attracted to her like she thought. That his being nice to her here was simply that: politeness and not motivated in any way by the same desire she'd been fighting ever since she awoke in this hold and realized the sexy, rugged, wounded Argonaut had saved her life.

Slowly, she eased back, breaking the kiss. He didn't speak. Didn't move. Just stared at her with those mismatched eyes that seemed to flicker just like the firelight. And in the silence her mind tumbled for excuses, for something she could say to ease the sudden awkwardness. She was a nymph, trained in the art of seduction by Sirens. Awkwardness wasn't supposed to happen to her. But then *he* wasn't supposed to happen to her either, and here she was, hoping for something that had absolutely nothing to do with her mission. Wanting—

"Where do you think you're going?" His arm snaked around her back and pulled her in close to the heat of his body. "That wasn't nearly enough."

Daphne drew in one quick breath before Ari's mouth closed over hers, but relief filled her lungs, seeped into her body, and made her more lightheaded than any wine. She opened instinctively, drawing his tongue into her mouth, groaning at the sweet, masculine taste of him filling her senses. His lips were soft, his mouth wet and alluring, and when he leaned closer and kissed her harder, she knew she was lost.

She let go of the blanket, pressed her hands against his chest, then shifted her weight and straddled his hips. The blanket fell to her waist. He didn't break the kiss, continued to nip and suck and lick like he couldn't get enough. Inching forward, she slid her fingers up his pecs then across his soft, scruffy jaw. His hands found her waist, tugging her even closer. His mouth turned greedy beneath hers. Hot. Wild.

Settling herself on his lap so she could rub against his rock hard erection, she let him take the lead, wanting only to taste him deeper, to feel him everywhere.

"Daphne." He pulled his mouth from hers and pressed kisses along her jaw as he swept his rough fingers up her back. "Daphne," he whispered again before nipping gently at her earlobe.

Desire enflamed every inch of her skin. She groaned, tipped her head back so he could trail his wicked teeth and tongue down the length of her neck, rocked her hips against the thick line of his cock straining to be set free.

He flattened his hands against her shoulder blades, trailed his lips down her neck and across her upper chest, then pressed forward with his forehead, forcing her to lean even farther back. "I know I shouldn't, but, gods, I want you."

She lifted her head. Watched as arousal danced across his flushed features. Wanted only that and more. Wanted to see him on the edge of control, like she was now. "Then take me."

His mismatched gaze slid back to hers. Held. Didn't once waver. And the way he watched her, as if she were the only thing he ever wanted, only made her heart beat faster in anticipation. He looked back down at her breasts. "You don't know what you're offering."

Oh, yes she did. Suddenly, she knew exactly what she was offering. And it had nothing to do with Zeus or the Sirens. It had only to do with him.

Capturing his face in her hands, she tipped his eyes back up to hers. "I know exactly what I'm offering. You're not the monster people say you are, and I'm not afraid of you. If I was, I wouldn't be here now. I wouldn't be wet just from the thought of you."

A growl rumbled from his chest, one filled with lust and hunger and need. Sliding his hand up her back to cradle her head, he pulled her mouth toward his and devoured her. She moaned and kissed him back. His fingers found the blanket at her waist and yanked. Then he rolled her onto the plush sheepskin rug and climbed over her.

Yes, yes, yes... Her legs fell open as he licked into her mouth. Her hands trailed to his shoulders and thick arms. He pressed kisses down her neck again. Kisses that made her hotter and wetter, and she arched her back, offering more, wanting everything. Gripping the fabric of his shirt, she pulled, needing heat, wanting skin. He eased away long enough so she could tug the shirt over his head, but when she reached for the snap on his jeans, he captured her hands.

"Not yet." His bare chest grazed her oversensitized nipples as he pinned her wrists to the floor above her head with one hand. "I'm not done exploring." He let go of her wrists, his lusty gaze scraping every inch of her skin, making her strain for his touch. "Don't move these. Or you'll regret it."

It was a warning, not a threat. And she hadn't lied. She wasn't the least bit afraid of him, not after the way he'd saved her life, healed her, and tonight shown her more compassion than she ever deserved.

A smile pulled at her mouth, and she wriggled against the carpet as his fingertips grazed her ribs and skimmed across her hip. "How will you make me regret it?"

He laved his tongue over her right nipple. "I won't let you come."

Her eyes slid closed. She arched against his wicked mouth as he did it again. Was already so close she was pretty sure he couldn't stop her.

His hand drifted across her thigh. The softest touch between her legs made her groan and lift her hips. "Oh, do that again."

He moved to her other breast, licked and laved, applied more pressure between her legs and swept his thumb over her clit. "Like that?"

"Yes." She rocked against his hand as he teased her breasts, desperate to feel him inside. "More."

He released her breast, slid down her body. "More here?"

The first swipe of his tongue along her steamy center sent tingles all through her body. The second raced along every nerve ending until she trembled. He licked and suckled, devouring her like a feast, and when electricity raced down her spine, she grasped his head and arched up to meet his tantalizing tongue.

He pulled away just before the orgasm hit. Gasping, Daphne reached for him, but before she could touch him he flipped her over, wrapped his arm around her waist, and lifted her hips off the rug.

"Stay there."

Daphne's hands landed against the carpet, and she pushed up, but his palm landed against her shoulder blades, holding her down. "I said stay there. You have trouble listening to directions, little nymph."

There was humor in his voice, and a hunger that supercharged her arousal. Fabric rustled behind her, telling her he was finally losing his clothes, and just knowing he was nearly naked sent white-hot excitement pulsing through her veins all over again. Curling her fingers in the rug, she pressed her cheek against the carpet and held her breath.

One bare knee nudged her legs apart. His fingers slid through her wetness again, making her groan. "Do you want more, little nymph?"

"Yes," she panted. "More."

He pressed his thumb against her clit. "How much more?"

She bit her lip to keep from crying out. Her fingers tangled tighter in the carpet. "You. I want you."

The thick head of his cock pressed against her opening. They both groaned as he filled her, at the tight slide as he drew back, at the friction when he plunged deep once more. His fingers dug into her hips. She braced her forearms against the carpet as she pressed back against him. They picked up a rhythm, one that made her see stars, one that pushed her closer to her release.

"Gods," he groaned. "This is how I imagined you."

His large hand slid up her spine and into her hair. Knowing he'd fantasized about her made her that much hotter. Her climax screamed toward her. White light flooded her vision. She opened her mouth to cry out. But just before she reached the peak, his hand closed around her hair and pulled. Not hard enough to hurt, but enough for a sharp sting to echo in her scalp and shoot down her spine, keeping the orgasm hovering just out of her reach.

"Not yet, sweet thing."

She gasped. Groaned. Rocked back into him, wanting more, needing everything. He wrapped his arm around her waist and pulled her upper body away from the carpet until her back was plastered to his chest. Letting go of her hair, he trailed his wicked hand down her chest and over her breasts.

"Wait for me, Daphne."

Sweat drenched Daphne's skin. She couldn't find the words to answer as he plunged inside her. All she could do was grip his forearm and brace her knees against the carpet.

"Just a little longer," he breathed against her, "and it'll be so good."

His fingers slid down her belly and into her wetness. She dropped her head back against his shoulder and groaned with every thrust, with every flick of her clit. He grew harder, pressed deeper, reached places she hadn't known existed. And when he drew her earlobe into his mouth and suckled, when he hit that most perfect spot, the orgasm she'd been chasing crashed into her and exploded.

He buried his face in her neck and kept thrusting while she rode the pleasure, driving deep again and again and again. Electricity raced down her spine, through her sex, and then it was there, another blinding orgasm, consuming her, dragging her down, making her melt. He whispered frenzied words she couldn't make out. His thrusts grew faster, harder, longer. And then he plunged deep and held, spilling himself inside her and quivering with his own release.

Daphne fell forward, the soft carpet almost painful against her sensitized skin. She turned her face toward the fire, dragged air into her burning lungs and tried to catch her breath. Ari's sweat-slicked skin slid along her back, then he collapsed next to her, struggling for his own breath as he wrapped an arm around her waist and drew her back against him.

She didn't fight the tug, didn't have the strength, didn't want to. His chest pressed against her spine, his hips to her ass, and though his flesh was hot, kicking up her body temperature, she didn't care. She liked the way he fit against her. Liked the way he held her. Liked the things he could do with his wicked hands and tongue and that super sexy hero body.

"You...are...a surprise...little nymph," he said in ragged breaths. "A very pleasurable...surprise."

He was too. A delicious surprise she never expected. She had no idea what she was going to do next, but she knew for certain that she wasn't finishing her mission or going back to the Sirens. And no matter what, she wasn't letting anyone else finish it either.

Smiling, Daphne reached for his hand at her waist and drew it to her mouth so she could press soft, wet kisses against his fingers.

Sliding her tongue along his index finger, she drew the digit away from the others, closed her lips around the tip, and sucked.

He groaned behind her and pressed his awakening erection against her ass. "A very wicked surprise."

Daphne's lips curved around his finger before she let go. She shifted around and looked up at him. "You like wicked? I can be wicked."

Sitting up, she pushed her hand against his shoulder and rolled him to his back. A lusty, heated grin curled his mouth as she climbed over him. His hands landed on her hips. "I'm almost afraid to ask what you have in mind."

She settled on his lap, then braced her hands on the ground near his head and leaned forward. "Everything. I have everything in mind for you, warrior."

His smiled faded. He slid his hands into her hair as his gaze skipped over her face and he looked at her, really looked at her, as if seeing her for the first time. And though she couldn't read his expression, she knew he was as moved by all of this as she was. And that something important had happened here tonight. Not just sex, but a connection. One that had the power to change everything.

"Show me," he whispered.

She leaned down and kissed him. And planned to do exactly that.

* * *

Wind howled past the windows of Stonehill Hold, but the chill didn't reach inside. Wrapped around a sleeping Daphne on the carpet in front of the hearth, Ari stared into the dying fire and watched wood crumble to ashes.

A pillow was tucked under his head, and a blanket covered their legs, but the warmth Ari felt came directly from Daphne, snuggled against him, her head resting on his bicep as she faced the fire, her hand clutching his at her waist. He knew he should wake her, carry her to the bed where she'd be more comfortable, but he didn't want to move. Moving meant he had to think, and thinking was something he was trying to avoid. Because thinking meant facing reality. And reality was hard and cruel and deadly.

The charred log slipped and fell into the smoldering coals, sending burning ash into the air. Ari watched a flake float and cool, turning from red to gray and finally white powder as it hit the stones of the hearth.

"Duty crumbles to ashes in the fires of love."

Daphne's voice echoed in his head. She was wrong. It wasn't love that destroyed duty, it was lust. Lust was the true deceiver, messing with the mind, fooling the heart. Lust for a female who'd never truly wanted him had destroyed everything Ari had held dear. And now, if he wasn't careful, lust had the power to destroy another life. Not his this time, but Daphne's.

He looked down at her sleeping against his arm, watched her eyelids flicker, and wondered what she was dreaming about. Wondered if she was dreaming of him. Her skin was like alabaster, her hair a warm mahogany that curled around his fingers like silk. His gaze slid over her cheek, down the long, lean line of her neck, to her succulent breasts he'd licked and laved and worshipped. And though all he wanted to do was worship her all again, a place deep inside his chest—a place she'd set free—knew he couldn't.

Bit by bit, Ari's good mood slipped away. Gently, so as not to wake her, he untangled his hand from Daphne's and carefully slid his arm out from under her head. A soft, sweet grunt slipped from her lips as she adjusted on the carpet and rolled to her other side. When her breathing lengthened and slowed, he pulled the blanket up to her shoulders then rose to his feet.

He tugged on his pants and headed for his office. After flicking on the lamp, he lowered into the chair and stared at the map on the wall across the room.

The sum of fifty years' worth of work. An obsession he'd prefer to forget but couldn't. He looked from flag to flag, marking the Sirens movements, and knew that even though he didn't want to, he'd go on tracking them. It was the only way he could stay semi-sane. He'd told Daphne about Penelopei, but he hadn't told her about the aftermath of Penelopei's death and what losing his soul mate continued to do to him even fifty years later. And as much as he liked Daphne's companionship, as much as he enjoyed being with her, he didn't want her to ever see him in the throes of one of his episodes. He'd barely survived seeing the horror in his son's eyes when Cerek had witnessed it.

There was only one way to keep that from happening. Rising, he walked to the window and looked out into the darkness. The wind had died down. By morning the storm would be gone. There'd be fresh snow, but he knew how to traverse the snowy landscape. And no matter how much he wanted to stay hidden in this hold, this time he couldn't.

Because by this time tomorrow, Daphne needed to be nothing but a memory. Not just for her sake, but for his as well.

* * *

Daphne awoke with a start. Blinking several times, she looked up only to realize she'd been shaken out of sleep by a firm hand.

"Sorry to wake you." Ari set something next to her on the floor and pushed to his feet. "The storm's broken. I took these from Silas's room. You should be able to make them work."

Groggy, Daphne watched him disappear into his closet. He was dressed, wearing jeans, a long-sleeved T-shirt, and boots, and he'd showered, the tips of his hair still damp where they brushed his nape. But he should still be lying next to her, not up and moving around.

She glanced at the items he'd left beside her and realized they were clothes. Clean clothes. Confused as to what he was doing and why, more importantly, he seemed to be avoiding eye contact, she pushed up on her arm and scanned the dimly lit room.

The fire beside her was nothing but smoldering embers. A backpack sat near the door, one that looked as if it had already been packed.

Apprehension slid down Daphne's spine. Tugging the blanket up to her chest, she ran her fingers through her hair, then pushed to her feet and wrapped the blanket around her. She moved toward the closet and leaned against the doorjamb as she watched him pull a box from the shelf above the rack and flip off the lid.

"You're up early," she said, trying to sound nonchalant. Nonchalant had never really been her specialty, but if there was one thing she'd learned from the Sirens, it was that morning-after awkwardness killed the mood like nothing else, so better to avoid it altogether. "Any chance you made coffee? I don't operate well unless I have caffeine. Well, food too. We burned off so many calories last night, I definitely need food."

She was rambling. But this time she didn't care. He seemed to like it when she rambled.

He pulled a black knit hat out of the box, replaced the lid, and set the box back on the shelf. Handing her the hat, he stepped around her and said, "I'll find you a coat."

Two things hit Daphne at once. He was definitely avoiding eye contact—or any contact for that matter. And he was getting her dressed for outside weather.

"A coat for what?" She snagged the sleeve of his shirt before he could get all the way past her. "What's going on, Ari?"

He gently pulled his sleeve from her fingers and moved back a step. "I'm taking you into town. You need to get back to wherever it is you came from and I need to get back to the way things always are for me."

He was pushing her away. The realization hit like a punch to the gut. Last night *had* meant something if he was kicking her out like this. She stepped away from the wall. "I liked last night, and I know you liked it too. I don't want to leave."

"Well, you don't get a say in it." He moved for the door. "It's safer for you if you just go."

Safer... Safer, she realized...from him.

She darted around him, stopping in the hallway, preventing his exit. "Silas told me about your blackouts. I'm not afraid of them. I know you wouldn't hurt me."

He turned his mismatched eyes on her. But unlike last night, they weren't soft and dreamy. They were hard and icy. "Silas should learn to keep his big mouth shut."

He tried to move past her again, but she stopped him with a hand on his chest. "He cares about you. That's why he told me. And they're not your fault."

Those steely eyes narrowed. "You don't know what they are, and you don't want to be around when they happen." He grasped her wrist and pulled it away from his chest, then stepped around her. "This isn't up for negotiation. We're leaving in fifteen minutes whether you're dressed or not. It's cold outside. I suggest you listen."

He stomped out of the room before Daphne could stop him, but as soon as he was gone, her stomach sank and all the excitement she'd felt last night leaked out of her like a balloon deflating. Dropping down to sit on the hearth, she clutched the blanket at her chest and tried to stop her silly heart from aching.

If he wanted her gone, there wasn't anything she could do to stop him from kicking her out. She wasn't strong enough to intimidate him, sex clearly hadn't worked to seduce him, and Silas was gone, so she didn't even have the half breed on her side to talk some sense into the Argonaut. But what really hurt was the fact she'd failed. Not at her mission—she'd decided last night she wasn't about to let Zeus manipulate her into doing his dirty work ever again—but at convincing Ari he wasn't the monster everyone thought him to be.

Her gaze drifted to the rug where they'd slept tangled together, then to the clothes he'd left for her. And as both blurred in front of her eyes, she realized something else.

Without the Sirens, without a purpose in her life, she had no idea where she would go from here.

CHAPTER SEVEN

The howling wind was nothing but a dull hum lost in the roar of the engine as Ari maneuvered the snowmobile around a tree. Unfortunately, it wasn't enough to distract him from the simmering heat at his back.

He tried to focus on the solid handlebars beneath his gloves, on his knees pressing against the seat between his legs. The machine was an extension of himself, the skis slipping over the pristine snow with ease, familiar and comforting. But the warm circle around his waist where Daphne held on for dear life kept distracting him. And the pressure of her thighs against the backs of his legs, the press of her breasts along his spine—even through the thick jackets they both wore—definitely wasn't comforting. It was arousing as hell, and every time she flexed her arms and moved even closer to hold on tighter, he remembered what it had felt like to have her wrapped around him last night. Naked and begging for his touch.

He zigzagged around trees, heading down the mountain toward the small town at the mouth of Lake Shannon. He had plenty of money to give her. From there she could catch a bus into Seattle then hop a plane wherever she wanted to go. Bottom line, though, was that where she went from here wasn't his concern. He was doing the right thing by making her leave. Getting her to safety before he snapped and did something he'd regret.

A heavy hand knocked into his shoulder. Realizing she was trying to get his attention, Ari turned his head, intent on telling her to sit still until they got to their destination. But one look was all it took to realize she was focused on something off in the trees.

Ari slowed the snowmobile. Before the machine came to a

complete stop, she jumped into the snow and tugged off her helmet.

He quickly pulled off his own helmet and grasped her by the sleeve. "Where do you think you're going?"

"I saw someone." She tugged free of his grip and darted into the trees before he could stop her, her too-big boots sinking into the new powder with every step.

"Skata." Ari dropped his helmet on the seat and followed, his own boots sinking all the way to his ankles. Someone could be some*thing*. She could have seen a damn daemon for all she knew. Yeah, she was ticked at him for making her leave, but this wasn't ticked. This was stupid. "Come back here, before I—"

His words cut off when he passed a large tree. A trail of blood stained the snow and led from the tree around a large boulder. A warning tingle slid down Ari's spine. He reached for the dagger he'd strapped to his thigh before they'd left the hold. "Daphne, come back to me right now."

A grunt echoed from behind the boulder. Ari gripped the dagger and bolted around the rock, then slowed when he saw the horror.

Daphne knelt next to a female leaning against the rock in the snow, the front of Daphne's pants and jacket red with blood.

His heart lurched into his throat, and he rushed forward. "Holy gods. Are you—?"

"It's not me," Daphne said quickly, tugging off her gloves. "It's not my blood."

She pressed her hands against the female's shoulder. Blood gurgled between Daphne's fingers, ran down the female's arm, and dripped onto the snow at her side. "She's hurt. We have to help her."

Relief that it wasn't Daphne's blood whipped through Ari, slowing his steps, but that relief waned when he turned his attention to the female. She was dressed in knee-high black snow boots, slim black pants, and a thin jacket. Nothing someone who spent a lot of time in the snow would wear. Her thick mane, a mixture of blonde and brown and red, hung past her shoulders in a sleek wave, and her brilliant blue eyes were guarded as she stared over Daphne's shoulder toward him. On the ground beside her injured hand, lay a very unique, very intricately carved bow. A bow Ari had definitely seen before.

Siren.

The word ricocheted in his head like a marble zinging around a track. He waited for the rage, for the blackness to overtake him, but nothing happened. Looking out over the trees, he searched for anyone else, but the snowy forest was cold and silent.

"Ari," Daphne said, her voice dragging his attention back to her. "She needs help."

Ari watched the blood bubble through Daphne's fingers. She wanted him to help a Siren, the same being he hunted.

Except...he wasn't hunting this one. He hadn't even known she was in the area, which totally went against everything he knew and understood.

"Ari," Daphne said again, looking over her shoulder with pleading eyes. "She's going to die if you don't help her. Please."

That duty that was ingrained in his DNA kicked into gear, forcing his feet forward before he could stop them. He knelt on the Siren's other side and rubbed his hands against the thighs of his pants. The female whispered something to Daphne he didn't catch. In response, Daphne said, "Shh... It's going to be okay. Trust me."

Ari wasn't so sure. He didn't know what would happen when he touched the Siren, but that duty wouldn't let him leave. Regardless of what she was, she was injured, and he had the healing gift that could save her. To Daphne, he said, "Move your hands."

The Siren's jacket was shredded in three long, angled lines, blood seeping through the garment and running down her arm. Ari reached for the Siren's ripped collar. The female's eyes grew even wider, and she jerked back against the rocks.

"He's not going to kill you," Daphne said, scooting forward and placing a hand on the Siren's arm to steady her. "I promise."

The Siren looked from Daphne back to Ari, and though fear reflected deeply in her eyes, she stilled.

She knew who Ari was. She'd probably been in these woods to kill him, and here he was about to save her life. The irony wasn't lost on him, and for a split second he considered getting up, dragging Daphne with him back to the snowmobile so the Siren could die as she deserved, but as soon as the thought hit, he knew he wouldn't do it.

"Damn duty," he muttered. Then louder to Daphne, "We need to get this jacket off. I can't reach the wound like this."

Daphne grasped the ripped fabric in both hands and pulled, tearing through the Siren's jacket so they could peel it away from the wound. Three large claw marks ran in a diagonal pattern over the Siren's shoulder and down past her collarbone.

"A daemon," Daphne said, staring at the wound.

That was exactly what it looked like to Ari. And where there was one, there was always more. He shifted closer to the Siren, intent on getting this over and done with fast.

"How many?" Daphne asked the Siren. "And what happened to them?"

"Th-three," the Siren answered. "We killed two. The third"—she cringed in pain and adjusted against the rock—"the third took...Rhebekah...into the woods."

Daphne closed her eyes for a quick second, then opened them. "Was she alive?"

The Siren shook her head. "I...I don't know."

Two Sirens in the area, and he hadn't sensed either. Ari didn't know what the hell was going on, but when Daphne turned to look at him with pleading green eyes, he knew they were done wasting time.

He reached for the Siren's shoulder. "Hold her still. This will hurt."

The Siren tensed, but Ari laid his hands over her wound before she could jerk away again. Heat gathered beneath his palms, penetrating the wound and stitching it back together. A warm yellow glow radiated from below his fingers and palms. The Siren cried out as the heat and energy shot through her body, but Daphne held her down, preventing her from moving and disrupting the process. Seconds later, it was over, the wound sealed. The glow subsided, and Ari lifted his hands to check the result. Nothing but thin red lines remained on her skin.

"Will she live?" Daphne asked, looking at what he'd done.

Unfortunately for him, yes.

Knowing Daphne wouldn't want to hear that, he pushed to his feet. "Her wounds weren't nearly as bad as yours." He glanced at the Siren. Her head was tipped against the rock, her damp hair stuck to her temple, her eyes half-lidded as she breathed through the remainder of the pain. "In an hour or so she should be fine."

"Thank the gods," Daphne breathed.

Ari didn't thank the gods for anything. But as he studied Daphne's profile, the strong jawline, small nose, and the determined chin, he remembered her horror last night at learning Zeus's Sirens had destroyed her village and killed her parents. She, of all people, should want to see a Siren dead, but here she was, relieved that he'd saved one.

That icy space in his chest that had warmed and expanded because of her grew even wider, making his heart beat harder, making his fingers tingle with the urge to reach for her, to drag her close, to ask her what the hell she was doing to him. But he knew this wasn't the time or the place, and he definitely didn't want to have that conversation in front of his archenemy.

"Stay here." He tugged off his jacket and laid it over the Siren. "I'm going to have a look around."

He made it three steps away before Daphne's hand captured his arm. Before he could ask what she wanted, she rose on her toes and pressed her cold lips against the scruff on his cheek. "Thank you," she whispered. "Thank you for helping her."

She let go of him, knelt back by the Siren, pulled his jacked up to the Siren's neck and whispered words Ari didn't catch. And as he watched, that cold space deep inside heated until only warmth remained.

* * *

"What the hell are you doing here?" Daphne whispered when Ari disappeared into the trees. "And what in Hades happened?"

Sappheire adjusted against the rocks, sitting more upright. "Athena sent us to find out what was taking you so long. We were looking for you."

Unease filtered through Daphne's belly. If Athena had sent Sappheire and Rhebekah, she could easily send more Sirens. She needed to think fast. "I hit a snag."

"No shit," Sappheire grunted. "What's going on, Daphne? Why did he heal me? He has to know what I am."

Daphne fixed the jacket over Sappheire's bare shoulder then sank back on her heels. "He does. I could tell by the way he looked at you. But he's not what you think."

Sappheire's brilliant blue eyes narrowed. "I don't understand. He should have killed me already."

Daphne brushed her hair over the shoulder of her jacket and braced her hands on her thighs. "He's not crazy, Sappheire. Not like they want us to believe. They lied to us—Athena, Zeus, all of them. He's not the monster they say he is. You've seen it for yourself."

Sappheire's eyes grew skeptical. "He's got you under some kind of spell. What have you been do—"

Ari's shout echoed through the trees, cutting off Sappheire's words. Frustrated that Sappheire so easily believed the lies they'd been fed, Daphne whispered, "There's no spell. I've simply opened my eyes."

She turned toward the trees where Ari appeared, stomping through the snow.

"I found two dead daemons and a trail of blood." He wiped his blade against his thigh, then sheathed it at his hip. "The third's no longer a problem." He looked down at Sappheire. "Your friend was dead by the time I got there. I'm sorry."

Daphne's heart pinched as she looked back at Sappheire. Daphne hadn't known Rhebekah long, but Rhebekah and Sappheire had been close. Emotions ran over Sappheire's face as she glanced around the snowy forest, clearly not seeing any of it. "I..."

"Are you sure there were only three?" Ari asked.

Brow drawn low, Sappheire finally looked up. "Three?"

"Daemons. Did you see any others?"

"No." Sappheire shook her head and swallowed hard. "No, only three. They surprised us. We heard voices over the ridge and went to look. It...it must have been them."

Ari glanced toward Daphne. "Voices could mean more. I can handle a handful of daemons on my own, but not an entire horde, not with you both here, and not with fresh blood in the area. We need to go."

Fear wrapped an icy hand around Daphne's chest and squeezed. She remembered all too well the horror of being caught with those daemons. She pushed to her feet. "Can the snowmobile hold all three of us? I can—"

"I'm not going with you."

Daphne's gaze snapped to her mentor. "Of course you are. You can't stay out here, especially if there are more daemons in the ar—"

"I'm not going with you," Sappheire said again. "I know how to get home on my own."

"But—"

"No buts." Gritting her teeth, Sappheire pushed up to standing. Her arm hung limply against her side as she leaned back against the rocks, but it was clear Ari's healing powers had worked. She looked past Daphne toward Ari at her back. "Thank you. For killing that last daemon. Where is she?"

Ari nodded toward the trees. "Fifty yards that way. You'll see the rocks. She's behind those."

Sappheire eased away from the boulder and took a step past Daphne.

"Wait." Panic pushed at Daphne's chest. They couldn't just leave Sappheire out here, not if there were more daemons in the area.

"I'm fine." Sappheire pinned her with a hard look. "I'm getting Rhebekah and taking her home. Go, Daphne, before anything else appears."

Before any other Sirens appear. Daphne heard the warning loud and clear. Sappheire was letting Ari go. But Daphne had no idea if the Siren meant to bring other Sirens back or if she'd tell Athena what she'd witnessed.

A new sense of urgency gripped Daphne. "She's right." She grabbed hold of Ari's sleeve and pulled him toward the snowmobile. "We need to go."

She picked up her helmet as they drew close, grabbed his and handed it to him. He was watching her curiously as she sat on the snowmobile and snapped her chinstrap, and she knew he was wondering what the hell had just happened, but she didn't have an answer, and she didn't want to get into it now. Now they just needed to put as much distance between them and this location as they could, in any direction.

"Come on," she said when he only continued to stare at her. "I thought we were going."

"She called you Daphne." His eyes narrowed. "I don't remember saying your name in front of her. Do you know that Siren?"

Oh shit...

Daphne's stomach drew tight as a drum, and her mind spun as she tried to think of an answer—any answer—that would make sense. But before she could latch on to one, Ari drew in a deep whiff through his nose and growled.

Startled, she looked up. And a new sense of fear consumed her.

His gaze was fixed on something far off in the trees. Every muscle in his body was tight and rigid. But more importantly, his eyes were no longer the mismatched green and blue she'd come to love. They were black. Deathly black, and one-hundred percent possessed.

"Sirens," he growled in a low, unfamiliar voice.

Daphne lurched to her feet and glanced over her shoulder. Six females—six Sirens—emerged from the trees. They were dressed in knee-high boots, slim pants, and tight, sleeveless shirts. All carried the familiar bow and arrows from Olympus, and all were as gorgeous and built as Sappheire. But a tingle of unease spread down Daphne's spine as she looked over the group. None of the females were familiar to Daphne, and she'd met every Siren on Olympus, even the newest recruits. More than that, though, the look in each of these Siren's eyes was both dark and evil. And it was a look she'd never seen from any of her sisters.

"Something's not right." She reached for Ari's forearm.

He pulled his gaze from the Sirens and looked down at her. And for a moment, the crazed, dark look faded and his eyes shifted back to their normal mismatched colors.

An arrow whirred through the air. Ari pulled Daphne off the snowmobile and shoved her to the snowy ground. Against her ear, he growled, "Stay down."

Her heart beat hard. Another arrow whirred through the air. Ari jerked to his feet before she could grasp him, that crazed look darkening his eyes once more and twisting his features until she barely recognized him.

"Ari." She reached out to draw him back to her. "Stop."

But he was already was gone, racing toward the females she knew instinctively had never been her sisters.

CHAPTER EIGHT

Ari was in hell. Burning in the fires of Tartarus, unable to escape from the heat. He turned, kicked, punched out at the flames, but they snaked over his body and danced toward his face as if he hadn't even moved.

He was going to die. Suffocate from the heat. From the smoke. And he deserved it after all the horrible things he'd done. After he'd left Daphne bloody and alone in those snowy woods. After he'd lost control and—

He bolted up, gasped in a breath, and stared into the flames across the room. A log rolled off the pile and sent a flutter of ash and sparks upward in the fireplace. Sweat slid down his temple and dripped along his spine as the crackle of wood echoed in the air, drowning out the sound of his heavy breaths, bringing consciousness slowly back into place.

His bedroom in the hold. He looked down at the soft bed, at the covers tangled around him. Kicking them free, he swung his legs over the side of the mattress, leaned forward, and dropped his face into his hands.

In. Out. He breathed deep as his heart rate slowly came down. He didn't know how he'd gotten here or what had happened, but that was nothing new. Whenever he had one of his episodes, he couldn't remember shit. All he knew for sure was that he was alive, he was naked except for a pair of boxers, and he was alone. But as soon as he closed his eyes, images flickered through his mind. The snowmobile. The Sirens. Arrows flying through the air. Daphne covered in blood, lying in the snow.

He jerked upright, walked across the room and back again so he didn't completely lose it, and racked his brain, trying to remember what had happened. He could only see bits and pieces, not the entire scene, and his mind kept tripping over Daphne in the snow, blood staining her hands and shirt and pants, reaching out for him, telling him...

He stopped. His brow dropped low. Telling him what?

"Ari, stop."

Her voice echoed in his head, the sound of her plea squeezing his chest so hard pain radiated outward from the spot. She'd been telling him to stop. To stop hurting her.

Bile slid up his throat. The walls closed in until he could barely breathe. Glancing quickly around the room, he spotted a pair of sweats he'd left on the chair days ago. With hands that shook so hard they barely worked, he pulled them on, needing air, needing to breathe, needing to run until the pain of disgust and regret loosened its hold.

He flung his bedroom door open, stumbled down the hall toward the great room and the wide deck beyond. Darkness pressed in through the tall windows. He had no idea what time it was, but he didn't care. All he could focus on was freedom. All he heard was Daphne's voice, echoing in his head.

"Ari, stop..."

"Oh my gods, that's it. That's...holy Hades, that's it."

His feet slowed just past the open library door. The first words had definitely come from his mind. A memory from the snowy forest. But the second...

He moved back to the library door and peered inside. A fire crackled in the fireplace, and in the middle of the floor, surrounded by books and notebooks, a slim female with dark, curly hair hanging past her shoulders sat cross-legged and scribbled on a piece of paper.

"Daphne?" he whispered.

Her head came up, and when her gaze met his, her green eyes twinkled. "Oh, you're awake. Good. There's something I want to talk to you abou—"

She wasn't covered in blood. She wasn't lying dead in the snow. Heart in his throat, Ari crossed the floor in three steps, grasped her at the shoulders and hauled her to her feet. The notebook and pen flew from her fingers. She yelped but he didn't let it deter him. He closed his arms around her and held her tight.

"Um. Okay." Her arms shifted around his back until they rested softly against his bare skin. "I guess that means you're happy to see me."

Relief was sweeter than any wine. He closed his eyes, breathed her in. Reveled in the fact she was whole, alive, not a single hair on her head out of place. And that she was here. With him. Waiting for him to come out of his nightmare.

He eased back, but he didn't let go of her. Wasn't ready yet. His gaze searched her face for answers. "How?" He drew away just enough so he could look down her body, so he could see for himself that she wasn't injured. Dressed in nothing but one of his long-sleeved T-shirts, the hem hitting mid-thigh to show off her shapely legs, she didn't just look healthy, she looked perfect. His gaze lifted back to her face. "What happened? The last thing I remember is seeing you bloody and hurt in the snow."

"I wasn't hurt." She slid her hands to his forearms, over the Argonaut markings he'd been born with. "That wasn't my blood. It was Sappheire's."

"Sappheire?" His brow wrinkled. "Who the hell is Sappheire?"

"The Siren you healed. She's upstairs. In my old room. Asleep."

A Siren was in his hold? He tuned into his senses. Didn't pick up a thing. If a Siren was close, he should know. He should be flipping out already.

Daphne's soft fingers landed on his jaw, tugging his face back toward hers. "Ari, you're not crazy. It's a curse. It's not your fault."

She was talking about his blackouts. His psychosis. Holy gods, she'd seen it. He let go of her and stepped back, for the first time realizing the kind of horror she must have witnessed.

"I know." He turned toward the fire, unable to face her. "It's the soul mate curse. Whenever I sense Sirens I can't stop myself. The need for revenge is too strong. I can't control it. I didn't want you to see that. I didn't—"

She stepped in front of him. "No, it's not the soul mate curse. It has nothing to do with your soul mate's death. If it did, you wouldn't have healed Sappheire. You'd be going after her now. And look at you, you aren't. There's not a crazed thing about you."

There wasn't. He felt as in control as ever. But that just meant his curse was growing more unpredictable, and unpredictable meant even more deadly. "I remember sensing them. I remember the rage and—"

"They weren't Sirens."

"They were Sirens. I was there. I saw them." He opened his eyes and stared down at her, ready to tell her to stop being so naïve, but the excitement in her gemlike eyes halted his words.

"Come here." She grasped his hand and pulled him around to her books, then drew him to the floor. "They weren't regular Sirens."

Her grip was strong, and he was still wrecked from his episode. He let her tug him to the floor. She grasped a book from her stack and handed it to him.

"Look here." She pointed toward a passage on the page. "They looked like Sirens. When they showed up in those woods, I thought they were. But then I realized they were different."

Ari glanced down at the book. A drawing of a female warrior dressed in leather breastplates, armbands, and boots, holding a weapon graced the page. "Different how?"

"At first it was the look in their eyes. There was a darkness there I'd never seen before on a Siren. But then I looked closer." She flipped the page. Another drawing of yet another female warrior filled the page. She was dressed the same as the first, except this one wore a sleeveless tunic. "It's subtle, but if you look closely..." She pointed toward the marking on the female's right bicep, flipped back to the first drawing. No marking there. She turned the page again. "Two S's in the shape of snakes, head to tail. Those females had this marking."

Ari was more confused than ever. "If they weren't Sirens, what were they?"

"I think they were the Sirenum Scorpoli. Zeus's secret band of Sirens. The ones he culls from the Siren Order to do his dirty work."

"That's no different from any regular Siren."

"It is different. The Sirens are tasked with policing otherworldy creatures in the human realm. Zeus's own private army. He can't control the Argonauts and what you do, but he can control the Sirens. The Sirens, however, are headed by Athena, the goddess of wisdom and war, so he can't use them in all the ways he wants. Enter the Sirenum Scorpoli. He can do what he wants with them, can command them to carry out any plot he deems worthy. And no one can stand in his way. Not Athena, not the Argonauts, and especially not his wife."

"What does Hera have to do with this?"

"Everything, I think." Daphne paged through the book in his

hands until she came to a chapter on the gods, specifically a passage about Hera, Zeus's wife. "'And the Fates decreed,'" she read aloud, "'that no person—mortal or immortal—shall be subjected to more than one curse by any god at any time.'"

He stared at the words, still unable to see her point. "You've lost me. What does this prove and why is it important?"

"It proves you're not hunting Sirens." When he glanced up at her, still completely confused about where she was going with this, she shook her head. "It means what happened to you isn't related to the soul mate curse. If it truly were the soul mate curse making you hunt down Sirens in revenge for your mate's death, you'd have gone crazy as soon as Penelopei died. But you didn't. Silas told me that you didn't start having these episodes until long after you'd faked your death and were living in the human realm alone."

Ari looked down at the page. That was true. His episodes hadn't started for several months after Penelopei's death.

"These blackout moments don't happen when you're around regular Sirens," Daphne added. "I think they happen only when you sense the Sirenum Scorpoli. And if that's the case, then I think it's highly possible Hera took advantage of your pain and depression after you lost your mate and cursed you a second time."

"You just said a person can't be cursed more than once by any one god. Hera is the one who established the soul mate curse."

"Right. But once an Argonaut's soul mate is dead, there is no more curse, now is there?"

Ari studied her smooth face in the firelight. Her eyes were filled with hope and promise, but he was wary. For fifty years he'd been fighting the soul mate curse. Hadn't he?

"I hear what you're saying," he said cautiously. "But there's no way to prove it. Just because I didn't flip out on the Siren upstairs doesn't mean anything. It could just be that the soul mate curse is changing, adapting, I don't know, fucking with me so I go even more nuts."

"I might have believed that myself until I saw the marking on your calf."

"What marking?" He reached for the edge of his sweats and pulled them up to his knee. "I don't have a marking on my leg."

"It's faint. I didn't notice it until I helped you out of your wet clothes and put you into bed. Here." She placed her hand on his leg and twisted so he could see the back of his calf. And the very faint mark, two inches long, so light and in a place he never thought to look, he'd never noticed it.

A feather. A peacock feather.

"The peacock is a symbol for Hera," Daphne said. "I looked it up. No other Argonauts have that marking. Which means this mark, this curse? It's unique to you."

Ari stared at the marking, his mind tripping back over every encounter he'd ever had with Sirens. He couldn't remember them. Couldn't see their faces or the markings on their arms. But even if Daphne's theory was true, it didn't change anything.

He set the book down, what little hope he'd foolishly built up crumbling at his feet. "Whether they're Sirens or this Sirenum Scorpoli, it makes no difference. I still hunt and I still kill and I still can't remember why."

"It makes all the difference." She grasped another book from the floor and set it in his lap. "According to this—this ancient text from Olympus that I found in your own library—the Sirenum Scorpoli are responsible for instigating most of the wars in the human realm. They stir up religious zealots. They prey on differences between cultures and emphasize those differences until people want nothing more than to kill each other. These pages are filled with accounts of the Sirenum Scorpoli stimulating one natural disaster after another with Zeus's magic, for causing diseases like the black plague and AIDS. Think about it, Ari. Zeus thrives on chaos. Chaos creates instability and instability leads people to pray. To pray to the gods. And that, more than anything else, is what he uses the Sirenum Scorpoli to do. To make people turn back to praying to the gods. Because the more humans who worship Zeus, the stronger his powers grow.

"Ari," she said softly, "You're not hunting unsuspecting good guys. You're hunting the bad guys. The Sirenum Scorpoli cause more bloodshed and death than any daemons. They're daemons trussed up like models."

Ari's chest vibrated with both hope and doubt. He looked down at the book she'd set in his hand. Didn't remember bringing it here. Didn't know where it had come from. Closing the book, he looked at the cover. The same double-S marking Daphne had seen on those females' arms in the woods was stamped into the leather.

A memory flashed. Bits and pieces of a battle he couldn't piece together. "I took this from them," he muttered. "After a fight. When they were dead."

"That's what I assumed. There's no other way you could have gotten your hands on something from Olympus." She glanced up and around the library. "It's been here a while. You had the knowledge the entire time. You just didn't know it."

A sliver of hope tunneled its way into Ari's chest, but he was too afraid to let it grow. "If this is true, why would Hera use me? What did I ever do to her?"

"Nothing. You did nothing to her. But if she saw you struggling with your grief after your soul mate's death, I'm guessing she saw a way to use you. To curse you again in a way you'd never know. To make you think it was simply an extension of the soul mate curse, when in reality, it was her way to get back at her husband. The god who's done nothing but humiliate her to the world."

Ari's heart beat hard and fast against his ribs. If what Daphne said was true, then he'd been used as a pawn in an immortal chess game. He'd lost his life, his home, his son, all because of the whims of the gods. But ironically, he didn't care. Suddenly all that mattered was the fact he might possibly be free.

He reached for Daphne's hand, warmth and hope filling his chest, making him feel light and alive. More alive than he'd ever felt before. "How did I get here?"

Daphne smiled as he pulled her toward him. A sweet, beautiful, electrifying smile that made his whole body tighten in anticipation of her touch. "I brought you here. Sappheire helped. She heard the commotion through the trees and came running to help. When she saw the Sirenum Scorpoli, she opened a portal and helped me get you through before anything happened. I told her how to get here."

He hadn't hurt anyone. Not even those evil Sirens. "And she just...saved me? Even knowing how many Sirens I've killed over the years?"

Daphne's eyes softened. "She saw what I saw, Ari. And she realized the same truth I already figured out. That she'd never known a Siren killed by you. She's served with the Order for nearly three hundred years. She's Athena's right-hand Siren. If you were really killing Sirens like Zeus and Athena want everyone to believe, she would have met at least one."

Ari glanced toward the fire and watched a flame dance over the log. Remembered his dream of burning in the fires of Hades. He wanted to believe Daphne's claim. Wanted to believe he'd been doing good all these years instead of bad, but something held him back.

"How do you know so much about the Sirens?" His gaze drifted to the shelves. "I haven't been asleep that long. You can't have learned it all from these books or the Siren upstairs."

A nervous look passed over Daphne's face. "That's the other thing I want to tell you." She pulled her hands from his, pushed to her feet, and crossed toward the fire. "Oh man. I can't believe I'm about to do this."

Ari's brow dropped low as he watched her, and a low buzz sounded in his ears. One that set his nerves on edge. One he didn't like. Sliding the book on the ground beside him, he slowly rose to his feet. "Do what?"

"Ruin everything," she mumbled.

Before he could ask what that meant, she turned to face him and straightened her spine. "I know about the Sirens because a week ago, I was on Olympus training to become one. I wasn't in that forest by accident, Ari, and our meeting wasn't by chance. Zeus sent me here to find you. He sent me to find you, to seduce you, and then, when you let down your guard, to kill you."

* * *

Ari didn't say anything. Just stared at her from across the room with blank, unreadable eyes.

Urgency pushed Daphne's feet forward, her stomach swirling with both dread and fear. Not fear that he would hurt her, she knew he'd never do that, but fear that she'd lose him if she didn't tell him everything fast.

"I was close to being inducted into the Order. I thought that's what I wanted. When Zeus gave me this mission, I couldn't say no. If I didn't do it, they would have kicked me out, and you know I have no family left. So I said yes, and I came here looking for you, and I pretended that I was running from a god, when the truth was, I was doing what he and Athena told me to do. But I quickly realized that you aren't at all what they said you are."

She knew she was rambling but she didn't care. All that mattered was making sure he understood the truth. "I didn't seduce you. I realized early on that I wasn't any good at seduction. I mean, I was trained in it. All Sirens are. But I guess none of it really stuck because when I tried to use it, you totally walked away. The only time you even seemed interested in me was when I was being my normal, rambling self, which, by the way, the Sirens do not like. I can't even begin to tell you how many times Sappheire's told me to shut the hell up. And I'd already decided that I wasn't going to do what Zeus and Athena sent me to do, but then I saw the map in your office and I learned what they'd done, and you were so nice and you comforted me, and...and I knew even more that you weren't the psycho they said you were."

She swallowed hard and met his eyes. They were guarded now, his gaze narrowed. And she still couldn't read what he was thinking. But those mismatched eyes of his were locked on her, and she took that as a good sign.

"I didn't sleep with you because I was trying to seduce you," she went on. "I slept with you because I wanted to. Because I'm attracted to you. Because you're the sexiest male I've ever laid eyes on. I mean, let's get real." She held out her hand toward his chiseled abs and muscular arms. "You're like...carved from marble. My knees went weak the first time I saw you in the gym downstairs, and that was when I thought you were a lunatic and when you didn't even want to have anything to do with me. I slept with you because you excite me. Because I'm crazy about you. Because..."

Heat burned her cheeks when she realized how insanely she was rambling now. But she forced herself to go on. "Because I...because I care about you."

No, she didn't just care. She loved him. The truth burned through her chest, stole her breath, and knocked her back a step. She'd heard that nymphs fell fast and hard when they met that perfect someone—her mother had once told her she'd fallen in love with Daphne's father in a matter of days—but Daphne had never experienced love before so she didn't know what to expect. Now, though, she did. Now, when her head grew light and her legs trembled, she knew exactly what it was from.

The room spun around her. Backing up, she reached out to steady herself but knew it was already too late.

Strong arms closed around her and pulled her against a hard chest before she hit the floor. Blinking several times, she gazed up into Ari's handsome face as that whoosh of emotion sped all through her chest again.

She really did love him. So much she no longer saw the scars on his jaw and neck, no longer saw the menace she'd first noticed in his mismatched eyes. She just saw a hero. Her hero. The only true hero she'd ever known.

She also saw someone who wasn't drawing her into him and professing his feelings right back.

He shook his head. "You're crazier than I am, you know that?"

Crazy. He'd said crazy, not beautiful, not amazing, not alluring, not dreamy. Just *crazy*.

Heat rose in her neck and enflamed her cheeks. A hard knot rolled through her stomach with the realization that she'd just made a giant fool of herself.

Pushing against his arms, she found her feet and stepped back, just enough so she could catch her breath. Just enough so she didn't humiliate herself even more.

Pull it together, Daphne. So he doesn't love you. Big deal. You still believe in him. You can still help him.

"So what if I am? Crazy, at least, is real. I could be all seductive and mysterious if I wanted, but I don't want to be. Just like I don't want to be a Siren. I never really wanted to be a Siren in the first place, but you can't say no to the gods, at least I didn't think I could. Now I'd tell them all to fuck off."

An amused expression crossed his features. One that only kicked her embarrassment up even higher. "And why are you smirking at me? Is what I'm saying funny? None of this is funny. I'm trying to tell you the truth. I'm trying to tell you—"

"Daphne." He grasped her by the shoulders and pulled her into him. "Stop talking, okay? I believe you. Any time you ramble I know there's no way you're lying."

Butterflies took flight in her stomach. "You do?"

He nodded, lifted one hand to her cheek, and brushed the hair away from her face. "And you are seductive and mysterious, and yes, even crazy. I've lived with crazy long enough to spot it." He slid his fingers into her hair and cupped the back of her head, pulling her toward him. "Which is probably why I can't get enough of you. Even when I know I'm the last person who should ever touch you."

"Oh..."

His lips brushed hers, and she groaned, immediately opening to his kiss. The taste of him rocketed through her body, bringing hope back to life. Tipping his head the other direction, he kissed her sweetly, slowly, with so much passion her head grew light. And, wanting only this, wanting only *him*, she dug her fingers into his biceps and just held on.

He broke the kiss. Rested his forehead against hers. Breathed deep as his thumb grazed her cheek. "All these years... All this time, and you're the first person who ever saw past the monster." He lifted his head and looked into her eyes. "Why did you even try?"

Tears filled her eyes. Tears filled with joy and love. "I didn't have to try. I just had to open my eyes. And when I did, I knew with you is the only place I ever want to be."

He groaned and kissed her again, his tongue sliding along hers, his mouth absolutely devouring her. She moaned, lifted to her toes, and wrapped her arms around his shoulders, giving him anything he wanted.

His hand slid from her hair, down her back and over the swell of her backside. He stepped into her, forcing her backward. Cool air tickled the fine hairs along her spine as he continued to kiss her, to drive her wild with his tongue, and she knew he was grasping her shirt, that he was pulling it up, that in seconds she would be completely naked. And she wanted that. Wanted more. Excitement pulsed through her. Excitement and heat and a desire that would never get old.

He broke the kiss long enough to tug the long-sleeved T-shirt she'd snagged from his closet up and over her head. The garment landed somewhere on the floor behind him. She didn't look to see where. Was too lost in the fiery heat in his eyes to care.

"This," he whispered as he slid his knuckles down her breast and around one straining nipple, "is all I want." He lowered to his knees in front of her. "Don't move."

Her stomach quivered as she looked down at him, and she remembered when he'd pinned her hands to the ground in front of the fireplace in his room and told her the very same thing. "Or what?"

He looked up at her, and mischief flashed in his mismatched eyes as he pressed his fingers against the inside of her right knee, forcing her to step open. "Or I'll tie you up and make sure you don't move."

A wicked thrill rushed through her just as he exhaled a breath of hot air over her mound. Her eyes slid closed, and she rocked forward, seeking his touch. She'd never been into the whole bondage thing, but with him she knew she could be. With him she had a feeling she'd be into everything.

His tongue parted her folds, slid along her center and flicked her already sensitive clit. Daphne groaned and pushed her hips against his mouth, wanting more. He did it again, this time flicking faster, circling the sensitive nub, then drawing it into his mouth to suckle.

Heaven. His mouth was pure heaven. His hands sliding over her skin absolute paradise. When he suckled her again, she groaned and dropped her hand on the back of his head, pulling him into her. Pleasure arced through her body. Before it could consume her, though, his fingers closed around her wrist. He pulled her hand away then twisted it around her lower back and pinned it to her body.

His threat echoed in her mind, and that naughty thrill whipped through her once more. But then he flicked his tongue against her again and it faded. She rocked her hips again and again, losing herself in the ecstasy. Her orgasm barreled close. She slid her other hand into his hair and pulled him in again. Pleasure rippled along her nerve endings and shot down her spine.

He jerked away before it could consume her and quickly rose to his feet. "I warned you, little nymph."

Daphne gasped, stumbled. Reached out for him. But Ari ducked down, and before she realized what was happening, he wrapped his arms around her legs and threw her over his shoulder. A grunt passed her lips. She pushed a hand against his back, opened her mouth to tell him this wasn't what she wanted—that she wanted his mouth, his hands, *him*—but the words never made it out. A whoosh of air brushed her spine, and the grunt turned to a screech. Then her back hit the couch cushions, and she stared up at his handsome, naughty, playful face.

Desire burned in his eyes. A desire that heated her blood and supercharged her need. "You like being in control, don't you?"

He smirked, a sexy, one-sided grin that made him look downright delectable. Straddling her hips, he pressed one knee into the cushions, leaned over her, and reached for the lamp on the end table beside the couch.

Unsure what he was doing, Daphne twisted against the cushions and looked over her head. He grasped the lamp at the base, pulled until the cord snapped free of the lamp and the light went out, then tugged the end out of the wall socket.

Daphne's gaze shifted back to him. Firelight danced over his features, making his skin look darker and his eyes even wilder. "You just ruined that lamp."

"I know." Grasping her hands at the wrists, he tugged them over her head so they hit the arm of the couch, then wrapped the lamp cord around her wrists and secured the cord to the leg of the table. "Does that hurt?"

Unrestrained lust consumed her when she realized what he'd just done. And though a little voice in the back of her head screamed giving up control was so not a Siren thing to do, she ignored it. Because she wasn't a Siren. And because she was so wet from just the thought of him having his way with her, she could barely think. "No."

"Good." His eyes sparked with heat. "Now, you can't move."

Oh yes...

Her gaze slid down his chiseled abs, directly in her line of site, then over the waistband of his sweats, sitting dangerously low, the V at his hips making her mouth absolutely water. "What do you plan to do with me?"

He leaned down toward her mouth but stopped a millimeter from kissing her. "Everything."

She lifted, aching for his kiss, but he drew away. His hand lightly skimmed her belly and moved across her mound. She whimpered. Then his talented fingers finally slid along her heat and pressed deep inside, and she groaned.

Her eyes slid closed. Energy raced along every nerve ending. She arched her back, tightened around his fingers, twisted against the cord pinning her hands over her head. Sweat gathered along her spine. Her orgasm rushed right back to the surface. Pleasure overwhelmed her. But before it could crest and drag her under, he pulled away once more.

"Oh gods." Fabric rustled somewhere close. Daphne pulled against her restraints. Frustrated. Hot. Aching. "Come back. I need—"

His lips captured hers. His chest grazed her sensitive nipples. His tongue dipped inside her mouth until she was breathless and right back on the edge. "You need me."

"Yes. Gods, yes." She tore her eyes open, stared up at him through hazy vision. His face was flushed with arousal, his muscles straining beneath his skin. Capturing her leg, he hooked it over his hip, then raked his lust-filled gaze down her naked body until he was staring at her sex.

Her body quivered at the heat she saw in his eyes. She bit her lip as his hand closed around his thick cock. He leaned forward, and unable to look away, she lifted her head and watched as he rocked his hips forward, as the blunt tip of his cock slid through her wetness and over her clit, as he groaned at the sight.

Fire rushed down Daphne's spine. She dropped her head back and moaned. He slid his cock through her wetness again, then circled her clit until she saw stars. Until she was rocking against him, growing hotter with every stroke. Until she was so close her body trembled.

"Not yet, little nymph." He pressed his lips against hers and then was gone. His cock slid down and pressed against her opening. "With me."

She cried out at the delicious fit. Lifted to hold him in. Groaned when he slid out then speared inside once more. He braced one knee on the couch between her legs for leverage. Drove deep again. Every thrust was heaven. Each slap of skin divine. Leaning close, he kissed her again, taking control of her mouth the same way he controlled her body.

His hand skimmed her ribs. He pinched her nipple between his thumb and index finger. Rested his forehead against hers as he drove her closer to the edge of oblivion. "Gods, I love being inside you. Could stay like this forever."

Daphne moaned at the thought, lifted her mouth back to his and kissed him crazy, wild for more. He skimmed his other hand up her body and grasped her wrists in his long fingers, squeezing to hold her arms still. His lips released hers. Sweat dripped from him onto her as their bodies picked up speed. And it was good—so good—but she wanted more. Wanted all of him.

"Surrender to me," he growled.

She wanted to—gods, she wanted to—but she didn't know how to do that. She tightened around him, lifted to meet every stroke, tried to grasp his hand with her fingers pinned beneath his hold against the arm of the couch. She was close. So close. And she knew if she could just go over she could drag him with her. But—

He pinched her nipple again. Pain ricocheted through her entire body, wiping away every other thought. She arched and cried out. But before the sound was even out of her mouth, the pain transformed into pure, mindless pleasure.

Daphne moaned and sagged into the cushions. Ari's cock grew even harder as he pushed into her deeper, faster, hitting that perfect spot again and again. She let go of the tension in her muscles, gave herself over to his thrusts and wicked touch. And the moment she did, she had a split second of clarity. Of his need to overwhelm her. To consume her. To own her so she was his. Which was everything she needed too. The orgasm exploded inside her without warning, a sea of white-hot, blinding light that absolutely devoured her.

Long moments passed, but slowly consciousness seeped back. Shaking, Daphne dragged air into her lungs. Her muscles felt like gelatin, her body a pile of bones under a heavy weight. Prying her eyelids apart, she looked up, but all she saw was skin.

Ari lay over her, one hand still closed over her bound wrists, his slick body resting on top of hers while he fought to catch his own breath. Tingles erupted everywhere they touched, warming her skin, bringing it back to life one millimeter at a time.

"I'll move," he breathed in her ear. "Just...give me a second."

His body was as limp as hers, and the realization made Daphne's lips curl in a self-satisfied smile. She'd done that. She'd completely and utterly wrecked him. As thoroughly as he'd wrecked her.

Slowly, he eased back and looked down at her. His mismatched eyes were still glazed from his own pleasure, but a look of pure contentment softened his features and smoothed the scars on the lower half of his face.

He glanced toward the table above her head and chuckled.

"What's so funny?" She twisted so she could see what had captured his attention, then gasped.

The table lay in pieces on the floor, the lamp shattered against the hardwood.

She whipped back to face him. "Did I do that? Oh my gods, I don't remember that. I'm sorry."

His grin widened. "Why? I like a female who can relinquish control so completely and forget about everything around her." He pressed his lips against hers and rocked his hips, proving he liked it a lot. He was already growing hard again inside her. "I like it so much, I want to make you do it again."

Oh... She wanted that too. Right here. Right now. Every day for the rest of her life.

"I'm the last person who should ever touch you."

His words echoed in her head. Groaning, she lifted to his kiss and lost herself in him all over again. He was wrong. He was the *only* person who should touch her. The only one who made her feel alive.

And somehow, she promised herself, she'd find a way to make him believe it too.

CHAPTER NINE

Ari lay in bed, his arm wrapped around Daphne's back, her naked body draped over his as she trailed her fingers along his ribs. Firelight from the hearth flickered over the ceiling in his bedroom, and he watched the shadows dance and move as he played with the ends of her hair and tried to convince himself keeping her with him was not a bad idea.

Nymphs were highly sexual creatures, free with their bodies in ways other races weren't. He wasn't stupid. Sex with Daphne would have been mind blowing regardless of the situation, but the fact she'd shared her feelings made it all the more sweet. Nymphs weren't known to declare their emotions. Penelopei hadn't once told him how she felt, and they'd been together for months. Then again, Penelopei had been manipulative and selfish, and Daphne wasn't. Even though Daphne had trained with the Sirens, she was the most selfless person Ari had ever met.

She rolled her luscious body on top of his, rested her palms on his chest, and looked up. "You're awfully quiet, Mr. Argonaut. What are you thinking?"

She was also highly perceptive. Something that struck him as odd because Penelopei hadn't once keyed in to his moods in all the time they'd spent together.

He brushed the hair over her shoulder so it ran down her sexy back in a sleek mass. "Sorry. I was thinking about home."

"Argolea?"

He nodded.

"You miss it, don't you?"

He toyed with the ends of her hair. "Yes, I do. I miss the

mountains and the ocean and the white marble of Tiyrns. But mostly I miss the people."

"Silas said you have a son."

"Cerek." His chest pinched with a familiar sense of guilt. "He'd be about a hundred and twenty-five years now."

She pushed up on his chest and stared down at him with wide eyes. "Good gods, your son is a hundred and twenty-five? You must be ancient."

Smiling, he rolled her back in the pillows and kissed her neck. "That's right. I'm older than dirt. You just got fucked by a senior citizen."

She giggled and slid her fingers into his hair. "Thank the gods your ass isn't saggy. How old is dirt, anyway?"

He moved to her earlobe. "Really old."

"Give me a number."

He stilled against her ear. She was only in her twenties. Nymphs had long lifespans, but not as long as Argonauts. Even though they both had roughly five hundred years left to live, he didn't want to shock her.

He also didn't want to lie. Not after the way she'd been so honest with him. He pressed a kiss to the soft skin behind her ear. "Two hundred and twelve."

Her hand shoved against his shoulder, knocking him back into the mattress. Sitting upright, she stared down at him with even wider eyes. "Holy Hades. It's a wonder you didn't break a hip with that last acrobatic stunt you pulled."

She had an adorable way of lightening the mood. One that put him at instant ease. Tugging her down onto his chest, he wrapped one leg around hers, locking her tight against him. "I have a stockpile of acrobatic stunts saved up." He lifted his head and kissed her. "And I heal fast. So if you break my hip, little nymph, I'll be good to go in only a few hours. Don't worry."

Laughing, she relaxed into him again, then laid her head back on his chest. "No wonder you're so attracted to me. You need someone to keep you young."

He sifted his fingers back through her hair and realized she was right. Isolating himself the way he'd done had only aged him beyond his years. Every day he felt the weight of loneliness wearing on his body and mind. He hadn't realized how much until Daphne had come into his life like a breath of fresh air, reminding him he was still a relatively young male.

"So when was the last time you saw Cerek?" she asked, drawing a lazy circle on his chest with the pad of her index finger.

His stomach instantly tightened, and an image filled his mind. A flash of that last day, when he'd set that fire. "Fifty years ago."

"In Argolea?"

"No. The human realm."

She didn't ask, but he knew she was waiting for more. And even though talking about it only brought back painful memories, he owed her answers after everything she'd given him.

"After my soul mate was killed, I wasn't much fun to be around. I was living in the human realm then, just trying to get from one day to the next. Cerek kept popping over to check on me when he should have been focused on his new position with the Argonauts."

"He took your spot after you left?"

"Yes."

"Do you have other children?"

"No. Just Cerek."

"And you miss him."

It wasn't a question but a statement, one that hit him hard beneath her hand where it rested on his chest. A lump formed in his throat. One he'd spent fifty years trying to get rid of but never quite could, one that made it hard to form words. He nodded.

She was quiet for several seconds, then said, "Since you said you were only with your soul mate a few months, and Cerek's way older than fifty, I'm guessing his mother wasn't your soul mate?"

He breathed out a sigh of relief, thankful they'd moved on from what a shitty father he was. "No, she wasn't."

Daphne looked up at him with narrowed eyes. "It's very hard to get information out of you, Mr. Super Secretive Argonaut."

There she went again, relaxing him when no one else ever really had. He brushed his hand down her hair, smoothing it over her lower spine. "It was right after I'd joined the Argonauts. I was young. She was interested in hooking up with a Guardian. It wasn't serious. When she discovered she was pregnant, we both knew our relationship wasn't going to last, but we remained connected through our son. We stayed friends."

"Does Cerek see her often?"

"She died when he was about ten. This was back when the borders of Argolea were more fluid. She and some friends crossed into the human realm and were attacked by a horde of daemons."

"I'm sorry."

He sighed and looked up at the ceiling, another whisper of guilt rushing through him because he hadn't been able to stop Gia. Hadn't been able to save her. "It was a long time ago. When she died, I mourned her, but it didn't break me. It was harder for Cerek. I had the Argonauts. He didn't. Somehow, no thanks to me, he got through it."

Ari's chest squeezed tight. Cerek had been dealt a crappy hand, and it was all Ari's fault. He hadn't done a thing to make life easier for Cerek, and when it all got to be too much, he'd walked away, leaving Cerek to pick up the pieces of a shattered family. That was Ari's greatest regret. That his son had paid for his mistakes. Was *still* paying for them.

"No," Daphne said softly. "I'm sure it's *because* of you that he got through it."

Startled by her words, Ari looked down at her. Her eyes were a soft green, her face filled with so much emotion, the pain in his chest slowly seeped away. She didn't know Cerek, didn't know how cocky and arrogant Ari had been back then, didn't know anything about his old life except what she saw now. And even after all of the horrible things she knew about him today, she still believed the best of him.

"Why do have such faith in me?" he asked quietly. "I'm not worth it."

"Do you really have to ask? I have faith because I love you."

For a moment, he was sure time stood still. Of all the things he'd expected her to say, that wasn't it. His heart beat hard against his ribs as he searched her face for the lie he knew had hidden somewhere inside her. But in her shimmering gemlike eyes he saw nothing but truth.

"Daphne." His pulse turned to a whir in his ears. "I'm pretty sure I'm not capable of love."

Bracing her hands on each side of his shoulders, she straddled his hips and leaned forward so her lips brushed his in the sweetest, softest kiss. "I don't believe that for a second. I can tell by the look in your eye and what you don't say that you love your son. And something tells me you didn't fake your death so Cerek would stop pestering you. You left to spare him from seeing his father in the throes of a nightmare he didn't understand. You can love, Ari. You already do."

She moved back to his side, rested her head on his chest, and curled into him. "Love is a blessing, not a curse. You just have to choose it."

Her breaths slowed as she drifted to sleep beside him, but Ari knew he'd find no sleep. Because as he looked into the flames on the far side of the room and her words of love echoed in the air around him, he knew he couldn't keep reality at bay any longer.

Zeus would never let her live. Not with the way she'd sacrificed her duty for his enemy. By now his Sirenum Scorpoli had probably already shared what had happened in those woods. And that meant every moment she spent in this hold put her life in that much more danger.

His chest pinched so hard it stole his breath. Rolling to his side, he wrapped his other arm around her and pulled her in tight to his chest. Gods, she awed him again and again. She believed in him when she had no reason to. Cared for him when others would turn away. Loved him even when he didn't love himself.

She was wrong. Love wasn't the blessing. *She* was the blessing. And he would do whatever he had to do to keep her safe.

Even if that meant becoming the savage she didn't believe him to be.

* * *

Daphne slid out of bed at dawn, tired but in need of caffeine. She hadn't been able to sleep much, thoughts of the Sirens and Athena and Zeus and the Sirenum Scorpoli sifting through her mind. She knew that wasn't the last they were going to see of Zeus's secret sect, and as much as she hated to leave Ari naked and asleep in that big bed of his, she needed to talk to Sappheire about what their next move should be.

She found one of Ari's huge button-down shirts in the closet, tugged it on, and headed for the hall. Voices echoed from the kitchen, and her brow lowered as she tried to figure out who Sappheire was talking to.

"And I bet that's something you do regularly on Olympus," a familiar male voice said.

"Actually," Sappheire answered, "it's not. I can't tell you the last time I went out on a date. The only males on Olympus are gods who aren't interested in anything but casual sex. And, no thanks, I don't need to be another notch on an immortal's bedpost. The males I encounter in the human realm won't even come near me when they discover what I am."

The male chuckled, then the refrigerator door opened and closed, and as Daphne listened, she realized it was Silas, back from his supply run a few days early. "Maybe it's not what you are but the way you look. Gorgeous females are more than a little intimidating to the average guy."

"It's not real," Sappheire said. "It's part of the whole Siren gig. Immortal glamour to create the perfect female. The old me isn't anything like this, believe me. Daphne's the only female I can remember in all the recent classes who wasn't altered. Nymphs are so genetically blessed. It's disgusting."

Silas chuckled again. "Something tells me you're wrong. Zeus doesn't pick the homely girls for the Siren Order. I'm sure he was fully impressed before your transformation."

"Well, I did always have great tits. Those didn't change."

"See?" The sound of a knife hitting a cutting board echoed from the kitchen as Daphne drew close, but it was the smile she heard in Silas's voice that piqued her interest. "There you go."

"Are you agreeing with me?"

"I'm definitely not arguing. They're more than nice from where I'm standing."

They both looked up when Daphne stepped into the room, Silas from the stove where he was cooking, and Sappheire from the counter where she sat on a stool sipping a cup of coffee with a silly grin. The Siren was still wearing the same pants she'd had on yesterday, but the light-blue T-shirt hanging off her toned shoulders had to be Silas's.

"Oh, there you are." Sappheire's smile wobbled as she set her mug down. "I was just telling Silas here about your irritating genetics."

Silas grinned. "She doesn't give her own genetics enough credit. Nice shirt, Daphne."

This wasn't one of the shirts Silas had picked out for her before he'd left, which meant he knew where she'd gotten it. And how. Daphne knew she should be a little embarrassed, but she wasn't. Not at all.

"How's the patient?" Sappheire asked.

"Fine." Actually, he was better than fine, but Daphne didn't want to share that with her friends. Some things were meant to stay private. She crossed to the far side of the kitchen, pulled a mug from the cupboard, and poured herself a cup of coffee. "He was more than surprised to learn you were here though, Sappheire."

"I bet he was," Sappheire mumbled, lifting her cup again. "Not as much as this guy though."

Silas chuckled. "You shocked me, I'll admit it."

"But it was a nice kind of surprise," Sappheire said with a smile in her voice. "Wasn't it?"

Daphne turned. Sappheire sipped her coffee, and looked right at Silas with that same silly, mischievous grin. His gaze held hers, and he smiled too, then went back to chopping. "Yes it was. A very nice surprise."

They were flirting. Daphne looked between the two, amused and, yes, surprised herself. Ari's caretaker and Daphne's mentor. Who would have guessed? In all the years Daphne had known Sappheire, she'd never known the Siren to flirt. Sappheire didn't even use seduction on her victims, like the other Sirens in her Order. Just arrows.

Silas's grin faded, and he turned toward Daphne. "Sappheire filled me in on what you discovered about Zeus's secret Sirens. It makes a lot of sense. Makes a shit ton of sense."

The secret Sirens. Right. Daphne needed to remember why she'd come in here, not get caught up in someone else's romance.

"The question is what are we going to do about it?" Sappheire asked. "No one's ever confirmed the Sirenum Scorpoli actually exist. That tells me right there that anyone who knows about them is dead. Which means we're at the top of Zeus's shit list. It's only a matter of time before he finds this place."

"I was thinking the same thing." Daphne bit her lip then looked toward Silas. "Ari's not safe here. The only place where Zeus can't get to him is Argolea."

"But his Sirens can," Sappheire pointed out. "That won't protect you or me from Athena's retaliation, or any of us from Zeus's evil bitches."

"No." Silas braced his hands on the counter. "It won't. And if Zeus sends his assassins into Argolea, it'd turn into a blood bath. Thousands of innocents would die."

Silence settled over the room as each of them considered. Finally, Daphne said, "We could contact the Argonauts. Ari's son serves with them. I know they would send help if they knew he was still alive."

"No one's contacting the Argonauts." Ari's voice echoed from the archway to the hall.

He'd pulled on loose-fitting jeans and a black T-shirt that stretched seductively across his broad shoulders, and as Daphne took in the sight of him, her skin warmed and all the delicious things they'd done to each other last night rolled through her memory. But there was a hardness to his mismatched eyes she hadn't seen last night, and remembering their conversation about his son, something in the back of her mind whispered not to push him too hard too fast. "It's the smartest option we have, Ari. I know you're not ready to go back to Argolea yet, but if Zeus comes here—"

"Then I'll deal with him." His gaze didn't waver from hers. "The same way I've dealt with his secret sect all these years. But you're right. The three of you need to leave." He looked toward Sappheire. "Take her back to Athena. If you tell her what happened, I'm sure Athena will protect her."

Oh no. He wasn't sending her away. Not now. Not after everything that had happened between them. He'd tried that once before and this time she wasn't leaving.

She set her mug on the counter, moved behind Silas, and crossed to stand in front of Ari, still in the doorway. "You're not getting rid of me that easily. If you're staying, I'm staying."

"This isn't up for discu—"

His words died as he lifted his head. Every muscle in his body went rigid. Before Daphne could ask what was going on, his eyes shifted from their mismatched blue and green to deathly black.

"Oh shit." Her stomach clenched with fear. For him. "Ari?"

He darted to the window and looked out at the early morning light.

"What's going on?" Sappheire slipped off the barstool. "Do you sense something?"

Ari darted to the next window, his gaze scanning the cliff beside them, then shifting to the valley far below. A low growl built in his throat. "Sirens."

Silas and Sappheire exchanged worried glances, but Daphne was too focused on Ari to care what they were thinking. Rushing to his side, she reached for his hand. "Ari, stay with me."

He rounded on her so fast she gasped, and when he looked down at her with those crazed eyes, his features twisted with fury, fear shot through her chest. But in her heart she knew this was the same male who'd touched her and loved her so thoroughly last night. And she wasn't about to let him forget.

She gripped his hand tighter. Forced him to look at her. "Stay with me. You can fight it. You fought it yesterday. Focus."

He squeezed her hand so hard, pain shot up her arm. But she didn't pull away. Instead, she watched his eyes for her cue. Held on. Said his name over and over. His eyes flickered between black and blue and green. Then slowly they shifted to the familiar colors she knew so well.

"Yes," she whispered, squeezing his hand, knowing she had him back. "I'm right here."

Before she could wrap her arms around him, he pulled his hand from hers and looked toward Sappheire. "Take her back to Athena *now*."

Panic pushed at Daphne's chest when she realized he meant to stay here and face Zeus's evil Sirens alone. She darted in his way, blocking his exit toward the hall. "I'm not leaving you."

He glared down at her. "Too fucking bad. You don't have a choice in this."

He tried to step around her but she moved in front of him again. "Yes, I do. I said I'm not leaving, and I'm not."

His jaw clenched down hard. His eyes flickered. She could feel the insanity bubbling just under his control, but she wasn't backing down. She hadn't been there when her village had been attacked. She wasn't leaving Ari now to the same fate.

"I'm not going anywhere without you," she said again.

"Yes, you are." His eyes flashed to black and held. "The Sirens trained you well, female. You were a good fuck and a decent distraction, but I don't have time for your games anymore, and the last thing I need is another person hanging on me, hoping for something I don't have the power to give them. I ditched my son for way less than you, so don't think for a minute that you're anything special. I don't want you anymore. Deal with it and get lost. All of you."

Daphne's mouth fell open, but he stepped past her before she could stop him.

Long, silent seconds passed. No one in the room spoke.

"We can't go to Olympus," Sappheire finally said quietly. "Athena will never side with us, not against Zeus. Not even if she knows about his secret sect. We wouldn't be safe there."

"We can't stay here," Silas said.

"No, we can't," Sappheire answered.

"I know who can help us." Strength gathered inside Daphne as she turned to face them. A strength she hadn't even known she possessed until just this very moment. "A Siren who would never say no to an Argonaut in need."

Sappheire's brow lowered. "You're talking about Skyla."

Daphne nodded.

Sappheire's jaw clenched. "She hates me."

"Doesn't matter. She's bound to an Argonaut. She'll be able to get the help we need."

Sappheire and Silas exchanged glances, then Sappheire looked back at her. "Are you sure about this? If we do this, they'll find out he's still alive, and he clearly doesn't want that."

"I'm more than sure. That little speech of his was complete bullshit. He might say he knows what he wants, but I know what he needs. We're not leaving him to Zeus alone."

"Well done, nymph." A slow smile spread across Silas's face. "Very well done."

CHAPTER TEN

"Come on." Cerek tapped his palm against his bare chest then held his arms out wide. "Hit me. Ever since you and Skyla were bound, you fight like a pussy."

A low chuckle rumbled from Orpheus across the mat, rising in the ancient gymnasium toward the upper seating levels of the oval-shaped stadium that showcased some of Tiyrns greatest sporting matches. The Argonaut tipped his head and shot Cerek a pointed look. "I know you're scared of females and all, big guy, but let me tell ya a secret. Pussies don't fight. The good ones give nothing but pleasure."

Cerek swiped the sweat out of his eyes with the back of his marked forearm and scowled. He wasn't afraid of females. His reasons for avoiding them were his own and no one else's. But just the fact Orpheus seemed to make it his personal mission in life to razz Cerek about his lack of female companionship only fueled Cerek's desire for blood. "Fine, then you fight like a fucking girl."

"My girl's a Siren." Orpheus grinned as he dropped his bare shoulder and shifted his feet on the mat. "Or was. She'd take that as a compliment."

Orpheus charged and plowed his shoulder into Cerek's ribs. Locking his arms behind Cerek's back, he lifted Cerek off the floor. Air whooshed over Cerek's spine just before he cracked hard into the mat. Pain spiraled across his back, but before Orpheus could get the upper hand, Cerek flipped Orpheus to his stomach, grabbed the back of Orpheus's head, and slammed the Argonaut's face into the ground.

"Son of a fucking..." Orpheus shoved his elbow hard into Cerek's ribs, knocking Cerek back a step. "That's my godsdamn nose, you prick."

"Let me guess." Skyla's voice echoed from the doorway that disappeared beneath the spectator area. "My mate was giving you a hard time."

Cerek pushed upright and glanced toward the former Siren. Skyla's blonde hair hung in a sleek wave past her shoulders, and her green eyes sparkled with amusement as she watched her mate roll to his back and pinch his nose to stop the gush of blood.

"I warned you not to taunt him," Skyla said to Orpheus. "Clearly, you didn't listen. Again."

A goofy grin slid across Orpheus's face as he peered up at Cerek. One that told Cerek loud and clear that the bastard had intentionally pushed him right to the edge just for the fun of it. "It's not really a workout if it doesn't get the blood pumping."

Fucking idiot. Orpheus was a deadly warrior in battle, but he liked to stir the shit at home. He always had.

Cerek held his hand out to Orpheus and pulled the Guardian up. "Next time I'll break your arm."

Orpheus flashed bloody teeth. "Next time I'll get my *girl* to break yours."

Skyla sighed. "My hopes for either of you to grow up just crashed and burned. Listen, children, we have a situation."

"What kind of situation?" Cerek's gaze snapped to Skyla, his focus zeroing in on the Siren and her real reason for being here.

"A very serious one." A female wearing slim black pants, boots, and the baggiest T-shirt Cerek had ever seen stepped up next to Skyla, her auburn hair, streaked with gold and brown, hanging past her shoulders like a luxurious mane. Beside her, another female moved into the room, this one much shorter, with long, dark hair, dressed in nothing but a man's oversized shirt.

"Whoa," Orpheus muttered. "Siren."

"Both of them?" Cerek's brow lifted in surprise. Sirens didn't often visit their realm. In fact, he could only remember one time in the last ten years that any Siren other than Skyla had shown up in Argolea.

"No, just the one on the right," Orpheus muttered. "The other's a nymph."

Cerek's gaze ran over the nymph, and his back tingled when her focus locked solidly on him. He'd never met her before but something about her made the hairs on his nape stand at attention and a whisper of worry rush down his spine.

"Don't get any ideas, daemon." Skyla shot her mate a pointed look. "The nymph's already spoken for." She turned toward the nymph. "Don't worry. He's harmless."

Grinning, Orpheus stepped off the mat and slid an arm around Skyla's waist, then leaned down and kissed her cheek. "Totally harmless."

"Ew." Skyla grimaced and leaned away from him. "You're covered in blood and sweat."

"Never bothered you before."

Skyla rolled her eyes. The Siren beside her looked Orpheus over with speculation. "*This* is the male you left the Order for?"

Skyla frowned up at her mate. "Yes. The one and only. Sometimes I can barely believe it myself."

Orpheus held out his hand toward the Siren. "Orpheus the great and powerful."

Skyla crossed her arms over her chest and huffed. "In your dreams, daemon."

Orpheus's bloody grin only widened. The Siren returned his handshake cautiously. "Sappheire."

"Whoa." Orpheus's stupid smile faded, and he looked back at Skyla. "The same Sappheire who—"

"Yes," Skyla answered quickly, turning toward Orpheus and widening her eyes in a shut-the-hell-up signal only a moron could miss. "The same Sappheire I served with on Olympus. Amazing, isn't it?"

From his spot on the mat where he watched the banter, Cerek couldn't help but chuckle. Even Cerek had heard Skyla's stories about the Siren who'd constantly challenged Skyla's status as Athena's right hand on Olympus. Leave it to Orpheus to stir the shit for his mate when the female in question was standing in the same room.

Orpheus looked back at Sappheire, his gaze sliding over her baggy shirt. "What are you doing here? That's not a sanctioned Siren uniform."

"No, it's not," the nymph said, finally speaking. "We're here because we need Cerek's help."

"Me?" Cerek glanced at the nymph once more, confusion tugging at his brows. "Why me?"

"Because Aristokles is in trouble." Her green eyes narrowed only on him. "Your father's alive, Cerek, but he won't be for long unless you help him."

* * *

Please don't let him die. Please, please, please...

As she traveled through the portal toward Stonehill Hold with the handful of Argonauts who'd joined them, all Daphne could think about were the multitude of ways they would find Ari's lifeless body.

Don't let him die. Please don't let him die.

She wasn't stupid. She knew why he'd said the things he had. Not because he meant them but because he was trying to get her to leave him so she'd be safe. But what he'd been too stupid to realize was that the only safe place for her was with him.

Her nerves vibrated as her feet connected with the frozen ground. As they couldn't flash through solid walls, they'd chosen a location on the hillside outside the hold. She said another prayer that they'd gotten here before Zeus's army, then opened her eyes and gasped.

The entire structure was on fire. Dark smoke rose to the gray sky above. Female bodies littered the ground, some missing their heads, others stabbed through the heart by random blades, even more burned as if consumed by flames.

"Oh my gods." Fear wrapped an icy hand around her throat as she scanned the destruction.

"Way to go, Ari," Silas said at her side.

Daphne whipped toward him with wide eyes, but when the half breed met her gaze, she discovered he wasn't horrified like her. He was impressed. "Why—?"

"Booby traps," he said. "Ari wired this place up good in the event we were ever attacked." He pointed toward a dagger sticking out of a dead female's chest. "A rain shower of blades. Dirty bombs." He glanced toward the charred remains on the hillside beside them. "Barrels of oil he could light on fire."

Daphne looked back at the burning structure, a new sense of terror ripping through her. "Are you saying he set this fire himself?"

"Maybe. Hard to know. Zeus could be trying to smoke him out of the safe room."

"Is there no other exit?" Cerek moved up next to Daphne, his features tight, his eyes a little wild. Wild, Daphne knew, because she'd told him his father was alive, and they'd just walked into a nightmare.

"If Ari's in the safe room, he can get out." Silas pointed toward the south. "A tunnel runs from there, through the mountain, and exits in a ravine on the other side of the ridge."

Hope leapt in Daphne's chest. She scanned the snowy hillside.

Cerek took a step in that direction, but Theron, the massive Argonaut with shoulder-length dark hair Daphne had learned was the leader of the Argonauts, stepped in his way and pressed a hand to Cerek's chest. "Be careful. If what the half breed said is true and Ari's in one of his episodes, he could be dangerous. Even to you."

Cerek's back tightened. "He's my father. I'm not afraid of him."

"I know you're not, but—"

"He can control it," Daphne said. They both turned her way. "He just has to focus. If I can get to him, I can help him."

The skepticism in Theron's eyes said he wasn't convinced. "Let's hope you're right, female." He glanced toward the other warriors who'd flashed in just after them, standing behind Cerek. "Zander, Demetrius, and I will take Silas around the south side of the building and check the hold. Skyla, you and Sappheire go with Cerek and Daphne to where the tunnel lets out and see if you can find him. Orpheus, Phin, and Gryphon are coming up from the west where the path leads down the mountain in case anyone's coming or going that way. I sent Titus to find Nick. He and Cynna are on holiday, but if we run into Zeus, we're going to need our own god on our side. Let's hope we get out of here before that happens. Everyone clear?"

Heads nodded. Blades were drawn. As a light snow began to fall, Daphne looked from face to face, both awed and relieved that so many had come to Ari's aid. He thought no one cared. If he knew what they were all willing to do for him—

"Good." Theron stepped past Daphne and headed for the burning hold. "Let's wrap this up before anyone gets hurt."

"That dumbfuck better be alive when we get to him," Zander muttered as the group parted and he followed Theron down the snowy hillside. "Or I'll kill him myself."

Cerek turned to Daphne. "Come on."

Daphne had so many questions, about the Argonauts, about their relationships with Ari, about Cerek and what he'd been through these last fifty years, but now wasn't the time to ask them. She and Cerek had spoken briefly regarding Ari before they'd left Argolea, about who she was to Ari and how she'd known to go to Argolea for help, and though she knew Cerek had a million questions of his own, he didn't ask them either. Both of them were lost in thought as they hiked through the snow.

Her throat grew tight and her hands trembled as she stepped around trees and boulders, trying not to sink into the snow, trying not to let fear get the best of her. Sappheire and Skyla were silent as they followed. But the closer they drew to the ravine, the harder it was for Daphne to keep her pulse steady and her breaths slow and even.

The sound of metal hitting metal reached Daphne's ears first. Her heart rate shot up when she realized blades were striking. Her legs pushed into a sprint.

"Daphne," Sappheire hissed.

But Daphne didn't stop. Couldn't. Her heart lurched into her throat.

Breathless, she reached the edge of the ravine and looked down. Ari stood in the bottom of the small, snowy valley, his blade clanging against the dagger of a Sirenum Scorpoli as she lunged and tried to slice him. His arms were a whir of black menace, his blade a violent weapon that beat her back. And though Daphne couldn't see his eyes, she knew they were black and crazed. Could tell by his jerky motions that he was in that moment where all he craved was blood.

Screams echoed from the other side of the ravine. Daphne's gaze jerked that way, toward the dozen or so Sirenum Scorpoli sliding down the snowy incline. Her heart rate went stratospheric.

"Holy gods," Cerek muttered at her side.

She didn't have time to respond. Before she could look his way, he was over the edge, sliding down the snow, yelling Ari's name and swinging his blade as he sliced through Zeus's assassins like paper dolls.

Skyla and Sappheire quickly followed him down into the ravine and joined the fight. She was trained for this very thing, and Daphne knew she should join them, but all she could focus on was getting to Ari. On grounding him before he turned his blade on the wrong person and did something he couldn't undo.

Dagger gripped tightly in her hand, Daphne slid down the hillside.

The sounds of blades slicing through flesh and bone echoed in the small valley, but she shut them out and focused on her target. Twenty yards ahead, Ari arced out with his blade and caught the Siren he'd been fighting across the jugular.

The female hit the rocks with a crack. Blood gurgled from the wound, choking her to death.

"Ari." Daphne raced up on Ari's right and gripped his forearm with her free hand as tight as she could. "I'm here, Ari."

His eyes were a sea of black, as possessed as she'd ever seen them. As if she hadn't spoken, he jerked his forearm free so he could move on to his next kill, but she knew if that happened, he might attack the wrong person. Frantic to get through to him, she dropped her blade on the rocks at her feet and grabbed on to his arm with both hands.

"Ari, dammit. Look at me."

Using every bit of strength she had, she jerked him around to face her. His crazed eyes couldn't seem to focus, skipped everywhere as if looking for the threat. But she held on, not letting go, and said his name over and over again. Until those black pools landed on her eyes. Until the glossiness started to fade. Until his eyes flickered from black to blue and green and back again, telling her he was still in there. That if she didn't give up, he could come back to her.

"That's it," she said softly while the battle continued to rage behind him. "I'm right here. Focus on me, Ari."

"D-Daphne?"

"Yes, it's me." Relief swept through her, stealing her breath, making the muscles in her legs grow weak. "I'm here."

His familiar, beautiful mismatched eyes skipped over her features. "What the hell are you doing here? I sent you to Olympus where you'd be safe."

Oh, she'd been so right.

"I'll never be safe on Olympus. Not when anyone who looks at me can see I'm in love with you. Did you really think I was going to let you do this alone?"

"Do what alo—" He turned to look over the ravine, then froze. "Holy skata."

Daphne glanced past him, toward Skyla, pulling her arrow out of a dead Sirenum Scorpoli, then to Sappheire, shaking her head at a body on the ground at her feet. Each and every one of Zeus's assassins who'd come over the side of that ravine was now dead. But Ari's shock had nothing to do with their victory.

His reaction had only to do with the fact his estranged son was striding right for him with a bloody blade held tightly in his hand.

* * *

Ari tensed. Cerek was exactly as he remembered. Fifty years hadn't changed the color of his eyes, or the slope of his nose that was so much like his mother's, or the square cut of his jaw that came directly from Ari. He was just as big as he'd been before, the same height and size as Ari, and his sandy brown hair was just as rumpled as it had always been when he was a kid. Even the small scar on his upper lip, the one he'd gotten when he'd fallen out of that tree, was exactly the same.

But he wasn't the same. Fifty years had aged him in a way that didn't show on his face, but reflected deeply in his light-brown eyes. Eyes that were now guarded and filled with disbelief.

Cerek stopped two feet away, his wide-eyed gaze skipping over Ari as if he'd seen a ghost. A splatter of blood was smeared across his cheek. His jacket was torn at the shoulder, and the blade in his hand dripped crimson red droplets onto the dirty snow. But Ari didn't move. Didn't speak. Didn't know what the hell he could say to make up for fifty empty years.

"I didn't think it was true," Cerek muttered. "I can't believe it's you. All these years..."

Ari's pulse whirred in his ears, and his hands grew damp against his side. He wanted to turn, to run, to disappear, but he couldn't. Not this time.

Say something, shithead. Do *something. He's your son.*

He swallowed hard. "Cerek, I—"

The blade in Cerek's hand clanged against the snowy rocks at their feet. Then he moved so fast, Ari barely had time to brace himself. But instead of the right hook to the jaw Ari deserved, Cerek closed his arms around Ari's shoulders, pulled him in, and held on tight.

The snow, the ravine, everything seemed to swirl around Ari as he stood still, embraced by his son. He heard Cerek's voice. Knew the boy was talking to him, but couldn't make out the words. Except for one.

One got through and wedged its way solidly inside that heart he thought he didn't have.

Pateras.

Every mistake he'd made, every wrong choice over the last fifty years no longer mattered. With tears stinging his eyes, Ari wrapped his arms around his son and hugged him back.

"I'm sorry," Ari managed, his throat thick with regret. "I shouldn't have left. I was wrong. I—"

"I don't care." Cerek drew back and clasped Ari's face in both of his big hands. Tears shimmered in Cerek's eyes as he shook his head. "You're back. That's all that matters to me." A beaming smile pulled at his lips. "You're back."

He hugged Ari again, so tight the air felt as if it were squeezed right out of Ari's lungs. But Ari didn't care. He didn't deserve redemption, but his son was offering it, and he wasn't about to let it pass him by.

Cerek finally let go and swiped his forearm over his eyes. "But you're an idiot for not contacting us sooner. What the hell were you thinking taking on Zeus's assassins alone? Good thing Daphne's smarter than you."

Daphne...

Ari's chest warmed at just the thought of her, and he turned quickly, desperate to find her. He didn't have to look far. She stood off to his right, her hair twisted into a knot on the top of her head, her body covered by slim black leggings, a fitted hip-length jacket, and boots that elongated her legs and reminded him what it felt like to be surrounded only by her. And her eyes, her beautiful, honest, innocent eyes, were focused right on him, shimmering with both love and forgiveness. Two things he didn't deserve. Two things that were now part of his life, all thanks to her.

He reached for her, slid his arms around her waist, then lifted her off the ground and buried his face in her neck. "I love you," he whispered. "I love you, I love you, I love you. Forgive me."

Her arms closed around his shoulders. "There's nothing to forgive." Her breath was warm against his skin, her words the sweetest thing he'd ever heard. "I knew you were just trying to protect me. I'm not stupid."

He couldn't stop the smile that spread across his mouth or the kiss he pressed against her cheek. "I know you're not. You're the smartest female I've ever met. Way smarter than me. Even my son knows that."

Her gemlike eyes sparkled as she eased back and looked up at him. "Don't forget it."

"I won't. No way I ever could."

"I should have known you were too much of a rat bastard to die," a male echoed from somewhere close.

The familiar voice ricocheted through Ari's mind, and he released Daphne just enough so he could turn and glance behind him. Zander, the oldest of the Argonauts and the Guardian Ari had served with the longest, strode across the snow toward him, all blond-headed and Adonis-beautiful, just as he'd been for the last eight hundred years.

Ari let go of Daphne and pushed her a step away, bracing himself for Zander's legendary rage, just in case. Behind Zander, he spotted other Argonauts, but he didn't have time to look closely. Because Zander captured him in a tight hug before he could, then slapped a hand on Ari's shoulder and drew back.

"You're an asshole, you know that?" Zander grinned and shook his head, that rage nowhere to be seen. "I fucking missed you man. Holy hell. I can't believe you're really here."

Friends Ari had thought he'd never see again stepped close, hugged him, then let go. Words of happiness echoed around him but he was too dazed to decipher what was said. He recognized his Argonaut brothers—Theron, Demetrius, Gryphon, Phineus, and Titus. Spotted a couple people he'd never met but who were now obviously part of the group—like the blonde holding a Siren's bow and the guy at her side with dark hair and mischievous eyes. And he saw others still—like Silas and Nick and Daphne and Cerek—people who were familiar. Whose friendly eyes and warm smiles told him that no matter where he'd been or how long he'd been gone, he was home.

Emotions closed his throat, and tears—joyous tears—filled his eyes. Wrapping an arm around Daphne's shoulder, he pulled her in to his side and smiled. Really smiled. In a way he hadn't smiled in at least fifty years.

She laughed at something someone said and slid her arm around his waist. But instead of the warmth he expected to feel, a chill slid down his spine and everything inside him came to a screeching halt.

"Ari?" Daphne's worried voice echoed close but he couldn't look at her. Because his mind was suddenly focused on only one thing.

"Sirens..."

The world seemed to spin in slow motion. Ari turned and looked up. A Siren stood on the top of the ravine, her venomous gaze pinned on him. She pulled the string of her bow back. The arrow whirred through the air. Screams erupted. Ari lurched to his side. His arm caught Daphne by the waist, and he dragged her to the ground. A grunt echoed from her lips. Opening his eyes, he expecting to see the arrow, zinging toward him, but a body darted in the way.

The arrow struck flesh and bone with a *thwack*. Cerek dropped to the snowy rocks with a crunch only feet away.

No. Ari's eyes flew wide. *No!* He scrambled from the ground and skidded to Cerek's side.

"Cerek..."

Someone screamed his name. He looked up just as the Siren on the edge of the ravine pulled another arrow back. Another whir sounded, but this one didn't come from the Siren's bow. Just before she released the arrow, a dagger struck her in the throat. Blood spurted from her neck, and the bow fell from her fingers. Her body hit the ground and slid down the side of the ravine.

Ari's head swiveled to the side, and in a daze, he realized Daphne had thrown the dagger. She rushed to his side, dropped to her knees next to him, and looked down at the blood drenching Cerek's shirt. "Oh gods."

Air clogged in Ari's lungs as he looked back at his son. He had to fix this. Grasping the fabric where it was torn, he ripped Cerek's shirt open, then wrapped his hand around the arrow and pulled, but it wouldn't release.

"Ari." Panic lifted Daphne's voice. "Ari look."

His eyes shot to the wound. To the blood that was already drying, and the gray lines streaking outward from the spot where the arrow was embedded into Cerek's flesh.

Ari placed his hand on the skin near the wound. It was hard. Hard and cold, like stone.

"No." He focused on his healing power, placed his other hand over Cerek's chest. Energy gathered beneath his palms, but it wouldn't permeate Cerek's skin.

He tried again, but still nothing happened. Voices muttered near him. Feet shuffled. Someone dropped to the ground on Cerek's other side. But all Ari could see was his son lying in the snow in front of him, his body slowly turning to stone with every inch those lines traveled.

"No." Ari's vision blurred. He moved his hands to yet another spot, only his healing powers weren't getting through. "This can't be. Someone help us. Someone—"

"*Pateras.*" Cerek's hand closed over Ari's on his chest. "Dad," he said in a weak voice, "it's okay. Stop."

Ari stilled his frantic movements and looked at Cerek's face.

"I'm okay," Cerek said. "There's nothing you can do. I'm... You have to let me go."

"No." Tears swam in Ari's vision. He pressed his hands harder against Cerek's chest but it was already hard and cold. *"No."*

"I'd do it all again for you," Cerek said, his voice fading. "Promise me...you'll finish what we started. Promise"—the streaks crept up his neck—"you won't let our line fail."

Tears slid down Ari's cheeks. He'd said those very words to Cerek just before he'd faked his death and disappeared. He'd wanted Cerek to take his place with the Argonauts, to fill the slot meant for his kin as the chosen descendants of Theseus. Never in a million years did he expect to hear his son say the very same words back to him.

"I...I promise," Ari choked out. "I won't let our line fail."

Cerek closed his eyes and drew a shallow breath. "That's...good. That's...the way it should b—"

The streaks crept over his chin and up his cheeks, hardening his lips mid-sentence. Ari grasped Cerek's stone shoulders and screamed "No!" but the streaks spread up his face until his skin cracked and hardened and what life force was left inside him turned to solid stone.

"Holy Hades," someone muttered.

"Gods Almighty," someone else said.

Through tears, Ari stared down at Cerek's lifeless body, unable to believe what he was seeing. There had to be a way to fix this. There had to be someone—

His frantic mind caught on Nick. Nick was a god now. Kronos's son. Ari had seen Nick's face only moments before. He turned quickly, scanned the crowd through blurry vision, screamed, "Nikomedes! Do something! Do something now!"

"Ari, man." Nick stepped close, his face drawn and somber, his dark gaze skipping over Cerek's stone body. "I'm so sorry. I can't—"

"He can't bring anyone back from the dead," a cold voice said from the top of the ravine. Ari's head jerked around, and he looked up to where Zeus stood staring down at their group with contempt and victory in his black as sin eyes. "No god can. Thank your fucking Fates for that, Argonaut."

"You." Ari's vision turned red. "You did this. You killed my son."

"Technically," Zeus answered, "my very special Sirens killed him. Their arrows were dipped in Medusa's venom. I'd much rather one struck you, but since your friends consistently choose war over peace, I guess I'll take any dead Argonaut I can get."

"You bastard." Ari lurched to his feet.

Zeus's eyes flashed. "Careful, Argonaut. The laws of the Fates don't allow me to kill you with my powers, but if you come at me, I'm more than happy to rip your head from your pathetic body."

Ari jerked forward, but Nick captured him by the shoulders and stepped in his way. "He's right. Dammit, Ari." Ari struggled against his hold. "You can't win against the king of the gods."

The other Argonauts moved between Zeus and Ari. Disgust filled Zeus's features. "Circling the wagons. Such a mortal thing to do. You needn't bother. I'm done here." He turned his soulless gaze on Daphne. "You'd all be wise to remember who caused this tragedy, though. Had the nymph finished the job I sent her to do, I'd have what I want and your son, Argonaut"—he looked toward Ari—"would still be alive."

Zeus disappeared in a poof of white smoke. Smoke billowed around the ground near Ari's feet as well. Startled, he looked around, wondering where it was coming from. Then Daphne screamed his name.

He swiveled and looked down, and as the smoke cleared, he realized the ground where Cerek had just laid was empty..

"He's gone." Daphne's wide-eyed gaze lifted to his. "He's just...gone."

"Fucking bastard," someone said. "He took him. He took all of them."

Ari glanced over the battlefield. The dead Sirens were all gone too, only blood-stained snow left in their wake.

Ari turned back to Daphne, his mind a mess of what, where, how... But the tears spilling over Daphne's lashes brought reality to a hard, gasping breath.

His son was dead. Cerek was dead. And there was nothing he could do, no way he could bring him back. He'd healed so many across the years, but he couldn't save the one person who mattered most.

The finality of the moment hit Ari so hard, the pain dropped him to his knees in the snow as if someone had stabbed him straight through the heart.

"I'm sorry." Somehow, in the sea of misery, Daphne was there, wrapping her arms around his shoulders and holding him close. "I'm so sorry. It's all my fault. I shouldn't have gone to him. I shouldn't have gone to Argolea. I—"

"No," he choked out even though just drawing breath hurt like the pain of a thousand daggers. "No, it's not. This wasn't you. This was...me. This was...oh gods..." That pain turned to a burn that consumed his entire chest. "If I hadn't taunted Zeus all those years, if I hadn't killed his Sirens—"

"No." Daphne grasped his face so he could look into her eyes. "That was Hera. Don't you dare blame yourself for this."

Her voice penetrated the pain. She was his strength, his rock, his last lifeline. And he wanted to reach for her, to hold on and never let go, but the guilt wouldn't let him.

"She's right, Argonaut."

Daphne turned toward the female voice and gasped. And when Ari found the strength to look, he glanced past Daphne and spotted the same thing she had—the elderly woman dressed in a diaphanous white gown who'd poofed out of nowhere and now sat perched on a snowy boulder.

The woman brushed her silver hair over one shoulder with wrinkled hands. "Hera cursed you to destroy her husband's secret sect and the power he wields through them and with them. It had nothing to do with you, Guardian. You were but a vessel for Hera's revenge."

Voices whispered behind Ari. Someone muttered, "That's her. It's Lachesis." But he didn't turn to look. Couldn't because the Fate who spun the thread of life was focused solely on him.

"I know you hurt for what you have lost." Lachesis's gaze skipped to the group behind Ari. "I know you all do. And I know you cannot see the purpose. But in time you will understand. All things happen for a reason. Cerek's sacrifice will have rippling effects. Ones you will realize before the end."

She looked back down at Ari. "I also know your heart, Guardian. I know you want revenge. But now is not the time. Now is for healing. And healing is power. Use that power and you will not fail."

She pushed to standing, but her feet didn't hit the snow. They hovered over the ground as if she walked on air. "I cannot remove Hera's curse, but know this. Every curse can be a blessing if viewed in the right light. I have faith you can put this curse to use for the greater good. If, that is, you follow through with the promise you made to your son." Her gaze drifted to Daphne, and a slow smile spread across her wrinkled lips. "This one, I have no doubt, will help you. Hold on to her, hero."

The Fate disappeared as if she'd never been there. And though her words drifted in the cool air, easing a little of the pain, the only comfort Ari wanted—the only person he needed—was already hugging him again, pulling him in and never letting go.

"I'm here," Daphne whispered. "I won't let you fall. I'm not letting you disappear from the world again. Cerek wouldn't want that."

"No." Ari sniffled. "He wouldn't."

"You can do this."

He wasn't sure. But for Cerek and for her—for the two people he loved and who believed in him enough to love him back—he was willing to try.

"Only with you." He rested his forehead against hers and gripped her arms at the elbows as he drew in a steadying breath. "I'm nothing but a savage without you. You brought me back to life. Stay with me, Daphne. Stay with me and be my strength. Help me honor Cerek and my promise."

She brushed the hair away from his temple and drew back just enough so she could meet his eyes. Love and duty twisted together in her shimmering gaze, giving him strength, telling him that even in death, there was life.

"Always," she whispered. "I will always be right where you need me."

EPILOGUE

The wind whipped Zeus's hair back from his face as he walked along the windy path up the slope of Mt. Olympus. "So he's rejoined the Argonauts."

"Yes, my king." The Argolean who fed him information on the Argonauts' movements stumbled over a rock then regained his footing as he hurried to catch up with Zeus's long strides. "He's taken the Argonaut Cerek's spot in the Order and vowed to finish his son's work. They've welcomed him back with open arms."

"Of course they have," Zeus muttered. "The prodigal son has returned and they all act as if he never betrayed them. What of the nymph?"

"She remains in Argolea. The two were recently bound."

Zeus's jaw clenched down hard as he walked. Had Daphne completed her mission, he'd planned to bring her into the Sirenum Scorpoli. He wanted her. Still wanted her. Her beauty and sexuality were unmatched, and since her mother had refused his advances, he *deserved* her. But she'd fallen for that asshat Aristokles, and now all his plans to have her writhing and moaning beneath him were ruined.

The Argolean stumbled again. Rocks spit over the side of the cliff that dropped straight down into the clouds. The pathetic male glanced downward with absolute fear. For a moment, Zeus considered pushing him over just to watch him scream, but restrained himself. He needed his spies.

"They—she—" The Argolean regained his balance and looked up at Zeus. "Everyone in the realm is enraged that you took the Argonaut's body. The funeral pyre releases the soul to the afterlife. He cannot join his ancestors."

"No, he can't." Smug victory rippled through Zeus as they rounded a bend in the path. A cave opened three hundred feet ahead, a slow, red light spilling from the opening. "And what of the Siren? Sappheire?"

"She remains in Argolea as well, my king."

His vision darkened with the familiar rage of betrayal, but it cleared as he eyed the cave. Soon he would have his just revenge. Soon the walls of Argolea would crumble and he would control not only the human realm, but the world of the heroes as well. And all who dwelt there.

"That is all." He held out his hand. "Bring me more information when you have it."

The Argolean's eyes brightened with an evil glow as he reached for the gemstone in Zeus's palm that glowed with a shimmering blue light. "Yes." He bowed, then scurried backward, closing the magical stone in a tight fist. "I will. I absolutely will, my king."

Zeus snapped his fingers, opening a portal for the spineless maggot. Energy popped and sizzled. The Argolean stepped through, then the portal closed with a crack.

Alone, a smile spread across Zeus's lips. The idiot thought he had a prize he could use for his own nefarious purposes. What he really had was one more element that would aid Zeus in his quest.

He moved through the cave, heading toward the red hue. The tunnel twisted through the mountain, the rocks absorbing the light and all but humming with energy. Rounding the last bend, he drew to a stop three steps from the stone altar where the female with fire-red hair spilling down her back in endless curls stood staring at flames crackling in a bowl set on a tall golden pedestal.

Zeus cleared his throat.

"I sensed your approach." Circe, the strongest witch in all the kingdoms, met his gaze with piercing eyes. "Your little friend's pathetic snuffling could be heard for miles."

Zeus ignored the comment about his spy and narrowed his eyes on the witch. She was drop-dead gorgeous, always had been. Her body was long and lean, her breasts heaving and perfect in the flowing green dress that matched her eyes. A wide ballet collar showed off her toned shoulders and milk-white skin, the stitching accentuated her slim waist, and the long skirt flowed around her feet on the ground like an offering, making her look even taller than her seven feet. Bell sleeves cradled her slim wrists and fingers. And the choker at her neck with the large oval red stone in the middle, one Zeus swore fueled her power, accentuated the long, feminine line of her throat.

Her beauty was unmatched, her sexuality greater than that of all the nymphs. But both came with a price. The red sorceress was the most venomous black widow he'd ever faced, and Zeus had learned long ago never to mix business with pleasure in his dealings with her.

She flowed down the stairs as graceful as water, the scent of jasmine floating in the air as she stepped past him, warming both his blood and libido. "You've come to check on your prize."

Of course she knew why he was here. The female knew everything. Reminding himself not to be drawn into her web, Zeus followed her through a dark archway and into another tunnel. "What of your progress?"

"Patience, my king." She stopped at a door, pressed her hand against the steel, and turned to look at him. "Good things are bestowed on those who wait."

Waiting was a virtue Zeus sorely lacked.

She pushed the door open. White light cast illumination all over the black stone floor and walls and shimmered in waves over the still gray body lying on the table in the center of the room.

Fucking witches... Zeus's vision darkened as he crossed to the body and knocked his knuckles against the gray stone. "This isn't what I'm paying you to do. I thought you'd have this situation remedied by now. I need to know the truth. Can you bring him back?"

Circe moved to the other side of the table and batted insanely long, gorgeous eyelashes. "I can bring anyone back. But as I said, magic takes time. And what you've asked for here..." She looked down at the stone face. "This is going to require more than just time. Reprogramming is not a simple process."

Time was something Zeus had plenty of. But he preferred to have things done on his timetable, not anyone else's. This, however, would turn the tides in his war against the Argonauts for good. And for that, he was willing to wait as long as it took.

But he didn't like it. He pinned her with a hard look. "I want this fixed. You know I'm an impatient god, and you know what happens when I don't get my way."

Her eyes flared red. "And you know what happens when witches are pushed and magic goes awry. Do not threaten me, *king*, or your magic will turn to ashes in your hands."

Energy gathered in Zeus's palms. The desire to unleash it on her overwhelmed him. But then he looked down at the stone body between them. And told himself to save his fury for the Argonauts.

Their time would come. It would come soon.

He turned out of the room. "Just get it done."

UNCHAINED

An Eternal Guardians Novella

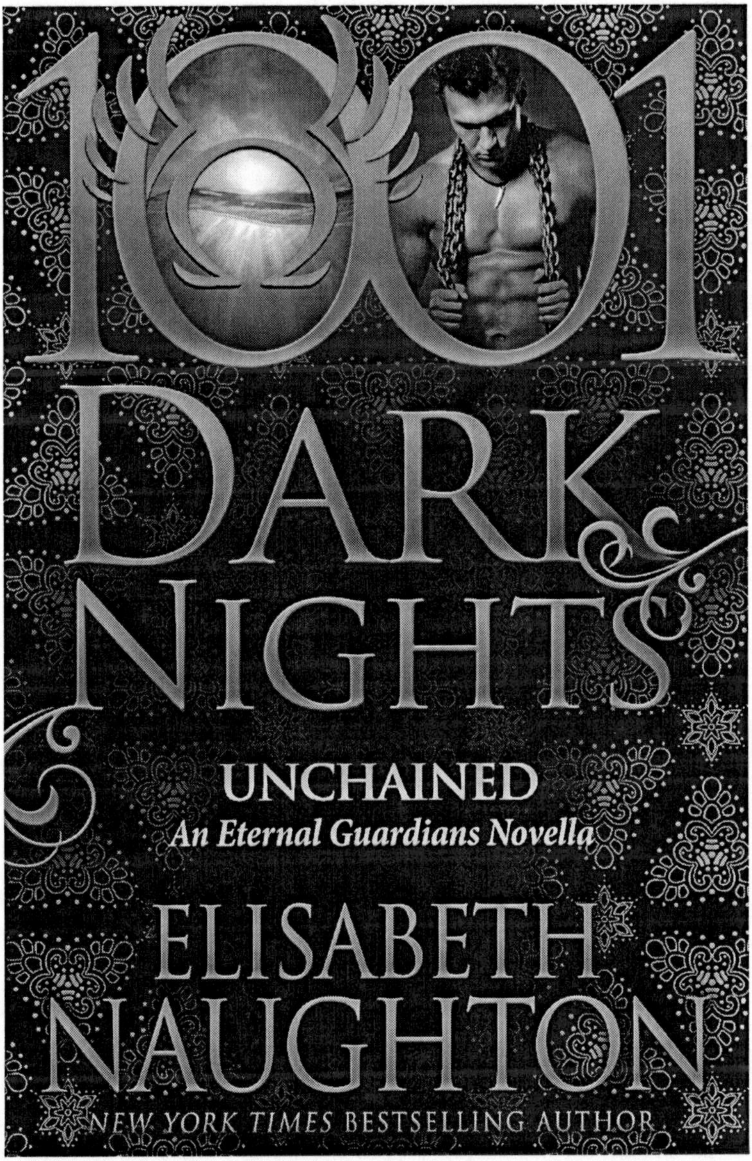

"There is the heat of love,
the pulsing rush of longing,
the lover's whisper, irresistible—
magic to make the sanest man go mad."

—Homer, *The Iliad*

CHAPTER ONE

"Find me. I'm waiting. I'm waiting only for you..."

The words echoed in Prometheus's head as he wandered the empty halls of the ancient castle high in the Aegis Mountains. He heard them in his waking hours now, not just when he was asleep. Heard them tickle the hairs on his nape, heard them whisper like a lover in his ear, heard them call like fire to his blood until he twitched with the need to find her and claim her as his own.

Her. The female with the flame-red hair and eyes like glittering emeralds he'd conjured with his mind. The female who was now more real to him than, well, him.

Damn, but he'd fantasized about her so often over the last few months he wanted her more than he wanted his precious isolation. But the voice wasn't real because *she* wasn't real. Not even a Titan, a god with the power to match that of any ruling Olympian's powers, could make her real. The only person in the cosmos who could summon life was the Creator, and the Creator had screwed Prometheus over so long ago, Prometheus knew there was no chance in this world or the next that he'd ever be blessed with a living version of his endless fantasy.

Life didn't work that way. Correction, *his* life didn't work that way. His life was a series of bad choices and never-ending repercussions. Which was exactly the reason he was determined to stay right here in this dank castle and *not* follow the sultry voice that made him so hard he could barely walk.

He waved a hand, using his telekinetic powers to light a torch along the wall in the cold, dark hallway as he moved. Maybe he was going mad. Maybe all these years of isolation were finally catching up with him. After the Argonauts—warrior descendants of the strongest heroes in all of Ancient Greece—had freed him from Zeus's chains, Prometheus had craved nothing but solitude. To do what he wanted, when he wanted—or to do absolutely nothing at all. But now, more than twenty-five years later, he was starting to wonder if his self-imposed seclusion in this ancient castle was at the root of all his problems. He was hallucinating, for shit's sake. Not just visions, but voices now, too. A sane person didn't do that. A sane person—mortal or immortal—recognized when he was standing on quicksand and got the fuck out.

"Find me. I'm waiting, Titos. I'm waiting for you..."

She always called him Titos in his hallucinations. A nickname that translated to fire. One that now brought him around to stare down the dark and empty hallway even though he knew she wasn't real.

Nothing moved. No sound met his ears. The castle was as silent as it had been since the day he'd arrived. But his spine tingled with apprehension, and his god-sense, something he rarely relied on because no one knew where he was, shot a warning blare straight through his ears.

The witches in the valley at the base of Mt. Parnithia had told him this castle in the Argolean realm had once belonged to an evil sorcerer who'd chosen darkness over light. That sorcerer's quest for power had cost him his life, and he now resided in the lowest levels of Tartarus, tortured endlessly by Hades much as Prometheus had been tortured by Zeus. His energy still lingered, though. A vile and murky energy Prometheus felt vibrating in his bones. As a divine being, Prometheus wasn't worried that energy would claim him—he was too strong for that—but he couldn't help but wonder if the sorcerer's dark energy was somehow affecting him. Could it be the source of the voice?

"Titos... I'm waiting..."

"Who's there?" he called.

Silence met his ears. His pulse ticked up as he scanned the darkened corridor, the only light coming from the torch behind him. Still nothing moved. Even the wind outside the castle walls had died down as if it too were afraid to utter a sound.

His imagination. It had to be. A hallucination or whatever the fuck he wanted to call it. Frowning, he turned away only to catch a flash of white out of the corner of his eye.

He whipped back. Some kind of gauzy fabric disappeared into the library, followed by the sound of laughter.

Sexy, feminine laughter.

Prometheus's stomach tightened as he rushed to the threshold of the room, grasped the doorframe, and peered inside. Shelves lined with books covered all four walls. A cold, dark fireplace sat across the distance. An empty couch, two side chairs, and a small coffee table lingered in the middle of the library.

Nothing moved inside the room. No fabric rustled. No laughter sounded in the cool air.

His stomach dropped when he realized he was hallucinating again, and he lowered his head into his hand and rubbed his aching temple. What had he said to himself earlier? A sane person recognized when he was standing on quicksand and got the fuck out? Maybe it was time he did that. Maybe it was time he moved on from Argolea and refocused on what he should have been doing these last twenty-five years. Namely, finding a way to screw Zeus over for everything the asshat god had done to him.

"I can help you."

Prometheus's head jerked up at the sound of the sultry feminine voice he'd heard so many times in his dreams. Only this time when he looked the room wasn't empty. This time a gorgeous female with hair as wild as fire and eyes like chipped emeralds peered back at him from the couch.

"I can help you exact revenge on Zeus," she whispered, sitting forward so her breasts heaved in the low-cut white gown. "All you have to do is help me first."

* * * *

"Help you how?" The Titan took one step into the library and stopped. "Who are you? And how did you get here?"

This was where she needed to be careful. Circe slowly pushed to her feet and brushed the thick curls over her shoulder. If he suspected too much, all her efforts would be for naught. She had to play this cool, had to stick to the plan, had to wait for just the right moment to strike.

"My name is Keia." Not entirely a lie, she figured. For thousands of years, humans had called her a goddess pharmakeia, which was just a fancy nickname for witch or sorceress. She was simply borrowing from that label. "But I am not here. I am only an apparition."

"I don't believe you." Prometheus stalked forward. He reached out to grab her but his wide palm and long fingers passed through nothing but air.

His hazel eyes widened as he looked from his hand back to her. "What the hell?"

He was only a few inches taller than her nearly seven feet, but he was bigger everywhere. A wall of solid steel that stood between her and eternity. Power radiated from his broad shoulders and chiseled muscles. A power that made her heart beat faster and her blood warm in a way it hadn't done in ages.

His dark hair was cut short, his jaw strong and square and covered by three days worth of stubble that made him look both dangerous and sexy. He was thousands of years old—like her—but he didn't look a day over thirty. And when his eyes narrowed and his luscious lips thinned, she had an overwhelming urge to dive into his mouth to find out if he tasted as good as he looked.

"How did you find me?" he said. "What do you want with me?"

Circe blinked, his voice pulling her back to the moment. She'd not been sexually attracted to anyone in so long, she'd forgotten what that rush of excitement felt like. Then again, she'd not had the chance to be attracted to anyone. Zeus kept her locked up tight and had for way too long.

Focus. Sexy as hell you can use to your advantage.

She lifted a foot-long length of heavy chain. "Look familiar?"

His face paled as he looked at the chain Zeus had used to bind him to that rock. The rock where he'd been tortured daily by a giant eagle that had torn into his side and consumed his liver day after day. "Where did you get that?"

"Find me and I'll tell you."

His confused gaze lifted to her face. "Find you?"

"You're a Titan. You have powers others don't. Find me and I can help you make Zeus pay for everything he's done."

He glanced over her from head to toe, a careful sweep of his green-brown eyes that was filled with both skepticism and interest. "Who are you?"

She could tell him she was a witch, but instinct made her hold her tongue. Prometheus was wary of all otherworldly beings. Many had known about his torture over the years, but none had dared rescue him from Zeus's clutches. None but the Argonauts.

"I'm no one of importance. Just a maiden who helped another and is now trapped because of it. Much as you were trapped for helping mankind."

Prometheus had given fire to humans. That was the big sin Zeus had punished him for. On a grand scale, she could see how his punishment made sense. Fire had led to the industrialization of man and the advancement of society. Zeus would have preferred man continue to worship and rely on the gods. Circe, on the other hand, had only helped free another of Zeus's prisoners, one who'd already fulfilled his required destiny for the king of the gods. But Zeus was determined to torment her forever for that crime.

She'd learned one very valuable lesson then. If you crossed Zeus you were fucked whether your offense was a major or minor violation.

She had to get out of here. She'd go mad if she had to spend eternity in this prison. Urgency pushed her forward. "Please help me."

"I can't. I don't know how." He looked over her again. "You're nothing but air."

"I—" Footsteps echoed close. Her pulse shot up. Zeus was back. Waving her hand, she broke the feed as she swiveled toward the sound. Prometheus's frantic "Wait," faded in the air as she faced the king of the gods.

Zeus strolled into her cave high on Mount Olympus and stared up the three stone steps where she stood next to the copper cauldron she used to conjure her magic. The flames in the bowl slowly shrank and eventually died out.

His black as night eyes narrowed. He was taller than most gods, over seven feet, and nothing but muscle. And though she supposed some probably found his dark looks attractive, Circe realized he paled in comparison to Prometheus.

"Well?" Zeus asked, hands on his hips and a perturbed expression across his angular face.

"These things take time, my king." She lowered her head in a reverent bow but gritted her teeth because just doing so made her want to scream.

"I grow tired of your lack of progress. I want the water element, and I want it now."

Of course he did. Ever since he'd stolen the Orb of Kronós—the magical disk that housed the four basic elements and had the power to unleash the Titans from Tartarus—from the Argonauts, he'd been pressuring her to figure out where Prometheus had hidden the last element. The god who possessed the Orb with all four elements intact could lord ultimate power over every living being. Forget controlling simply the heavens. With the water element, Zeus would finally control every realm and each being in them.

Circe was determined not to let that happen. Though Zeus was allowing her to contact Prometheus with her powers so she could find the element for him, she was really planning to convince Prometheus to break her free from this hell. Because it was hell. Being trapped in this mountain, even though she was allowed to use her magic, was as much a prison as any other. She was tired of doing what Zeus wanted. Tired of being his yes-witch. Tired of living half a life tucked away from the world.

"My magic cannot be rushed," she said, careful not to give her plans away. "We've discussed this before. You must be patient."

Zeus's jaw clenched down hard. "Do whatever you have to do to get me that element. But you'd better get it quickly because I'm a god of only so much patience. If I don't see results soon, witch, things are going to change."

Circe lifted her chin as he turned to leave. He couldn't threaten her. Because of him, she was the strongest witch who'd ever lived, and he knew that. Oh, she'd get results, but they'd be for her, not him.

When his footsteps faded in the tunnel that led out of her cave, she turned back to her cauldron and bit her lip. She couldn't go on visiting Prometheus as an apparition. He was already fascinated by her. She needed to step up her game.

A wry smile pulled at her lips as an idea formulated. One that would take him from fascination to obsession and set the wheels of change in full motion.

CHAPTER TWO

Prometheus sat on the top of a knoll in the summer sun, his elbows resting on his updrawn knees, a stalk of wheat between his teeth as he looked across the valley. Sunlight beat down, filtering through the leaves of the oak above. With his enhanced eyesight he could see his daughter Natasa in the field far below, summoning her gift of fire as she entertained the handful of young around her.

Knowing she was healthy and happy warmed a place inside his heart. Because of him she'd endured a very hard life, but the last twenty years had been good to her, and he was thankful for that. She was mated with the Argonaut Titus, and their bond only seemed to be strengthening. They didn't have young of their own yet, but Prometheus knew it was only a matter of time. Natasa loved children, and even though Titus had always been resistant to forging a family, the Argonaut was slowly coming around.

Prometheus watched Natasa form a fireball in the palm of her hand and send it swirling toward the sky. Excitement and glee shown in the eyes of the youthful faces around her. At Natasa's side, Titus smiled and slipped an arm around her shoulder while the young laughed and pointed. No, she might not have young yet, but she would be an incredible mother one day, and Prometheus was bound to be here when that happened.

He sighed as he watched the happy scene. She was the real reason he stayed in this realm. So he could make sure she was safe. So he could watch over her the way he should have watched over her long ago. A paternal urge to join her in that field pulled at him, but he ignored it. His daughter had long ago forgiven him for being the world's shittiest father, but that didn't mean he deserved to be part of her life.

"Find me. I'm waiting. I'm waiting only for you..."

The throaty feminine voice caused Prometheus to turn his head. All other sound drifted to the background as he focused on one thought:

She was back. The mystery apparition from his dreams. The one he'd desperately wanted to touch and taste and devour yesterday in his castle.

"Find me..."

He pulled the stalk of wheat from his mouth, dropped it on the ground, and pushed to his feet. A flitter of white disappeared in the trees.

His heart rate shot up. Like a moth drawn to a flame, he followed, his blood warming with every step. He'd lain awake long into the night rationalizing she was a hallucination. At best, he figured she was a ghost. Either way, he wanted to know why she was haunting him, and there was no better time to find out than right now.

The light faded as he entered the copse of trees. Leaves rustled in the warm breeze. Grass and rocks gave way to a carpet of moss. The rippling edge of white chiffon disappeared behind a tree, the fabric's movement like a lighthouse beacon drawing him home in the dark of night.

He stepped around the trunk of the tree and drew to a stop when he spotted her, standing barefoot in the distance, the straps of the white gown hanging from her delicate shoulders, following the curves at her waist and hips. Ribbons of sunlight filtering through the canopy caught in the fire-red hair spilling down her spine in gentle curls, the color of heat, of flames, of desire and passion.

Slowly, she turned and smiled at him with candy-red lips and eyes that gleamed like emeralds. Her nose was straight with a tiny flare at the tip, her cheekbones high, her skin so pale it looked like newly fallen snow. And even before she spoke he felt himself falling under her wicked spell all over again. The same way he had in his dreams. The same way he did every time he closed his eyes. The exact same way he had yesterday when she'd begged for his help then poofed out of his library with no explanation.

"Who are you?" he whispered, stepping forward.

Her smile faded. "Yours. I'm yours. Find me..."

Her words lingered in the air as she turned and ran.

His adrenaline shot into the stratosphere. "Wait!"

She didn't stop, didn't slow, and without even thinking he pushed his legs forward to follow.

She was fast for a hallucination. His muscles burned as he hustled to keep sight of her through the forest. She weaved her way around brush and trees. A small river rippled somewhere to the right. She darted in that direction, following the meandering water along its bank. He rounded a corner and slowed when he spotted the end of the path. A waterfall loomed ahead, the ground rising on both sides. Past the waterfall, a stone bridge spanned the river, and in the distance, a stately gazebo with marble columns and a domed ceiling overlooked the pristine sight.

Prometheus's breathing slowed as he searched for the female, but he couldn't see her. Long seconds passed with the only sound the water tumbling over rocks. Panic pushed in; panic that he'd lost her, that he'd never see her again, that—

A blur of white rushed across the bridge, moved into the trees, and zigzagged up the hillside toward the gazebo.

His heart kick-started all over again, and he looked toward the cliff ahead. The forest was dark here, but the rocks seemed to form...

Yes, they formed steps leading up the cliff face.

He moved toward the steps, climbing steadily until he reached the top. His legs moved as if they had a will of their own, driving him over the bridge and up the hill until he stood at the base of the gazebo.

It towered above, all ancient stone and marble, with ornate carvings and scrollwork, more temple than garden structure. Energy vibrated from inside, an energy he didn't recognize. Pausing to catch his breath, he stilled and listened to the forest around him, tuning in to his god-sense for any indication of a threat.

"Find me, Titos..."

Her voice slithered over his skin like a sensual caress. Common sense told him to be careful, that he didn't know who or what she really was, but desire pushed his feet up the steps and brought him to a stop at the doorway.

His fantasy stood in the middle of the octagonal room, flame-red hair curling down around her shoulders, gemlike eyes pinned on him, candy apple red lips curved in a wicked, for-his-eyes-only smile.

Forbidden images swept through his mind—the flimsy white gown slipping free of her delectable body, her hands coming up to caress her plump, perfect breasts, a catch of her breath as she slid one hand down her toned belly and into the thatch of red curls at the apex of her thighs.

Blood rushed into his groin, making him instantly hard. A moan echoed in his head...hers, his, he couldn't tell which.

"Come, Titos."

The words were a command he couldn't ignore. He stepped one foot into the gazebo, and another. Her smile grew wider. Heat and the sweet scent of heliotrope surrounded him as he drew close.

"Touch me and make me real."

Yesterday she'd wanted him to find her. Now she was telling him to touch her and make her real. Confusion pulled at his brows. "I don't know how."

She moved closer, until she was mere inches away, and lifted her chest so his attention dropped to her breasts heaving with her breath in the low-cut white dress. "Just touch me. Your Titan powers in this place will do the rest."

His hand lifted as if guided by some unseen force, and as his fingers drew close, he thought he heard her whisper. His gaze darted toward her face, and he watched in a trance as her ruby-red lips moved quickly, the words barely audible.

Ancient Greek. He recognized the tongue, not what she was saying. His hand stilled. Her chanting grew louder. Just as he was about to pull back, she stepped into him, and his fingers passed through what should be her shoulder.

A flash of light illuminated the inside of the gazebo and quickly faded. Prometheus blinked several times and looked down only to realize the warm flesh and solid bones beneath his hand were real.

His gaze darted right back to her face. "Who are you?"

"I told you yesterday. My name is Keia."

She stepped back, away from him, and in a daze he realized the gazebo was no longer dark and empty but illuminated by dozens of candles around the periphery that seemed to have appeared out of nowhere when he touched her. A thick rug made of red and gold swirls lay beneath his feet, a gold chaise with plump red pillows sat ahead. He turned to find two more plush chairs and dozens of soft, luxurious pillows scattered across the floor.

"What just happened?" he asked. "What is this place?"

"You're a Titan." She moved to a small table, uncapped a decanter and poured red liquid into two goblets. Handing him one, she stepped close once more and said, "Don't tell me magic is new to you."

He looked into his goblet as she sipped from her own. Wine, he guessed from the fruity scent, but it might just as well be poison. His gaze narrowed on her flawless features once more. "I'm not in the mood for games."

"Neither am I. You've made me real. In this place, at least. For that I'm thankful." She moved to the chaise and gestured to one of the chairs. "Sit and talk with me for a bit before it's time for me to go. It's been ages since I've had the chance to converse with anyone."

He was having trouble keeping up. And that sweet scent of heliotrope combined with the rich scent of the wine was making him lightheaded. Or maybe *she* was making him lightheaded. He wasn't sure which. "What do you mean before it's time to go? And how are you real here when you weren't at my castle?"

She sighed and lifted her wine to her lips once more. "I suppose an explanation is in order, but there are rules I must abide by. Not all things are allowed to be revealed." She sipped her wine and lowered the goblet to her lap. "I have certain powers."

His eyes narrowed with understanding. "You're a witch."

"Some may call me that. Others call me an enchantress. Regardless of the label, I created this gazebo with my magic. When you touched me within these walls, your Titan powers altered my apparition into flesh. Here I am real."

He wasn't exactly fond of witches. They'd never done anything for him. But magic was a very real thing in their world, and he was in no position to judge. "And when you leave this place?"

"I exist only in this realm in solid form within this gazebo."

He stepped toward her. "I don't understand. You said you were trapped. Who's trapped you? And why—"

"That I cannot tell you, per the rules. What I can tell you is that I've long been fascinated by you, Prometheus. You were watching the Argoleans in the field earlier. Do you have the same affection for them as you do humans?"

She was switching topics way too fast. "Watching me, how?"

"With my magic, of course. It gives me the ability to look through windows. I do a lot of looking because of my confinement. What do they call it in the human realm? Oh yes. People watching." A faraway, almost sad look filled her eyes. She shook her head and blinked several times, a weak smile curling the edges of her plump lips. "I much prefer being real with you here than watching you through that window."

He sat beside her on the chaise, close enough to feel her heat surround him, but not quite close enough to touch. Though he wanted to touch her. He was itching to run his hand over her bare shoulder again. To slide his fingers through her luxurious hair. To pull her in and find out for himself if her lips were as soft and tempting as they looked. "Why me?"

Her smile widened as she turned to face him, and this close...gods, she was more beautiful than he'd expected. Her flawless features took his breath away.

"My, but you are full of questions," she said.

Realizing he probably sounded like a ten-year old, he frowned. "I guess you could say it's been a while since I've had anyone to talk to as well."

"That's why I've been watching you. Because we are so similar." She sipped her wine again. "You didn't answer my question about the Argoleans. In the field."

All he wanted to do was go on peppering her with questions about why she was here, why she'd come to him, and how he could make her stay. But there was something about her... Something that made his pulse tick up and his body feel alive in a way it hadn't in thousands of years. And if she had to leave soon—for whatever reason, he didn't want to waste what little time they had left frustrating her, or him.

"The male in the field was an Argonaut. The female with him was my daughter."

Keia's eyes narrowed in question, then slowly relaxed as if she'd suddenly made connections in her mind. "Ah yes, your daughter. I almost forgot you had a daughter. And her mother? Are you—"

He shook his head. "A one time thing. She died thousands of years ago. She was a nymph who came across me during my imprisonment and eventually went on to marry an Egyptian prince."

"Io?" A knowing light filled Keia's eyes. "Your daughter's mother was Io? I didn't realize that."

He nodded. This witch knew more about him than he'd thought. A voice in the back of his head warned him to be wary but he ignored it. "I didn't even know Natasa existed until several years ago. Because of me, she suffered greatly. I'm in this realm because she's here. Watching out for her is my way of...I don't know, making up for a little of the pain I caused her."

"That's a very fatherly thing to do."

He frowned. "Don't get any ideas. I'm not a good father. Not even close."

"I'm sure you're a better father than you think."

He huffed, lifted his wine. Paused when it was an inch from his lips and stared down into the goblet.

The sweet sound of feminine laughter floated around him. "Worried that cup is poisoned?"

His gaze slid her direction, and he caught the playful gleam in her eyes and the soft spray of freckles across the bridge of her nose he hadn't noticed earlier. "I'd be lying if I said the thought hadn't cross my mind."

Smiling, she leaned forward and took the goblet from his hand, her slim fingers grazing his in the process to send sparks of electricity all through his arm. "Watch, Titos."

She brought his cup to her mouth and sipped, her eyes locked on his the entire time. Lowering the goblet, she licked the droplet of wine from her bottom lip, then bit down gently with her top teeth until the succulent flesh darkened.

Heat spread through his whole body and shot into his groin, bringing his cock to life in a way it hadn't been alive in thousands of years.

"See?" She handed the wine back to him. "No poison. Just decadent pleasure."

He grew hard at the sexual innuendo, but there was still just enough common sense left in his head to make his eyes narrow. "Maybe it doesn't affect you. You did say you were created from magic."

"No, I said magic made me flesh and blood in this place so we could be together." She leaned forward again, drawing his attention right to her delectable cleavage. "I assure you I am a living, breathing female in another realm, not just a figment of your imagination."

Her eyes were hypnotic, her voice sultry and so damn erotic he could go on listening to her talk about anything. Somehow he pulled his attention away from her perfect breasts and looked deep into her emerald eyes. "What realm? Tell me where you are flesh and blood at all times so I can find you."

"That would break the rules. And if we are to see each other again, I can't break them. As for what I want, though..." Her breaths grew shallow as she drew even closer and her gaze dropped to his lips. "I think this want burning inside me is the same one that brought you to this place."

Her hand landed against the back of the chaise, and she angled her face up toward his. The heat of her body surrounded him, consumed him, infused him with need. He lifted his hand to her neck, felt the soft, silken flesh beneath his fingers, and was powerless to hold back.

His mouth lowered to hers as if they were magnets, drawn together by a force neither could resist. Her supple lips brushed his...warm, sweet, tender yet intoxicating at the same time. He had an overwhelming urge to take her, to claim her, to make her his own, but he didn't want to do anything to spook her, and he was still so confused about what and who she was. So he kissed her slowly. Slid his fingers into her sleek hair. Held back from the passion he wanted to release.

She sighed against him. Brought one hand up to rest against his chest. Warmth circled the spot, shot sparks of electricity straight into his groin. Sliding his tongue along the seam of her lips, he coaxed her to open, to let him in, to give him a taste of what he'd been dreaming about for far too long.

She drew back quickly, breaking their kiss before he was ready. His hand dropped to her thigh as she looked to her right.

He didn't care about whatever animal outside the gazebo had distracted her. He only wanted more. He reached for her. "Keia."

"He's back." She pushed to her feet before he could kiss her again. Her gaze stayed locked on something to her right. "What is he doing back so soon?"

"He who?" A little of Prometheus's lust faded when he saw the worry rushing over her features. He stood and reached for her. "Keia?"

She glanced his way. But this time he didn't see heat in her gemlike eyes. He saw fear. True fear. "He's not alone. I have to go."

"Wait." He stepped toward her. "Tell me where you—"

His fingertips grazed her sleeve, but she vanished before he could grasp her.

* * * *

Circe extinguished the flames in her cauldron just as three of Zeus's Sirens—his Barbie-doll like warriors, dressed in skintight black tops, fitted black pants, and knee-high kickass boots—moved into her cave and spread out around her.

"What is the meaning of this?" Circe straightened her back and looked past the Sirens toward the tunnel. "Where is Zeus?"

"Zeus is busy," the one in the middle with blonde hair falling in waves to her shoulder blades said. "He sent us to inspire you."

The brunette to Circe's right chuckled and ascended the steps toward her.

"Stay back." Circe lifted a hand, a chant growing in her mind, but the Sirens moved with stealth speed and were on top of her before she could summon a spell.

They jerked her arms behind her back. "No chants for you," the redhead said, clamping metal cuffs around her wrists. "Not right now anyway."

Circe grunted as the weight of the cuffs pulled on her wrists. But more than that, she felt the power in the metal. Adamant, she realized. The strongest metal in all the realms. A groan echoed from her chest.

"That's right," the Siren to her right said, pushing her forward so she stumbled down the steps. "These cuffs were forged by Hephaestus himself. Your spells won't work so long as they bind you."

They led her out the tunnel from which they'd come. The adamant cuffs didn't just block her magic, they made it impossible for her to fight back. Sunlight spilled into the cave as they grew close to the opening, and Circe tensed. Zeus had trapped her in this cave with his powers. She couldn't leave. If she tried to cross into the light, an invisible force field would jolt her back with an electrical current. The Sirens didn't lead her into the light, though. They turned just when she was sure she was going to be zapped and drew her into a tunnel she'd never noticed before.

Darkness surrounded them. The tunnel circled down into the depths of the mountain. Unable to struggle, Circe followed, unsure where they were leading her. The air grew cold. Ahead, a flickering orange light beckoned.

Unease rolled through her. She'd never been in this part of the mountain, but the hairs on her nape standing straight told her whatever was down here could not be good. The ground finally leveled out as they entered a large room. The Sirens at her back drew her to a stop. The one at her front crossed toward a lone torch lit on the far wall, removed it from the holder, and walked back toward Circe.

The Siren tipped her head. "Zeus has decided you need a little something to inspire you to work harder." Her gaze skipped past Circe. "Ladies?"

The Siren on Circe's right let go of her and stepped away, into the darkness. Metal groaned, and in a heartbeat of understanding, Circe realized the sound was a door opening. A rusted, metal door. And this wasn't just a cave. It was a dungeon.

The Siren at her left maneuvered her into the darkness.

"Wait." Circe tried to push back with her weight, but the adamant cuffs stopped her momentum.

They shoved her into the cell. One uncuffed the manacles from her wrists. The other lifted her boot to the small of Circe's back and thrust her forward.

Circe lifted her hands just before she hit the hard rock wall of the cell. Metal groaned and clanked. Whipping around, Circe spotted the three Sirens standing outside her cell, the one in the middle holding the torch to shine light all around them.

"Don't waste time trying to conjure a spell to free yourself," the brunette said. "These walls are infused with adamant as well. Your powers won't work here." She looked to the redhead, and then the blonde. "We should go before he wakes."

"Wait." A bolt of fear shot down Circe's spine, and she rushed to grasp the bars. "He who?"

The brunette smiled. "You'll find out. Come on, girls."

The light faded along with their footsteps. Darkness pressed in, stealing the air from Circe's lungs. Shivering, she stepped back, holding out her hands until she felt the cold stone wall at her back.

"Don't freak out," she said aloud to keep the fear at bay. "Zeus is just trying to scare you. He'll let you go in a few hours."

A roar sounded outside her cell. Circe's gaze jerked in that direction, and her pulse shot into the stratosphere.

That didn't sound like a Siren. Or a god. It sounded like a monster.

She swallowed hard and told herself the adamant in the bars of the cell door would protect her from whatever was out there. But a clicking sound echoed close. Like nails clawing at the ground. Growing faster. Louder. Coming closer...

She held her breath and went completely still.

The heavy steel door of her cell crashed open. Circe swallowed her scream and slid down the wall, arms and legs shaking, hoping she blended into the darkness

Something drew in a long sniff and growled. "I smell you, witch."

All she saw was the whites of its eyes before it lunged.

CHAPTER THREE

Circe's cell door clanged open hours later. Footsteps sounded across the stone floor. Too weak to lift her head, she groaned and pried her eyelids open only to wish she hadn't.

Torchlight filled the room. A Siren scrunched her nose in distaste as she held the torch and waited in the doorway while the king of the gods crouched in front of Circe and brushed the blood-matted hair away from her face.

"Gesenius was extra rough with you." Zeus clucked his tongue. "Looks like you fought back. Bad idea, witch. A shade is nothing to mess with."

A shade. A death shadow. That's what had attacked her. She would have realized that sooner but the pain had been too great to think through.

"He liked you," Zeus said. "Then again, your blood turned him back into a human for a day. Who wouldn't like you?"

Sickness rolled through Circe's stomach. She closed her eyes again, not the least bit interested in his gloating. Her body was too busy trying to repair itself from the shade's damage.

"Oh now, don't be like that," Zeus said. "You brought this on yourself, Circe. We had a good thing going until you decided to take your own sweet time. Lucky for you I'm a forgiving god."

He wasn't forgiving. He had no intention of living up to his "deal," and she knew that now. He was never going to release her from his service because she was now the most powerful witch in all the cosmos. And to him, she was nothing more than a prize, just as Prometheus had been his prize so long ago.

Prometheus...

He was her only chance now. She had to find a way to convince him to free her completely. And the only way to do that was to make him so obsessed with her, he had no other thought but to come after her.

She needed to move up her timeline. Needed to work faster. Needed to seduce Prometheus now rather than later.

But first she had to get out of this cell so she could get back to her magic.

Groaning, she pushed up on her hands, cringed at the pain in her neck and down her side, but somehow found the strength to shift so she leaned back against the wall. Her dress, damp with blood, fell open across her breasts but she didn't bother to fix it. "What do you want?" she asked, her voice raspy and weak.

"I want that element, witch."

Lead him on. Tell him what he wants to hear.

"I could have gotten it...for you. But your Sirens...interrupted me."

"No, my Sirens clearly inspired you." Zeus's dark eyes narrowed. "You need to work smarter." He brushed another lock of bloody hair back from her cheek, almost tenderly. "I told you I was a patient god, but I have limits." His licentious gaze drifted over her ripped gown and exposed flesh. "Either get me the results I want, or the hell you just lived through will be your new normal." His gaze lifted back to her face. "The clock is ticking, witch."

He rose and looked toward the Siren. "Move her into a cell where she can work. Bring her food and new supplies. Then send someone to clean up this mess. It stinks like death in here."

He stalked out of the room, followed by a smug-looking Siren. Closing her eyes once more in the dark as the metal door clanged shut, Circe shuddered against the cold stone floor.

Your new normal...

Understanding sent bile sliding up her throat. He was going to torture her the same way he'd tortured Prometheus. Painfully. Horrifically. Daily until she gave him what he wanted. And when she did, he might free her from the shade, but he'd never free her from her imprisonment.

Breathing in and out slowly, she fought to regain her strength for one blinding purpose.

To find Prometheus. Because he truly was her last hope.

* * * *

A thick fog covered the forest floor in the dead of night, illuminated only by a sliver of moonlight filtering through the thick foliage above. A shiver raced down Prometheus's spine as he scanned the dark trees that looked almost ghost-like in the dim light.

She was out here. Somewhere. He'd heard her voice in his head. Always calling him. *"Find me, Titos..."*

His heart raced as he stepped forward, his boots disappearing in the fog, his god-sense on high alert. An owl cried above. The high-pitched chirp of bats flying in the distance echoed to his ears. He knew she was out here. Had felt her. The shiver told him something else was out here too. A faceless danger he couldn't see but which hunted her.

A flutter of white darted through the trees. He whipped in that direction, his pulse going stratospheric.

He pushed his legs into a run, darting around eerie gray tree trunks in the forest, jumping over logs and boulders his god-sense picked up beneath the fog. The ground rose steadily upward. His muscles burned as he ascended the hillside. The trees slowly dissipated the higher he ran, finally opening up until he stood on a long flat plateau of rock high above a valley.

Keia stood at the edge of the cliff, overlooking the valley and its meandering river, her thin white gown blowing in the gentle breeze, her fire-red hair fanning out behind her. His breaths came fast and shallow as he slowed his steps, as he tried to figure out why she'd lured him here.

"Keia?"

She turned and faced him, her eyes as green as he'd ever seen them, her face as pale as the moon. "Find me, Titos."

His pulse beat strong and fast, and he stepped toward her. She wasn't real. He knew she wasn't real. She was only real in the gazebo. But he reached for her hand regardless. Then sucked in a breath when his fingers curled around solid flesh and bone.

His gaze dropped to her hand then up to her face. "What's going on? Why did you bring me here?"

She closed both of her hands around his and squeezed so tight pain shot up his arms. "Because you are mine."

Her eyes shifted. They were no longer the color of shimmering emeralds but morphed to hard black cinders. And her voice...it was different. Deeper. Masculine. A voice he'd heard long ago.

She stepped back to the edge of the cliff and pulled him with her. "And you will always be mine, Titan."

The ground fell away. Prometheus's body sailed over the edge. Before he could release her, the ground rushed up at what felt like a million miles per hour.

Prometheus sat upright in a puddle of sweat, the sheet tangled around his legs, his heart racing as his gaze darted around his dark bedroom suite.

No sound met his ears. No voices. His gaze angled down, to the mattress beneath him, to the floor, and finally the window that looked out into the darkness.

Not a cliff. He was in bed, not falling to his death. Not that a Titan could be killed by conventional means, but it *was* possible. Especially where magic was involved.

Magic...

Keia...

That voice...

He knew that voice. It was Zeus's voice. The god who'd imprisoned him and left him to a daily torture that still haunted his restless hours. Throwing his legs over the side of the bed, he drew in deep breaths that did little to settle his racing pulse, let them out slowly, tried to make sense of the dream.

No, not a dream. A warning. His god-sense was picking up something...something he needed to key into before it was too late.

Urgency pushed him across the floor. He pulled on jeans and a T-shirt, shoved his feet into boots, and moved for the dark corridor that led to the stairs. He didn't care that it was the dead of night. Didn't care that common sense was telling him it had just been a dream. He knew what he'd felt, and his senses were going apeshit over the threat he knew lurked somewhere out there in the dark.

He made his way into the trees. A low fog hovered over the ground as he headed toward the gazebo Keia had lured him to only yesterday. Moonlight slanted through the canopy to illuminate the woods in an eerie white glow. Déjà vu trickled through him, but he fought it back and pushed onward. He could flash to the gazebo—he had the power to flash in any realm—but didn't because if danger really did lurk in that magical place, he wanted to surprise it. Minutes later he crossed the bridge and moved silently through the trees toward the dark structure.

Nothing moved inside. No light, no sound came from within its walls. The gazebo was as eerily quiet as the air. He listened, didn't pick up anything out of the ordinary with his heightened senses, but knew not to drop his guard. Magic could cloak danger just as magic could create an alternate reality. Moving silently up the gazebo's steps, he stood at the threshold and peered into the dark room.

The chaise, the pillows, the dozens of candles—now dark—were just as he'd left them yesterday after Keia had disappeared. He stepped into the gazebo and looked over each item, searching for something—anything to explain the warning echoing in his head. Still, nothing stood out.

His heart rate slowed. And little by little the tingles across his spine lessened. It had just been a dream. Brought on by hallucinations, not enough sleep, and impending madness. His years of isolation were taking a toll on him. He turned to leave, was at the point of believing he'd made the whole thing up—even Keia—when he spotted a pool of blood on the floor to his right.

He kicked a pillow away, crouched near the puddle, and slowly touched the edge of the blood.

Electricity shot into his arm, across his chest, and up his neck. Blinding pain radiated outward from the left side of his throat, knocking him off his feet to slam against the ground.

He gasped and quickly swiped his bloody fingers against his pant leg. The pain slowly lessened until it was nothing but a twinge in his flesh.

Reality and fantasy intermingled in his mind until he didn't know which was which. And in the distance he heard Keia's voice calling to him.

"Find me, Titos. Find me before it's too late..."

* * * *

By daybreak, Circe's strength had returned enough so she could conjure her magic. She wasn't a hundred percent yet, but she couldn't wait until her body completely healed. Zeus had made it clear the shade could return at any moment. She needed to step up her plan with Prometheus if she had any hope of breaking free from this prison.

She placed the length of chain Zeus had given her in the cauldron, held her hands over the bowl, and summoned her spell. The chain was her link to Prometheus. It had been a part of him so long it still possessed part of his lifeblood. With it, she could find him wherever he was in the cosmos. And with it she could make herself ethereal and lure him to her.

The rock walls around her faded, revealing stone columns and the sound of leaves rustling in the early morning breeze, birds chirping in the forest, and water rushing over the falls. The scents of moss and wood filled her senses as she turned, confused why the spell had brought her to the gazebo already. She wasn't supposed to start out here. She was supposed to start with Prometheus and tempt him to follow her to th—

The thought halted when she caught sight of him, lying on his side on the chaise, his hands tucked up near his face, his eyes closed, and his chest rising and falling with his deep breaths. Something beneath her ribs tightened at the sight of him. Something other than lust. Fast asleep, his long dark lashes feathering the skin beneath his eyes, he looked more innocent than godly, more angelic than dangerous. And for a fleeting moment she pictured him chained to that rock in the blistering sun, unable to move, unable to do anything but wait for the giant eagle to swoop down and rip out his liver only to come back and do it all again the next day.

He'd only escaped that living hell because of the Argonauts. Because his daughter's mate had rescued him so Prometheus could save her life. Zeus had been pissed when Prometheus was freed. Circe remembered all too well how he'd marched into her cave and ordered her to bring Prometheus back. It had taken her several hours to convince the king of the gods that her witchcraft didn't work that way. Luckily—for her—Zeus had finally abandoned that order, but she knew he was waiting for the moment when he could make Prometheus suffer. Zeus's memory was long. When someone bested him, he never forgot. And Prometheus had bested him more than any other.

Was Zeus planning something she didn't know? Was he using her as bait? Circe was well aware that the king of the gods wanted the water element more than anything else, but he also always had an agenda. Was Prometheus at risk because of her?

His eyes fluttered open and held on hers. And that tightness beneath her ribs rolled and swirled as he stared at her as if seeing her for the very first time.

He pushed up on his hand, dropped his legs over the edge of the chaise, and blinked several times. Sunlight slanted through the arches to highlight his hair and the dark scruff across his jaw, making him even more handsome than yesterday. He was dressed in jeans and a black T-shirt that pulled across his chest, and when he moved she caught the flex of muscle in his arms. Suddenly, she couldn't help but wonder what his carved shoulders and toned body looked like under all that fabric.

"Keia," he said in a voice still thick with sleep. "You're here."

"I'm here," she repeated, growing hotter with every passing second. She moved toward him. Pain echoed across her neck and shoulder, but she bit back the wince so he wouldn't see. Lowering herself to the chaise, she sat beside him, close, but not too close. Not yet anyway.

He turned to face her, confusion darkening his eyes. "I was looking for you."

Her plan was working. A coy smile twisted her lips as she brushed a hand down the bodice of her green dress, the one she'd conjured to match her eyes and make them appear even darker. "I like that you were looking for me. I came here to find you as well."

"I saw it in the night. Blood. And pain."

Circe's smile faded, and a tingle of apprehension shot down her spine.

"You were scared," he went on. "I tried to help you. But when I reached you, you grasped my wrists like chains, and a voice that was not yours fell from your lips as you pulled me over a great cliff."

Circe's heart beat hard and fast, killing whatever arousal she'd felt earlier. "Who's voice did you hear?"

"Zeus's."

Circe's fingers shook as she pushed to her feet, crossed to the edge of the room and stared out at the water rushing toward the falls. Zeus's voice. How could he have heard Zeus's voice?

Fabric rustled at her back. "What's going on? You said you were trapped. Who has trapped you and why?"

Her mind spun. She couldn't come right out and tell him. Not yet, anyway. He was on the verge of becoming obsessed with her, but he wasn't there yet, and if she revealed too much too soon, she risked losing him altogether.

She had to play this strategically. Had to be smart. Fixing an amused smile on her face, she turned his way. "It sounds like a dream."

"It was a dream. But it was also real. The blood was real, right here on the floor of this gazebo."

He held out his arm, and Circe's gaze followed until she spotted the dark stain on the wood floor. Her breath caught.

"I touched it," he said in a low voice. "I felt it."

Her gaze darted to his features, and in his eyes she saw truth. Through her blood he'd felt her pain and suffering.

He stepped toward her, eyes dark and very focused. "Tell me what's going on here."

"I..." Words faltered on her tongue. She didn't know what to say. Didn't know how any of this was possible. Her two worlds were not supposed to converge. Magic kept them apart. "It wasn't my blood," she lied. "Some kind of animal must have wandered in and—"

His big hands closed around her biceps. "Zeus is involved with whatever's going on with you, isn't he?"

"I don't... I can't... There are rules."

"Fuck his rules. What does he want from you?"

"He wants..." *Don't tell him the truth.* "He wants to punish me."

"Why?"

"Because..." *Think, dammit!* "Because I helped someone."

That wasn't a lie. She had helped someone. When the princess of Argolea had snuck into Olympus and come to Circe in her cave a few months ago, Circe had helped the female find an Argonaut Zeus had imprisoned. Zeus had been pissed when he'd discovered how Circe had betrayed him. Was still pissed. And Circe knew that was part of the reason Zeus was stepping up his pressure on her now to find the water element. But she couldn't tell Prometheus that because his daughter was mated to an Argonaut. If Prometheus was at all privy to what the Argonauts were up to, telling him that would give away who she was, and he might turn away from her for good.

"Someone Zeus was using so he could gain more power," she went on, figuring that was a safe explanation. "I didn't want to help Zeus but I had no choice. He's the king of the gods. When one is in his service, one cannot just say no. I might not age because of my powers, but I'm not immortal like the gods. If Zeus wanted to kill me, he could."

Prometheus's shoulders relaxed, but he didn't let go of her arms, and she liked his hands on her. Liked the warmth of his skin against hers and the way he made her feel small. "The gods can't take life. That goes against the natural order."

She frowned. "They can dictate it though. He keeps me isolated from others. I'm allowed to use my magic—which is how I found you—but that is the extent of my freedom."

She wanted to add that her freedom was limited by what Zeus allowed her to do. She could watch anyone through her mirrors, but she couldn't contact friends or family—not that she had any anymore—without an object linked to their lifeblood. But, of course, she couldn't tell Prometheus that either because then he would know Zeus was aware she was contacting him now, and he'd grow suspicious.

Gods, her life was one major lie after another. Frustration bubbled through her. Frustration and anger and...helplessness.

"Why did you find me?"

Warmth crept up her neck and into her cheeks, distracting her from thoughts of Zeus, from frustration over her imprisonment. Part of what she was about to say was a lie, but truth also lingered in her words. A truth she wanted him to hear. "Because you captivated me. You survived thousands of years of torture at the hands of your enemy, and you didn't just survive it, you came out whole and sane on the other side. I needed to see for myself that was possible."

Unease passed over his features as he let go of her arms, and she tried to fight the disappointment the loss of his touch caused but couldn't mask it completely. "I'm not whole. And I'm not anywhere close to sane."

Panic pinched something in her chest. A panic that came from the reality that he honestly believed what he was saying. She moved closer. "Yes, you are. And you're a hero. As much a hero as any of those Argonauts in the capital city far below us."

He scoffed.

"It's true." And this time there was no lie in her words. "I watched, from my mirror, when you helped the Argonauts twenty-some years ago. I saw how you risked yourself to save your daughter. You were willing to face Zeus, to do anything to save her, even knowing you might be chained again, all because you believed what you were doing was right. I want to be like that." She shrugged, thinking back over the hundreds—no, thousands—of things she'd done in her lifetime for no one's gain but her own. "I wanted to know what that felt like. For once."

His gaze narrowed and held on hers, and as he studied her, she felt as if he were looking all the way inside her, right to the edge of her soul. "How did you end up with Zeus?"

Truth was a bitter pill to swallow, but she didn't want to lie anymore. This, at least, she needed to be honest about. "A long time ago, Zeus made me an offer I couldn't refuse. To amplify my abilities so I would become the strongest witch in all the realms. I took it, thinking my powers would grow. But what I didn't know then was that the king of the gods was playing me. The offer came with a catch. My powers did grow, but only in the cave where I'm confined. By the time I realized what he'd done, it was too late. I was trapped."

"So you exist in that cave—"

"No longer doing what I want, only what he commands. And over the last thousand years I've come to realize that what he wants is ultimate power. Much as I did, only the difference is he has no conscience about the things he orders me to do, and I've developed one. Power means nothing if it's used for evil instead of good."

He stared at her a long beat before saying, "I've often felt the same, which is why I rarely use my powers unless a situation is dire."

"I know." That too was true. She'd learned a lot from watching him. Learned what she should be. She moved closer still, until his heat and heady scent of pine and something citrusy surrounded her. "I was not always a good witch, Titos. But I want to be one. I hope you believe that."

His gaze skipped over her features. "I'm not sure what to believe when it comes to you. You're doing something to me. Something I don't understand."

Her heart beat faster. It was exactly what she needed to hear to put her plan in motion, but that wasn't why her stomach was tingling and heat was suddenly rushing low in her belly. No, this excitement came from knowing he felt the same things she did. "You're doing something to me, too. Something I like far too much."

Her fingers drifted to his forearm, barely grazing the dark hairs and the strong muscles beneath his skin. And when she saw the way his eyes darkened and his breaths picked up speed, that warmth slid down between her legs to send tingles all across her sex.

"You're the only thing I have to look forward to, Titos," she whispered, running her fingertips up his arm to his thick, muscular biceps. "I know it's not fair to you, but I think about you all the time. Even when I shouldn't."

"You do?"

She nodded. "Do you think about me?"

"Far too much."

Her lips curled. And her fingers continued to trace a lazy pattern against his scintillating flesh. She moved closer, until only a whisper of breath separated their bodies and heat was all she felt. "Do you think...? I mean, I know it's probably bold of me, but would you mind if I kissed you again? It's been ages since I felt—"

He moved so fast she barely saw him. One minute he was staring at her with lust-filled eyes that she knew had to mirror her own, and the next his mouth was on hers, making her breath catch, making her body tremble, and her heart race like the wind.

His hands captured her face, slid into her hair, and when he groaned against her, she opened to him, drawing his tongue into her mouth and his heat and life deep into her soul.

He tasted like mint. Like heaven. Like sin and paradise all rolled into one. And she was desperate for more. Desperate to touch and taste and know him as no one ever had. Desperate to lose herself in him for as long as she could before reality dragged her back to the abyss.

His tongue stroked against hers, inundating her with long, wet, deep kisses she felt everywhere. Her breasts grew heavy, her nipples tight, and an ache built between her legs, one she knew only he could assuage. Groaning into his mouth, she moved closer, until their bodies were plastered together from chest to knee, and his growing erection pressed hard against her belly.

Gods, she wanted him. More than she could ever remember wanting anyone in her 2200-year life. She hadn't lied. She'd been a conniving witch before Zeus had trapped her on Olympus. She hadn't cared who she'd hurt in her quest for power. She'd seduced immortals who could grant her extra powers, then tossed them aside when their usefulness to her was spent. And she would have done the same to Zeus if he hadn't double-crossed her. But imprisonment had taught her a very valuable lesson. That all life had value. And when she'd stopped scheming, she hadn't even missed sex or companionship. Until now.

"Keia..." He whispered her name as he changed the angle of their kiss, as his hands slid down her hair, over her shoulders, and along the length of her spine.

Keia. His whispered word penetrated her hazy mind as his hands reached her waist and he pulled her tighter to him. Not Circe. Not her name. He didn't even know who she was. He was falling under her spell, and she was letting him. A spell she'd cast for her own gain, just like all the other spells she'd cast before her imprisonment.

Her hands drifted up to his shoulders and over to his pecs, and she groaned at how hard and carved he was beneath her palms, but she told herself not to be distracted. Somehow she found the power to push against him and step back, breaking the kiss she only wanted to get lost in.

His face was flushed as he looked down at her, his lips swollen from her mouth, his eyes glazed and so close to gone. "What's wrong?"

"I..." Her heart cinched down tight, sending pain rippling along her ribcage. A pain she'd never felt before, not even when that shade had attacked her.

She had to tell him the truth. She couldn't go through with this lie. If she did, she was no better than Zeus. If she did...it meant she'd not learned a single thing in the thousand years she'd been trapped on Olympus.

"I can't—"

The unmistakable sound of claws scratching against stone sounded somewhere close, shooting Circe's pulse into overdrive. She darted a look to her left, not seeing the gazebo or forest but seeing the bars of her cell in the bowels of Olympus.

"Keia?"

"I have to go," she said quickly, stepping further away from him. "I can't stay any longer."

She broke the feed and swiveled toward the sound. Prometheus's frantic "Wait," faded in the air. The gazebo dissipated. Dank rock walls appeared around her. She jerked back, knocking the bowl she'd been using to conjure her magic from the pedestal in the middle of the room. It clattered against the hard stones. The flames snuffed out. Hot, red cinders scattered across the floor and paled until they were nothing but cold black coals.

Her heart raced as she flattened her body against the rocks and prayed he moved past, that today she'd be spared.

Her cell door clanged open. She closed her eyes and held absolutely still, knowing there was no use in fighting. Remembering when she'd struggled yesterday and the blinding pain that had followed.

Before she had time to conjure a protection spell, he snarled and lunged. His big body slammed into hers, knocking her head against the hard stones. Pain ricocheted across the back of her skull. Even though she told herself not to, she tensed and cried out. His fangs sank deep into her throat, ripping through her flesh.

She somehow forced herself to relax so he wouldn't tear her to pieces. As the shade feasted on her blood, tears streamed down her cheeks. Tears of horror. Tears of agony. Tears of blinding, bitter madness.

This was her fate. To be punished day after day after miserably long day.

Just, she remembered as her vision darkened, as Prometheus had been punished so long ago.

CHAPTER FOUR

He couldn't stop thinking about her.

Prometheus paced the length of the library in his lonely castle, his blood humming with lust as he remembered the kiss he'd shared with Keia in the gazebo. She hadn't appeared to him in two days. Not in his dreams, not in his waking hours. Hadn't once called to him in all that time, either. He'd yet to hear her voice since she'd poofed out of his arms in the early morning light, and he was going nuts waiting for her to contact him again. Not only because he didn't like the thought of her anywhere near Zeus, but because he itched with the need to touch her. To taste her. To feel her everywhere.

This need was stronger than anything he'd ever felt. Not just lust, he knew, but something more, something primitive, something so all-consuming it was all he could focus on.

His mind skipped back over the blood he'd found in the gazebo, and his steps slowed as he remembered the way she'd abruptly left him—twice now. She'd told him the blood had been animal, not hers, but he couldn't stop wondering if they were somehow connected. She'd said she was a prisoner. He, better than anyone, knew how the king of the gods treated prisoners. He thought back to her creamy flesh in the low-cut green gown and her flawless face. She hadn't appeared hurt when she'd come to him, but she knew how to use magic, and if Zeu—

Voices sounded from the corridor, bringing his head around. His heart picked up speed when he realized one voice was female. Was it her? Was she back? He stepped toward the door, excitement burning like fire in his blood, only to draw to a stop when his daughter Natasa and her mate, Titus, appeared at the threshold of the room.

Disappointment swept through him, a disappointment he tried to mask.

"There you are," Natasa said with a smile as she crossed toward him, slid her arms around his waist, and pressed her cheek to his chest. "Hi, *pateras*."

Pateras. Father. He didn't feel much like a father. He felt like a failure when it came to her.

His arms drifted around her slim shoulders, and he hugged her back, but when he looked down and caught sight of her flame-red hair—red thanks to the fire element he'd hidden from the gods in her blood hundreds of years ago and which had caused her intense pain until she'd been reborn in the flames—the guilt he always felt around her consumed him again.

She was safe, he told himself. No longer suffering. And she was happy. His gaze drifted to Titus, standing with his hands tucked into the front pockets of his jeans, his dark wavy locks tied at his nape with a leather strap, a bemused expression across his face.

Titus loved Prometheus's daughter. Would do anything to protect her. Their bond was strong and real and deep.

His gaze drifted back down to Natasa. To her flame-red hair. Hair that was as red as Keia's.

Urgency pushed in again. He needed to find Keia. Couldn't go on waiting. Why the hell hadn't she appeared to him yet?

Natasa eased back and looked up. "We came out to invite you to dinner tonight."

His daughter was speaking to him but he could barely make out her words. All he could think about was the witch.

"*Pateras*?" she asked. Then, "Titus?"

Footsteps sounded close, followed by Titus's quiet voice. "He's blocking me. I can't tell what he's thinking." Then louder, "Prometheus? Dude, are you feeling all right? You don't look so good."

Prometheus blinked several times and finally focused on his daughter's worried face, then looked past her to her mate's narrowed hazel eyes. Titus stood behind Natasa, his hand resting on her shoulder, the ancient Greek text that marked his and all the Argonaut's forearms visible in the lamplight.

The male wasn't wearing his ever-present gloves. Titus had the ability to not only hear others' thoughts, but to pick up their emotions through touch. That ability, Prometheus knew, was one Titus had always considered a curse. But with Natasa he liked knowing what she was feeling. One look at his daughter's face told Prometheus she was feeling fear and confusion...all because of him.

That knowledge jolted him out of his trance. Fixing a relaxed look on his face—as relaxed as he could manage considering his focus remained locked on Keia—he smiled. "I'm fine. How are both of you?"

Natasa's worry fled, and she reached for her father's hand. "Good. Titus has to leave on a mission in the human realm with the Argonauts day after tomorrow so we thought we'd cook dinner for you tonight. It is your birthday, you know."

His birthday. He'd totally forgotten it was his birthday. At his age, one didn't celebrate birthdays anymore. Especially when one's life was as empty as his. A birthday was just a reminder of the passing years and the life he wasn't living. But today he wanted to celebrate. Just not with his daughter and her mate. He wanted to celebrate with Keia.

A renewed urge to find her rushed through him. To see her. To touch her and taste her. To make sure she was okay. If she wasn't going to come to him, he needed to go to her. He'd go back to the gazebo. Find a way to contact her. There had to be something in that gazebo that could draw her back to him. He didn't know what but maybe if he used his Titan powers he could—

"*Pateras*?" Natasa said again. "You're starting to worry me."

Prometheus blinked again and looked down at his daughter. But inside, his heart was racing.

"No need to worry." Grasping Natasa at the biceps—careful not to graze Titus's fingertips in the process—Prometheus pressed a kiss to the top of her head and released her. "Thanks for the invite but I actually have plans tonight. And I'm already late so I should get going."

"You do?" Natasa's brow lowered as Prometheus stepped around her and Titus. "With whom?"

"With a female."

Surprise and approval lit Natasa's eyes as she looked up at her mate, then back at Prometheus. She knew he never made plans. "Who is she?"

Stopping at the threshold of the library, he looked back. "A witch.

And before you say anything, I know what I'm doing."

"I'm sure you do. Have fun, I guess." A wry smile spread across Natasa's lips. "And don't do anything stupid."

Before he knew what he was doing, he smiled back. "I won't."

And he wouldn't. Because what he planned to do with Keia wouldn't be the least bit stupid. It would be hot and wild and, if she let him, mind-meltingly satisfying for both of them.

* * * *

She couldn't keep doing this.

The reality of Circe's situation was a heavy weight on her shoulders as she focused her powers to bring the gazebo into focus. Zeus's shade had hit her again just as her strength had returned from the attack that had pulled her away from Prometheus two days ago. She never knew when the shade was going to come, which made it impossible for her to prepare herself for his assault. If she had any hope of surviving this nightmare she needed to spend her time focusing her powers to protect herself rather than wasting them building this fantasyland.

That knowledge caused an ache to spread out from the center of her chest. Not because it meant she was going to disappoint Zeus by not getting him the element he wanted, but because it meant no longer seeing Prometheus.

She'd thought long and hard about this decision while her body had been healing. When she was stronger, when she knew how to fight the shade, then she could come back and find Prometheus again. But right now she needed to protect herself or she'd never have the strength to go through with her plan.

"Keia."

Fabric rustled behind her in the fading afternoon light. Startled out of her thoughts, Circe turned to see Prometheus rising from the chaise and striding toward her. Her pulse shot up as he drew near. His hazel eyes were a little bit wild, a whole lot hot, and when he reached her and his hand brushed her elbow, electrical impulses shot from the spot straight into her belly.

She swallowed hard, told herself to be tough. That she'd come here to say good-bye for now, not get lost in his immortal good looks and fabulous scent of pine and citrus. But her resistance wavered as he pulled her in, as his long, lean body brushed hers, and his mouth lowered to draw her into a blistering hot kiss.

His lips were just as fierce as his eyes, and the moment his tongue dipped inside to stroke against hers, all the reasons she'd told herself she couldn't have him faded in the ether.

Her hands slid up his chest and around his neck. Her breasts tingled as she leaned into him, as she kissed him back, as she melted in his arms like honey. A moan rumbled from his chest, and he tightened his arms around her, drawing her even closer to his heat and energy and life. Her fingers drifted into the silky hair at his nape. Desire turned to a frantic urge she couldn't resist. In a haze, she realized she was moving, being drawn forward as he moved back, but she didn't care. All she could focus on was his desperate kiss, his commanding hands turning her in the gazebo, the way his erection pressed against her with a heedless need of its own.

"Gods, Keia." His fingers found the line of buttons down her spine as his lips moved to her jaw. Shivers rushed over her as he breathed hot across her skin and pressed a wicked line of kisses down her throat. "I haven't been able to think about anything but you since you left."

His hands made quick work of the buttons on her dress as she trailed her fingers down his muscular back and up and under the black T-shirt he wore. Sparks of desire coiled in her belly, made her thighs tremble in anticipation. Her eyes slid closed as she traced the carved lines of his abs and savored the sensation. "Me too." Oh gods, she couldn't think when he kissed her like that. "I mean you. Titos...don't stop doing that."

A primitive growl—a sound laced with a burning passion she felt all the way to her toes—echoed from his chest. He drew a breath away, grasped the pale blue dress at her shoulders, and pushed it down her arms. Cool air washed over her breasts as he bared them to his view. Her nipples tightened, and when his eyes darkened and his approving gaze swept over her, those tingles in her belly ricocheted straight into her sex.

"I think I'm going mad, but I don't care." He palmed her right breast, lifted it in his hand as he lowered his head. "I need to taste you."

"Oh, yes..."

His tongue swept over her nipple, and she groaned and threaded her fingers back into his hair, reveling in the wicked sensations and heady desire spinning around her.

He licked and laved her nipple, sending her need into overdrive. With his other hand, he palmed her left breast, pushed them together and teased both nipples with his tongue. Her breaths grew shallow and fast. Her sex contracted with the need to feel him everywhere. Sliding her hands back down to his shoulders, she somehow managed to find the hem of his T-shirt and pull the garment up his spine.

He drew away so she could tug the shirt off. Tossing it on the ground, she reached for him again but he moved quickly, his hands bunching in the fabric at her waist. Before she knew what was happening, he pushed the dress all the way to the floor and moaned.

"Oh, Keia..."

She was naked beneath the dress. In her haste to get here and tell him she was leaving for good, she hadn't thought to conjure undergarments. Something in the back of her mind warned this was her last chance to leave. That she needed to get out of here before this went too far. But as he lowered to his knees, her sex clenched and she knew she was lost. There was no way she could leave now. Not when he was looking at her like she was the only thing he'd ever wanted.

He coaxed her to lift one foot out of the fabric at her feet and step back. The chaise brushed against her calves. He pushed the dress aside, inched forward on his knees, and grasped her hand in his, pulling her down to sit.

"Turn, Keia." His hands landed on her knees, pushing her legs apart. As she turned slightly, he slid one hand under the back of her knee and lifted her foot to the seat. Her spine pressed into the plush cushions as he positioned her. Then he was moving closer, his hands trailing up the insides of her thighs, his hot breath fanning her sex until she was trembling with need.

He parted her with his fingers, stared down at her as if she were a feast he couldn't wait to devour. Her stomach quivered with anticipation. Her hands shook against the seat of the chaise. When he didn't make a move, she knew she couldn't wait any longer. On a desperate breath, she reached for him, wrapped her hand around the back of his head, and pulled him closer. "Taste me, Titos. Don't make me wait."

"Yes," he breathed against her. Then his tongue swept over her clit, sending shards of pleasure all through her core.

She moaned. Lifted her hips to his wicked touch. Shivered as he circled her clit then trailed his tongue down to her opening and pressed inside.

Her eyes slid closed as she leaned back. All she knew was his touch, his tongue moving against her to drive her mad, his hands sliding up her belly to cup and tease her breasts. Heat prickled her skin, made her need that much hotter. She lifted and lowered her hips in time with his frantic strokes, moving faster as the orgasm built. And when he drew her over-sensitized nub between his lips and suckled, the wave of ecstasy broke over her like a tidal wave cresting the mountains.

She cried out, trembled against his lips as the pleasure raced along her nerve endings. The wave slowly faded, and vaguely she became aware of her surroundings, of the darkness pressing in from outside the gazebo, of the soft cushion beneath her, of her knees open, one leaning against the back of the chaise. But then his lips moved over her hip, her belly, trailing a line of hot kisses up to her breasts, and she forgot about everything but him.

Her hands found his shoulders. Her fingers pressed against his strong muscles. She lifted her head, grasped him and pulled, forcing him up from the floor. Finding his mouth with hers, she kissed him with everything she had in her, wanting to give him exactly what he'd given her. Wanting him to know pleasure like nothing he'd ever known.

He groaned into her mouth as he rose over her. Her hands slid down to the waistband of his jeans while she flicked her tongue against his and sat upright. Finding the button, she popped it free then slipped her hands beneath the fabric and pushed it down his hips.

He kissed her harder. One hand moved to the back of the chaise, the other slid into her hair to tip her head so he could kiss her deeper. As she worked the fabric down his rock hard thighs and past his knees, he moved closer, rested one leg on the seat of the chaise so she could tug the garment free and throw it on the ground, kissing her the whole time as if he couldn't get enough.

Need resurged within her as she drew her hands up the backs of his thighs, over the soft layer of hair on his legs, then around to his front. Licking into his mouth, she closed one hand around the base of his cock. He groaned again. His fingertips dug into her skull. Sliding her hand up the thick cylinder of flesh, she cuffed the end and squeezed. A bead of fluid slid from the tip, making her mouth water. With her thumb, she spread it over the sensitive underside of the head and drew her hand down and back up.

He drew back from her mouth. Pulsed in her fist. "You make me weak," he rasped. Letting go of the back of the chaise, he trailed the pad of his thumb along her wet, bottom lip. "I want to feel these lips around my cock."

"Oh yes..." She grew wet and hot and achy with his words. Her hand shifted up to his ass, and she pulled him closer, forcing him higher above her as she angled forward and drew his cock toward her.

She breathed hot over his erection, watched it twitch. He trembled as she flicked her tongue against the tip and squeezed the base, teasing him with the lightest of touches.

"More," he growled, shifting closer. A vein pulsed in his neck. His face flushed with arousal. "Taste me. Suck me, Keia."

She groaned as she looked up at him. And when his hand drifted to the back of her head, she finally closed her mouth over his length and sucked.

He groaned long and deep. Pushed forward with his hips until he breached her throat, then drew back. Licking the underside every time the tip passed over her tongue, Circe pleasured him with her mouth, wanting him to find the same release he'd given her, wanting to give him everything. He grew harder with every suck, with every lick, with every press and glide and retreat.

"Yes, Keia." His fingertips tightened in her hair. "Don't stop."

She didn't. Flicking faster with her tongue, she sucked deeper as his thrusts picked up speed. Her other hand found his balls and squeezed. She did it again and again, until she felt his cock begin to swell. And when she sensed he was on the edge, when she felt his climax about to peak, she drew him all the way in and swallowed around his sensitive head.

His pleasure erupted into her mouth. A long, guttural groan echoed from his chest. His fingertips dug into her skull as he thrust once, twice, three more times and trembled.

She continued to work him with her mouth, swallowing every drop, bringing him down slowly. His hips angled back long seconds later, releasing him from her lips. Breathing deeply, she swiped the back of her hand over her mouth and looked up with a smile of satisfaction, of pride, of her own pleasure that she'd been able to give him what he'd given her.

He moved quickly, sweeping his arms around her, lifting her from the chaise. Her smile morphed to a gasp. In a rush, he slid beneath her, and before she realized what was happening she was straddling his hips and his mouth was beneath hers, drawing her right back into a kiss that was so blisteringly hot, lust resurged within her.

He tugged her down and devoured her mouth. His rock hard erection slid through her wetness, reminding her he was a Titan. He could go for days without growing soft if he wanted. A fact that now sent a shiver of excitement down her spine.

"Take me," he mouthed against her, lifting his hips until he pressed against her opening. "Ride me. Use me. Fuck me. Now."

She couldn't say no because that was all she wanted now too. Grasping the back of the chaise, she lowered her weight. Her tongue swept into his mouth just as his cock pressed into her core. Groaning, she tightened around his length until he was seated so far inside they became one.

"Oh, fuck, yes." His hands landed against her hips. He used them to help her lift and lower. Flexed his hips so he drove in deeper. Against her mouth he groaned and kissed her again. Pleasure arced all through her body as she rode him, as their passions grew together, as he pressed into her with long, deep, blinding thrusts.

A frenzied high the likes of which she'd never known hovered just out of her reach. She moved faster. Kissed him harder. Needed to reach it. Needed to drag him into the abyss with her. Needed everything. Sweat beaded her skin, melded with his. She groaned, lifted, lowered, trembled as he hit that perfect spot again and again. Pulling her mouth from his, she dropped her head back and gave herself over to the moment, to every touch, to the way it pushed her right to the edge.

"Come for me, Keia." His hot breath washed over her neck. One hand closed around her breast, and then his mouth was there, suckling her nipple. Shards of ecstasy shot from her breast into her sex. Light blinded her. She cried out. And as the orgasm consumed her, she realized the pleasure she felt with him was better than anything she'd ever felt, not because he was a Titan or even a god, but because he was the first person in ages that mattered.

Slowly, she became aware of the gazebo once more. Candles she didn't remember lighting blazed around them. Somehow she'd ended up on her back on the chaise with Prometheus's heavy weight pressing into her from above, his sweat-slicked skin plastered to hers. She didn't remember him flipping her, didn't remember much of anything besides the most delicious orgasm of her life.

"Holy Hades, witch," he breathed against her neck. "You totally wrecked me."

No, he'd wrecked her. More than she'd thought possible. Nerves echoed through her belly and chest, a feeling she didn't understand. What was happening to her? Was she falling for him? She wasn't supposed to fall for him. She was supposed to use him. And if she couldn't stomach using him, she was supposed to walk away. But right now she didn't want to walk away. She just wanted a repeat of the wicked pleasure he'd given her only moments ago.

Her throat grew thick as she looked up at the shadows dancing over the ceiling from the candles, so similar to the shadows she watched on the ceiling of her cell as she lay on her measly blanket when the flames in her cauldron died out. A bitter reality circled around her.

Nothing had changed.

No, that wasn't right. Her chest pinched. Something had definitely changed.

Her heart had changed.

No matter how badly she wanted to be free, she wouldn't risk him. Not now, not when she knew she was falling for him. If she told him the truth about her imprisonment—now or when she'd learned to fight the shade—she had a feeling he'd come after her. He might succeed in freeing her from Zeus's hell by doing so, but he'd put himself at risk. Zeus had a long memory. Yes, the king of the gods wanted the water element in his quest for ultimate power, but he would also love to see Prometheus suffer once more. And nothing would make Prometheus suffer more than being chained all over again.

She couldn't let that happen. Which meant she wasn't just going to walk away for now. To save him, she needed to walk away forever.

Something hot burned behind her eyes. Something she wasn't used to. She blinked several times, knowing more than anything that she just wanted to go on lying there in his arms, but couldn't.

She shifted beneath him. Taking her hint, he rolled to his side on the chaise, propped his elbow on the cushion and his head on his hand, and smiled down at her. "That was amazing." His hand drifted from her shoulder, across her collarbone, and down the center of her chest, right between her breasts, sending tingles over her skin. "I love this body. And I plan to have it each and every way tonight before you have to leave."

Her eyes slid closed as his warm hand drifted lower, over her belly button and down her lower abs. Gods, that was all she wanted too, but she knew if he started that wicked plan, she'd never have the strength to leave.

Capturing his hand before it could slide between her legs, she lifted it to her mouth and kissed his palm. And then, pushing up so she was sitting, she moved his hand to his naked hip, pinned it there, and leaned in to feather a kiss against his luscious mouth. "I wish I had time for that, but I don't."

She rose, found her gown on the floor, and pulled it on.

"You have to go already?" Confusion drew his brows together as he sat up. "But you just got here. I haven't seen you in days."

"I know." She reached back and buttoned her dress, turning away so she wouldn't have to see the disappointment in his hazel eyes. "And I'm sorry. Believe me. If I could stay, I would."

"Keia."

The floor creaked behind her. His hands landed on her shoulders, turning her to face him. "I want more than these brief visits. I was sort of hoping you wanted more too."

Her heart squeezed tight as she looked up at him. She did want more. She wanted everything. But that wasn't her future, and she had no one to blame for this gigantic mess but herself. "Titos, this is the last time I'm going to visit you."

Panic widened his eyes, and his fingers tightened around her shoulders. "What?"

She pushed back the pain, unwilling to let it consume her. When she was alone in her cell again, then she'd wallow in it. But now she needed to be strong. For him, but mostly for her. "I can't keep coming here. It's not fair to either of us. It's too draining on my powers, and as you said, it's disrupting your life."

"Since meeting you, I finally have a life." His intense gaze swept over her features. "Tell me where you are. I'll come find you."

The pain she'd tried to fight back lanced her chest. His declaration was exactly what she'd wanted when she'd hatched this crazy plan, but now there was no way she could let it happen. "You can't."

"Yes, I can. I'm a Titan. Tell me where you are. I'm not afraid of Zeus."

"I know you're not," she whispered, lifting to her toes and pressing her lips against his for one last kiss. "But I am." She lowered to her heels as tears filled her eyes. Tears that were as foreign to her as this heaviness in her chest. "I'm sorry, Prometheus. I'm sorry for everything."

Before she could change her mind, she cut the feed. The dank rock walls of her cell replaced the gazebo's ornate columns. Prometheus's frantic, "Come back," echoed in her ears as the agony of loss settled deep into her bones. And in a moment of clarity she knew the shade wasn't the greatest threat to her life.

Caring for someone else—caring for Prometheus and never seeing him again—would decimate her far worse than that monster ever could.

CHAPTER FIVE

The last time...

Prometheus stood in the middle of the gazebo long minutes after Keia disappeared. Something had happened to spook her. Something over the last two days when she'd been away. He'd been so obsessed with touching her—with having her—that he hadn't picked up on her signals when she'd finally appeared.

The dream—or had it been a vision?—which he'd had days ago, drifted through his mind. He had the gift of foresight. He could see alternate futures. But those futures were often hazy when they involved himself. This one had been clear, though: Zeus, controlling her, leading him to his death. Only he was a Titan. He couldn't be killed. Not by conventional means. He could be captured, though.

A warning tingle rushed down his spine as he turned a slow circle, looking over the gazebo in the early evening light but seeing none of it. Was she a plant by Zeus? Was this a trick to lure him to imprisonment once more? He didn't want to believe it but she herself had said she'd made a deal with the king of the gods. He'd been so obsessed with her he hadn't pushed that issue when he'd seen her last. Then he'd gotten lost in her sweet, seductive kiss.

Her words—before she'd been pulled away the last time—echoed in his mind: *"You're the only thing I have to look forward to, Titos. I know it's not fair to you, but I think about you all the time. Even when I shouldn't."* Followed by the memory of that blood and the blinding pain he'd felt when he'd touched it.

His heart sped up, beating a bruising rhythm against his ribs. None of that could be a trick. He'd felt the desperation in her kiss, heard the truth in her words, and the blood...she'd said it was animal, but he knew in his gut it had been her blood. He wasn't sure how he knew, he just did. And the pain he'd felt when he'd touched it had been hers as well.

She was in danger. She was with Zeus, in some kind of cave, he remembered her saying at one point, and she was in danger of—

"Holy shit." His eyes flew wide. He'd heard his daughter and Titus speak of one witch who lived high in the caves of Mt. Olympus. One who'd helped the Argonauts not long ago. Only she didn't go by the name Keia.

He pictured the Argolean castle in the heart of the capital city of Tiyrns and teleported into the foyer of the marble structure. As a god, he had the power to flash through walls, something the Argolean people could not do. The guards stationed at the main doors turned at the sound of his appearance. Their eyes grew wide as they drew their swords. In seconds they were rushing toward him.

He didn't have time for this nonsense. Wanted nothing more than to backhand the guards into next week. The only thing that kept him from doing so was the fact his daughter was invested in this realm and that he didn't want to make things worse for her.

Six guards surrounded him, swords and spears drawn and pointed right at his heart. Holding up his hands in a nonthreatening way, Prometheus said, "I want no trouble. I've just come to find the Argonaut Aristokles."

The guards didn't back down. Voices echoed in the three-story entry. Just when Prometheus's patience was about to hit its limit, he heard Titus's voice from the balcony above.

"What in Hades?" Titus rushed down the wide, curved staircase, waving the guards back with his hand. "He's with me. He's fine. Let him through."

The guards slowly lowered their weapons and stood at attention. Titus drew close, his hair pulled back, his hands covered in those ever-present gloves, a look of bewilderment across his weathered face. "What's going on? Why are you here?" Panic rushed across his features. "Natasa isn't—"

"No," Prometheus said quickly, recognizing that quick shot of fear in Titus's eyes...the same fear he was feeling for Keia. "I'm not here about Natasa. I haven't even seen her. I need to speak with Aristokles."

"Ari?" Titus's brow wrinkled. "He's not here. He's in the human realm. On a scouting mission."

Shit. "Where?"

"I don't know. He hasn't checked in since last night."

Frustration pummeled Prometheus from every side. "What about the princess?"

"Elysia?"

That was her name. He was so far removed from the politics of this realm, he barely paid attention to who was related to whom. "Yes. Where is she?"

"In a meeting with the queen and the Council. Prometheus, what's this about?"

Prometheus swiped a hand against his suddenly sweaty brow. "It's about Olympus. I need to know what Aristokles and the princess saw when they went to Mt. Olympus."

"To rescue Cerek?"

"Yes."

"Why?"

Holy Hades. Prometheus liked Titus for the most part, but right now he was ready to shake some sense into the Argonaut. "Because someone's life might be in danger thanks to that rescue."

Titus clearly didn't understand, and Prometheus was past the point of wanting to explain. "Where's Cerek? Is he here?"

"Yeah, he's in the training center with Max."

Prometheus turned on his heels. "Maybe he can help me."

The training center was a domed structure on the castle grounds. It consisted of a gym, weight room, medical facility, and classrooms. Searching rooms, Prometheus finally located Cerek in a medical bay having his shoulder stitched up by a healer.

Prometheus didn't bother to wait until the Argonaut was done, just stalked into the room without waiting for an invitation. The healer glanced over with an annoyed look. Cerek, shirtless and seated on an exam table, looked up as he and Titus entered. "Hey," he said as the healer placed a bandage on his arm. "What's up with you two?"

"What happened?" Titus asked, nodding toward Cerek's arm.

"Nothing. Just took my eyes off Max when I shouldn't have."

Max was an Argonaut in training, Prometheus remembered from a conversation with his daughter. Young. Cocky. A little bit reckless.

He'd spent time in the Underworld as a kid. That had to fuck a person up.

"Where is he now?" Titus asked.

"With Zander. Probably getting a lecture about taking it easy on the old folks."

Titus nodded. The healer said, "You're done. Just keep this dry for a few hours so it has time to heal."

"Thanks." Climbing off the table as the healer left the room, Cerek reached for his shirt. "So what's going on?"

"That's what I'd like to know," Titus muttered.

Prometheus's jaw clenched. "Aristokles and the princess mentioned a witch on Olympus when they went to rescue you. I need to know why she's there."

Cerek glanced at Titus and back to Prometheus with a perplexed expression. "She's there because she works for Zeus. She's the one who reprogrammed me."

Zeus's Sirens had shot Cerek with a poisoned arrow twenty-five years ago. The Argonauts had all thought he'd died, but the poison had preserved his body in stone. Zeus had taken him to Olympus and wiped his memory so he didn't know who he was or where he'd come from. He'd only recently regained his memory when he'd been rescued by the princess and the Argonauts. "In a cave?"

"Yeah." The wrinkle in Cerek's brow deepened. "On Mt. Olympus. Why?"

Prometheus's conversation with Keia days ago ran through his memory.

"What does he want from you?"

"He wants to punish me."

"Why?"

"Because I helped someone. Someone Zeus was using so he could gain more power."

"What was her name?" he asked.

Cerek frowned as if it were common knowledge. "Circe."

Circe was the daughter of Hecate, the goddess of witchcraft and the strongest sorceress to ever walk the earth. She'd never been as powerful as her mother, but Prometheus knew from his interactions with the immortal world before his imprisonment that the daughter of Hecate had craved power as much as Zeus himself.

Keia. Goddess pharmakeia. That's what the commoners had called Circe for years. His eyes widened with understanding. She'd told him who she was with that name, and he still hadn't clued in because he'd been so obsessed with her.

"Find me, Titos..."

She worked for Zeus. She'd sought him out, appeared to him, seduced him so the king of the gods could recapture him. And he'd fallen for it. Even told her he'd risk facing Zeus to find her.

"Why the sudden interest in Circe?" Cerek asked. "Is she in danger?"

Prometheus turned away, his heart pounding hard with both adrenaline and utter stupidity. No, the witch wasn't in danger. He was.

"I don't know," Titus muttered. "But there's clearly something going on. And before you ask, no I can't read him."

Silence stretched over the room as Prometheus thought back over every interaction he'd had with the witch.

"Elysia's had nothing but regret about leaving Circe in that cave," Cerek said long seconds later. "She didn't have to help us, but she did. I guarantee Zeus has come up with some twisted form of punishment for her because of us. He keeps all kinds of sick monsters trapped in the bowels of Mt. Olympus."

The memory of that blood hit Prometheus again. He turned to look back at the Argonauts. "What did you just say?"

Cerek met his gaze. "I said Zeus is probably punishing her because of us. That witch is as much a prisoner as I ever was."

As much as Prometheus ever was.

"I was not always a good witch, Titos. But I want to be one. I hope you believe that."

He'd felt the truth in those words when she'd said them, did believe them even if she'd kept her identity secret, and every time he though about that blood, each time he remembered the agony he'd felt when he'd touched it, he knew Cerek was right. She was being punished for helping the Argonauts. And judging by the way she'd been pulled away from Prometheus during the times they'd been together, that punishment had happened right before his eyes, and he hadn't realized it.

He'd been punished daily by Zeus. Chained to a rock in the blistering heat of the sun, unable to move as he waited for a giant eagle to slice into his side with its razor sharp beak, rip out his liver, and leave him in blinding pain until the wounds slowly closed and consciousness returned.

Yes, Zeus could come up with all kinds of horrendous punishments. For a witch who'd helped the Argonauts, Prometheus knew the king of the gods would not hold back.

The urge to find her, to save her, to rescue her from the same kind of hell he'd lived through overwhelmed Prometheus. "You're certain she's on Mt. Olympus."

"Yeah," Cerek answered. "She can't leave there. Her magic's confined to the mountain."

"Where? Where is her cave?"

"At the top. There's a path that winds all the way up."

Prometheus's mind spun. He could transport to Olympus. The minute he stepped foot into the realm of the heavens, though, Zeus would know. The king of the gods would sense him. He wouldn't have much time to find Circe and transport her to freedom.

"Thank you." Plans ricocheted through Prometheus's brain as he turned away from the Argonauts.

He made it two steps before his daughter's mate stepped in his path and held up both gloved hands. "Hold up. You're not thinking about going to Olympus to get her, are you?"

"No, I'm not thinking about it." He'd already decided.

Titus's jaw tightened. "You're walking into a trap. You know that, don't you? All for a witch."

He might be, but he didn't care. Witch or not, Circe made him feel alive in a way nothing and no one had in over a thousand years. Regardless of why she'd sought him out—whether it was her doing or Zeus's—he wouldn't leave her to the same torment he'd endured.

Before Titus could stop him, he pictured Zeus's precious mountain and flashed.

* * * *

Mt. Olympus was cold and dark when he arrived.

The sun had set. Night pressed in from all sides as Prometheus stood behind a rock outcropping, staring toward a dark cave opening. There had to be more than a hundred caves on this damn mountain, but he'd yet to pass a single one. This had to be the right place.

He hoped it was, at least, because Zeus had probably already been alerted to an outside force in his realm. It wouldn't take long for the king of the gods to zero in on that energy and locate Prometheus.

"You'd better be there," Prometheus whispered beneath the starry sky.

He moved away from his shelter and into the tunnel. Cool air washed over his cheeks, sending a shiver down his spine. It was dark, but his Titan eyesight picked out every bump and ridge on the rock walls. He followed the tunnel around twists and curves until it opened to a vast room with a raised platform and a pedestal topped with a copper bowl. No sound echoed from the space. No movement to cut the silence. He climbed the steps and circled the bowl, recognizing it as a cauldron. Circe's, he guessed.

He lifted his gaze and scanned the room. Two arched doorways opened off the space. Moving in that direction, he peeked into a bedchamber and another room that housed rows and rows of books, a small sitting area, and a basic kitchen.

This was where she lived. Where Zeus had trapped her for over a thousand years to conjure her spells under his bidding. But she wasn't here now. His heart pounded hard as he rationalized where she could be.

Cerek had said she was confined to this mountain. That because of Zeus's curse she couldn't leave. She had to be here. He hadn't seen any other cave openings when he'd wandered up the path. That didn't mean they weren't out there but—

His mind shot back to the moment he'd stepped into the tunnel and the burst of cool air that had washed over his face.

It had come from the left. There'd been another tunnel.

He rushed back to the opening, found the second tunnel and realized why he'd missed it. It curved at a right angle, leaving the appearance of nothing but rock. Moving around the corner, he followed the second tunnel down as it wound deep into the center of Mt. Olympus.

The air was colder down here. Musty. Water dripped along the rock walls, puddled over the ground. He placed a hand on the cool stones as he followed the path, scanning the tunnel for changes, for threats, for Zeus himself.

The tunnel widened to a central, circular space. Several doors made of metal bars lined the room. One was dark and empty, opening to another tunnel that led deeper into the bowels of the mountain. His gaze skipped back to the doors. Cell doors, he realized. The trickle of liquid running under one drew his attention. He stepped toward it. Looked down. Realized the liquid wasn't water, but blood.

"Circe?" Panic tightened into a fist around his throat. He grasped the bars and pulled. The door swung open easily, creaking on its hinges.

A groan echoed from inside.

Prometheus's gaze sharpened, and he spotted a shadow on the floor against the far wall. "Keia?"

The shadow shifted, and another groan echoed. Blood trickled through the rocks along the floor. In a terror-filled heartbeat, Prometheus knew it was her.

He rushed to her side, knelt, and gently turned her away from the wall where she lay curled. She cried out in pain. "I'm sorry," he whispered. "I didn't mean to—"

Blood covered his hands in the dark. As she turned onto her back and whimpered, he saw the giant gash in her neck, still spilling blood.

"Hold still." Heart racing, he placed a hand over the wound at her neck. "This may hurt, but I promise it will help."

He closed his eyes, called on his gifts. As a Titan, he had the ability to heal. It was how he'd survived that giant eagle's attack each day. He could transfer that ability to another if he focused, but this particular gift wasn't always reliable, as he didn't often use it anymore.

Who the hell was he kidding? He never used it because he isolated himself from others in that castle high in the Argolean mountains.

"Hold on," he whispered, focusing harder. Warmth gathered in his palm, permeated her skin. A golden glow radiated from where he touched her, the power of regeneration fusing her skin back together. Sweat beaded his brow. His muscles grew taut and rigid. What should already be healed wasn't. He could feel the cells binding beneath his fingers, but it was taking much too long. Something was slowing him down. Something—

"Adamant," Circe rasped, as if reading his mind. He opened his eyes to focus on her pain-filled face. Blood matted her hair and stained her white dress. "This cell is lined...with adamant. He drags me in here to keep me from casting...a spell to stop him."

His gaze shot up to the rocks. Adamant was the strongest ore in all the realms. It didn't just block her spells, it was weakening his gift, keeping him from healing her.

A clicking sound echoed from beyond the open door. His gaze shot in that direction. Beneath his hand, Circe stiffened.

"It's him," she said in a shaky voice, one filled not just with fear but with terror. "He's come back. He's early. You have to leave. You have to go before—"

A low snarl sounded from the doorway, followed by a growl that was both man and beast at the same time. "The witch is my prize. Back away."

Prometheus let go of Circe and slowly pushed to his feet. She reached out, trying to stop him, but she was so weak from the blood loss, her fingers grazed his arm and dropped away. Focusing his eyesight, Prometheus zeroed in on the monster only to realize it was human.

No, not totally human. Part of it reeked of death. It was a shade. A death shadow that preyed on blood. It had attacked her. Continued to attack her, Prometheus realized when he remembered the way she'd been abruptly drawn away from him several times.

"Leave her or there will be consequences," Prometheus said to the shade. A promise, not a warning.

The shade moved into the room, its long nails clicking an ominous sound against the floor. "And who will provide them? You? Your powers are useless down here, god. Adamant doesn't affect the dead, but it does the living."

"Titos," Circe called in a frantic voice.

"Then it's a good thing I'm not just any god. I'm a Titan."

The shade's eyes widened, then it snarled and lunged.

CHAPTER SIX

The shade knocked Prometheus back into the rocks. His head hit the wall with a crack. Near his feet, Circe shrieked.

The shade was strong from drinking the witch's blood. Prometheus, on the other hand, was weakened thanks to the adamant in the walls around him. Grasping the shade at the shoulders, he managed to keep the beast from ripping into the flesh of his arms and shoved the monster back.

His Titan strength may be weakened, but that didn't mean he still wasn't stronger than this piece of shit.

The shade hit the far wall, bounced off, growled, and charged again. Prometheus waited until it drew close, then captured it by the waist, whipped around as he lifted it off its feet, and slammed it to the ground.

The shade whimpered but struggled under Prometheus's hold.

"The only way...to kill a shade," Circe managed from the corner of the room, "is to pierce its heart."

Pierce its heart. That clearly could only be done when it was in human form. Which meant Prometheus had to work fast before it used up Circe's blood reserved and morphed back into a death shadow. Which it was doing quickly as it exerted its strength to fight.

Pressing his weight into the shade to hold him still, Prometheus scanned the room for anything he could use to stake the fucker. The room was empty except for a wooden chair in the opposite corner from where Circe sat.

Dragging the struggling shade with him, Prometheus shoved the shade against the wall with one hand, held it tight by the throat, and broke a leg free of the chair with the other.

The shade snapped and snarled as the rest of the chair fell into a pile of wood against the floor. "What do you think you're going to do with that? You can't kill me. I'm already dead."

"You're right. I can't kill you. But I can send you to Hades once and for all for what you've done." He jammed the chair leg straight through the shade's heart.

The shade's eyes went bug wide, then its entire body disintegrated into ash and fluttered to the floor.

The stake crashed against the ground. Coughing, Prometheus fanned the ash away from his face and quickly moved back to Circe's side.

"Careful," he said when she reached for his arm. "You're still bleeding." Placing his hand back over the wound in her neck, he focused his gift so the tissue could begin to heal.

"You're not safe here," she rasped. "You have to go."

"Shh." He wrapped his arm around her and held her while he let his gift work. "Don't move too much just yet."

She stopped trying to turn and sank into him. "How did you find me?"

"The Argonauts." When her brow wrinkled, he added, "Cerek."

"But how did you know who I was?"

"I finally used my superhuman brain." Her frown deepened in such an adorable way, he chuckled. "Okay, it's not so superhuman. I just put your clues together. Keia. Goddess pharmakeia. I remembered that was what the commoners used to call the witch Circe. And when I thought back to what you'd said about Zeus punishing you for helping another, I realized you were the witch who helped rescue Cerek from Zeus's service."

Her green eyes softened in the dark. "I'm sorry," she whispered. "I wanted to tell you who I was, but I couldn't. There are rules."

"I know." He lifted his hand, checked the wound beneath. The bleeding had stopped. The wound was still fresh, but a layer of new skin was already beginning to form. "And I'm not upset. I understand why you couldn't tell me." His gaze drifted to her face. "Though you should have told me about that shade."

Tears filled her eyes. "I wanted to, but I couldn't. I couldn't put you in danger."

"I'm a Titan, Circe. Even weakened by adamant, I can kick a

shade's ass."

"I see that. But it's not the shade I'm worried about."

Zeus. She was talking about Zeus. "He can't hurt us anymore."

"Titos—"

"Come on." He pulled her to her feet. "We need to get back up to the surface so we can get the hell out of this realm. There's not enough adamant in these walls to immobilize me, but there is enough to prevent me from teleporting."

She pushed a hand against his chest, her feet shuffling over the ground as he maneuvered her toward the door. "You don't understand. It's not the adamant keeping me here. It's—"

"It's her love of power," Zeus said from the doorway.

Prometheus drew to a stop, his arm around Circe's waist. Against him, Circe froze and whispered, "Oh gods."

"Stay behind me," Prometheus said in a low voice, pushing her back.

"There's no need for that, Titan." Zeus stepped into the room. "We're all friends here, right, witch?"

Behind Zeus, five Sirens rushed in, bows drawn, arrows poised at Prometheus's heart.

"Just so we're clear," Zeus said. "Those arrows are made from adamant. So if you decide to bolt, Titan, you won't get far."

Prometheus's jaw tightened. His dream had become a reality, the alternate future he'd ignored. He was trapped. Again. Only this time it wasn't just him. "Let the witch go. You used her as bait and it worked. She means nothing to you and we both know it."

"Oh, she was bait," Zeus answered, lacing his fingers together behind his back. "But willing bait."

"Titos," Circe whispered in a pained voice at his back.

"Go on." Zeus lifted a hand toward the witch. "Ask her yourself. Ask her about our deal. Her freedom from this mountain in exchange for seducing you into giving her the water element."

Shock rippled through Prometheus as he turned and stared into Circe's green eyes. "Is that true?"

Guilt rushed over her flawless features. "Yes, at first. But that was before I knew you. You have to believe me. I changed my mind."

The pain of betrayal lanced his chest, as swift and sharp as that eagle's beak had ever been. He turned away from her.

"Never trust a female, Titan." Zeus clucked his tongue. "I thought you would have picked up that tidbit over your long lifetime."

Anger and betrayal and stupidity swam in Prometheus's veins. "When would I have picked that up? When I was chained to that rock?"

Zeus grinned. "It was a nice rock. You miss it, don't you?"

Prometheus's vision turned red. An image flashed in his mind, his hands wrapping around Zeus's throat, his arms ripping the god's head from his body and flinging it at his precious Sirens. But he'd never do that no matter how much he wanted to. Because attacking Zeus would guarantee the witch would never be freed. And even though she'd betrayed him, he still didn't want her to suffer the way he had. Wouldn't wish that kind of torment on anyone.

Anyone but Zeus, that was.

"Well, this has all been fun, but it's time to get on with things." Zeus sighed. "Sirens, take him."

"Wait." Circe jerked in front of Prometheus. "Take me instead. He told me where the water element is. You don't need him anymore. Take me."

Prometheus's gaze darted to the back of her head as the Sirens moved up behind him and tugged his arms behind his back, cuffing him with the adamant shackles that would severely limit his powers. He'd never told her where the water element was located. They'd never even discussed the water element.

"Did you really think this was about the water element?" Zeus lifted his brow in amusement. "He doesn't even know where the thing is. He scattered those elements over the earth on purpose so he'd never be able to tell another god where they're located. I know that." He angled his chin Prometheus's direction. "He knows that. You, witch, are the only one who was stupid enough to fall for that ruse."

A gasp rushed out of Circe's mouth. Zeus turned away, but she rushed after him. "I can get you what you want. I can use the chain. Access his god essence in the metal and look back into his past with my powers to see where he scattered the elements. You don't need him. You have me."

Zeus whipped back to her so fast she stumbled, then his hand closed around Circe's injured throat like a vise, and in one swift move he lifted her off the floor. Her face turned red. Her eyes bulged as she struggled to pry his hands free to no avail. Prometheus's muscles flexed and he shifted an inch forward, but the adamant cuffs held him in place. And the Sirens' daggers suddenly pushing against his side kept him from trying. "I'll always have you, witch. You think you're getting out of this cave? You're never doing anything but what I say."

He shoved her back into the wall and released her. Gasping, she fell to the floor and lifted a hand to her injured throat.

"Bring him," Zeus said to the Sirens, turning for the tunnel.

The Sirens pushed Prometheus forward. His gaze shot to Circe on the ground, tears streaming down her cheeks.

"I'm sorry," she whispered. "I'm so sorry."

Before he could answer, Zeus barked, "And bring her, too. She can watch as my new eagle feasts on the Titan's flesh."

* * * *

Circe watched in horror as the Sirens shackled Prometheus vertically to a flat rock, his arms outstretched above his head, his feet together against the ground. They were somewhere in the human realm, though she didn't know where. The landscape was dry and barren, the hills around them littered with rock outcroppings baking in the sun.

She tried again to move her arms, but her hands were cuffed together at her back with a length of adamant chain, preventing any kind of movement. She couldn't conjure a spell without her hands. Couldn't even contact Prometheus's daughter in the Argolean realm and tell her where her father was trapped. Finally, she was free from that cave, with all the power in the world within her grasp, yet she was unable to access it and save the male who'd come to mean more to her than any other.

"You know," Zeus said in a cheerful voice as the Sirens checked Prometheus's chains one last time to make sure he couldn't move. "When Circe and I hatched this plan to lure you out of hiding, Titan, I had no idea it was going to be quite so easy." Brushing a lock of hair away from Circe's cheek, Zeus smiled down at her almost sweetly.

Sickness brewed in Circe's stomach at the lies he was telling. Lies Prometheus was believing.

"She really is a find, isn't she?" Zeus went on. "As seductive as any Siren, but as cunning and manipulative as the gods. Any male would be lucky to have her on his side. And I will have her on my side." His eyes darkened with a heat that made her skin crawl. "And on her back, and on her hands and knees, all too soon. Finally, witch, you're going to submit to me the way you should have submitted long ago."

"I never agreed to this." Rage simmered along Circe's nerve endings, but she didn't pull away from Zeus's touch. Knew she wouldn't be able to even if she tried. "And I'll never submit to you. Not willingly."

"Oh, you will." Zeus's grin faded, and he dropped his hand. "Because I have your lover, and if you don't do exactly what I want this time, I'll make his torture that much worse. Do you think I'm clueless? I knew all about your plan to double cross me and have Prometheus rescue you. I even knew when you gave up that plan and decided to sacrifice yourself to that shade so selflessly in a lame attempt to spare his life. I'm the god of the heavens, witch. I know everything. I let you think you were in control. And do you know why?" His eyes narrowed on Circe as he pointed toward Prometheus. "Because his suffering is going to be that much more satisfying when that eagle's ripping into his flesh and he's thinking about all the ways I'm fucking the female who's fallen in love with him."

In love with him? Was she? Panic rushed through Circe's chest but turned to a warm liquid feeling that gave her strength.

Yes, she was in love with him. Quickly, madly, deeply in love with a Titan.

Zeus turned back to Prometheus with a smug grin. Circe's gaze followed and rested on the Titan, chained to the rock wall, and bile slid up her throat at what Zeus had planned. But Prometheus's hazel eyes weren't on Zeus. They were locked on her. And they no longer brimmed with betrayal. They swam in a sea of regret and sorrow and pain.

I'm sorry, she mouthed to him, tears filling her eyes. Did he feel any of what she did? She'd never know. Not when she was Zeus's prisoner on Olympus and he was trapped here.

Prometheus shook his head slightly, telling her in one brief motion that it wasn't her fault, that he didn't blame her, that he was sorry too.

That he *did* feel at least some of what she did.

The pain in her heart grew exponentially until it choked her throat.

"Where the hell is that eagle," Zeus said, his voice growing impatient as he glanced past Prometheus toward a dark cave opening Circe had tried—and failed—to ignore.

Almost as if on cue, a screech echoed from inside the cave.

"That's more like it." Zeus grinned down at Circe once more. "Let's get this show on the road so we can get on to other, more enjoyable activities."

Sickness threatened to overwhelm Circe, but she kept her gaze locked on Prometheus. Refused to give Zeus even a fraction of her concentration. Wanted him to know that she wouldn't leave him until forced.

Light flashed to her left. Zeus muttered a curse and turned in that direction. Voices echoed—several, male—dragging at Circe's attention. She finally looked that way, eyes widening when she spotted two, three, no seven Argonauts, their arms and hands covered in the ancient Greek text of their forefathers as they drew their swords and rushed toward Prometheus.

"Stop them!" Zeus screamed. Lifting his hand toward the heavens, he grasped a lightning bolt out of thin air and hurled it toward the Argonauts.

The six Sirens who'd accompanied them to this place abandoned Prometheus and reached for their bows, readying for battle. The Argonauts jumped out of the way of Zeus's lightning bolt and continued streaking toward them. Shock widened each of the Sirens' eyes. Only one was able to grasp her bow in time. The others quickly reached for their secondary weapons, the daggers strapped to their thighs.

Zeus continued hurling lighting bolts, barely missing one of his Sirens. The Argonauts darted away from his bolts, rolled across the ground to avoid being singed. Argonaut clashed with Siren, the sound of a battle rising in the air. Unable to move, to do anything to help, Circe looked back at Prometheus and spotted a flash of red out of the corner of her eye, rushing his way.

Seconds later the entire rock outcropping was engulfed in flames, consuming Prometheus. A scream tore from Circe's throat before she could stop it.

Zeus whipped back, saw the flames and growled. "Fucking Argonauts." His gaze shot back to the battle where several Sirens were already on the ground, pinned by the Argonauts. "They're not going to win. Not this time."

He wrapped a hand around Circe's biceps and jerked her into him. "I still have you, witch."

* * * *

"Natasa..." Prometheus's eyes grew wide as the wall of flames surrounded him and his daughter drew close. "What are you doing here? How did you—"

She knelt at his feet and laid her hand over the chain at his ankles. "Titus figured out you were going to Olympus. We followed and found Circe's cave thanks to Cerek."

The chain grew red beneath her hand, and he hissed in a breath as the heat of the fire element inside her melted the adamant chain as if it were nothing. It broke open and dropped to the ground, freeing his legs. "But how—"

"I fanned the flames in her cauldron." Pushing to her feet, she grasped a piece of the rock wall sticking out and climbed two feet off the ground so she could place her hand over the chain above his right arm. "Her spell was still active. It showed me where to find you."

The chain above his head broke free. He dropped his arm, rolled his shoulder to stretch his sore muscles as she moved around him and did the same to the last chain pinning him to the rocks.

"Zeus set this all up," he said as the final chain melted, freeing him. He rubbed at his sore wrist, a growing panic rising in his chest. "He tricked her. He wants me to suffer, and he's using her to make that happen."

"I know." Natasa moved to stand in front of him, the wall of flames crackling around them a barrier even Zeus couldn't penetrate. "Which is why this just got a whole lot trickier. We'll only have one shot to get her away from Zeus."

His gaze narrowed. "What are you thinking?"

"Something that's only going to happen with Circe's help. How sure are you that she's on our side?"

* * * *

Circe fell against the hard wall of Zeus's chest with a grunt. Zeus's black eyes reflected the flames as he squeezed her upper arm, sending pain all through her biceps.

"You'll pay for this, witch," he growled. "You'll pay for all of this."

Her gaze shot to the flames as she felt Zeus's energy build around them. Zeus was going to flash them back to Olympus. Before she would ever know if Prometheus was alive or dead.

Panic clawed at her chest. "Titos," she whispered.

The wall of flames parted. Prometheus's large body launched through the opening and smacked into Zeus. The king of the gods jerked her forward, but the force of Prometheus's blow broke his hold on Circe, and she stumbled before finding her footing.

The two gods rolled across the ground, a tangle of arms and legs, swinging fists and bunching muscles. Zeus gathered electrical energy in his hand and zapped Prometheus's shoulder, causing the Titan to lurch back. Before he could zap Prometheus a second time, a fireball that seemed to come out of nowhere struck Zeus's hand, tearing a screech from Zeus's throat.

Circe's eyes grew wide, and she staggered back from the fight, from the flames. Her back hit something hard.

"Hold still," a female said behind her.

Warmth gathered around Circe's wrists, followed by a burn that cut across her skin. She cried out, but before the sound fully escaped her lips, the chains at her wrist fell to the ground, freeing her hands.

She whipped around and looked into Prometheus's daughter's eyes. "How did you—"

"We don't have time for that. These chains were forged by Hephaestus, correct?"

"Yes. They're made of adamant."

"So if we get them on Zeus, he won't be able to break free, will he?"

Circe saw where this was going. Grunts, the sounds of fists hitting bone, and blade clashing with blade, echoed around them. "Yes. Yes, that's right."

"Then do your thing and get them on Zeus's wrists." Natasa rushed past her, held out her hand. A fireball formed in her palm. She watched Zeus and Prometheus, rolling over the ground. When Zeus shifted on top, pinning Prometheus beneath him, Natasa launched the ball, hitting Zeus in the back. The god's shirt erupted in flames.

Zeus shrieked, released Prometheus, and lurched to his feet. Knowing this was her only shot, Circe held her hands over the chains that had just fallen from her wrists, closed her eyes, blocking out all that was happening around her, and summoned forth an attraction spell.

The chains rattled. Zeus growled somewhere close and said, "She'll die for this, Titan. She and your precious offspring will both die for what you've done here."

Circe's focus honed in on the chain, on the spell, and with the last uttered word, she felt the chain rise from the ground and shoot to her left.

"*Noooo*!" Zeus's shocked voice echoed in the air, followed by a *thwack* and a grunt.

Opening her eyes, Circe turned to look. The king of the gods lay on his back on the ground, his bound wrists shackled at his front.

"You can't do this. You can't!" Zeus screamed as Prometheus pushed to his feet, sweaty and dusty as he crossed to stand over the king of the gods. Zeus's dark eyes shimmered with retribution. "Sirens!"

"Oh, you mean those Sirens?" Prometheus angled his head to his left. Circe's gaze drifted to the battle—or what was left of it. Bows and daggers littered the ground out of reach of the six Sirens standing in a circle, surrounded by the Argonauts with weapons drawn, just in case. "They're out of commission."

Fury twisted Zeus's face. "You'll pay for this. Do you hear me? You and all the fucking Argoleans will pay."

"Not today we won't." Prometheus grasped Zeus by the arm and hefted the king of the gods to his feet. "Natasa?"

Prometheus's daughter rushed over and helped him maneuver Zeus to the rock wall where Prometheus had been chained.

"What are you doing?" Zeus's eyes grew so wide, the whites glowed all around his coal black irises as they jerked his arms over his head and chained him to the rocks. "What do you think you're doing?

You can't leave me here."

"Can and will." Prometheus stepped back as Natasa latched the last chain to Zeus's feet. "You like torture so much, I think it's about time you got a taste of it yourself."

A screech echoed from the cave to their left. Zeus's eyes grew even wider as he looked in that direction, panic and true fear rushing over his features. "Release me. Release me right now!"

Natasa rose and stepped back. Looking toward her father, she said, "We're good here. Go to her."

He squeezed his daughter's hand. Then turned to face Circe.

Circe's breath caught as Prometheus headed toward her. Dust covered his hair, his ripped shirt, and torn pants. A track of blood from a gash in his forehead stained his cheek but the wound was already sealing from his Titan genes. He stopped a foot away from her, and as he looked at her—really looked at her as he'd done in their gazebo—her heart sped up, tripping over itself until pain ricocheted all through her chest.

There were so many things she wanted to say to him, so many things she needed to make him understand. So many things she needed to make up for. "Titos, I—"

"Can you cast a spell on those Sirens so they think Zeus is dead?"

Confusion drew her brow together. That wasn't what she'd expected him to say. "Yes."

"Do it before that eagle comes out and we run out of time."

Turning away from him, she looked toward the Sirens and held out her hands. The Argonauts kept their weapons drawn but stepped back. She tuned out the sound of Zeus's continued threats, ignored the pain still burning her wrists from that melted chain, and tried not to be so aware of Prometheus standing close, but not close enough.

But as the cloaking spell fell from her lips, she knew she'd never be unaware of him. She cared for him. Would always care for him because he made her a better person.

"There," she said when the spell was done. "It's cast."

Prometheus looked toward the Argonauts, blocking the Sirens' view of Zeus, and nodded. Blinking, Circe watched as the Argonauts opened a portal and took the Sirens and Natasa through.

When the portal closed, she gathered her courage and turned to Prometheus. "I'm so sorry. I didn't mean for any of this to happen. I didn't mean for—"

He moved before she saw him. And when his mouth closed over hers and his hands encircled her wrists, lifting them to rest against his chest, she gasped.

The gasp turned to a sigh as he drew her into a kiss that finally felt...free.

"I'll kill you for this," Zeus screamed in a crazed voice. "I'll kill you all, do you hear me?" The ground shook, followed by another shriek, this one not from a god but from a beast. A giant, winged, sharp-beaked beast.

"Oh, fuuuuuck," Zeus hollered just before the sound of flesh tearing echoed in the air.

Circe never had time to look because she felt herself flying, and when Prometheus finally drew back from her lips and she looked up into his mesmerizing eyes, she realized she wasn't in a barren desert anymore. She was in her gazebo—*their* gazebo—surrounded by the lush green forests of Argolea.

She glanced around the familiar surrounding and listened to the soft trickle of water rolling over the rocks in the river below. "You brought us back here."

He let go of her wrists—wrists, she realized, that were no longer burned but healed from his magical hands—and slid his arms around her waist. "Seemed like the perfect place for both of us to start over. Together, if that's what you want."

Her gaze shifted back to his. Warmth gathered in her chest, pushing aside all the fear and doubt and longing she'd lived with for far too long. "I do want. Oh, do I want, Titos. But...the spell I cast on those Sirens won't last. Athena will be able to tell they're charmed. Zeus will be free before long."

"I don't care."

"You have to. He'll come after you. What will you do?"

"What I should have done a long time ago. Help the Argonauts find the water element so Zeus can't use the Orb."

Her heart swelled. He might be a Titan but he was every bit a hero as the Argonauts.

"We're safe here," he said, gazing down at her with soft eyes. Eyes she could see a future in. A real future. "Zeus can't cross into this realm, and his Sirens are no match for me...or us."

Her heart skipped a beat. "Are you sure you want me? Knowing everything you now know about me?"

A sexy half-smile curled his lips, and he tightened his arms around her waist, pulling her against the heat and life of his body. "Yes, I want you, Keia. In case you haven't noticed, we're the same, you and I. And the intensity with which I want you has not changed in the last day. If anything, it's only amplified."

She smiled because she definitely felt that intensity amplifying against her belly. "You won't grow tired of me? Witches aren't the easiest of beings to get along with."

"Neither are Titans." Flexing his hands against her lower spine, he pulled her in closer and leaned down toward her mouth. "But I have a feeling we have plenty of time to work all of that out."

They did. Sighing, she lifted to her toes and threaded her fingers through his silky dark hair as she opened to his kiss.

Thanks to him, nothing but eternity stretched before her, and she intended to spend every moment of it with him.

HUNTED

An Eternal Guardians Novella

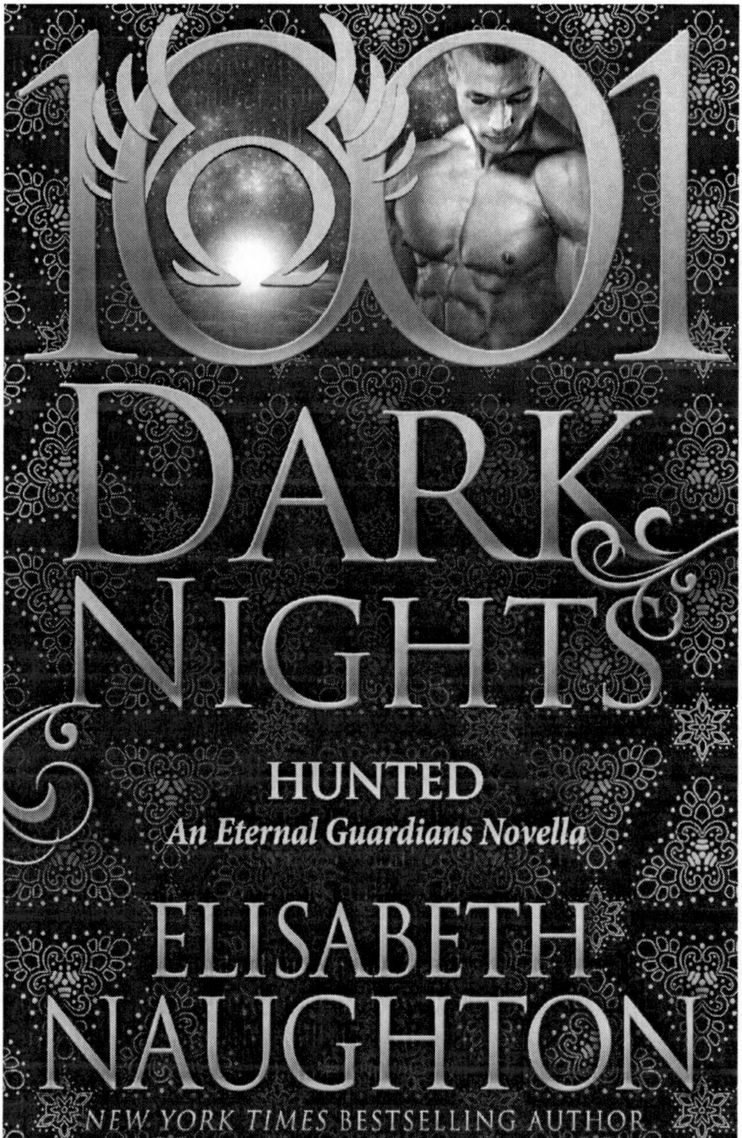

"From the deepest desires often comes the deadliest hate."

—Socrates

CHAPTER ONE

One thing Erebus could say for the Sirens—they sure made their trainees feel special. So special they couldn't even refer to them by name when they crashed and burned and Zeus decided it was time to hunt them down and snuff them out.

Not that Erebus cared all that much. He knew his place. He was a minor god in service to Zeus only because Hades had lost him in a bet to the King of the Gods. He didn't particularly enjoy serving, but it was better than the alternative: being decimated altogether like his kinsfolk or spending eternity suffering in the pits of Tartarus. While he'd been spared the same fate as his family thousands of years ago, his time in servitude to Hades in the Underworld had shown him just what happens to prisoners in Tartarus—at both the hands of Hades and Tartarus's most famous prisoner: Krónos—and he had no desire to get stuck in that living hell as an inmate himself.

A flash of blonde hair to his left caught his attention as he ran through the dark forest. His target—Trainee #429745—was close, but then he knew that already. His god powers were strongest in darkness, and his hearing, smell, even sight were amplified when night disadvantaged other hunters. He could hear her labored breaths echoing in his ears, could smell the lemony scent of her skin in his nostrils, but seeing the flash of long blonde hair had surprised him.

He hadn't looked at her picture before he'd left Olympus for this hunt. He'd memorized her trainee number, read through her file and made mental notes of her trainers' mostly average comments about her hand-to-hand combat and warfare skills. Had questioned the stupid guards she'd overpowered at the gates of Olympus when she'd fled, and who were now suffering their own just fates. And he'd located the portal she'd used outside the gates to cross into this forest in the human realm. But he'd purposefully not looked at her image.

Putting a face to a number gave his prey a human quality he didn't need to concern himself with. His orders from Zeus were clear: "*She failed her last Siren test and ran. Hunt her down and bring her back to me.*" It was not Erebus's place to question Zeus's command. The King of the Gods could have ordered Erebus to kill the trainee—which he'd done in the past and would do again when called upon *because it was his duty*—but Zeus hadn't. That made Erebus's job this time a helluva lot easier, and for that he was thankful.

But that flash of blonde...

He'd seen it somewhere before. Or hair like it. Not a white blonde. Not a honey blonde. Not even a multicolored blonde like many of the Sirens sported on Olympus. This hair had been a golden blonde so bright it had looked like a gilded waterfall in the darkness of the forest when she'd whipped past him through the trees.

Not important.

What she looked like had no impact on his current assignment. Clearing his mind, he shifted direction and picked up his speed, heading toward the flash of blonde he'd seen. Her labored breaths grew louder. Her scent stronger. Ahead, that golden blonde flashed again, whipping behind her as she turned to look into the dark forest at her back then angled forward again and ran faster.

Leaves and pine needles slapped him in the face. The forest floor was damp and soft beneath his boots. She wasn't particularly fast for a nymph, but she zigzagged around trees and brush quite a bit, changing direction so much it was hard to anticipate her next move. He'd researched this forest in preparation for this hunt, though, and he had a good idea where she was headed. Instead of chasing her maze of steps, he shifted to his right and ran at an angle away from her.

He calculated distance and speed in his mind. The ground rose and fell in the mountainous terrain. Somewhere above, an owl hooted and the whir of bat wings echoed like background music to his steps. When he'd run far enough, he cut back to his left. The terrain gave way to a small clearing between the mountains. Just as he predicted, she came tearing down the hillside to his left and emerged from the trees, that blonde hair a blur around her face as she repeatedly glanced over her shoulder to check his position.

Victory flared hot in his veins. He increased his speed and shot into the clearing at her right. Her surprised gasp met his ears when she spotted him, but she didn't have time to react. Lowering his shoulder, he slammed into her, knocking her off her feet to fly through the air ten yards before hitting the meadow grasses with a grunt.

He slowed his steps as he approached and looked down. She groaned and rolled onto her side away from him in the grass. That oddly familiar golden hair covered her face, triggering a sense of déjà vu, but he ignored it. He ignored everything except what he was here to do.

His pulse slowed now that he'd captured his prey. "Your fun's over now, nymph." Leaning forward, he reached for her arm. "On your feet."

His hand closed around her biceps. She still wore the typical training attire: knee-high kick-ass boots, slim black stretch pants that molded to her muscular legs, and a fitted black tank that showcased her curves and plump breasts. Heat from her bare skin burned into his palm as he wrapped his hand around her upper arm, but she didn't immediately climb to her feet, which irritated him. And something about her scent... It was warm and familiar, like a summer breeze blowing through a lemon grove at dusk.

Like a lemon grove at dusk? He gave his head a swift shake, knowing the hours he'd spent hunting her were catching up with him. Fuck him. He was the god of darkness. It was in his DNA to be moody and short-tempered, not romantic and idealistic. The sooner he got this insolent nymph back to Olympus, the sooner he could catch a few hours of shut-eye to recharge his dwindling energy reserves. He might be a god, but he still had needs. And after he dumped Trainee #429745 in Zeus's lap, he needed to gear himself up to instruct the newest class of Siren recruits. The ones who were even more inept than the last set Zeus had sent him.

He was tired, grouchy, and in need of a little R and R before he had to deal with more bratty Siren trainees who thought they were all the shit. The fact this one was causing him so much trouble didn't do a thing to ease his perpetual bad mood.

"I said your fun is over, nymph." He jerked on her arm.

A blur of golden hair whipped in front of him, and he saw the briefest flash of silver in that blur. But he had no time to react. Hot metal pierced the flesh of his upper arm and stabbed deep before his brain clued in to what the silver meant.

Pain ripped through his arm. His hand reflexively released her, and he jerked back. The recruit yanked the blade of a dagger free from his arm, lurched to her feet, and faced him with both malice and fury in her brilliant blue eyes. "Wrong, asshole. I say when it's over."

Her features registered the instant she found her footing, and in a flash he realized where he'd seen that unique blonde hair before, where he'd smelled that exotic, hypnotic scent.

During her one-on-one training sessions.

During their highly specialized time alone together.

During her extremely erotic, immensely pleasurable seduction sessions, directed by him.

Seraphine. Sera. *His* Sera. He'd been her seduction trainer twelve—no, eighteen months ago.

He blinked, barely believing what he was seeing. She looked different from what he remembered. Every other time he'd been near her she'd been dolled up with sexy makeup, her hair perfectly styled, her voluptuous body wrapped in whatever arousing attire he'd picked out for her. Now she looked more like a warrior than a Barbie doll, but he still recognized her. Knew not just from her scent and that unique hair, but from the way his blood heated and rushed straight into his groin as a rash of memories of her wicked hands, her sinful mouth and tight body consuming his flooded his mind.

All nymphs were easy to train in the Siren ways of seduction, but this one had been a natural. She'd been able to suck and fuck better than any other recruit he'd worked with in his last hundred years serving Zeus as a Siren trainer, and that was saying a lot, considering Zeus handpicked the females he wanted in his Siren Order from across every race and realm.

The pain in his arm faded from his mind. In her familiar eyes he saw a flash of recognition that pushed him a step closer and caused him to reach out for her. But just as his fingers grazed her skin, she kicked out with her leg and nailed him in the side of his head with the toe of her kick-ass boot.

The force of the blow knocked him off his feet and set him flailing toward the grassy meadow. Pain spiraled up his spine as he hit the hard earth and grunted. Opening his eyes, he blinked several times, shocked that she'd gotten the jump on him. Blonde hair flashed in his line of sight once more, followed by the icy glare of her crystal blue eyes as she leaned over him with her blade held high.

And holy shit, that was hot. Hotter than he ever remembered her being.

"If you think this is fun, *god*," she said in a low voice, "then you're more useless than I thought."

Oh, but this was fun. Staring up into her challenging gaze was more entertainment than he'd had in months—no, years. And anticipating what the little vixen would do next didn't just fuel the flames already rising inside him; it made him hard as stone.

* * * *

Of all the hunters she'd expected Zeus to send after her, Erebus had been the last.

Sera probably should have struck while he was down, but something had held her back. She'd told herself it was because he was a minor god, which meant he was immortal. Any further attack on her part wouldn't kill him, only enrage him, and she didn't want to tangle with the god of darkness out here in the dark. So instead she'd decided to take advantage of his shocked expression and ran. But that niggling voice in the back of her whispered that wasn't the real reason she'd held back.

She shook the voice away as she pushed her legs harder through the dark forest. Erebus was nothing to her now but one of Zeus's henchmen. She didn't care what her stupid heart had once felt for him. She only cared about putting as much distance between her and the asshole as she could now.

Her muscles burned as she darted around trees and brush, over downed logs and across a narrow stream. He would chase her, she knew. He would probably catch her. Her only hope at this point was to make sure he didn't catch her with *it*.

A searing pain tightened her lungs as she slowed her steps in the darkness and scanned the forest. Dried leaves and fallen twigs crunched under her boots as she searched for something—anything—that would help her. Panic spread through every cell, and she started to run again, squinting to see, hoping—

Her boots skidded to a stop when she spotted the decaying log lying across the forest floor ten yards to her right. Rushing in that direction, she dropped to her knees near the base and felt around, searching for any kind of hole. The instant she found one, she silently rejoiced, pulled the medallion from her pocket, and shoved it deep into the log where no one would accidentally find it.

Pounding footsteps echoed through the silent forest at her back. Her adrenaline surged.

She lurched to her feet and tore off to her left, zigzagging around trees and brush. The medallion didn't look like much—a coin slightly smaller than the palm of her hand, stamped with the imprint of Heracles and surrounded by the traditional Greek key design. Even if some hapless person did manage to find it in that log, she hoped it would be so covered in dirt and grime that they wouldn't know what it was. But Erebus absolutely could not find it because one look and he would know. He'd know the power a person could wield with it, and she knew without a doubt he'd take it right back to Zeus.

Her heart pounded, feeling as if it had taken up permanent residence in her throat. Sweat slicked her skin even though the fall night was cool and damp. She ran harder, faster, intent on getting as far from that log as possible. She couldn't go to the half-breed ruins now as she'd planned. She couldn't risk Erebus following her there. Couldn't risk his interfering with her only chance to contact her friend Elysia in Argolea.

Something hard slammed into her from the side, knocking the air out of her lungs and the thoughts from her mind. She grunted as her body sailed to the right and smacked against the hard earth. A groan tore from her throat. Pain spiraled through every cell in her body, and her vision wavered.

She rolled to her side. Groaned. Tried to get up. Tried to find her feet so she could run. But he was on her before she could even push up on her hands.

His big body straddled hers, and he dropped to his knees, his massive tree-trunk-like thighs pressing against her ribs. She lashed out with her hands to claw him off her but he captured her wrists easily and pinned them to the ground over her head. "Enough!"

Hearing his voice so close colored everything in red. She kicked out with her legs and thrashed from side to side, trying to throw him off, but he was too strong. Her hair whipped across her face as she fought harder, not wanting to hear his deep voice, now wanting to feel his hard body against hers, not wanting *him* ever again.

He squeezed his thighs so tight against her ribs, she gasped, and his fingertips dug into the skin of her wrists until pain shot straight to her brain, slowing her fight. "I said *enough*, nymph."

Breathing hard, she glared up at him through wisps of sweaty hair, hating that he was here now. Hating even more that he was just as handsome and enticing as he'd been a year and a half ago when she'd seen him across the Siren training field for the first time. Jet black hair, dark eyes, mahogany skin, and a body that was an almost seven-foot wall of solid muscle.

She knew those muscles intimately. Had traced them with her hands and fingertips and tongue during their steamy sessions when he'd been her seduction trainer. Only for her it hadn't just been seduction. Because of those erotic nights and the things he'd made her feel, he'd ruined her ability to think about or even look at another guy without remembering his whispered words against her overheated flesh and the way he'd been able to make her melt with just one carnal look. And then he'd cast her aside as if she'd never meant a single thing to him at all.

Which she hadn't, she realized as she glared up at his narrowed black-as-night eyes. He hadn't even used her damn name when he'd ordered her to stop fighting. Knowing him, he probably didn't even recognize her.

And why would he? He'd fucked hundreds, probably thousands of trainees in his time serving Zeus as one of the Sirens' trainers. She'd been nothing special to him. She'd just been the stupid nymph who'd foolishly believed every bullshit lie the gods—him included—had fed her.

Fury coiled tight in her veins, and her chest rose and fell with her quick breaths, but she didn't fight. Didn't look away either. He might have caught her, but he didn't have the medallion. And the second he loosened his grip, she'd be gone.

"That's better," he said, his voice losing that edge of rage she'd heard when he'd pinned her to the ground. "I've spent the last twenty-four hours tracking you, and I'm tired."

She didn't buy that for a second. Not that he hadn't spent that amount of time tracking her—he was a god known for hunting down Zeus's most menacing foes—but that he was tired. He was a fucking *god*. Gods didn't get tired. They were Energizer bunnies raring to go at the slightest provocation, as she'd learned multiple times when he'd fucked her until she'd passed out.

He lifted his weight off her and hauled her to her feet with one hand wrapped tight around her biceps. "Get up."

She stumbled. Gasped as he jerked her up and against the hard wall of his chest. Tried to push away. But he kept her close so she was forced to inhale his natural badass scent of snapdragon skull flowers, leather, and hints of cognac.

He glanced around the dark forest as if searching for something. Or someone.

With his hand still wrapped tightly around her upper arm, he turned to the left and hauled her with him. "This way."

His legs were way longer than hers, and she had to hustle her steps to keep up so she didn't trip and fall. And as she did, she couldn't help but wonder why he hadn't searched her for the medallion. And why she wasn't already dead.

She wasn't stupid enough to ask those questions, but she wasn't exactly upset over that fact, either. Since he hadn't killed her, it meant she still had a chance. Her mind spun with every step, her eyes scanning the darkness for something—anything—that would offer the opportunity to flee.

They reached the top of the rise, and he slowed his steps. Light was already rising on the eastern horizon, just enough for her to see the massive lake surrounding a small island housing some kind of crumbling structure far below. "There it is."

"There what is?" she mumbled, glancing around the dark forest and the steep mountains that rose out of the crystal blue water.

"Where we're going."

He pulled her with him down the hillside toward the lake.

"Wait." She grunted as her boot hit a rock, and she stumbled, hoping he wasn't taking her where she suddenly thought he was taking her. "Where *are* we going?"

"Somewhere we can be alone."

His hand tightened around her arm, and his gaze drifted down to her. But this time when he looked at her, his eyes were no longer enraged. They glowed with an erotic light. One she recognized well. One that sent a new kind of fear and anger swimming in her veins.

"I've got plans for you, Seraphine. Big, hard, very wicked plans."

Shit, she was right. And the fact he'd used her name meant she was in serious trouble because this male knew her every weakness.

Unless some kind of miracle happened in the next few minutes, there was no way she could hold out against what he had planned next.

CHAPTER TWO

Motherfucker, he was hard.

Not just from the feel of her hot little body plastered to his side as he hauled her down the mountainside, but from the way she'd very nearly kicked his ass out there in the trees.

Darkness closed around him as he dragged her into a cave that opened to a series of tunnels, which provided passage beneath the lake to the island beyond—a darkness that only made his dick throb harder. Darkness turned him on. Danger made him hard. This minx's reactions and the way she was still trying to fight him made him absolutely ache with the need to take her and tame her and show her who was really in control. Especially when he remembered how responsive she'd been during their training sessions and how easy it had been to drag her into all the dark, dirty filth that got him off.

"I want to know where you're taking me," she said as he pulled her around switchbacks in the tunnel, her breath heavy at his side, her skin so hot against his he was starting to sweat.

He didn't owe her an explanation. She was lucky he hadn't decided to kill her after the way she'd lashed out. Or taken her to Zeus already. The second he'd recognized her he'd decided not to do either, though. Not because she didn't deserve one or both but because he had his own plans for her. Plans that didn't include the King of the fucking Gods, at least not yet.

Eventually he knew Zeus would want her back for punishment, which could include anything from having her reassigned as a servant or handmaiden or even a sex slave. And though Erebus wasn't wild about any of those options—especially the last, unless she was *his* sex slave—he knew he had time. Time to have his own fun before his life-long obligations to Olympus drew him back.

Hell, he deserved some fun after the years he'd spent in servitude, didn't he? As far as he was concerned, he deserved more than a little fun simply because he had to deal with Zeus's incompetent Siren trainees on a daily fucking basis.

"I'm taking you to the half-breed ruins," he said, tugging her around another corner in the dark, deciding he didn't want her completely defiant. Oh, he enjoyed an adrenaline-amping fight now and then, but it was so much more enjoyable when he could coax a female's reluctance into cries of sensual pleasure. With Sera's nymphomaniac tendencies, he knew it wouldn't take much persuading.

"No one's there," she argued. "The half-breed ruins have been empty for twenty-some years."

Exactly. No one was there. No one could hear her screams from inside its walls. No one would even know a minor god had gone off the grid there with a cheeky little nymph who made him so hard he hurt.

She tugged against this grip. "Erebus, please. This is a bad id—"

It was the *please* that brought him around. Or maybe it was the way she said his name. He wasn't sure which, but something in her voice made him whip back and push her up against the cold rock wall.

She gasped as he moved in close at her front. Blood rushed straight into his cock at the reaction, making him even harder. He knew he shouldn't tease her, that he was only tormenting himself by doing so, but he didn't care. She was like a drug making him high, making him want. And it had been so long since he'd wanted anything purely for himself, he couldn't seem to force himself to stop.

"I like it when you beg, Seraphine." He leaned in close and traced the line of her ear with the tip of his nose. She trembled, which shot his blood even higher. "I love it when you beg me. Do you remember when I had you tied to that bed in the training center, when you begged me to fill you, to fuck you, to make you come?"

Her throat worked in the darkness as she swallowed, and her hands landed against his chest. Hands that were warm and soft and so much more than he remembered. He wanted them on his skin. Wanted to feel them wrap around his cock. Wanted her to draw him toward all her warm, wet heat all over again as she pushed him over on that bed, as she straddled his hips, as she rode him to a blistering climax that had been better than any he'd had in a thousand years.

She didn't answer, but the way her breath sped up, the way her hands curled into the fabric of his shirt and didn't push him away told him she was already acquiescing.

A smile curled his lips as he lowered his face to her neck and breathed hot over her scintillating skin. "I remember, *oraios*. I remember the way your fingers clawed at my back after I released your bindings and you screamed for me to give you more." He drew in a deep whiff of her rich, citrusy scent. A scent that was so intoxicating it had made him wild on Olympus anytime she was near and still haunted his dreams to this day. "I remember the way you flipped me to my back, the way you scored your nails down my chest until you drew blood, the way you made *me* scream."

She groaned, a sound that caused his erection to twitch against his fly and him to rock against the wicked heat of her lower body.

She bit down hard on her lip. Her fingers curled tighter in his shirt as she fought what he knew was her own growing desire to press back against him. But instead of giving in to her needs as he wanted, she whispered, "Why are you doing this to me?"

He drew back just enough so he could see her face. It was pitch black in the tunnel, so dark he knew she couldn't see his face, but one look was all it took to see she wasn't peering up at him. Her eyes were tightly shut, her face scrunched as if in pain. But not the same pain of lust and desire swirling like a vortex inside him—this was another kind of agony. An emotional torment he didn't understand and which dimmed his craving until it was a manageable ache instead of a burning demand.

He eased back a step, putting space between them, and released her arm. As cool air swept over his body, he watched her eyes flutter open. Watched her head turn and her gaze narrow as she tried to see him. Watched that silky blonde hair he'd enjoyed fisting flutter over her slim shoulders.

His heart hammered against his ribs, and his blood was still up from a hunger that hadn't been satisfied. But the heartache he'd seen in her features moments ago continued to resonate inside him, keeping him from touching her again.

Conflicting thoughts raced through his mind. She was a nymph, a Siren recruit, Zeus's *property*, so he shouldn't care what she was feeling besides lust. But he did. As his heart continued to beat in long, steady thumps, he realized he cared more than he liked. Even now, when all he wanted to do was strap her down and ravage her until they both screamed, he cared. Because his desires where she was concerned were rooted firmly in pleasure, not pain. He wasn't a sadist, regardless of his darkness. He wasn't Hades. He wasn't even Zeus. And even though he'd fucked hundreds of Siren recruits, all in the name of training, he remembered now what it was about Sera that had resonated so strongly with him then.

She had been different. She hadn't just wanted sex, as so many of the other recruits did the moment they saw him. She'd wanted to talk. She'd spent time getting to know him. As they'd lain in bed together after her sessions, she'd made him smile with tales of the recruits' antics in the barracks and on the field. At times she'd even made him laugh, as she had when she'd tried to bind him to that bed and hadn't been able to tie a knot that would hold.

In the long, lonely years of his life, for brief flickering moments, she'd been a light to his darkness. A breath of fresh air. An oasis in the middle of a desert whose grains of sand were nothing but years of servitude to the gods. And he wanted *that* nymph back. He wanted to see her smile. He wanted to hear her laugh. He wanted her wild and willing and begging and *his*. The way she'd been his before she'd been wrenched from his grasp and he'd been reassigned to another recruit.

The force of that want was strong. So strong he turned away from her, swiped a hand down his face to cool himself down, then reached for her arm again—but only when he knew he wouldn't give in and try to force her to want him back.

"Come on," he said, pulling her away from the wall, this time tugging gently. "We're almost there."

Confusion pulled her brows together. He saw it from the corner of his eye.

And he knew she was wondering why he'd stopped his advances and what he had planned next.

He frowned because...he was suddenly wondering that too. His so-called plans had just changed. Oh, he still wanted her, still intended to have her, but the ways in which he would get there were now swirling in his mind. Along with just what he needed to do to remind her just how much she'd wanted him long ago.

How much the woman he'd awakened inside her years ago still wanted him now.

* * * *

Sera was unnerved. Unnerved and confused and more aroused than she wanted to admit.

That moment in the caves, when Erebus had pressed all his succulent heat against her and whispered those dark and naughty things in her ear, echoed in her mind, replaying like a silent video set on repeat. He was a highly sexual beast. She'd seen that on Olympus. She'd felt it moments ago in the caves. And she knew exactly why he'd dragged her into these ruins and what he intended to do to her.

She knew and she hated him for it.

She knew, and she trembled with anticipation over when it would happen.

The half-breed colony had once occupied an abandoned castle on an island in the middle of a glacial lake. As Erebus drew her into the structure and up several flights of stairs, she'd realized that the tunnel he'd pulled her into had led to the island. Walls were blackened and burned. The ceiling was open and missing in places from some kind of fire, but the rock of the castle remained, as did several floors that had been built out of stone. Now, after twenty-odd years left abandoned, plants and vines had crept into the space, making the ruins their home.

Erebus ignored the main floor with the broken wide windows that looked out over the early morning light rising above the lake and dragged her to an upper room. To what she recognized had once been a bedroom suite but was now scattered with broken furniture, dirt, and dried leaves.

She swallowed hard when she spotted the enormous bed, the old, worn mattress covered in a layer of dirt and slashed in the middle, stuffing falling out to mix with the debris on the floor. Though she tried not to be turned on by the presence of that bed, heat built in her veins and her treacherous body tingled to life.

Her whole body tensed as he tugged her toward the bed, but instead of tossing her onto that dingy mattress and having his way with her as she expected, he backed her up against one of the four posts. "Put your arms down at your sides."

Her heart beat faster. Some instinct deep inside warned her not to obey, but she did as he said, not wanting to do anything to set him off. He was twice her size, the epitome of darkness as she'd seen when he'd attacked her in the forest, and she was a nymph who hadn't completed her Siren training and who was currently without weapons. But that wasn't the only reason she'd acquiesced, she knew. The other reason was because her lascivious body liked his touch. Her traitorous mind craved his commands. And that submissive part of her lineage—the part straight from her nymph heritage—yearned to please him as she had eighteen months ago on Olympus when he'd been her seduction trainer and she'd done every dirty, erotic thing he'd demanded.

Anger welled inside her as she watched him pull a length of thin rope—rope that didn't look like it was strong enough to hold a cat, let alone a person—from somewhere in his pocket. Anger and disgust with her own body. He hadn't once looked at her since they'd left the darkness of the tunnels. Wasn't looking at her now as he wrapped the rope around her torso and the bedpost several times. Didn't even glance at her face when he tied it off at her back and finally stepped away.

He'd ignited a slow-burning fire inside her with his words in the tunnel, and now he was letting that fire smolder. Tormenting her in a new and torturous way.

He moved to the far side of the bed, and she heard the sounds of fabric rustling, then the bedpost shook at her back. Excitement surged inside her. An excitement she didn't like. Knowing he was distracted, she shifted her shoulders and tried to move, but the rope held her tight, and she realized belatedly that the rope had to be charmed by some kind of otherworldly force.

Of course it was. He was a freakin' god, after all. Had she honestly thought escaping would be easy?

He stepped around her with a pile of filthy sheets and moved toward the door without another word.

Confusion drew her brows together. "Hey," she called as he reached the threshold. "Where are you going?"

He didn't answer. Just turned the corner and disappeared.

Panic pushed in. She didn't like being confined. Strapped down and ravished was one thing. Bound and deserted was something altogether different. "You can't leave me like this!"

The only response that met her ears was the sound of his boot steps fading down the stone corridor.

Alone, she heaved out a sigh. He'd be back. He hadn't dragged her all the way to these ruins to abandon her. While she knew she should be thankful he wasn't tormenting her with his hands and lips and sinful body as he'd done in the caves, part of her couldn't help be disappointed. Yes, she hated him for so easily ditching her on Olympus all those months ago, but she couldn't deny that sex with him had been earth shattering. Just the memory of how he could seduce without even touching made her whole body tremble. And the things he could do with that mouth...

Her skin grew hot. She cleared her throat to fight her body's natural response to him. Instead of thinking about hot, sweaty, satisfying sex, she needed to stay focused on why she was here. Why she'd been out in that forest in the first place. Not for herself, but to set right a wrong that been done a hundred years ago and to prevent what had happened to her world from happening to someone else's.

She glanced over the suite, searching for any kind of escape route. This room had avoided the fire that had charred other parts of the castle. A dark fireplace fronted a ratty couch, what used to be a side chair, and an old coffee table. The door on the far wall looked as if it might open to a bathroom, but she couldn't see inside to be sure. Peering over her shoulder, she caught the movement of gauzy white curtains, frayed and hanging in front of what looked to still be solid windows. Beyond, the rising light of morning told her the view was from several stories up, and unless she planned to jump to her death, her only way out was the main door Erebus had left through.

She frowned and looked back to the fireplace. At least she wasn't going to freeze to death when the chill of night swept back over the castle. But even that was a small comfort as minutes turned to an hour and still there was no sign of her captor.

Where had he gone? What was he doing? He'd said he had something big, hard, and very wicked planned for her. She'd felt that big, hard, wicked bulge in the caves and knew he'd been close to giving it to her there. But now, when she was bound, and—thanks to her licentious body—aching for the same damn thing, he was nowhere to be found.

She struggled against her bonds, but soon decided all she was doing was exhausting herself. As daylight warmed the room, the last few hours—the last few days caught up with her, and her muscles grew limp.

It had all started when she'd heard rumors in her training class of the Sirens' recent discovery of a medallion with special properties. Something about the location of the discovery had seemed oddly familiar, and she'd gone to the Hall of Sirens during her free time to research. Little had she known that research would trigger her memories—memories that had been blocked by the Sirens when she'd been handpicked by Zeus to train with his elite female warriors. And that those memories would reveal a deception so great, she was sure only the gods could conceive of something so heinous.

In retrospect, she probably shouldn't have confronted Athena, the leader of the Sirens. That had been a bad idea and had led to Sera being tossed in the Pit—a black hole in the ground on Olympus where Sirens were often punished—for a week. At least she hadn't told Athena she'd regained her memories. Doing so would have resulted in her immediate death. But it had made her realize that everything she'd been told from the moment she'd arrived on Olympus was a lie. When she'd emerged from that black hole of despair, she'd pretended to step back in line, but behind the scenes she'd plotted her revenge.

Of course, that revenge had landed her here—in this cold castle in the middle of nowhere, wondering where the hell Erebus had gone and when the heck he was coming back.

She heaved out another sigh and glanced up and around the room. No wonder she was tired. She'd barely slept in the last two weeks, and her adrenaline was rapidly crashing. As much as she didn't want to encourage Erebus and his nefarious plans, she wished he'd tied her to the mattress before he'd left so she could sleep. Wished he'd had the sense to tie her lower to the post so at least she was sitting and could rest her weary legs.

Her eyes grew heavy, and her head drooped. Thoughts of Erebus and the sensual way he'd held her against the cave wall in the dark swirled in her mind. Whatever he had planned, she knew she would endure it. Just as she knew she'd likely enjoy it. The key would be making sure she found a way to escape as soon as his body was sated and he dropped his guard. Because staying, and ultimately letting him haul her back to Olympus, was not an option.

She hadn't sacrificed her future to fail now. Too much depended on her success. Erebus might be the master of seduction, but she wasn't going to let her treacherous heart fall for him again. She was going to escape.

Or, the Fates help her, she'd die trying.

CHAPTER THREE

Erebus took his time finding somewhat clean sheets and blankets. While the castle hadn't been used in years and a good portion of it was in ruins, he'd been surprised at how much was still useable.

The sheets, blankets, and even a few pillows he'd discovered in the back of a cupboard on an upper floor. In the bowels of the castle, he'd found a gas-powered generator and enough fuel to supply the north wing, where he'd left Sera, with lights and running water. Firewood was easy to locate—there was plenty of wood thanks to destroyed furnishings—and a quick trip down to the lake provided him with berries and fish he'd be able to cook for dinner.

Thoughts of Sera flittered through his mind as he finally headed back up to her room several hours later. Wicked, hot, erotic thoughts he had to tamp down because he didn't want her to see them on his face as soon as he walked in. He'd save overwhelming her like that for later. Sure, Zeus might be pissed it was taking him so long to track the little nymph down, but he didn't care. He'd take her back to Olympus soon enough. Tonight was for him—and her too. After all, there was no telling what Zeus's punishment would entail. It could be her last chance for fun for a good long time.

Unless he plans to execute her. Then it's her last chance for fun ever...

His brow wrinkled as he moved up the stairs. The last time Zeus had executed a recruit it had been for something much more sinister than simply failing the Sirens' tests. Over the last twenty to thirty years that Erebus could remember, recruits who failed a checkpoint were reassigned to various jobs. Of course, none of those recruits had run, he realized.

Would Zeus consider running grounds for execution?

His head said no—after all, she was a quick learner, bright, and highly erotic. Even though he didn't like the idea, Erebus could easily see her being reassigned as a pleasure slave to any one of the gods. But his gut... His gut said yes, Zeus would see her going AWOL as prime reason to execute her, if for no other reason than to make an example of her to other recruits who might be considering the same thing.

He needed to find out why she'd run. Peppering her with questions would likely dampen the seductive mood he wanted to set, but perhaps if he knew why she'd taken off he could come up with a way to help her. Or, at the very least, maybe it would give him an idea how he could put in a good word for her with the King of the Gods.

Afternoon light shone into the room as he stepped under the doorjamb, but the first thing he spotted was Sera hanging limply from her bonds, her head forward, her golden hair covering every inch of her face. Panic pushed him across the room in two steps. He set his bundle down and grasped both sides of her face, lifting so he could see her eyes. "Sera?"

She grunted. Her eyelids fluttered. And in a moment of clarity he realized she wasn't dead, just asleep.

The pressure in his chest eased. Yes, he'd been away from her most of the day, but it was unusual for a Siren—even a recruit—to drop her defenses enough to sleep when she was in a hostile situation, which he knew she considered this to be. Carefully, so he didn't wake her, he lowered her head once more and watched as that mass of blonde covered her features all over again.

Had the instructors on Olympus worked her so hard she wasn't sleeping? He managed most of the Siren instructors and knew their schedules. Granted, he'd been immersed with a new class the last few months and up to his ears with newbies who didn't have a clue, but Sera's class—almost two years into their training—should have been well adjusted to the physical demands of the Sirens by now.

Something didn't add up. With questions swirling in his mind, he went to work remaking the bed. He'd flipped the mattress before he'd left, and the underside wasn't nearly as disgusting as the top had been. When he was done, he threw the covers back, carefully untied Sera from the bedpost, and hefted her into his arms.

She weighed practically nothing, and that erotic scent of citrus and vanilla floated around him once more, as enticing as anything had ever been. Her head lolled against his shoulder as he moved and laid her on the fresh sheets. This time her eyes didn't even flitter. The second her body hit the mattress, her head lolled against the pillow and a soft snore echoed from her lips.

It took every ounce of strength he had to tug off her boots and nothing else. To pull the covers up around her shoulders and *not* climb into that big bed with her. But he was determined to make this good for both of them, and there were things he needed to do first for that to happen. For a moment he considered tying her wrists to the headboard, but then dismissed the idea. She was dead to the world right now, and from here on out he didn't plan to leave her alone. Which meant there was no reason to bind her—unless of course she asked to be bound.

That thought shot a burst of wicked heat all through his body, which lingered as he used the broken wood in the room to build a fire, then found a broom in a nearby closet and went about sweeping the floor of dust and debris. In an upstairs kitchen area, he'd found candles, a frying pan, plastic plates, utensils, wine glasses, and even an old bottle of wine. He had no idea if the wine was still any good, but he figured anything to help set the mood—and relax her enough to get her talking—was a plus.

The sheets rustled on the bed behind him just as he was finishing cooking the fish. One glance over his shoulder at her confused expression told him she was shocked at what he'd done.

He smirked. "Good morning, sleepy head." He pulled the frying pan from the heat and slid the two trout he'd caught onto the plates. "Or should I say good evening." Pushing to his feet, he grabbed two forks and the plates and crossed toward the bed, where she eyed him like he'd grown a horn right in the middle of his forehead. "Here."

"What is that?"

"Dinner."

"Why?"

"Because it's rude to eat in front of someone." He pushed the plate closer to her hand. "Take it."

She glanced from the plate up to him, and he didn't miss the skepticism in her blue eyes.

He frowned. "It's not poisoned. If I wanted to kill you I'd have done so already."

The expression on her flawless face said she wasn't so sure of that, but she hesitantly took the plate and lowered it to her lap, carefully watching him as he walked back to the club chair he'd hauled in from another room and sat.

Her gaze skipped around the room while he started eating, and from the corner of his eye he caught the surprise in her features at what he'd done while she'd been asleep. She glanced at the bedpost where she'd been tied, then chanced a look over her shoulder at the wood headboard. "Why am I no longer restrained?"

Heat rolled through him all over again. He cut another piece of fish and stabbed it with his fork. "Do you want to be restrained? If so, I can easily play along."

Her gaze narrowed to a glare. Several moments passed where all she did was glower at him while he ate. Then slowly, she set her untouched plate on the far side of the bed, then threw back the covers.

He leaned back in his seat, eyeing her warily as she pushed to her feet. "Where do you think you're going?"

"I need to use the restroom."

His stomach tightened at the bite in her words.

She rounded the bed and scowled deeper when she spotted him standing with the plate in his hand. "Unless you want my bladder to explode, of course. In which case I could just sit here and we could wait for it to happen. Then you could clean up the mess. Which will it be?"

Her tongue had definitely sharpened in the time she'd been away from him and with the Sirens, a fact he didn't like. Part of what he'd been most drawn to eighteen months ago was how sweet she'd been.

He eyed her boots where he'd left them by the side of the bed. Even if she did bolt, she wouldn't get far in bare feet. He stepped back and held his arm out toward the bathroom door. "Be my guest."

She huffed and stepped past him.

"But, Sera…"

She paused when she reached the darkened bathroom doorway but didn't turn to face him. A fact that for some reason only heightened his desire for her.

"When you come back out," he said calmly, "we're going to talk about the real reason you were running. And then we're going to finish what we started in the tunnels."

* * * *

"We're going to talk about the real reason you were running..."

Erebus's words pounded in Sera's brain as she closed the bathroom door and leaned back against the solid wood. But it was the second part of his command that made her heart thump even harder. *"...then we're going to finish what we started."*

There was no way she was finishing anything with him. She'd seen what he'd done to the room out there and knew he was maneuvering her just where he wanted her. Her entire body was already vibrating with the need to feel his touch. She knew if she let him that close she'd melt under the weight of his erotic commands. But more than that, just the fact he'd said anything about the "real reason" she was running was a giant red flag telling her she needed to get as far from the minor god as possible. Because if she melted the way he wanted her to, she didn't trust herself not to accidentally let the truth slip out. And the second he discovered she'd stolen the medallion from Zeus, any sexy mood he'd had toward her would turn to malice.

Her fingers shook as she hit the lock on the bathroom door, then darted toward the window. It hadn't been opened in over twenty years and she had to grit her teeth and pry up on the wood until her fingertips turned white. It finally gave, and she breathed easier as she pushed it up an inch, but as the crack of old wood separating echoed through the bathroom, her anxiety shot through the roof, and she froze.

She listened, waiting to see if he'd heard it. When nothing but the sound of her own heart pounding met her ears, she let go of the window, rushed to the sink, flipped on the water to drown out any more noise, then moved back to her one shot at freedom.

Her fingertips burned, and the muscles in her arms ached as she forced the window higher. When it was open far enough for her to crawl through, she pulled herself out and onto the small rock ledge that ran the length of this wing of the ruins.

Wind whipped her hair around her face. Dusk was just settling in, shrouding everything in an eerie gray light, but she could still make out the waves of the lake crashing against rocks three stories below. And glancing up, she spotted another four stories above her and spires that reached for the darkening sky.

It had once been an amazing castle. Still could be with a little work. Though she wasn't sure why it had been completely abandoned after the inhabitants had obviously beaten back their invaders, she told herself that wasn't her concern. Her only concern now was getting away from Erebus, retrieving the medallion she'd hidden in the woods, and taking it somewhere Zeus and the Olympians could never find it.

Her stomach tightened as she leaned back against the wall and used her hands to help guide her to her right. The ledge was only six inches wide, and more than once her bare feet stumbled over chipped and broken sections. When she reached another closed window, she slid down the wall until she was crouched on the ledge, reached over and tried to pull the window up. Like the one in her bathroom, though, it was sealed tight. There was no way she could pry it open from out here, not without falling to her death in the process.

She kept going. Her pulse thumped hard and loud in her ears as she moved faster, hoping and praying that Erebus wouldn't suddenly realize she'd been gone too long and appear on the ledge beside her.

Three windows down from the one she'd exited, she finally came to one that was broken, the glass jagged and half-covering the opening. Victory pulsed in her veins. Without shoes or long sleeves, she had nothing to shield herself from the glass, but she figured a few cuts were a small price to pay for freedom.

She positioned herself in front of the broken window, turned sideways, and gripped the casing on both sides to steady herself. Then she held her breath and shoved the knee of her pants through the rest of the glass.

A burn spread across her knee and thigh. She knew she'd torn her pants, was fairly certain she'd cut her leg, but she didn't stop to look. Gritting her teeth against the pain, she knocked the rest of the glass away, then carefully lowered herself into what looked to be a sitting room for another suite.

The room grew darker with every passing second, but somehow she managed to avoid stepping on shards of glass with her bare feet. Pulse racing, she rushed to the door, pulled it open a crack, and peered out into the dim hallway.

Nothing moved. No sound met her ears. A golden glow to her right indicated the door to the room Erebus had taken her to was still open, the fire and candles continuing to burn bright.

She couldn't go that way. Couldn't risk his seeing her. She glanced to her left. This castle was huge. There had to be a back set of stairs that led to the main level.

Deciding that was her best bet, she crept out into the hallway and moved as quietly as she could, stepping over debris littering the space. Something moved in the shadows ahead. Her heart rate spiked again, and she stilled. But when no sound met her ears and nothing else moved, she realized it had to have been some kind of small animal, not Erebus, as she'd feared.

She didn't know how long he'd wait before checking the bathroom to see what was taking her so long. Reaching a set of back stairs, she hustled down as quickly as she could. At the main level, she looked around, trying to remember which way they'd come. The castle was surrounded by a lake. Her only hope for escape was to backtrack through the tunnels.

She pushed her legs into a jog, searching for the stairs that led down. Just remembering those tunnels made her think of the way Erebus had backed her up against the rock wall in the dark, how he'd made her whole body tremble with just a few simple words. He'd always been able to do that to her, and she hated him for that. Hated him even more because her stupid heart was still hung up on the minor god who clearly didn't feel anything for her besides lust. She'd been nothing to him but another recruit he could use to get his rocks off. He was still trying to use her for that, evidenced by the seduction scene he'd set up in that room upstairs. She was a complete fool for ever thinking he'd cared for her. An even bigger fool for falling for him when she'd known better.

Disgusted with herself all over again, she found the stairs and hustled to the lowest level. Once there, she stepped over debris in what looked as if it had once been an anteroom, and moved out into the darkened tunnel.

Her pulse jackknifed. The tunnel was pitch black. When Erebus had first led her into the caves, the cool air moving across her skin from different angles had made her think there were other tunnels jutting off from the main route. Without a light she could be lost down here for weeks. She needed to go back into the ruins. Needed to find a candle of some kind so she could see where she was going. She turned back toward the ruins. The stairs she'd just come down creaked, causing her to freeze.

"Sera!"

Erebus's voice sent her heart straight into her throat. This time there was no hint of seduction in his voice. Only rage.

Knowing she didn't have time to find a light, she whipped back toward the darkness of the tunnel, swallowed her fear, and pushed her legs forward. Rocks and debris dug into the soles of her feet, but she ignored the pain. All she could do was hold her hands out in front of her so she wouldn't slam face-first into a wall. All that mattered now was ignoring everything except the instinct echoing in her head to *run*.

* * * *

When Erebus reached the main cavern, he used his heightened sight to search the darkness for Sera. Several tunnels veered off from the main route. She could be in any of them, and though he could see well in the dark, he couldn't see around twists and turns and through solid rock.

He stilled and focused on his enhanced hearing. The sound of heavy breaths and the rustle of cloth echoed from the tunnel to his right.

He darted in that direction, not even questioning if it was her. It *was* her. It had to be her. No one else was down here in these blasted caves.

The tunnel curved to the right, then left. He pushed his legs harder, racing around the corners without slowing. This wasn't the same tunnel they'd used to enter the ruins, and he had no idea how she was moving so fast. It was pitch black and he doubted she had any kind of light. She was being spurred on by pure panic. Panic, he sensed, that had little to do with him and what he wanted to do to her upstairs in that bedroom and everything to do with what Zeus wanted from her.

Zeus's intentions swirled in his head as he zigzagged through the cave, ducking under low-hanging rocks. The King of the Gods was nothing if not secretive. If he wanted to terminate Sera for running, he could have ordered Erebus to simply find her and kill her. But he hadn't. And her panicked reaction now told Erebus there was more going on here than met the eye. More than what he'd been told on Olympus. Way more.

He passed a small opening that looked like it led to a new tunnel. Something moved in the darkness, and he slowed his steps, wondering if she'd shifted direction and was trying to hide. Bracing one hand on the rocks above, he leaned down to peer through the archway, but saw only more rock. He listened for the sound of her rapid breaths, the beat of her heart, the rustle of fabric that told him she was in there. The cave was silent. Silent but for a faint clicking noise he was sure did not come from her.

To his right, a flutter of blonde hair caught his attention and then was gone. Ignoring the animal he'd stumbled across, he tore after her. The sound of her labored breaths met his ears along with the thump of her footfalls on the uneven rocks and the roar of blood rushing through her veins.

His adrenaline surged. He ran faster. And heard the unmistakable sounds of rushing water.

Motherfucker...

Running water meant some kind of underground river. Since he couldn't see any puddles in this cavern, that meant the underground river was below them, accessible through a hole or fracture in the floor ahead. And he'd bet his position as a trainer with the Sirens that she didn't know what she was about to run straight into.

Blonde hair flashed ahead of him again. The roar of the water grew louder. He was gaining on her, but not fast enough to stop her. "Sera!"

Whipped around to look back at him. Gasped. Stumbled when she realized he was closer than she'd thought. A panicked look crossed her features as she twisted away and burst forward.

The roar of the river grew louder. He reached out to grab her. His fingertips brushed the ends of her silky blonde hair.

Then she slipped through his fingers and her scream rose up around him.

CHAPTER FOUR

Erebus skidded to a stop at the edge of the sinkhole and stared down at the rushing river thirty yards below. Sera's scream was drowned out by a splash of water that echoed in his ears.

His heart lurched into his throat as he used his enhanced sight to scan the river for any sign of her. *Come on, come on, come on...*

The surface of the water broke twenty yards from where she'd gone in, and a gasp echoed up to him.

He didn't pause to consider what could be in the river below. Just stepped off the cliff and fell feet first into the frigid liquid. Water bubbled above his head. Something green and totally out of place flashed in the corner of his vision, but he didn't have time to see what it was. Instinct urged him up toward the surface.

His head popped out and he sucked in air, treading water as he turned and searched for her. The current was strong, quickly sweeping him downstream. He whipped right and left, scanning the darkness. The sound of labored breaths met his ears. He twisted back around and squinted. Then spotted her clinging to a boulder, fifteen feet away on the edge of the river.

Relief overwhelmed him, forcing air into his one-size-too-small lungs. He swam toward her, but the swift current slammed his body against the boulder she clung to before he could stop it from happening.

He grunted. Pain shot up his spine. Ignoring it, he worked his way around the rock to her side, then wrapped an arm around her shivering body and drew her against him. "*Agápi?* Talk to me."

Her eyes were closed. She sagged against the rock. Water dripped from her hair over her face. She opened her mouth to answer but no sound came out. And when her arm slipped from the boulder and slumped into the water, he realized she was losing consciousness. He grasped her before the current could whisk her away.

"Shit. Stay with me." He tugged her with him as he climbed out of the water and hauled her up onto the rocky ledge.

Blood dripped down her temple. Her head lolled to the side. Before he even let go of her, she started to shake, not just a shivering shudder of muscles, but full on tremors that told him she was going into shock.

Nymphs weren't immortal, not like the gods—not like him. Her race had been blessed with a long life-span—over five hundred years in most cases—but her body was still fragile and she could definitely die from injuries and hypothermia. Moving quickly, he tugged off his shirt and pants, then went to work stripping her of her clothing. Once she was dressed in nothing but her bra and panties, he pulled her onto his lap so her slim body was pressed up against his chest and he could close his arms and legs around her. As he leaned back against the rock wall for support, he grasped his wet T-shirt and held it against the wound on her head to slow the blood flow.

"You're okay, Sera. I've got you. I'm going to get you out of here."

Long minutes passed where she continued to tremble, and it felt as if his heart had taken up permanent residency in his throat. But slowly, as the heat of his body seeped into hers, her shakes slowly subsided, and she relaxed against him. He took that as a good sign. Lifting the shirt from her wound, he breathed easier when he saw the blood flow had lessened. She was going to have a nice-sized goose egg, but swelling outward from the impact was better than swelling inside the brain, and he knew that was an even better sign.

His pulse inched down. Glancing at her familiar face resting against his shoulder, he brushed a lock of wet hair back from her cheek, and as he did something warm and sweet slid through his chest. An emotion he hadn't felt before. A yearning that wasn't just sexual.

The feeling was so strong, so foreign, it threw him off kilter. He didn't *have* emotions. He was a god who'd learned long ago that emotions were dangerous. And yet... Somehow he recognized the feelings taking up space inside him now had been spawned by fear. Not fear that she was going to drop to her death and that he was going to miss out on the rough, hot sex he'd been envisioning since the moment he'd recognized her in the woods, but fear that something bad would happen to her. That he'd never see her again. That he would lose her.

Sweat broke out along his forehead, and an odd tingle started in his chest. He told himself it was her heat making him feel weird. Not denial. Not anything else. But even that didn't sound right, and he had no idea what the hell he was supposed to do next.

"Sera." The word was a whisper, a plea, a demand. "Sera, wake up and look at me." He needed to see her eyes. Needed her to explain what was happening to him. Needed to know if she felt it too.

She didn't move. He knew she was breathing. Knew she wasn't in any real danger. But the danger to him was suddenly all he could focus on. "*Agápi.* Open your eyes. Look at me, baby."

She sighed and snuggled closer. But the reaction didn't fire him up and make him ache to take her as he expected. It brought a calm over him that was more unsettling than the fear he'd felt before.

He didn't know what was happening. This female was doing something to him he didn't understand. He needed to get her back upstairs and into a bed. Needed to give her time to rest before he decided whether he was going to go ahead with his seduction plan or haul her back to Zeus without touching her. And he needed to think. Because the only thing he knew for sure at the moment was that he wasn't ready to let her go. And he had no idea what that meant or how it was going to impact his service to Zeus.

You can't take her back to Zeus...

The thought circled in his mind, unwilling to disappear. He glanced back down at her again, wondering just what the hell was really going on and why Zeus wanted her so bad.

"It's female," a raspy voice said in the darkness.

Erebus's head came up, and his adrenaline surged all over again.

"We haven't had us a female in forever," another low voice answered.

He squinted through the darkness, searching for the source of the voices, and spotted two sets of beady eyes peering out from behind a large boulder. Two sets of gnarled fingers wrapped around the stone. Two sets of claws, digging into the rock.

Fuck me.

Kobaloi. The gnome-dwarves who mined and protected Hades's invisibility ore. Erebus's gaze shot back to the river, and he easily picked out the spots of green glowing from the bottom of the riverbed that he'd noticed when the water had rushed over his head, but which he'd ignored because he'd been so intent on getting to Sera.

His jaw clenched down hard at his stupidity. The green glow was the ore, the therillium that powered Hades's invisibility cap. No wonder this colony was now fucking empty. Because Hades had discovered it sat right over his precious ore. The kobaloi clearly had free run of the ruins. He'd sensed another creature in the tunnels with him when he'd been chasing Sera. While they weren't particularly dangerous in small clusters, they often congregated in hordes. And while he knew he could fight off two or three or even ten, a thousand gnome-dwarves with razor-sharp teeth and knife-like claws could spell imminent doom for Sera.

He pushed to his feet, hefted her in his arms, and held her close to the protection of his body. Oblivious to the sudden threat in front of them, she sighed again, hooked an arm around his neck, but otherwise didn't wake.

"It's not just a female," Erebus declared in a deep voice, hoping it would scare the shit out of the scavengers and make them scurry. "And you do not want to mess with me."

A hiss echoed in the darkness, followed by a rapid clicking sound. "Erebus," a voice growled. "His scent was masked by the female."

Yeah, you better cower, dumbass.

"Hades wants him back," the other murmured. "This will bring us great reward."

The cavern filled with hundreds of rapid clicks, telling Erebus there weren't just two or three kobaloi hiding behind those rocks, there was an entire horde.

His adrenaline went sky-high. Stepping back toward the river, Erebus glanced up at the ceiling toward the hole Sera had fallen through. Options, strategies, possibilities ignited in his mind.

"We'll take him to our lord," a voice growled, closer this time but still hidden behind the stones. "And then the female will be ours."

Fuck that. Erebus tightened his arms around Sera. She was his. And this time no one was taking her from him.

* * * *

Sera was in a dream. A hot, sweltering fantasy that was extremely arousing.

She opened her eyes, blinked several times against the warm glow, and tried to focus. A fire burned across the room, which made zero sense since the last thing she remembered was darkness, running, and the bitter bite of frigid water.

She glanced down at her hands and spotted the comforter wrapped around her body. Rolling to her side, she realized she was in a bed. A comfy, soft, soothing bed that seemed to cocoon her in safety. And at her back? Something solid, warm, and muscular that felt incredibly tempting.

She rolled to her side, then stilled when she spotted Erebus lying on his side facing her, sharing space on her pillow. His dark eyes were closed, his shirtless torso relaxed, and his arm was entirely too possessive wrapped around her waist, holding her against him.

The beat of her heart turned to rapid fire in her ears, pounding blood through her veins. She'd been running. He'd been chasing her. Not because he'd wanted her as he'd led her to believe when he'd pressed all his succulent heat against her in the caves on their trek to these ruins, but because Zeus wanted her back so he could get his slimy hands on the medallion.

Panic condensed between her ribs. She needed to get up. She needed to run. He was asleep. Now was her chance to escape.

She rolled to her opposite side as quietly as she could. Lifted her head from the pillow. Reached out one hand and gripped the sheet a foot away to pull herself across the mattress.

His arm immediately tightened around her waist, and he tugged her backside into firm contact with his hips. "Should be sleeping, *agápi*."

She froze. *Agápi*? My love? She *had* to be hallucinating. No way he would ever call her that.

Her pulse roared in her ears, but she knew she was stuck at least until he drifted back to sleep. Trying not to do anything to wake him further, she breathed deep and worked puzzle pieces around in her mind to figure out what the heck he was doing.

Where was she? Why was he in bed beside her? And why the heck couldn't she remember what had happened?

Pain lit off behind her skull, and she lifted a hand to rub at the spot, only to realize a bandage covered part of her forehead near her hairline on the right side.

The arm across her waist lifted, and he gently tugged her hand back to the mattress. "Let that heal. It'll be better in the morning."

A flash of something green flickered in her memory. She remembered hitting a rock. Remembered...voices.

"What did you do to me?" Her voice didn't sound like her own. And her accusation clearly wasn't threatening because he only wrapped his arm tighter around her waist, pulling her even tighter against him.

"Rescued you," he said in a sleepy and sexy-as-hell voice.

Holy gods. Stop thinking he's sexy. That will only make things worse.

"From what?" she asked, ignoring how warm and perfect he felt pressed up against her back.

"Kobaloi. Shouldn't run off without me, *agápi*. All kinds of bad shit out there trying to take you from me."

Gnome-dwarves? Her eyes widened.

Okay, she was seriously dreaming because gnome-dwarves weren't even real. And he'd called her *agápi* again, which made zero sense, especially when he claimed things were trying to take her from him. *He'd* been the one to toss *her* aside on Olympus, not the other way around. If he'd wanted to hold on to her, he'd had plenty of opportunity long before this.

He sighed and pressed his face into her hair. His warm breath tickled the hairs on her neck and sent a shiver straight down her spine. A shiver that felt way too damn good. "Sleep, Seraphine. You wore me out. Need to rest before you get all feisty with me again."

Feisty? He thought she was feisty? Another shiver rushed down her spine, only this one wasn't because of his sexy breath but because his words had sounded like a compliment.

Logic told her to get up. To climb out of this bed. To run while his defenses were down and she had a chance. But her head was already drifting, her limbs heavy, her body too warm and comfortable to move. And his heat at her back was exactly what she'd been missing for so damn long, part of her just didn't want to go.

Not even if leaving meant saving the world.

* * * *

The second time Sera woke, she knew she wasn't in a dream. Her head was clear, her limbs still heavy and sore, but there was a realness to the room as she glanced around, a recognition that told her she was back in the suite at the half-breed ruins where Erebus had taken her.

Slowly, she pushed to sitting and slid the covers back. She was dressed in a black tank and cotton pajama bottoms he must have found in another room. They were old and musty, but surprisingly soft. The fire smoldered, but the curtains on the wide windows were pushed back to let late afternoon sunlight spill across the floor.

The last time she'd awoken—if she could call that being awake—she was sure it had been night. She didn't know if a day or more had passed since then, but when she lifted a hand to her forehead, the bandage she faintly remembered Erebus telling her not to touch was gone and a thin, one-inch long scab ran along her hairline. She pressed all around the scab, trying to recall what had happened. The skin was tender but not swollen, but she couldn't remember anything other than running, darkness, and falling.

Falling...

Pressure condensed beneath her ribs. Before she could figure out why though, footsteps sounded to her right. She looked in that direction just as Erebus appeared in the doorway carrying something flat in his big hands.

"You're awake. Good. I won't have to wake you." He rounded the bed, balancing whatever he was holding in one hand, and reached for the pillow at her back. "Lean forward."

Sera's stomach tightened. She had no idea what he was doing, but she couldn't find the words to ask because something kept spinning in her head. A word. Spoken in his voice. Repeated several times. Something that started with a...

The word was on the tip of her mind but wouldn't formulate into something solid she could reach. Had he said it when he'd been chasing her? Had she imagined it in her dream?

"There, you're good. Lean back."

One glance over her shoulder told her he'd fluffed her pillow against the wooden headboard and added another. Confused, she glanced up at him, then stared down as he set a tray of food on her lap.

It was some kind of soup, hot and steamy. Basil and rosemary drifted to her nose, and her stomach rumbled as if on cue.

Erebus chuckled and stepped away from the bed, stopping to use the poker to move the embers in the fireplace. "Sorry there's no bread. Baking is not my specialty."

Sera had absolutely no clue what was going on or what his end game was here, but she was suddenly too hungry to care. When was the last time she'd eaten? Before she'd stolen the medallion. Before running from Olympus. Long before she'd been tackled by Erebus in that meadow.

She reached for the spoon, ladled a bite of the warm broth, and realized there were carrots, celery, noodles, and some kind of white meat in the soup. Bringing it to her lips, she sipped slowly, in case it was too hot. The broth was warm, not scalding, and it stimulated her salivary glands. She took a big bite and moaned before she could stop herself.

Erebus glanced over his shoulder and grinned. And even though she was looking down at the soup, she caught the mesmerizing smile and the way it brightened his entire face, transforming him from devil-may-care to absolutely irresistible.

"Guess it's safe to say you like that." He turned back to the fire and added another log to the flames.

Sera's brow wrinkled. She wasn't sure what she liked. She wasn't sure of anything at the moment except that she was hungrier than she'd ever been.

She finished off the soup, and when there was nothing left but a spoonful of broth she couldn't quite scoop up, she set her spoon down, lifted the bowl in her hands, and poured what was left into her mouth.

It wasn't until she set the bowl down and used the napkin that she realized Erebus was standing at the end of her bed. His hands were tucked into the pockets of his jeans, his head tipped to the side, and he was watching her with a very amused expression. Not one smoldering with heat like she remembered from before, but one that was rooted in something else. Some kind of tenderness she didn't understand.

Erebus? Tender? Those were two words that definitely did *not* go together.

Nerves bounced around in her stomach as she lowered her napkin to the tray. He was her captor, nothing more. She needed to stop looking at him like some kind of hero—*because he isn't.*

Ag... Agi...Aga... Shit. Whatever word he'd said in that husky sex-god voice of his kept pinging around in her brain, unwilling to leave her memory. Or fantasy, or...hell, she didn't know what now.

She cleared her throat, working for nonchalant when she felt anything but. "So what did you do to me?" Her fingers drifted to her forehead again, and she felt the edge of the scab, knowing without a doubt that whatever had happened was totally his fault. "And how much time has passed since you did it?"

Instead of growing angry, as she expected, the corner of his lips curled. "You've been asleep for two days. You had a concussion. Hit your head pretty hard when you fell into an open cavern in the tunnels and tumbled into an underground river."

His words shot hazy memories through her mind. She remembered climbing out of the bathroom window, rushing down to the tunnels beneath the ruins, running in the dark. She remembered his voice calling her name. She remembered him chasing her. She remembered air whooshing past her face, something ice cold cocooning her body, then...absolutely nothing.

She'd fallen into a river. Knocked herself unconscious. Gotten a concussion. And he'd rescued her?

He must have read the confusion on her face because that amusement twisted his lips even higher. "You look surprised."

That he'd rescued her and *didn't* look like he was about to jump her bones? Hell yeah, she was surprised.

His expression took on a serious note. "There are kobaloi in the tunnels beneath us. I barricaded the door into the ruins, but I'm fairly sure I trapped a few in the castle with us, ones that were skulking around in here unnoticed. You don't need to worry, though. I lit fires in every fireplace from here to the kitchen, and I'll keep them all going. Kobaloi don't like flames. They'll keep their distance. Plus, they won't risk coming out where they could get caught in sunlight."

That didn't exactly put her at ease. She racked her brain for what she'd learned about kobaloi on Olympus. The gnome-dwarves were thought to be a fable, but if Erebus had seen them, that meant they were real. Her brow wrinkled. "All the tales I've heard about kobaloi claimed they congregate near therillium."

"Hades's invisibility ore. Yep. Those tales were correct. It's beneath us." He looked up and around the bedroom suite. "There's no telling how long this colony existed without Hades even realizing the half-breeds were perched right on top of his precious ore. Kind of fitting, don't you think? A way for the half-breeds to stick it to the god-king of the Underworld."

The fact he found amusement in that unsettled her. Erebus was a minor god *from* the Underworld. He'd served Hades for a thousand years before being lost in a bet to Zeus. There'd been a time—when she'd been so enamored by him during her seduction training—that she'd convinced herself he wasn't the epitome of darkness she eventually realized he truly was. But why would something created from darkness seem happy to know his true master—Hades—had been duped?

She couldn't come up with a logical answer. And that damn word...*agi, aga, agap*... It wouldn't leave her stupid brain. The only thing that remotely made sense was that this story about the kobaloi was just that...a story. A ploy to convince her she was safer *with* him than without him.

She knew how to take care of herself, dammit. She didn't need him.

Except...

The way her chest tightened when she looked up at him told her she *was* safe with him. Way safer than she'd been in years. And that didn't just unsettle her, it completely unnerved her.

Hands suddenly shaking, she moved the tray to the far side of the bed, tugged the covers up to her chest, and leaned back into the pillows. Her instincts screamed to get up, to retreat into the bathroom, to escape again, but her muscles wouldn't listen. Yes, she felt better than the last time she'd awoken—and now she was almost sure that hadn't been a dream. But she wasn't anywhere near a hundred percent, and if she ran like this, he'd easily catch her. Which meant she needed to rest. To think. To plot. And act on that planning later.

She closed her eyes, not because she was anywhere near falling asleep again but because she couldn't keep looking at him, not when she had no clue what was really happening and why he was being so damn nice. "Thank you for the chicken noodle soup. I don't know where you found the ingredients but it was very good. I'm just more tired than I guess I realized."

Liar.

Okay, why did she feel guilty about lying to him now?

"You're welcome." A shuffling sound echoed from the far side of the bed, and the mattress jostled, just enough to tell her he'd picked up the tray. Footsteps faded as he crossed the room, and she exhaled, thankful he was leaving. "It wasn't chicken, though. It was rabbit."

Oh great. On top of all the other stuff in her head, now she'd be thinking of boiled bunnies the rest of the night and that old movie she'd watched when she'd been with the half-breeds in Russia. The American one about the guy who'd had the affair with the psycho woman who tormented his family.

"I'll let you get some sleep," Erebus said. "When you wake later you can tell me what test you failed on Olympus."

"I didn't fail a test on Olympus."

"You didn't?" His footsteps silenced. "Zeus said you failed your last benchmark."

Her eyes popped open wide. And in a rush of understanding she realized that Zeus had lied to him about why he wanted her back and that she'd just given herself away.

Shit.

Shiiiiiiit.

Stay calm, Sera. If you accidentally spill the real reason you escaped Olympus and what you left with, you're as good as dead. Forget about how nice he's been to you tonight. Forget about that stupid imagined emotion in his eyes. His loyalty is to Zeus, the king of fucking everything, not you.

"Fail?" Her heartbeat whirred in her ears, but somehow she found the strength to close her eyes and breathe deep, feigning exhaustion. Rolling to her side away from him, she tucked her hands up by her face and added, "I thought you said fell. My balance improved quite a lot on the training field after you moved on to a new class of recruits."

Silence met her ears, but she knew he was still there. Staring at her back. Wondering what the hell she was hiding. Her pulse raced even faster.

Stay calm...

"Can we talk about the Sirens and my failures later?" She faked a yawn and forced her muscles to relax so it looked as if she were about to drift to sleep. "I'm really tired again."

Still no response from him. But seconds later the sound of his receding footsteps drifted to her ears.

She lay still a long time after he'd left, listening, waiting, afraid if she looked he'd still be there. But when she finally rolled to her back and peered toward the doorway, it was empty.

She threw back the covers and lurched to her feet. The room swayed, but she grasped the post at the foot of the bed and waited until her blood pressure regulated. When she felt steady, she scanned the room, searching for her clothes.

They were gone. He'd taken them, probably to prevent her from running again. Her boots were missing too.

Dammit.

Her heart raced with indecision but she decided it didn't matter. All that mattered was getting away from him before he learned the truth.

She bolted for the open door and headed for the back stairs she'd used before to escape. And hoped like hell *this time* she chose the right tunnel to freedom.

CHAPTER FIVE

Sera was hiding something.

Erebus didn't know what, but he was now convinced the story Zeus had fed him about why she'd escaped Olympus was total shit.

"I didn't fail on Olympus."

The way she'd said that, off the cuff, as if she'd been shocked he'd even assume such a thing, kept circling in his head as he sat in what used to be the main gathering room of the castle. He'd dragged the chair in from another room and set it in front of the fire. Staring into the flames as he swirled an ancient glass of brandy—the bottle another treasure he'd found in storage—he thought back to the Sera he remembered from those early days with the Sirens.

Before she'd been assigned to him for seduction training, Sera had pretty much sucked at marksmanship, agility, hand-to-hand combat, and warfare strategy. She'd been at the bottom of the class in almost every category. But by the time she'd moved on from his seduction training, she'd already been steadily improving in all the areas of the field. He'd told himself a well-satisfied Siren made a better warrior, but the truth had little to do with him. A confident Siren made a much better warrior, and he'd watched her confidence grow over the months they'd been together, not just in their steamy seduction sessions, but out on the field as well.

Which was why when Zeus had pulled him aside only days ago and told him he had an AWOL Siren, Erebus hadn't once considered it could possibly be Sera. By the time she'd moved on to the second phase of training and he'd been assigned to a new set of recruits, he'd been sure she'd adapt to every one of her training routines and pass each of her upcoming benchmarks. And remembering back to the way she'd almost kicked his ass out in the woods when he'd been hunting her proved she could hold her own. Shit, the way she'd scaled the side of this freakin' castle and very nearly escaped from him down there in those tunnels proved she wasn't just confident as hell but completely capable.

She was definitely hiding something. And he was determined to find out just what that something was.

Creaking floorboards echoed from the hallway. His head came up, and he looked into the darkened corridor. Night had spread over the lake and ruins, and although he'd checked the barrier he'd erected where the tunnels opened to the ruins, that didn't mean there weren't kobaloi hiding in the shadows inside the castle, now looking for a way to get back into the tunnels where they were safe.

Another floorboard creaked, the sound pushing him to his feet. Setting his half-empty glass on a side table he'd dragged in along with the chair, he quietly moved toward the dark hall. A shadow moved, heading slowly toward the stairs that led down to the tunnels. A shadow that was definitely not small enough to be kobaloi.

Amusement spread through him. Amusement and challenge, and a tiny bit of disbelief that she was trying this *again.*

As a god, he could flash in any realm. He wasn't limited by laws of physics or solid walls, like mortals. Gathering his energy just as he'd done when he'd flashed Sera out of that cavern and away from that horde of kobaloi, he envisioned the top step of those stairs and appeared directly in front of her before she could take that first step down.

"Going somewhere?" he asked.

Sera gasped and scrambled back. "Erebus." She pressed a shaky hand to her chest. "Y-you scared me."

"Uh huh." He didn't buy that for a minute. "You were looking for me, I assume."

Panic flashed in her eyes, and she took another giant step back, the pajama bottoms he'd dressed her in pooling around her bare feet. "I... Well, yes. I didn't know where you'd gone."

Liar...

He moved up the step, eyes locked on her, and stepped forward. "I was sitting in the main room. In front of the fire. You couldn't have missed me."

She scrambled back another step, glanced over her shoulder toward the glow from the fireplace, then quickly looked back, only this time the panic was stronger in her sweet blue eyes. "Oh, I... I heard a sound. I didn't even look in the main room. I just assumed you were downstairs."

Two days ago, if she'd fed him this line of B.S., it would have enraged him. Now all it did was entertain him, because even when she knew she was caught red-handed, she still wasn't backing down.

He had to admire her for that. Had to admire that even after escaping Olympus, nearly falling to her death, and suffering a concussion, she was still willing to take on a god. A minor god, albeit, but a god who was still a hundred times more powerful than her.

"Since you're out of bed," he said, drawing closer, "you must be feeling better."

"Better?" She inched backward until her spine hit the wall. Pressing her hands into the stone behind her, she sidestepped to her left, toward the glow of the main room. "I-I wouldn't say better, per se. Just...worried."

Worried? About him? He wished she was, but considering she looked like a cornered animal at the moment, he was calling bullshit. "Well, for what I have planned I don't really need you better, just able to stand upright."

Her eyes widened. "What you have planned?"

Was that excitement he heard in her voice? Oh, he definitely liked that.

He braced a hand against the wall over her shoulder and leaned toward her seductive heat. She immediately tensed, but didn't try to move away. And he liked that even better. "Why do you think I nursed you back to health? So we could finish what we started the other day."

She sucked in a breath and held completely still as he pressed his face into all her silky hair. "You don't mean—"

"I mean exactly that, female." He bent at the knees and hefted her over his shoulder. Holding her tight, he ignored the yelp that passed over her lips and headed straight for the main staircase. "We have unfinished business, and now that you're well enough, we're going to get back to it."

Her hands landed against his back. Warm and small and so damn enticing. She tried to push herself upright, but he held on tighter, keeping her immobile as he carried her up the steps.

"B—but," she sputtered. "I have a concussion!"

"Then I guess you should have stayed in bed."

A warm glow emanated from the fireplace in her room, bathing the corridor in an eerie orange light. Dropping her to her feet in front of the same corner bedpost he'd tied her to originally, he reached for the charmed rope that was still wrapped around the wood and pressed her back. "Hold still."

"Erebus, you can't do this!"

She struggled but was no match for his strength. Satisfied she wasn't going anywhere, he stepped back, perched his hands on his hips, and eyed her carefully. "This looks very familiar. Though this time I'm going to do more than just leave you alone to plot your escape."

Her eyes shot daggers into his as he grabbed a chair, dragged it in front of her, turned it around, and straddled the seat. Resting his forearms on the back, he watched as she struggled to break free, smirked at the way her long, silky blonde hair fell over her eyes and the delicate skin of her face, and smiled as she grew more outraged by the second.

"We can do this the easy way or we can do this the hard way, Sera, but know this, you're not getting away from me until I'm ready to let you go. And I have no intention of letting you go until you give me what I want."

She glared hard in his direction. "I'm not giving you anything. If you want it, you're going to have to try to take it from me."

Excitement pulsed inside him because that was exactly the answer he'd hoped for. After twiddling his thumbs the last two days, waiting for her to heal and regain her strength, he was more than ready for some fun. He could have gone back to Olympus during that time and checked in with Zeus to let the King of the Gods know he was still looking for the nymph, but he didn't want to risk giving Zeus a reason to reassign him and send another hunter after Sera. Plus, if memory served, fun with Sera was hotter than anything Erubus had experienced before or since her, and he wasn't about to let anyone else near her.

Grinning, he pushed up off the chair. "I guess we're doing this the hard way then. Good thing that was my first choice." He crossed the room, reached for a pair of scissors he'd found in a dresser drawer downstairs, then moved back to stand in front of her. "Okay, nymph, where should we start?"

Her eyes zeroed in on the scissors and grew so wide the whites could be seen all around her sexy blue irises. "W-what are you planning to do with those?"

"Get you naked, of course." He reached for the hem of her shirt. "Top or bottom, *agápi*? Where we begin is all up to you."

* * * *

The statement—the implication—should have enraged Sera. Only it didn't. It didn't because all Sera could focus on was that one word...*agápi.* The same word she'd heard him utter in her dream, when she'd been groggy and wounded and he'd been lying in the bed beside her, holding her close as if she were...precious.

Precious.

Her.

To a minor god who didn't give a shit about anyone or anything.

Agápi...

Holy hell. The ancient endearment registered, and her breath caught in her throat. He *had* called her "my love" in the tunnels. He was calling her "my love" now too.

He tipped his head, and a mischievous smile curled his lips. "You look confused."

She wasn't confused. She was way the hell freaked out. He'd never called her *agápi* when he'd been fucking her senseless on Olympus. Why the hell was he using *that* word on her now?

Her mouth was so dry she wasn't sure she could form words, but somehow she mumbled, "W-why are you doing this?"

"Because nothing else seems to grab your attention. All you want to do is run."

She glared down at the ropes, then back up at him. "Well, I obviously can't run now, can I?"

"No, you definitely can't." His heated gaze swept over her chest where the ropes bound her to the post above and below her breasts, causing them to push out even more. "Though I can't complain. I like you like this."

Using the scissors, he sliced into the bottom of her tank. Cool air washed over her belly as he pulled the hem of her tank away from her skin and cut through the thin material.

Her pulse shot straight up. "Erebus. Stop."

"Hold still, *agápi*. I don't want to accidentally cut you."

He snipped again, and with every swish of the scissors tingles shot across her skin. Tingles that weren't all laced with fear. Even as he came dangerously close to nicking her flesh, her blood heated and an excitement she knew she shouldn't be feeling flared in her veins.

He pulled the scissors away, then tugged the bottom four inches of her tank free all the way around, leaving her stomach exposed to his view beneath the bottom rope holding her in place.

"Mm." He set the scissors on the seat of his chair and skimmed his gaze over her exposed flesh. "You've been working out, *agápi*." Drawing close once more, he brushed the back of his knuckles down the center of her abs. "I like this line right here."

She sucked in a breath. Tried to move back from his touch. Knew she couldn't get away from him. Knew also that part of her didn't even want to try.

Dammit, *this* was why she needed to run. Because the son of a bitch wasn't going to force her. He was going to seduce her, just as he'd done on Olympus. And her traitorous body would enjoy every single moment of it, even knowing when it was all over that he was going to haul her ass back to Zeus and abandon her.

"Please don't," she whispered.

His knuckle grazed the sensitive skin just beneath her belly button, sending tiny electrical arcs straight between her legs. "Please don't what?"

"Don't touch me like that," she managed, but the words were so soft even she had trouble hearing them, and there was no heat behind them. Just a quivering, aching need.

His hand stilled, and his head lifted. Holding her breath, she chanced a look up, and in the silence as their eyes held and nothing but the crackle of the fire sounded in the room, she had absolutely no idea what he was thinking.

There'd been a time when she'd been so head over heels in love with him on Olympus that she'd thought she knew what went on in that gorgeous head of his. That she could predict his reactions. Then she'd discovered he'd barely thought about her at all outside that farce of a bedroom where he'd screwed her blind in the training center, and every one of her beliefs had changed.

That realization had hurt, but it hurt more now because, even though she'd told herself she'd gotten over him, one gaze deep into his eyes here in this room and she knew she'd never be over him. It didn't matter what he had planned. It didn't matter what he did to her next. It didn't even matter that he was going to turn her over to Zeus when he'd had his fill of her. All that mattered was that she was a fool for ever thinking someone like him could love her back. At his core, regardless of what he'd done to "save" her, he was immortal. A god. As selfish as the Olympians. As emotionally void as Hades himself. As deserving of love as that bastard Zeus.

"Go on," she whispered, looking away, resigning herself to something she ached to feel, didn't really want, but knew she wasn't about to fight. "Just get on with it already."

"Okay," he said just as softly. "Since you asked so nicely."

She tensed, anticipating his touch on her breasts or between her legs, but it didn't come. Instead, he lifted the strip of black fabric he'd cut from her tank and used it to cover her eyes.

With swift movements, he tied the fabric behind her head so all she saw was darkness. "Where I want to start, *agápi*, is with the truth. You didn't fail any benchmark test with the Sirens, did you? You ran from Zeus for another reason. Before I untie you from this post and give you what we both want, you're going to tell me why."

Give you what we both want... The words echoed in her head and were so arousing, she suddenly wanted his hands everywhere she'd just told herself she didn't want them.

She waited for him to say more. Waited for him to cut away more of her clothing. Waited for that touch that would make her melt in ways she'd hate herself for later, but it still never came.

Neither did his voice. The only sound she heard was the squeak of leather.

"Erebus?"

"Right here. Waiting."

His voice was feet away. Lower than her ears. As if he were sitting in that chair again, watching her.

Without her sight, her other senses heightened. Everywhere the rope bit into her, her flesh heated, aching for more contact. The gentle push and pull of his breath sounded over the crackle of the fire—steady and even, not fast like hers, as if he had all the time in the world to sit and wait. And his scent—that hypnotic blend of leather and cognac and skull flowers—filled her nostrils, making her light headed in ways she didn't expect.

What the hell was he doing now? Making her suffer so she'd *beg* for his touch?

She clenched her jaw. "Erebus, what's going on?"

A shuffle sounded, like a boot scraping the floor, and heat flared in her veins all over again. She braced herself for the feel of his fingers against her skin—all but *ached* for it—but the touch never came.

"Erebus?"

"I heard you, *agápi*." His voice was still coming from that damn chair. The bastard *was* making her suffer. "But I'm still waiting for you to tell me what I want to hear."

Shock rippled through her. Shock and disbelief that he wasn't seducing her, wasn't taking her as she'd expected him to do.

The muscles in her stomach quivered, and between her legs—though she couldn't believe she was reacting this way—her sex grew heavy and tingly. "Erebus, take this blindfold off me."

"Why?"

"Because I don't like it."

Another scrape of his boot across the floor. "And I don't like you avoiding my questions. Tell me why you ran, and why Zeus is so pissed."

Holy hell, he was going to sit there and stare at her until she gave him what he wanted. And dammit, why was that suddenly a worse kind of torture than his seducing her?

Because you want him to seduce you. You're envisioning it now. You're getting all hot and bothered just thinking about it.

Dear gods, she was. Damn her nymph bloodline. Damn her body's natural reaction to sexual taunting.

"Come on, *agápi*. Give me what I want, and I'll give you what you need."

Her sex tightened at the sound of his deep voice caressing that term of endearment, and she ached to have his hands caress her hypersensitive flesh in the same way.

"I'm a very patient god, you know." His chair squeaked again. "I could watch you all night. All day tomorrow if that's what it takes. And the day after that and the day after that. I do love watching you."

Her stomach clenched, and against what was left of the black tank, her nipples pebbled with the thought of his heated, needy eyes roving over every inch of her.

She swallowed hard, knowing he'd do exactly what he threatened. Knowing just as surely that it would make her absolutely throb with need.

"*Agááápi...*"

He drew the word out until she wanted to scream.

"Fine," she blurted out. "You win, okay? I ran because I found out Zeus is a sonofabitch."

He chuckled. "That's not exactly news."

Anger burned inside her. Anger that she was about to tell him anything when she should just keep her mouth shut.

But maybe if she gave him a little information it would encourage him to untie her from this stupid post. And with any luck, when that happened, she'd be strong enough to squash this growing desire for a god who'd always been her greatest weakness.

"You want to know why I ran?" she said. "I ran because I remembered. I remembered everything the Sirens wiped from my memory when they kidnapped me and brought me to Olympus. I remembered that Zeus murdered my parents, that he destroyed my home, and that he wiped out my entire race. All because he's an asshole who doesn't give a shit about anyone but himself. And I ran because I wasn't about to stay another second in a realm with a god who hunts women down like dogs and gets a sick thrill out of turning them into his brainless Siren bimbos."

She drew a deep breath. "Now, are you happy?"

CHAPTER SIX

No, he wasn't happy.

Erebus stared in shock at Sera, blindfolded and tied to the corner post of the bed. Firelight flickered over the smooth skin of her belly and the gentle features that made her look more like an angel than a warrior. But it wasn't her sexy-as-hell body or even her looks that held him entranced right now. It was her words.

"Zeus destroyed your people?" he asked. "Who were your people?"

She pursed her lips, every muscle in her body tight. And for a heartbeat he was sure she wasn't going to answer. Then she said, "Atlanteans. I'm from Atlantis."

No fucking way...

"I thought you were a nymph."

"I am," she said with a frown. "Don't you know anything about genealogy? Atlanteans are descended from water nymphs."

Holy shit...

"My father was the first knight of the queen's guard," she went on when he didn't respond, still clearly perturbed. "My mother was a handmaiden in the queen's castle. When my father discovered that the queen of Atlantis was having an affair with Zeus, he warned her Zeus would tire of her eventually and that the affair would not end well. She ignored him. My father was worried about Zeus's intentions regarding the queen, so to keep his loved ones safe, he smuggled me and my mother out of Atlantis and into the human realm. Half-breeds from the Russian Misos colony took us in. My father was duty bound to return to the queen's guard and couldn't stay with us, but it was only a few months later that we got word his fear had come true. In a fit of rage, Zeus destroyed Atlantis and all who dwelt there, including the queen and my father. Not long after that, Zeus's Sirens showed up looking for us. They slaughtered my mother and many of the half-breeds who tried to protect her. The leader of the colony managed to hide me away during the attack, but I spent the rest of my childhood knowing I was the last of a race that had been nothing but collateral damage to the King of the Gods."

Erebus's heart rate slowly increased as he listened to Sera's story, and though disbelief churned in his brain, he was already racing back over everything he'd ever heard about the utopian society of Atlantis. He knew Zeus'd had a hard-on for the Atlantean queen and her realm. He also knew that the queen had strung him along, giving him just enough to appease him—in this case, as Sera had pointed out, her body—but that she'd refused to give him what he really wanted, which was the entirety of her realm to command and corrupt.

"How did you remember all that?" he asked. "Every Siren recruit has her memory wiped before her training begins."

Her shoulders stiffened. It was a very subtle reaction, but he caught it. And he didn't have a clue what it meant.

"I don't exactly know," she said, a touch of her anger gone. "I just know that I overheard Athena and another Siren talking about Atlantis one day in the mess hall. Their discussion about the Atlantean queen triggered something in my memory. As soon as my training was finished that day, I rushed to the Hall of Sirens and researched everything I could about Atlantis. And the more I read, the faster the memories rushed back."

Humans thought the utopian society of Atlantis was a myth. Those who believed it had actually been real thought it had been destroyed thousands of years ago. But Erebus knew the truth. Atlantis had been a thriving, advanced, self-contained realm hidden in plain sight in the human world, and it had continued to exist as recently as a hundred years ago. Atlantis had only fallen to destruction very near the time Hades lost Erebus in that bet that had plucked Erebus from the Underworld and dropped him on Olympus.

His hands grew damp against the back of the chair, and he pushed to his feet. "If what you say is true, it means you're not a twenty-three-year-old nymph Zeus randomly chose for his Siren Order."

"No. I'm not." Her jaw tightened again. "I'm a hundred and

fourteen years old. After about eighty years with the half-breeds and no repeat attack from Zeus's Sirens, the leaders of the colony figured Zeus didn't know about me. They decided it was safe for me to leave their walls. Even though I'd lived as one of them, I'd never felt as if I belonged there. And part of me wanted to leave. To live near the ocean, as my people had for thousands of years. I ventured out across Europe and finally settled on an island off the coast of Italy. I taught music to children. I built a life of my own surrounded by humans who had no idea who or what I really was. And I met a man who made me feel safe. But that safety was fleeting because Zeus found me there. He was screwing some human on that island and spotted me walking on the beach one day. His Sirens killed the human I'd been living with, destroyed my music studio, and wiped my memories. And then they took me to Olympus and told me I was a twenty-year-old nymph with no family who should be grateful she'd been chosen for the Siren Order. But there was no randomness to my being there. Zeus knew exactly what I was. He knew who I was. And instead of just killing me like he did my mother and the rest of our people, that sick fuck got off knowing he'd turned me into the very thing that had destroyed my entire world."

Pressure built in Erebus's chest. Pressure and warmth and an emotion he'd felt in the tunnels below this castle only days ago but hadn't understood. A feeling he knew now wasn't just sexual. It was rooted in a connection he never could have predicted that bound them together.

She tensed as he moved toward her, hearing or sensing him, he didn't care which. And when he lifted his hand to her soft cheek and tipped her face up, she sucked in a surprised breath.

But it didn't deter him. Heat flared in his belly. Heat and life. Without hesitating, without asking, he lowered his mouth to hers and kissed her.

She froze. Didn't kiss him back. Didn't even move. But he felt the jump in her pulse against his skin, and he heard the tiny moan she tried to stifle echo in his ears like fireworks.

He didn't demand more. Didn't coax her mouth open to deepen the kiss. Just let go of her jaw as he softly skimmed his lips against hers again and untied the blindfold from her the back of her head then tugged the ropes free at her back.

He half expected her to push away as soon as she was free, but she didn't. She lifted her hands to his chest and broke their kiss, drawing back just far enough to peer up at him with confusion and heat in her cerulean eyes. Eyes that were the same color as the seas around her homeland.

And filled with so much damn heat his blood pounded straight into his groin.

"W-why are you kissing me?"

"Because I didn't know." He lifted his hand back to her face and caressed her silky cheek. "Because I now understand. We're the same, you and I. The last of our people. I thought the reason I couldn't get you out of my head was because you were just better at seduction than any of the other recruits I'd trained. But I know now that wasn't the truth. The truth is that my soul recognized yours long ago, Sera. I was just too blind to see what was in front of me."

The lines in her forehead deepened and were so damn adorable he couldn't stop himself from pressing his lips against them and inhaling her sweet lemony scent.

"I'm older than Krónos," he confessed, moving to her temple. "I'm a primordial deity, spawned from Chaos."

Against his chest, she gasped. "Th-that makes you nearly five thousand years old."

"Older." Gods, he liked the sound of that gasp. Couldn't wait to hear it when she was in the throes of ecstasy. "I existed for many years before Gaia and Uranus created the Titans."

He shifted his fingers to the soft skin of her nape and gently massaged, part of him still unable to believe all that she'd told him, another part shocked he hadn't recognized their connection sooner. "The primordial deities had no idea the Titans were power hungry, thus they had no defense against the Titans when they were stripped of their human forms. My father, my siblings, they all ceased to exist as I had known them. But me... Krónos kept me as I was because he wanted my darkness. He wanted to use it to control the other Titans. And he did for a very long time. Until his own children overthrew him."

She drew back once more and gazed up at him. Questions still swirled in her hypnotic eyes, but he also saw awe. An awe that electrified him.

"I don't remember my life with my family," he said. "Just like Athena does with the Sirens, Krónos stripped my memories so I would never question my servitude to him. Then he bound any powers I had that were stronger than his. Unlike you, though, I'll never regain those memories. What I know of my past came from Hades. After Zeus, Hades, and Poseidon overthrew Krónos, Hades kept me for himself. I was duty bound to serve him in the Underworld. He's the one who told me of my past. And he made certain to point out how lucky I was to still be alive. But he didn't do so to educate me. He did it so I would never be inclined to release Krónos from his prison in Tartarus, and so that I would never fall victim to Krónos's lies and deception."

Her mouth fell open, but it was the empathy he saw swirling in her spellbinding eyes that cut right to the heart of him.

He dragged his fingers back to her face and gently traced the sleek line of her jaw, mesmerized by her all over again because he never thought he'd ever meet anyone in the long years of his life who knew what it was like to be alone. "What Zeus did to you was wrong. What he did to your people was wrong. I know what it's like to lose everyone and to be the last of your line. If I had known about your past..." His gaze dropped from her eyes to her lips. "If I had known, things would have been different. I never would have let you be hunted. After all you've been through, *agápi*, you deserve to be cherished and protected. Because you're special. Precious. You are the epitome of rare and irreplaceable and unique, and I won't ever let anyone hurt you again. I'll do whatever I have to do to keep you safe. I vow this to you here and now."

Shock rippled through her eyes, and then those eyes darkened to a warm deep blue just before she lifted to her toes and pressed her mouth to his.

He opened to her kiss. Slid his fingers into her hair and stroked his tongue against hers. Drew her scent and taste and essence deep into his soul. Into a place he hadn't known existed until this moment. Into the very core of who he was and wanted to be.

And as her hands slid up and around his neck and she tipped her head to kiss him deeper, he promised himself that no matter what Zeus or any of the other ruling gods wanted, this time he wasn't letting her go.

* * * *

She shouldn't be kissing him. She knew she shouldn't be kissing him. But Sera couldn't make herself stop.

He tasted like darkness, like sin, like seduction and salvation. And though she knew there was a chance he could be lying to her, that he'd just made up that entire story to coax her into bed, something inside her believed him. Something in her heart went out to him. Something in her soul latched on to his and was unwilling to let go.

He wasn't the emotionally closed-off minor god she'd convinced herself these last eighteen months he really was. He was the male she'd fallen for all those nights ago on Olympus. The one who'd been able to ignite passion in her with just one look. The one who'd been able to melt her with a single touch. The one whose words had echoed in her head for months and months after he'd left her bed.

Agápi...

She was wrong. She *had* heard him say that to her on Olympus. In the dead of night—on their *last* night—when she'd been drifting to sleep and he'd been wrapped around her like a warm blanket. She remembered it now. Remembered it like it was yesterday. Couldn't believe she'd ever forgotten.

She kissed him harder. Pulled her body flush against his so there was no space left between them. And groaned at the thick, heavy pressure of his arousal growing larger against the bare skin of her belly.

"Sera..." He turned her away from the bedpost. Nipped at her bottom lip. Kissed her cheek, her jaw, and breathed hot over the sensitive skin behind her ear as he maneuvered her to the side of the bed. "Sweet, stubborn, sassy Seraphine."

Emotions closed her throat. Made her desperate to touch him, everywhere. She grasped the T-shirt he wore, drew back from his lips, and wrenched the garment over his head. He did the same to her tank, then reached for her face and pulled her mouth back to his, all the while groaning as her bare breasts grazed his chest.

Her nipples hardened. Electricity arced between her breasts and into her sex. He wrapped an arm around her waist and lifted her up onto the mattress, then knelt over her and claimed her mouth. Claimed what was left of her resistance as well.

It was wrong. She knew it was wrong. She'd only told him a

fraction of the truth and was sure if he discovered the rest he wouldn't be frantic to take her and taste her and have her at all. But she couldn't stop. She didn't want to think about the consequences. Didn't want to think about Zeus or Hades or what anyone else wanted. She only cared about this. About him. About holding on to the absolute pleasure only he'd ever been able to draw from her and giving it back to him tenfold while she could.

She arched up to meet him, licked into his mouth, and opened her legs so he could press that heavenly erection right where she wanted it most. A groan slid from her lips as he rocked against her core, but all she could hear in her ears was the word *more*.

Her hands slid down his chiseled abs and found the button of his jeans. She flicked it free, then slipped her fingers beneath his waistband to graze the carved vee of his hipbones. He groaned into her mouth, pulled his arm from around her waist, and closed his hand over her right breast. Pain and pleasure shot from the spot and arced straight between her legs, causing her to rock against his length and tremble with primal need.

"Oh, *agápi*." He trailed a path of fire from her lips to her jaw, down her throat and across her collarbone. "You feel so good. So much better than I remember."

Her heart fluttered, a reaction she warned herself she needed to contain. She could feel. She could enjoy. She could give and even take. But she was not going to fall in love with him again. She couldn't and still survive.

Wrapping one leg around his hip, she rolled him to his back on the mattress. Surprise registered in his sinful eyes as she climbed over him and straddled his hips, lowering the heat of her pelvis against his already straining cock. A surprise that quickly morphed into eager anticipation.

Her palms landed against his chest. She pushed her weight back and ground herself against his groin. His eyes darkened, and between the layers of fabric between them, she felt the pulse of his need right where she wanted it most.

"Is this what you remember?" She trailed her fingers to his nipples and gently squeezed the dark tips.

"Oh yes." He rocked up to meet her downward thrust. His hands shifted to her hips as she teased and rolled his nipple, and his fingers slid beneath the waistband of her thin cotton pajama bottoms. "Keep doing that, *agápi*."

She had no intention of stopping.

Her skin was shades lighter than his, ivory where his was obsidian, and she loved the contrast. "What else do you remember?" she asked, moving to torment his other nipple, continuing to rock and grind and rub against his swollen erection.

"I remember your mouth, *agápi*. Devouring me."

The husky sound of his voice, the rolling heat filling his eyes, it all coalesced inside her to make her absolutely ravenous. Before he could push her pajama bottoms down her ass, she lowered her mouth to his nipple and laved her tongue all around the pebbled tip.

He groaned, lifted his big hands to sift into her hair, and arched up against her. "More."

She moved to his other nipple, licked and laved, then scraped her teeth over the sensitive tip. He hissed in a breath and flexed his hands, trying to pull her mouth back to his, but she easily slid from his grip and trailed her lips lower, across his carved abs, over his belly button, and down to lick the soft skin just above the open waistband of his jeans.

His stomach caved in. She shifted back, pushed his legs open with her knees, and climbed between them so she could grasp his waistband and tug his jeans down his thick thighs.

His cock sprang up, hard and thick and proud. Her gaze shot right to it, and her mouth watered as she tugged his pants the rest of the way off, dropped them on the floor, then climbed back onto the mattress to take her first sinful taste.

Her tongue brushed the flared underside of the head, and he groaned deep in his throat, his heated eyes watching her every movement. "Oh, yes, *agápi*. Do that again."

She licked all around the head, savoring the taste of him, then closed her lips around him and sucked.

This time, his groan was a mix of pleasure and pain, and when his fingers threaded into her hair and tightened, she took the hint. She drew him deep, wiggling the flat of her tongue along the underside until he breached the opening to her throat.

"Fuck, yes, Sera." His big hands helped drag her head back so the tip of his cock almost slipped free of her lips. Then he flexed his hips and thrust deep all over again. "Suck, just like that."

She remembered exactly what he liked and gave him precisely what he wanted. Used her tongue to drive him wild. And while he fucked her mouth with long, deep, penetrating strokes, she relaxed her throat and trailed one hand down to scrape her fingernails against his balls.

Pure pleasure tightened his features. Her breasts grew heavy as she watched him. Her sex throbbed, and the erotic sounds of pleasure he made as he used her mouth filled her ears, making her ache to bring him to a blistering climax so she could taste his release on her tongue. She sucked, licked, took him deep again and again and let him use her however he wanted. His fingertips tightened against her skull, and she felt his cock swell in her mouth. His thrusts grew faster, deeper. Relaxing her gag reflex, she gave herself over to his desire and let him breach her throat. And when he grunted and plunged in even harder, she swallowed all around the head, knowing it would send him right over the edge.

His whole body shook, and he grunted through his release. She didn't let up, continuing to suck and lick and swallow until there was nothing left. When his hands finally released her and his massive body relaxed against the mattress, she slowly worked her way back up his length, flicked her tongue around the head one last time until he twitched, then released him.

A satisfied smile curled her lips as she took in the thin layer of sweat all over his body and the way he lay completely wrecked beneath her.

She'd done that. She'd made him absolutely limp. He might have taught her a thing or two about seduction on Olympus, but she'd always been able to rock his world right out from under him. Right from the first night they'd spent together.

"Is that what you remember?" She squeezed his thigh and breathed hot against his still engorged cock.

Something else she remembered. He was a god. He didn't need any down time. Which she'd never been more thankful for than she was right at that moment.

His eyes drifted open and locked on her still kneeling between his legs. Eyes that were glossy from his orgasm but not nearly satisfied. "That's a good start, *agápi*."

Heat flashed in his sinful eyes just before he sat up, grasped her shoulders, and dragged her up his body so he could devour her mouth. She groaned, sucked on his tongue, reached for him. But before she could straddle his hips, he lurched out from under her, slid to her back, and pushed her to her belly.

She grunted as her face pressed against the mattress. In one swift move, he stripped the pajama bottoms from her legs then pushed her to her knees. "Ass up, *oraios*." When she tried to push up on her hands, he placed one big palm between her shoulder blades to hold her down. "*Only* your sweet ass."

Excitement swirled inside her when he used the ancient word for beautiful. And between her thighs, which he was already pushing apart with his knees, her pussy trembled.

Long, thick, torturous fingers slid along her swollen flesh, and he groaned. "Oh, you naughty nymph. You're already wet and dripping. Let's see what I can do about that."

She didn't know what he had planned, but when the bed bounced, that excitement inside her flared even hotter. Then she felt the flat of his tongue flicking over her clit and sliding through her heat, and all she could do was press her forehead into the sheet and groan.

Yes, yes, yes... That was exactly what she wanted. She rocked back, loving every moment of his attention. Decadent pleasure teased every nerve ending. He licked her again and again, until she was thrusting against his tongue and desperate to feel him slide inside her aching sheath. With one hand she squeezed her breast. With the other she gripped the blanket above her head and simply held on. The orgasm she'd been so close to feeling since the moment he'd dragged her into this room barreled toward her at light speed, and the instant he drew her clit between his lips and suckled, it consumed her like a fireball engulfing everything in its path.

Her whole body shuddered, and her knees gave out so she landed on her belly on the bed. But even before her powerful climax faded, he was pulling her hips up with his hands, pushing his knees between her legs, and brushing his monster erection right where she needed it most.

"Don't pass out on me, *agápi*. Not yet. We're not finished."

The head of his cock stretched her pussy so wide it was a mixture of pleasure and pain she'd only ever felt with him. A groan rumbled from her throat, one that was rooted in both ecstasy because of the way he made her feel and relief that with him she never had to have that awkward discussion about safe sex. Otherworldly beings—her included—were immune to human viruses and diseases. And thanks to her long life span, she was only fertile once every couple of years. She knew the signs when her fertility was active—as did he, being a god—and thankfully it was nowhere close now.

She tightened around him, trying to drag him deeper into her slick channel. Felt his fingers digging into her hips, felt the rough scratch of his leg hair brushing the backs of her thighs. And then he was there, shoving in so deep all she could do was gasp and curl the fingers of both hands into the blanket while she hung on for the ride.

"Fuck, Sera..." He drew back, shoved in even harder, and moaned. "So tight. So good." He slid back out once more, then thrust home all over again. "I forgot how hot and perfect you were."

Every time he drew almost all the way out, her sex contracted to hold him in, and each time he thrust deep, the head of his cock slammed against her G-spot and sent tiny electrical arcs all through her body. Her eyes slid closed. Her mouth fell open as he fucked into her again and again. She spread her knees and pushed back against every thrust, wanting more, wanting everything, wanting to pull him with her into mind-numbing ecstasy.

He leaned forward so the hard plane of his chest brushed her back, wrapped one arm around her waist, then slid his fingers into her wetness and flicked her clit in time with his thrusts. "Tell me how much you like this, *agápi*."

"So much." She arched her back so he could drive even deeper, so he could hit that perfect spot even harder. "Oh, god, so, so much."

"I am your god, Sera. Don't you forget it." His thrusts picked up speed until he was pistoning into her and the edges of her vision turned black. "Don't you forget it, baby."

Another orgasm, this one even bigger than the last, steamrolled straight for her.

"Oh yes, *oraios*. Squeeze me. Just like that. Don't let up. I'm going to make you come. I'm going to make you come so hard you'll never want anyone but me."

Her mouth dropped open in a silent scream, and just before her climax hit she had one thought.

She didn't want anyone but him. She hadn't wanted anyone else since the moment she'd tasted him eighteen months before. And she knew she'd never want anyone after him, even when this night was just a memory.

The orgasm consumed her, making her whole body jerk and quiver. A scream registered in her ears. Her scream. But all she could feel was blinding ecstasy.

Her cries of ecstasy faded and were drowned out by his grunt of satisfaction and a low growl as he said, "That's it. That's it right there, *agápi*. Fuck yes, that's exactly what I've been missing."

She wasn't sure when he came. When she finally tore her eyes open, all she knew was that she was flat against the mattress on her belly and that Erebus lay across her back, his rapid heartbeat pounding into her spine.

Every single muscle in her body was limp, her skin slicked with sweat, her brain completely wrecked. His heavy weight pressing into her made it painful to draw air, but she loved it. Loved the feel of him against her, around her, *inside* her. And even though it made her weak, even though she knew fucking him into exhaustion wasn't physically or emotionally smart, she didn't care. He was right. She'd missed this. And holy hell, as soon as she regained even a fraction of her strength, she wanted to do it all over again.

He slid off her back so she could breathe but didn't roll away from her. Though his heavenly erection was no longer inside her, she felt it lying semi-hard against the back of her thigh as he draped his leg over hers. Just the thought of rousing that magnificent beast back to attention made her pussy twitch with need all over again.

He pushed her hair to one side and trailed his fingers down her sweaty spine. "Are you still alive, gorgeous?"

Groaning, she turned her face toward his and found his mouth temptingly close. So close she could feel the heat of his breath across her swollen lips. "Barely."

A smile cut across his dark face, making him look absolutely beautiful in the low firelight. "That's the way I like you. Completely ruined from my touch."

"It's not just from your touch." She pulled her arm from beneath her, shifted it to her back so her fingertips grazed his hip, then closed her hand around his length, wet and slick from her body where it lay across her. "It's from what you can do with this magical monster."

His eyes darkened as she used her moisture to stroke him base to tip until he was hard and hot and ready all over again.

He groaned low in his throat, then the hand on her spine grasped the back of her head and dragged her mouth to his. And as he kissed her, he rolled her to her back and climbed over her.

Oh yes. That was exactly what she wanted. For however long she could have it.

She opened to his kiss, to his touch, to his every want and desire. Knew she couldn't hold back. Knew she'd never been able to. His big hands cradled her head. His body pressed her back into the mattress. His glorious cock settled between her legs and teased her aching sex.

She wound her arms around his shoulders and held on, but instead of thrusting deep like she expected, he drew back from her mouth and stilled his taunting movements between her legs.

His eyes held hers, hot and insistent and filled with so much emotion her chest tightened. "I'm not letting you go, Sera."

She inhaled slowly, fighting the feelings coursing through her chest. They were the words she'd longed to hear for ages, but they'd come too late to make a difference in her life. Focusing on his lips so he couldn't see what was going on inside her, she said, "I'm not yours to keep."

"Yes, you are," he whispered. "You always were. And this time I'm going to prove it to you."

He lowered and took her mouth just as his cock took possession of her body, and she gave him both without question. Gave him everything even as tears burned her eyes because he was right.

She was his. She'd been his from their first touch on Olympus. She'd always be his and forever curse the fact she'd finally gotten exactly what she'd always wanted but that fate still wasn't on her side.

Because the truth would come out, and the moment Erebus discovered what she'd stolen from the King of the Gods, he'd have no choice but to haul her back to Olympus.

He thought he had free will, but he didn't. He was a servant to the ruling gods. No matter how much she loved him, she would never again be a pawn in any of their games.

CHAPTER SEVEN

Erebus was warm and content and more relaxed than he'd ever been.

The fire crackled in the fireplace as he dozed with Sera beside him in the big bed. She'd fallen right to sleep after he'd brought her to a fourth blistering climax—or maybe he'd been the one to drift to sleep; he wasn't sure. Regardless, now, as he drifted in that space between sleep and consciousness with her heat warming the coldest places inside him, thoughts echoed in his mind. Thoughts he hadn't considered until this very moment.

His draw to Sera—not just here but eighteen months ago on Olympus—made so much sense now. She was from Atlantis, the enlightened race, the golden utopian realm, and he was from darkness. She was everything he wasn't—light instead of dark, selfless instead of selfish, resourceful instead of resigned. She balanced him in ways no one he'd encountered before her ever could. And he knew with her, he could lift himself to a place he'd never been able to reach on his own.

He wasn't giving her up. He didn't care what the Sirens said. He didn't care what Zeus wanted. He needed her, and he'd do whatever it took to keep her with him.

He rolled toward her, reached across the space between them to draw her back against his body, and faltered when his hand met nothing but cold sheets and blankets. Tearing his eyes open, he lifted his head and looked across the bed, surprised to see her side empty.

He pushed up to sitting and glanced across the room illuminated only by the dying fire toward the darkened bathroom. His pulse picked up speed, and he quickly climbed out of bed, telling himself the whole time she was in there, only the room was empty when he reached it.

Panic shot through his chest, chilling all those places that had warmed because of her. One look at the closed window told him she hadn't gone out that way. Turning back into the room, he spotted the open bedroom door, and reality hit him hard in the chest.

She hadn't run. She'd walked right out of this room. And he'd been too blinded by pleasure to stop her.

His fingers shook as he dressed. He didn't know how long she'd been gone, but he had to find her. Why the fuck would she run? They'd reconnected tonight. He'd seen it in her eyes, felt it in that space that hurt like a motherfucker in his chest right this moment. She was his. She knew she was his. What had spooked her into running when he knew she'd felt everything he had?

Zeus.

Fear stabbed like a knife straight through his heart, stilling his feet on the stairs.

Zeus could scare the fuck out of her and make her run. If the King of the Gods had been privy to what they'd done, if Zeus had any idea what Erebus was planning, he could have shown up here. He could have threatened Sera. He could have taken her.

He pushed his legs into a sprint and shot down to the tunnels. His enhanced sense of sight scanned the main corridors for any sign of her but he already knew she wasn't in any of them. She was gone. She was outside the ruins. All he could do was hope and pray he got to her before Zeus took her back to Olympus.

The forest was dark and damp when he raced out of the tunnels and stilled in the silence to search for her. He couldn't see her through the thick trees, but faintly he picked up the crashing of brush. Picked up racing heartbeats. Recognized heavy breaths and pounding footfalls.

Most were animals. He sensed elk not far away. A raccoon was in a tree a quarter mile to his left. And a cougar roamed the hillside to his right. But there was no sign of Sera.

He closed his eyes and focused on her, able to find her now because of his connection to her. Tuning in to his hearing, he searched the area for the familiar sounds of her breathing, the memorable scent of her skin. And located her a mile up the mountain to his right, not far from that cougar.

Using his god senses to zero in on her position, he flashed to that spot, muscles tight and ready to step between her and the King of the Gods. Except when he appeared at her back there was no sign of

Zeus. No sign of anyone else but her. And she wasn't running away as he'd expected. She was crouched on the ground with her hand inside an old, decaying log.

"Come on," she muttered with no clue he was behind her. "I know you're in here."

Erebus had no idea what she was doing, but something about the scene, about her hair shining almost silver in the moonlight set the hairs on his nape straight to attention.

"There you are." She exhaled what he recognized as a relieved breath and pulled something out of the log. He tilted his head to see over her shoulder and watched as she brushed dirt from a palm-sized silver coin.

"What are you doing, Sera?"

She jerked to her feet and whipped around to face him. Wide-eyed, she closed her fist tightly around the coin, hiding it from view. "Erebus. I—you scared me."

"I see that." He didn't like the guilty look on her face or where his thoughts were going at the moment. "Tell me you have a good reason for running this time. Right out of my bed when I thought you'd enjoyed that as much as I had."

"I..."

Warning signals fired off in his head when she couldn't even formulate a simple answer, and that darkness inside surged right to the forefront. Warning signals that screamed she hadn't felt any of the shit he had in that room tonight. "Start talking, Sera, before I come up with scenarios you don't like."

She swallowed hard and pulled whatever was in her hand against her chest. Her feet shuffled backward, and fear replaced the guilt in her eyes. The only thing that stopped her from bolting was the log at her heels that slowed her movement.

Before she could step back and over it, he grasped her wrist, pulled it away from her chest, and pried her fingers open. She yelped and tried to push his hand away, but he blocked her and stared down at the silver coin that was no bigger than her palm and stamped with an image of Heracles surrounded by the traditional Greek key design.

"I've seen this before," he said in a slow voice, lifting it so he could turn it in the moonlight.

"Erebus... Don't."

"This is the Medallion of Heracles. The key that opens the doors of Argolea, the realm of the ancient heroes, to any being who possesses it." His brow lowered in disbelief as he glanced back at her. "Where did you get this?"

She swallowed hard, and her gaze shot to the medallion still in his hand. "Just...give it back. Please."

Something didn't make sense. What the hell was she doing with the key to Argolea? He'd heard of its existence when he'd been with Hades, but it had been lost for years.

His jaw tightened. "Start fucking talking, Sera, because I can't think of a single reason why you, the last surviving Atlantean, would have this key. Unless you stole it from someone and plan to sell it to the highest bidder."

"Okay, just listen. And don't do anything rash until I tell you everything, okay?" She lifted her hands in what he knew was a pleading move, but it did little to settle the darkness inside him. "I did steal it. From Zeus. That's why he sent you after me. Not because I failed any of the Siren tests, but because I took the key so he couldn't use it."

His eyes flew wide. Not just because of what she'd done but because he hadn't known the King of the Gods had come into possession of the key. Zeus despised the Argoleans and could do serious damage with this key. He bet Zeus also wouldn't think twice about doing serious damage to the person who stole it from him.

"You know the story about the creation of Argolea, right?" she said quickly. "How Zeus created the realm of Argolea for his son Heracles to keep Heracles and his descendants safe from Hera's wrath? When Zeus created Argolea, he created a border that was impenetrable to the Olympians. He thought that would protect Heracles and all the others. And it did, but it also prevented Zeus from crossing into Argolea whenever he wanted. To get around that, Zeus had Hephaestus forge a special key, that medallion in your hand. It grants the bearer of the medallion the ability to cross into Argolea, regardless of race. For hundreds, thousands of years, Zeus had no reason to use the key so he kept it hidden. And the place he chose to hide it was in the one realm he knew Hera had no interest in visiting: Atlantis."

She wrung her hands together and glanced at the medallion. "He gave it to the queen of Atlantis to hold in safe keeping. It was hidden in my realm for ages, long before I or my parents were born. Zeus kept close tabs on it by seducing each and every queen so he could retrieve it whenever he wanted. But he made a mistake with the last queen. She sensed Zeus would one day use it for evil purposes, so she gave it to my father, and she told him to hide it in the human realm, someplace Zeus could never find it. And he did. He sent it with me and my mother to that half-breed colony in Russia. But Zeus discovered the queen's deception. That's why he destroyed Atlantis. That's why he murdered my father and sent the Sirens to murder me and my mother. So he could get his precious key back and get rid of anyone who knew what had happened to it."

Erebus's gaze strayed to the medallion between his fingertips. It looked like a coin, but even he could feel the power vibrating inside the small metal disk. And he knew if Zeus caught wind he had it, the King of the Gods would do to him what his father Krónos had done to Erebus's ancestors.

"Don't you understand?" Sera said. "Zeus is looking for the water element. He needs only that to complete the Orb of Krónos, the circular disk that holds all four classic elements and has the power to start the war to end all wars. He stole the Orb from the Argoleans. It already holds the three other elements—air, fire, and earth. Zeus is convinced Prometheus, who created the Orb, hid the water element in Argolea, where the Olympians cannot cross, and Zeus is frantic to get into that realm and find the last element."

She stepped toward him. "Erebus, if Zeus does that, if he finds the water element, he'll be able to release the Titans from Tartarus. He'll be able to command Krónos to wield all his evil powers for *his* purposes. And if he can do that, he'll control every realm—Olympus, the Underworld, the oceans, Argolea, and even the human world. No one and nothing will ever be able to stop him."

Understanding swirled in Erebus's mind. And visions of Zeus wielding unlimited power burst like fireworks behind his eyes.

"Erebus." Her soft fingers landed against his forearm, squeezed, gently. "If Zeus does that, he won't just destroy the other realms as he did Atlantis. He'll bring about death and destruction in ways even Hades cannot comprehend."

She was right. With this key, Zeus had almost everything he could ever want. And every race would be enslaved to him...exactly as Erebus had been enslaved to the Titans and Olympians since his family had been stripped of their human forms.

"If what you say is true and Zeus had this, then why didn't he use it immediately? And how did you even know Zeus had it?"

She exhaled a slow breath. "Remember I told you that I overheard Athena talking to one of the Sirens in the mess hall? That was true. But they weren't just talking about Atlantis. They were talking about this key. The Sirens have been searching for it ever since he annihilated Atlantis and discovered it was missing. He figured my father must have hidden it with me and he was right. It was at that Russian half-breed colony. They were protecting it. When I left there, I thought it would be safe. I never thought his Sirens would find it. That's what I overheard them talking about on Olympus. Something about the half-breeds registered as familiar, and after I left the mess hall that night, I went to the Hall of Sirens to look it up. That's when my memories came back. That was the trigger for me. I remembered everything then. Everything I told you about hiding with the half-breeds for eighty years and Zeus eventually finding me on that island off Italy was true. I just didn't tell you about this key."

His gaze shifted to her face, cast in the shadows of the trees, and he searched her eyes for lies. But he only saw truth. A truth that made his spine tingle. "Why? Why did you keep this secret?"

She swallowed again and glanced at the medallion. He could tell she was itching to take it back but knew she wasn't fast enough or strong enough to wrestle it from his grasp. "I-I wanted to tell you. I did." Her gaze shot back to his. "But you work for Zeus. And you were sent to bring me back to him."

Disbelief churned in his gut, a disbelief rooted in the knowledge that she didn't trust him. "You think I want Zeus to have this kind of power?"

"Don't you?"

His jaw clenched down hard. "Are you seriously asking me that question?"

"I—"

"I'm nothing but a fucking slave to Zeus. That's all I've ever been to the Titans or the Olympians. That's all I *will* ever be."

Her shoulders sagged, and relief filled her eyes as her fingers tightened around his arm. "Then we have to make sure he never gets his hands on it."

She was right, and yet he didn't like the fact she hadn't trusted him. Even after everything he'd seen in her eyes and the connection he'd felt with her, she still saw him as the personification of darkness. To her, he would likely *always* be only darkness because he came from Chaos and had served the three gods she considered the big evils: Krónos, Hades, and Zeus.

Motherfucker. Stupidity echoed through every cell in his body. He was good for a hot and dangerous fuck now and then but not for the truth.

"Why hasn't Zeus used this already?" he demanded.

"I'm not sure. I don't think he's able to. There's magic in it. Magic that is not from Olympus but from witchcraft. I remember my father and the queen discussing it. They thought Hephaestus had Hecate cast a spell over it that prevented Zeus from using it. From what I could gather, Hecate never wanted him to be able to use it either, so she cursed it. But it was only a matter of time before he broke that curse. Which is why I had to get it away from him."

That made sense. But before he could say so, another thought hit him. One he definitely didn't like. "And just how did you get this from Zeus?"

Her face flushed a gentle shade of pink, and for the first time since she'd started this plea to draw him to her side, she dropped her hand from his forearm. "Well, ah, I located its likely position on Olympus by following Athena, and then, well, I, um..." She scratched the back of her head and glanced down at the ground beneath her bare feet. "I overpowered the guards protecting it."

His gaze narrowed on her nervous features. She'd said *guards.* Not Sirens. "Overpowered them," he repeated slowly. "How?"

"With my Siren skills."

A vibration lit off low in his gut. "Which Siren skill?"

She bit her lip, seemed to debate her answer, then finally said, "Seduction."

Oh, no godsdamn way... "You fucked them?"

Her irate gaze shot up to his. "I didn't fuck them. I just distracted them with seduction skills *you* taught me. Then I immobilized them with the hand-to-hand combat I'd learned, and I stole the medallion. Isn't that what Sirens are supposed to do?"

Yes. But not *his* Siren. He didn't care that she hadn't actually fucked those guards. He didn't like the thought of her using her seduction skills on anyone but him. Which he knew was completely hypocritical considering all the Siren trainees he'd fucked during his time on Olympus, but he didn't care. They hadn't meant a thing to him. She meant everything.

He closed his fist around the medallion and swept his other arm around her waist, yanking her tight against his body. She gasped and braced her hands at his chest, but didn't try to push away.

"You're not seducing anyone else, *agápi*. Got that?"

Her fingertips curled into his T-shirt. "Does that mean you're not taking me back to Olympus?"

"That's exactly what it means. You're mine."

"And what about you? Does that 'mine' thing work both ways?"

"Absolutely."

Something softened in her eyes. Something he wanted to believe was trust, but a niggling voice in the back of his head whispered it wasn't. "And the medallion?"

"Zeus can't have it."

The tension in her muscles eased where he held her. "We have to take it to Argolea. It's the only place where it will be safe. You remember Elysia, right? The Siren trainee who escaped Olympus with Damon?"

Damon had been one of the Siren trainers Erebus had worked with. He'd always liked the mortal and had been oddly disappointed when he'd learned the guy was really an Argonaut who'd been duped by Zeus and that he wasn't coming back. "Isn't Elysia's the Argolean princess Damon broke out of the Siren compound?"

"Yes. She's in Argolea with him. But his name is really Cerek. They're our way in. They'll know what to do with the key and how to keep it safe from Zeus. That's why I came here, to the half-breed colony, because I thought maybe there would be a way to signal the Argonauts from here. They allied with the half-breeds for many years before that colony was destroyed."

Erebus knew all about the Argonauts. Do-gooders Hades—and Zeus—had bitched about in his presence on more than one occasion. "I know how to signal them."

"You do?"

The excitement in her voice didn't thrill him. He didn't want her around any so-called heroes who might try to take her away from him, but he knew in the center of his gut that they weren't getting back to any sort of seduction until they got rid of this medallion. "Yes, but I'm not about to call them unless you agree to one thing."

Unease filled her blue eyes. "And what's that one thing?"

He leaned close to her lips and breathed hot over her mouth. "That you promise to stop fucking running from me. I am not the one you have to fear. I'm the one who's going to save you."

* * * *

"I'm the one who's going to save you..."

Erebus's words in that damp forest echoed in her head as they crossed the portal into Argolea. She didn't need him to save her. Didn't need anyone to save her. She'd been on her own long enough to know how to save herself.

And yet, something inside her recognized that he *wanted* to be the one to save her. Which was a totally new experience for her and left her completely uneasy.

No one had ever cared enough to want to save her...no one but her parents. Sure, the half-breeds had kept her hidden and safe from Zeus's Sirens for eighty years, but not because they'd cared for *her*. They'd done that simply because they didn't want Zeus to have the key to Argolea, and quite possibly because they'd been afraid she might reveal their location and put them all in danger if they didn't protect her. She'd had to beg and plead her case to finally get them to agree to let her leave the confines of the colony, and even then they hadn't been thrilled with the decision.

That unease turned to a burst of guilt when she thought of the Sirens finding the Russian half-breed colony and destroying it, but at least she knew that hadn't been her fault. She'd never told the Sirens a word about the half-breeds' location. Now that she had her memory back, she was sure of it.

Erebus released her hand as their feet hit solid ground in the protected realm of the ancient heroes. Getting to Argolea had been a heck of a lot easier than she'd thought. Erebus, being a minor god, knew more about the key than she'd assumed. He'd flashed them to a mountaintop in Northern Greece and led her to a cave that looked as ordinary as any other she'd ever seen. He'd explained that the cave was actually the tomb of Heracles, and just inside there had been a small circular indentation that was the exact size of the medallion she'd stolen from Zeus. Anyone who didn't know what it was for would have easily overlooked it, but when Erebus slid the medallion into the slot, a flash of light erupted around them and the portal to Argolea opened.

Four guards dressed in armor and carrying long spears rushed toward the raised dais where they appeared. Behind them, the portal lights slowly faded until there was only an ancient stone arch above them.

Sera stiffened, but Erebus slipped the medallion into his pocket and immediately stepped in front of her, shielding her as he held up his hands in a nonthreatening way. "Careful, boys. Pretty sure you don't want to do that."

The guards' eyes flew wide. They clearly recognized he was a god, even if they didn't know which one. As a unit, they crouched down in fighter stances, their spears held out menacingly in front of them, and shouted to each other with rapid words Sera didn't catch. Another guard, one who must have heard the commotion, came running from another room, saw Sera and Erebus on the dais surrounded by spears, and sprinted toward a different archway flanked by columns.

"I don't think we're as welcome here as you thought we'd be," Erebus muttered under his breath.

"They're not used to people just appearing through the portal unannounced." Pressing a hand against his forearm, she stepped around him.

"Sera—"

"We're not here to cause any harm," Sera said to the guards, ignoring Erebus's warning. He might think he needed to save her, but he was the threat to these people, not her, and this time she was the one who was going to do the saving. "I'm a friend to your princess. Princess Elysia."

The guards exchanged confused glances, and Sera knew she had to get them to understand if they were going to believe her. "We trained together on Olympus."

The guards shouted again and shoved their spears forward. Sera's adrenaline shot up as they jerked toward her, and she yelped and stumbled back into Erebus.

His arms closed around her as he pulled her against him and moved back three steps. "Not a great idea to mention Olympus," he hissed in her ear.

He was right. She hadn't thought that one through. Her mind spun with options. She didn't want to take the key back to the human realm, where Zeus could possibly find them, but she didn't see another option at this point. Living was better than being skewered two steps into this realm. "Can you use the medallion to open the portal again so we can get out of here?"

"I'm not sure." He let go of her with one arm and reached for the medallion in his pocket. "I don't know how it works on this side. If I can't, we might have to make a run for i—"

"Holy Hera," a voice exclaimed from across the room. A voice Sera vaguely recognized.

Footsteps echoed, and Sera looked toward the arched doorway, where a very familiar face peered up at them.

"Damon," Erebus said in surprise, seeing the muscular blond male as well.

For the first time since they'd stepped into this realm, Sera breathed easier. "No, not Damon. Not anymore. He's Cerek." Her gaze dropped to his marked forearms, visible where his long-sleeved gray T-shirt was pushed up to his elbows, the ancient Greek text that identified him as one of the chosen warriors of the great heroes visible in this realm.

Cerek moved into the middle of the room, his eyes filled with confusion and disbelief. "Erebus? Is that you? Why—? When—? How the heck did you get—"

A horde of footfalls filled the room, and Sera glanced from Cerek to the other massive males rushing up behind him, each sporting the same holy shit expressions and the very same markings that identified them as Argonauts.

"Yeah, it's me," Erebus said, releasing Sera and moving up to her side. "And I'm not here to cause any trouble, so you can tell your guards to relax."

"Stand down," Cerek said to the guards. "The Argonauts will handle this."

The guards looked less than thrilled, but they did as Cerek

commanded and cautiously moved back to their posts, though Sera noticed their attention never left Erebus and they watched every single movement he made.

The Argonauts fanned out around Cerek, murmuring words to each other Sera couldn't hear. Still clearly in shock, Cerek climbed the steps of the dais until he stood in front of them. "I don't understand what you're doing here. Or how the heck you even got here."

"It's a long story." Erebus reached for Sera's hand and glanced down at her at his side. "You remember Sera, don't you? She was in the same training class as Elysia."

Cerek's gaze slid Sera's way for the first time, and recognition flared in his brown eyes, but they were still laced with a helluva lot of confusion. "Yeah," he said slowly, glancing back to Erebus. "Though I'm not quite sure what you're doing here with a Siren."

Sera's back went up. "I'm not—"

"She's not a threat either," Erebus said, cutting her off as he squeezed her hand, telling her without words to let him handle it.

She closed her mouth and let him take the lead, but frustration surged inside her that he didn't think she was capable enough to deal with an Argonaut. As sweet as it was that he thought she needed him to save her—which was still not exactly something she'd ever expected from him—she didn't like being brushed aside as if she were fragile and incapable.

"But she is the reason we're here," Erebus went on, clearly oblivious to what was going on in her head. "And when you hear what she did for you and your realm and everyone in the human world as well, I think you're going to be pretty damn impressed. Just as I was."

Cerek looked down at her, expectantly awaiting an explanation, and from the corner of her eye she spotted Erebus gazing down at her as well. But she couldn't think of any words to fill the awkward silence because all she could focus on were Erebus's last words.

"Well then," Cerek finally said, sensing she wasn't going to speak. "I can't wait to hear what you did. I'm sure Elysia would like to hear it as well. She's back at the castle."

The Argonaut was still talking. Sera could hear him speaking over his shoulder to the Argonauts and introducing them to Erebus, but she didn't catch his words. She was too hung up on what Erebus had said.

He'd been impressed? By her? By what she'd done for this realm and the human world? He hadn't seemed impressed in that forest. He hadn't seemed anything but ticked she'd left his bed, then frustrated he'd been dragged into this mess. The god of darkness was all about seduction and control and domination when he wasn't in Zeus's presence, so his being impressed by anything other than sex when he was with her seemed completely out of character.

Somehow she found the strength to glance up at him. Voices continued to echo around her, but she didn't hear them. And when her eyes met his, she didn't see irritation or darkness or even a hint of that domination—sexual or otherwise—in his dark eyes. She saw awe.

An awe that told her he hadn't lied when he'd said he felt a connection between them. An awe that completely rocked the ground right out from under her feet.

CHAPTER EIGHT

After two days in the protected realm of the heroes, Erebus could see why Zeus was so hot to get his ass here.

It wasn't Utopia, at least not the kind written about in fantasy novels. The country had its fair share of problems, which included political strife and class delineations, along with a little bigotry and misogyny thrown in—mostly spurred on by the aging male Council members who technically advised the monarchy but who Erebus had learned were secretly scheming to overthrow their queen.

But if a person could look past all that? Yeah. Erebus could see exactly what was so special about this place. Soaring mountains, a vast ocean, an ancient city with massive marble buildings and spires that reached to the sky. Not to mention the people. Everyone he'd come in contact with since arriving in this realm had been real. Not the fake, ass-kissing opportunists who lurked around every corner on Olympus. Sure, some of them weren't thrilled he was here—like the Council members and a few of the city's inhabitants who'd seen his size and stature and immediately assumed he was evil. But the others—like the queen and the leader of the Argonauts and Cerek's mate Elysia, and hell, everyone in the damn castle—had welcomed him with open arms once they realized just what he and Sera had brought them.

His gaze drifted to Sera walking twenty yards ahead of him in the trees as they headed toward the Kyrenia settlement far outside the walls of the capital city of Tiyrns. He watched as Sera glanced toward Elysia at her side, smiled at something the female said, then linked her arm with Elysia's and lifted her face toward the sunshine.

Next to Erebus, Cerek droned on about the Misos ruins where Erebus had caught up with Sera, but Erebus barely listened. He'd barely been listening for the last hour as Cerek and Elysia had shown them around Tiyrns and the major points of interest in the realm. His focus was locked solidly on Sera and the twinkle in her eye as she laughed at something Elysia said. At the way she smiled. At how relaxed she seemed now in this realm where Zeus couldn't follow them.

Gods, she was stunning, her blonde hair picking up the light filtering through the trees in a way that made it almost sparkle. The way her pale skin glowed in the sunlight. The way her lips were so plump and perfect and soft he ached to kiss them and lick them and devour them as he'd devoured her last night.

Tingles rushed from his chest to his belly, and memories lit off in his mind—meeting with the Argonauts and the queen to discuss the key he and Sera had brought them. Being shocked not only at the way they'd all accepted him, but also offered him a place to stay. Elysia taking them to a suite in the castle that night, and the way Sera had launched herself into his arms as soon as the outer door closed and they were finally alone.

Oh yeah, last night she'd smiled. Except then her smile had been laced with heat and need and a passion only he could sate. He was definitely planning a repeat performance as soon as they were alone again, but tonight he wanted more. Tonight he wanted to make sure she knew that she was his and that no matter what the queen decided to do with the key, she would still be his.

"After Hades joined forces with Zagreus and they attacked the Misos colony," Cerek said as they emerged from the trees and crossed into a field with knee-high, undulating wheat, "the colonists were transferred here." He pointed across the vast field toward a city wall made of stone and wood. "That's Kyrenia. It used to be a witch settlement, but now it's home to witches, Misos, and any others looking for life outside Tiyrns."

There were no marble spires. No towering white columns. No castle gleaming in the sunlight, but Erebus figured that was the point. Not everyone wanted to live in a giant city. Hell, not even him. Fancy wasn't his style. That was part of the reason he'd enjoyed the times Zeus loaned him to the Sirens and he could get out of the stuffy temples on Olympus. As nice as the Argolean queen's castle was in Tiyrns, someplace like Kyrenia was a lot more his style.

"Are there other villages in the realm?" he asked, wondering where Sera would prefer to live. She'd pretty much been a refugee her whole life. He had a hard time envisioning her settled in Tiyrns for long.

"Yes." Cerek swiped at a stalk of wheat and plucked it from the ground. "Smaller ones in the mountains. Kyrenia is the closest to the capital, and the most aligned with the monarchy. The queen is committed to protecting it from Council interference."

Ah yes, the infamous Council of Elders. Those old, bigoted men who wanted this realm to revert back to its patriarchal ways as it had been before their exalted King Leonidas had passed and his headstrong daughter Isadora assumed the crown and started making changes that promoted equality. How dare she?

"How many live here?"

"Thousands," Cerek said. "The population grows every day."

That was a lot of people fleeing from the confines of the Council. "And what kind of protection does the monarchy provide them so the Council doesn't exert authority?"

"Not a lot," Elysia answered from ahead. She and Sera had both stopped and stood looking back at them as they approached. "The monarchy doesn't need to provide protection because they have Nick."

Erebus's belly warmed all over again as his gaze locked with Sera's and he saw the spark of hunger in her eyes. A hunger he couldn't wait to feed.

"And who is Nick?" he asked, unable to look away from her brilliant blue eyes.

"A god." At Sera's side, Elysia smirked. "One stronger than you."

Erebus's feet stilled as they reached the females, and he finally tore his gaze from Sera and looked toward Cerek for confirmation. "Another god? In this realm?"

Cerek nodded and slung an arm over Elysia's shoulder. "Krónos's bastard son. He's the half-breed leader, and he and his mate Cynna manage the settlement. He's also as strong as Zeus and Poseidon and Hades, and we've got him on our side."

"With you," Elysia said, "we now have three gods on our side."

The "*we*" in the princess's statement hit him hard. Right in the center of his chest. He'd never been part of any "we." Even though he served the ruling gods, he'd never aligned himself with them. Serving wasn't his choice; it was his duty.

The thought spun in his head as he glanced from Elysia back to Cerek. "Sorry, did she say three?"

"We also have Prometheus," Cerek supplied, "though he's kind of a recluse and doesn't show his face all that often. He and Circe have a place up in the mountains. He tends to keep to himself, but he's been known to help out now and then when we need him."

Holy shit. A Titan and one of the most powerful witches in the cosmos were also both hiding in this realm. Erebus remembered vividly how pissed Zeus had been when Prometheus had broken free of his chains and the temper tantrum that had followed when Prometheus had then broken Circe out of her prison high on Mt. Olympus. He just hadn't realized they'd both come here, to Argolea.

"See," Sera said softly at his side, sliding her arm around his and leaning all her sultry heat against him. "You're not the only immortal being who finally saw the light and decided to side with the good guys."

Erebus's heart pounded hard as his gaze dropped to the nymph at his side. Was that what he'd done? Betrayed the ruling gods and declared himself a rebel like the Argonauts? Sided with the enemy?

It was, he realized as his pulse beat faster. By coming here and not delivering Sera back to Zeus, he was basically saying "fuck you" to the gods and making himself a target to be hunted for all eternity.

Sera, Elysia, and Cerek continued to chat around him but he couldn't focus on their words. All he could focus on was the fact that staying in this realm wasn't an option. Yes, he was immortal, but even immortal beings could be punished for disobeying orders. He'd served Hades in the Underworld for thousands of years. He knew what kind of penance awaited him if Zeus decided to turn him over to the god-king of the Underworld as a prisoner. But that wasn't his biggest fear. His biggest fear was suffering the same fate as the other primordial deities who'd been banished from this world when the Titans had come into power. To be stripped of his human form and cast into nothingness. To remain conscious of all that happened around him but forever be unable to react, to breathe, to live.

That wasn't something he was willing to risk. He liked living too damn much.

His hands grew damp. He needed to get the hell out of this realm.

To return to Olympus before anyone realized what he'd done. He still had time to fix this. He could tell Zeus he hadn't found Sera. He could say he'd heard she'd crossed into Argolea before he'd been able to locate her. Now that the key was safe with the queen, Zeus couldn't follow Sera here. He couldn't take the key. Sera was safe. The key was safe. There was no reason not to return to his duty.

And yet...

His gaze strayed to Sera at his side. She smiled at something Elysia said, then glanced up at him. And as their eyes met and held and his pulse slowly regulated, his chest filled with a warmth that burned everything else to ashes in his mind, and he realized... He didn't want to go back to Olympus.

He didn't want to leave her. For the first time in his long-ass life, he had something of his very own. Something not linked to duty and service and what the gods wanted, but something pure and special and his. He didn't want to let that go. He didn't want to walk away from her and forget the way he felt right now. He wanted this. He wanted her. He wanted a chance to finally—and maybe for the first time ever—truly *live*.

Sera's brow slowly wrinkled, and a worried look crept into her eyes. "Are you all right?"

His heart beat strong, steady, thumping pulses against his ribs. But they didn't hurt. They felt good. Spreading heat and life through his veins to give him strength. A strength that told him this decision—choosing *her*—was the right one.

"Yeah." Unable to stop himself, he slid a hand under all that gorgeous hair of hers, grazed her nape with his fingertips, and tugged her mouth toward his. "Yeah, *agápi*. I'm perfect."

Her lips were soft and sweet where they brushed his, but not nearly enough. And as she slid her arms around his waist and kissed him back, all he could think about was getting her back into that suite where they could be alone, where he could pin her to the mattress and make her his all over again.

"*Skata*," Cerek said at his side. "Uh, guys? We've got a problem."

Irritated by the interruption, Erebus lifted his head to tell the Argonaut to mind his own business but froze when he spotted the four females standing on the edge of the forest fifty yards away.

All four were decked out in fighting gear. All four looked like something straight off the pages of a *Victoria's Secret* magazine. And all four were staring at him kissing Sera across the field with wide, shocked eyes.

Those weren't trainees. Those were the real deal.

Sirens.

In Argolea.

Fuck.

Sera glanced over her shoulder and gasped. At Erebus's side, the unmistakable *shiiiing* of Cerek's blade being drawn echoed in the air.

"Get back to the castle," Cerek said, pushing past Elysia. "Tell the queen they're here."

"How the hell did they get here?" Erebus asked, pushing Sera to his back. His adrenaline surged as he watched the Sirens bolt back into the trees.

"Probably through the moving portals." Cerek pulled two more blades from his hips, these daggers not nearly as long as the parazonium he'd unsheathed moments before—the ancient Greek blade all Argonauts carried—but big enough to do some major damage. He handed the daggers to Erebus. "They're manned by the witches. While this realm is blocked to the Olympians, it's not to Zeus's warriors. The Sirens monitor where the moving portals open and close in the human realm and have jumped through before."

Grasping Elysia at the arm, Cerek pressed a hard kiss to his mate's lips. "Go. Get back to the castle. Tell the queen. We can't let them reach the portal. If they do, Zeus will know Erebus and Sera are here."

A worried look passed over Elysia's face, but she whispered, "I will." Cerek glanced at Erebus and nodded toward the trees, then took off at a run.

Elysia reached for Sera's hand. "Come on."

Erebus was just about to follow Cerek when Sera said, "No. I can fight." She struggled out of Elysia's grip and looked up at him. "You need me. We can't let even one of them make it through the portal."

He did need her. He needed her to live. Now that he'd decided he was staying here with her, he didn't want her in any situation where she could get hurt. But he was smart enough to know if he tried to convince her of that right now, they'd never catch up with those Sirens before it was too late.

His pulse raced with both fear and worry as he grasped her at the waist and pulled her tight against him. And when his lips met hers in a fierce kiss, he knew if he lost her now, just when he'd finally found her, it would ruin him for all eternity.

He drew back and met her gaze, hoping she saw with her eyes what he couldn't say in his words. "Stay with us and don't do anything stupid. I didn't betray the gods so I could be stuck here in this realm alone."

She took one of the daggers from his hand and grinned. "Not a chance, *omorfos*. And don't worry. I'm a lot better with a blade than I was when you were my trainer."

She slipped out of his arm and ran after Cerek.

Holy hell. He sure the hell hoped so because if Zeus found out they'd brought the key to Argolea, he'd unleash everything he could on this realm even if he couldn't cross into it himself.

* * * *

"There were four," Cerek said to the queen as he stood in the middle of her office in the castle of Tiyrns. "We took all four down before they reached the portal, but odds are good more will be coming when Zeus realizes these four aren't returning."

From her spot where she stood leaning against the wall with her arms crossed, Sera glanced from face to face at the people in the room. After stopping the Sirens from crossing the portal, she, Erebus, and Cerek had returned to the castle to update the queen and the Argonauts. She was sweaty and dirty from the fight, but her blood was still up, and more than anything she was still vibrating from the reality she'd played a part in killing four of Zeus's Sirens. Sirens who'd once been her trainers even if they'd never been her friends.

At her side, Erebus leaned toward her ear and whispered, "Are you okay?"

She shifted her feet and in a low voice answered, "Yeah," but she didn't look at him. Because she wasn't okay. Not really.

It was true—those Sirens had invaded this realm and instigated that fight, and from the first it had been clear that they were not going to allow anyone to take them prisoner. But still, knowing there'd been no other choice and living with the fallout from that choice were two completely different things.

A heavy weight pressed down on her chest. There was absolutely no going back to Olympus for her now. No going back to the Sirens. But she'd already accepted that the second she'd stolen the key to Argolea. Now all she could do was hope that no one in this realm was hurt because of what she'd done.

The queen pursed her lips. "The Sirens slaughtered the inhabitants of the witch's tent city when they kidnapped Elysia eighteen months ago. Brute force was warranted here to prevent another massacre. If Zeus cries foul, we make that clear. He doesn't know we have the key; therefore we had just cause to protect our realm. You did the right thing, Cerek." She looked toward the leader of the Argonauts. "What are our options at this point, Theron?"

Theron crossed his meaty arms across his broad chest. "Just cause or not, Zeus will retaliate. He already thinks Sera and the key are here."

"Zeus will send more Sirens," the tall Argonaut at the queen's side said, the one Sera was pretty sure was Elysia's father. "He's convinced Prometheus hid the water element in Argolea, and he wants the key so he can get into our realm, find the last element, and complete the Orb of Krónos. He won't stop until he has the key, which means no one here is safe until that key is destroyed."

"It always comes back to those damn elements," the queen said on a sigh.

Sera knew from Elysia that no one—not even Prometheus—was sure where the water element had landed after he'd scattered the four basic elements across the realms. Water was the most fluid of all the elements, and over the thousands of years since Prometheus's imprisonment for not choosing Zeus's side against the Olympians' war with the Titans, the water element had moved and morphed and changed location. It could be here in Argolea, but it could just as easily be hiding in plain sight in the human realm.

Regardless, if Zeus suspected the key was in Argolea, he would send as many Sirens as it took to get it back. And once he had it, he would sweep into this realm and destroy everything until he either found that element or annihilated the realm, exactly as he'd done to Atlantis.

Warmth radiated against Sera's lower back, interrupting her thoughts. Warmth and a soft, kneading pressure where Erebus rubbed his fingers gently along her spine.

For a moment, while the queen and the Argonauts discussed the situation, she zoned out and focused on that one spot. On how good his hand felt, how relaxing his touch was, and just how much she liked that he was here now—even on what had turned out to be a pretty shitty day.

His spicy scent surrounded her, and without even thinking, she leaned her head against his strong chest and just let his touch and scent and comforting presence calm her. Against the top of her head, she felt his lips press a kiss to her hair, and then he shifted her in front of him so she could lean back against his chest and those big, tempting hands were massaging the stress from her shoulders.

Oh, heavens... She could get so used to this. Her eyes slid closed, and she drew one deep breath, followed by another. And as the heat of his body seeped into her back and warmed the last cold spaces inside her, all kinds of visions about how he could relax her in their room filled her mind, making her anxious to get him alone.

When he pulled her back against him, she wiggled her ass against his lap, feeling his erection spring to life. She bit her lip to hold back a groan.

"Naughty little nymph," Erebus whispered near her ear. "I think they've got this handled on their own. Why don't we go back to our room and get cleaned up? Then I can handle you."

A wide smile spread across her lips, and heat exploded in her veins. She glanced over her shoulder at him and lifted her brow. "I'm up for that."

"No, *agápi*." He flexed his hips, and she felt his impressive arousal against her backside. "I'm the one who's going to be up."

Yes, yes, yes... Frantic to feel just that and more, she reached for his hand and pulled him with her as she stepped away from the wall.

"I'm telling you," the long-haired Argonaut who always wore the gloves said to the queen as Sera and Erebus drew closer to the group on their way toward the door and utter bliss. "That's the only way. In Phlegethon."

Erebus's hand slipped free of Sera's, and when she turned, she realized he'd stopped near the group. A perplexed expression crossed his face as he looked at the long-haired Argonaut. "What about Phlegethon?"

Sera frowned at the interruption and tried to pull him back to her, but he was like solid stone and wouldn't move.

The queen glanced up at him, looking absolutely tiny surrounded by the Argonauts and a god. "The key was forged by Hephaestus and is charmed by the powers of Olympus. The only way to make sure no one can ever use it again is to destroy it. And the only way to do that is to cast it into the river of fire in the Underworld. Phlegethon is the only heat strong enough to melt Hephaestus's weaponry."

Erebus looked from the queen to each of the Argonauts. "How do you know this?"

She nodded toward the long-haired Argonaut. "Because of Titus."

When Erebus's confused gaze swung Titus's way, Titus said, "I'm a descendant of Odysseus."

The Argonaut Sera had heard the others call Orpheus crossed his arms over his chest with a frown and leaned back against the queen's desk. "Don't question it, Erebus. Titus's forefather blessed him with enhanced knowledge about tons of ancient shit. He's right on this. He's always right. And it's getting really fucking irritating."

Titus cast Orpheus a smug grin but it faded when he glanced back at the group. "Someone has to take the key into the Underworld and toss it in Phlegethon." He looked back at Orpheus and lifted his brows. "O? You're the only one of us who's been there—besides Gryphon, of course, and I think it's pretty safe to say he's not volunteering to go back there anytime soon."

Orpheus huffed. "So because I was there once I get the job? Screw you, Rapunzel."

Titus chuckled.

The queen brushed her blonde hair back from her face and rubbed her forehead, looking like she had a massive headache. "Before we start talking about who should take the key into the Underworld, let's talk about how we even get there. Orpheus, you said the cave you and Skyla used to access the Underworld was destroyed when you left there with Gryphon. Who else knows how to get there?"

"Prometheus," Theron answered.

"Yes, but there's no guarantee we can even find Prometheus right now," the queen said with a frown. "He and Circe have been exploring the Aegis Mountains, searching for any sign of the water element. He could be on the other side of Argolea right now."

"Even Natasa isn't sure where he is at the moment," Titus said.

Sera was still trying to piece together who was related to whom in this realm, but she remembered Elysia telling her that Titus's mate Natasa was Prometheus's daughter. She wasn't sure how that was possible, since Prometheus had only been freed from Zeus's chains a handful of years ago and Natasa was older than that, but at the moment she was too focused on the key and this conversation to try to figure it out.

"There is someone right here who would know," Orpheus said.

All eyes turned toward Erebus.

Of course. Erebus. Sera's brow lifted as she looked up at him.

But instead of the gentle, helpful friend he'd been to Cerek and the others since they'd arrived in this realm, his stiff posture, hard jaw, and narrowed gaze skipping from face to face told her he wasn't feeling the least bit friendly at the moment.

"I brought you the key," Erebus said in a low voice.

"*We* brought you the key," Sera corrected, confused about the reason he looked ready to pound someone into the floor.

Erebus glanced down at her and nodded, then glared back at the group. "We brought you the key. What you do with it from here is up to you. I'm not getting involved with that."

Surprise shot through Sera. He wasn't here to help them? She thought that was *exactly* why he was here. It sure as hell was the reason she was here.

"No one's asking you to take it to the Underworld," the queen said.

"Though actually..." the leader of the Argonauts started.

"Actually, that's not a bad idea," Orpheus finished for Theron, uncrossing his arms and focusing on Erebus. "It's the perfect way to get around the prophecy."

"What prophecy?" Sera asked, her gaze swinging to Orpheus.

"The one that says he who destroys the key will be trapped in the Underworld for all eternity." Titus rested his gloved hands on his hips and looked at her. "That's why your ancient queen in Atlantis didn't just destroy the damn thing as soon as Zeus gave it to her. It's why none of your queens did. Because in order to destroy it, someone has to offer up a sacrifice. In this case, that sacrifice is being stuck in the Underworld after you do the deed."

Erebus's whole body stiffened. And, okay, yeah, if that was the case, Sera could see why he wouldn't be thrilled to help them with this.

"But Erebus isn't mortal," Orpheus pointed out. "He wouldn't get stuck there."

Oh....true. Sera's brow lifted once more.

"According to who?" Titus tossed back. "The prophecy says nothing regarding mortality."

"Maybe not," Orpheus countered. "But he already served Hades in the Underworld. He wouldn't be tortured there like any of us. And I'm betting he wouldn't even be stuck there. I guarantee Zeus charmed that thing with some special back door loophole which prevents it from impacting an immortal. We all know how Zeus loves back doors."

That was true as well. Sera was all too aware of how much the gods loved fucking with mortals but were reluctant to do anything to harm each other.

"Titus?" the queen asked.

Titus rubbed a hand across his jaw and considered for a moment. "It's possible. It's highly likely, actually. Zeus wouldn't risk bringing harm to an immortal because doing so could cause the other gods to join forces and rise up against him. He definitely doesn't want a repeat of the Titanomachy with him on the losing side. For once, O's logic is sound." When Orpheus frowned and flipped him the bird, Titus grinned, then looked back at the queen and added, "Though I can't confirm for sure. That part isn't in any of my enhanced knowledge. But if it's true then, yeah. Erebus would be the logical choice. Especially since he can cloak himself in darkness to slip into the Underworld unnoticed. If Prometheus or even Nick were to try to destroy the key, Hades would spot them immediately."

The queen looked toward Erebus with an expectant expression. And slowly, one by one, each of the Argonauts in the room did as well. "I know it's a lot to ask," the queen said. "But you're the only one who can do this without repercussions."

Sera's gaze followed, and hope gathered in her belly. But it shattered like a glass against the floor when she saw the slice of steel that was his jaw beneath his skin. The one that told her loud and clear he wasn't thrilled to be the center of attention. And that he had no intention of doing anything to help those in this realm. Her included.

"I'm not going to the Underworld," Erebus said in a low voice.

"Not for you or anyone."

He left the room without another word.

The Argonauts quietly whispered about what was up with him and why he wasn't willing to help them when he'd so easily turned his back on Zeus, but Sera barely listened. All she could focus on was the reality swirling like a vortex in her head.

He hadn't come here to help anyone but himself. As soon as he'd held the medallion in his hand, he'd known what it was. He'd known what it protected from the gods. And he'd seen his way out. A way to hide from Zeus and do whatever—and whomever—he wanted out from under the control of the gods.

She shouldn't be surprised. He was, after all, the personification of darkness. And darkness, as everyone knew, was immoral and selfish and absent of any kind of light that illuminated the soul.

CHAPTER NINE

The door crashed against the wall as Erebus shoved it open and stalked into the suite he'd shared with Sera last night, trying like hell to calm the roaring vibration still buzzing inside him.

Of course they'd all assume he was the perfect one to sacrifice eternity for them. He was the god of darkness. He probably liked the Underworld, right?

They could all piss off as far as he was concerned.

The door to the suite slammed shut, and footsteps sounded across the floor before coming to a stop at Erebus's back. He didn't need to look to see that Sera had followed him. He could smell her lemony scent and all but feel her own anger seeping from her.

The vibrations slowly lessened. Knowing she was just as outraged as him eased his rage.

"When were you going to tell me your plan?" she said at his back.

Confused, not just by the question but by the bite in her voice, he turned to look at her.

But her eyes weren't the compassionate eyes he'd hoped for. These were like blue ice chips, cold and staring at him as if she were looking at a stranger.

"Excuse me?"

"You heard me. You never cared about helping these people. You only came here with me because you saw it as an opportunity to get away from Zeus. To take a break from your duties and fuck me for a while. But now that you know the Argoleans are going to destroy the key, that changes things, doesn't it? Are you planning to take it back to Zeus tonight?"

His eyes widened in disbelief. "*What?*"

"You heard me." Fire flared in her eyes but it didn't warm that icy chill brewing in their cold blue depths. "I can't believe I was so stupid when it came to you. You duped me once before, and you're doing it again right now."

He couldn't believe she thought so little of him. He couldn't believe that after everything he'd done for her, she could even ask such a question.

He reacted before he could stop himself. Crossing the distance between them in two strides, he grasped her by the arm. "You're right, nymph. That's *exactly* why I came here. I serve Zeus. I must be the same selfish asshole he is, right? Why else would I bother?"

Her chest rose and fell with her heavy breaths, and a whisper of doubt crept into her eyes. "Let go of my arm."

Something dark burned inside him. Something dangerous he knew he needed to stop but couldn't seem to tamp down.

"Why?" He moved a step closer, using his size to tower over her. "You knew why I came here. You said it yourself. I came here to fuck you. And you didn't put up any sort of fight to stop me. In fact, ten minutes ago, if you'd been wearing a skirt, you'd have let me fuck you right there in that office in front of the Argonauts. So why don't I do that one last time before I leave? I want it. I know you want it too; otherwise you wouldn't be here."

Her eyes widened as he pressed her up against the wall. She lifted her hands to his biceps and pushed, but she wasn't strong enough to budge him. "If you even think about raping me—"

"Rape you? Oh, *oraios*. In sixty seconds you'll be begging for me to fuck you blind."

"In your dreams."

Anger swelled inside him. Anger and a burning desire to make her pay. "Since I'm going back to Zeus, dreams are the only thing I'll have left of you, so I might as well get as much as I can right now."

He lowered his face to the hollow in her neck and drew in a deep whiff of her scent. Lemon and vanilla and something that made him fucking high. "Gods, you smell good." He bit down on the tender flesh—not gently, not hard—and she whimpered, which was exactly what he wanted. "Taste even better."

Her fingers dug into his biceps, but he ignored the pain and kicked her legs apart so he could press himself against her heat. Then he licked the spot he'd just bitten and sucked until her cry of protest turned into a groan of desire.

The sound supercharged his blood and made the darkness inside rush right to the surface of his control. She thought he would rape her? She thought he'd still side with Zeus? He'd been sure she was the one person in the cosmos who understood him, but now he knew the truth. She was just like the gods, using him for her own selfish needs, then discarding him when she had what she wanted, casting him aside as if he were nothing.

He rocked against her and lifted one hand to squeeze the soft mass of her breast. "Tell me you don't want this, *agápi*."

She swallowed hard, pushed against his arms again, but not with the force of before, and against him he felt her muscles already relaxing. Felt her body giving in to the heat of his and melting beneath him. "I-I don't."

"You lie." He lifted his head and closed his mouth over hers. Her fingers fisted in his T-shirt, and she grunted as his tongue swept into her mouth, demanding and unforgiving. But she didn't try to push him away, and as he stroked her tongue and pressed his hard body into hers against the wall, she tugged on his shirt and pulled him closer.

That's it. Just a little more...

He slid one hand over her side and across her lower back, then down to squeeze the soft right globe of her ass. She moaned into his mouth and lifted her leg, hooking it around his hip so his cock could press against her clit. Her hands swept up to his face, then she tipped her head and kissed him deeper, rocking her hot little body against his until he was hard and achy and ready to explode. Until he knew he had her right where he wanted her.

He trailed a line of hot, wet kisses from the corner of her mouth to her jaw and then to the sensitive skin behind her ear. "Tell me you want me, Sera."

"Oh gods." She grasped his face again, pulled his mouth back to hers, and kissed him.

"Tell me," he breathed against her lips, squeezing her ass with every press of his groin against hers. "Tell me and I'll give you exactly what you deserve."

"Erebus." She drew back from his mouth, nipped his bottom lip, swept her tongue over the spot and suckled until he groaned. "Yes, I want you. Take me."

Primal need pumped hot inside him, but he wasn't about to let it free. Not with her. Not ever again.

He jerked back from her mouth, let go of her with his hands, and moved away so cool air rushed across her overheated body. "Not even sixty seconds. You're a predictable little nymphomaniac. I should have seen how manipulative you really were from the start. Zeus did pick you himself, after all."

He moved for the door. At his back he heard her gasp of shock and disbelief, but he ignored it, wanting only to get as far from her as possible. To get out of this castle and out of this fucking realm before all that darkness inside him burst free and made him do something he knew he'd regret later.

Inches from the entry hall of the suite, his foot hooked something hard, and his weight went out from under him. He hit the carpet with a grunt. Before he could process what he'd tripped over, strong hands flipped him to his back, and the sexy little nymph who'd tormented his body and consumed his thoughts these last few days climbed over him.

She slapped her hands against the carpet near his head and glared down at him. "You're not leaving."

"The hell I'm not."

He shifted his hands to her waist and lifted his torso to shove her off him, but she dropped her weight onto his hips and wrapped her legs around his waist as he sat up, locking her in place against his hard, aching cock.

She leaned in to breathe hot against his ear. "You're not leaving because we're not done here." Her teeth sank into his lobe, then she traced her wicked tongue around the rim of his ear. "You said you were going to fuck me blind." Against his straining erection, she rocked her steamy sex until he saw stars. "Fuck me, Erebus. Fuck me, now."

The darkness inside him burst free. He didn't know what game she was playing but he was past the point of caring. Past the point of thinking. Past the point of stopping.

A growl echoed in the room, one he knew came from him as he pushed her to her back on the carpet, then drew away long enough to rip the pants from her legs. She gasped but didn't miss a beat, wrenching the shirt over her head and throwing it off to her side with jerky movements.

His blood roared in his ears as he flipped her to her belly. She grunted and pushed up on her hands and knees. Blonde hair spilled across her bare spine and tickled his frantic fingers as he unhooked the white lace bra and pushed it down her arms. She helped him by wriggling out of the garment, then groaned as he ripped the panties from her hips and the sound of tearing fabric filled the room.

With one hand, he unhooked the button at his waistband. With the other, he swept his fingers between her legs and across her hot, steaming flesh. Kicking her knees wider with his, he growled, "Is this what you want?"

She rocked back against his hand so his fingers swirled over her slick clit. "Oh yes... More."

He drew his fingers down, to her opening, then thrust up inside with two. "This?"

"*Yeeees...*" She dropped her head forward and moaned, then rocked her hips back, fucking his fingers with long, deep strokes. "Gods, that's good. But I want more. Give me more."

Fire roared inside him. Fire and a blazing need he couldn't ignore, one that shoved aside the darkness until the only thing he knew was this moment.

He yanked his fingers from her body, and flipped her to her back again. She grunted and reached for him as he reached inside his waistband to free his erection. "You want more? You want this?"

"Oh, yes..." She hooked her legs around his waist and lifted her hips, her hot, tight channel finding the tip of his cock until she sucked him in a fraction of an inch.

Every nerve ending in his body flared in that one spot. "Say it," he growled.

"I want your cock. I want you. Fuck me. Fuck me, Erebu—"

He claimed her mouth at the same time he slammed himself inside her. His name erupted on a scream that only shot his blood higher.

He drew out until she whimpered, then drove deep again, grunting at the way her sheath contracted around him as he kissed her.

"Is this what you wanted?" He breathed hot over her lips. Bracing one hand on the floor, he used the other to hold her head still while he shoved deep again and again, fucking her with hard, long strokes that made her whole body shudder.

"Yes, yes..." Her fingertips dug into his shoulders.

She was leaving bruises, he was sure, but he didn't care. All he could focus on was thrusting deeper, faster, proving to her that he wasn't at all what she thought.

"Don't stop," she rasped. "Gods, don't stop..."

He couldn't. He was too far gone.

Shifting his weight to his knees, he grasped both of her legs and shoved them forward, then drove even deeper. "Say you like fucking me," he growled.

Her eyes slid closed. "I do. Gods, I do."

A frenzy rose up in his mind. One that told him to prove to her she wasn't at all what she thought either. "Say you're a dirty nymph who likes to be fucked by the gods."

"No." She tossed her head from side to side and her channel grew impossibly tight around him. "Just by you. Only you. Ah, gods, Erebus. Don't stop. Please don't stop."

Electricity raced down his spine and gathered in his balls. He plunged into her harder, unable to do anything but what she demanded, hating that she was still manipulating him, even now. "Say it," he growled, his fingers tightening around her knees where he held her open to him. "Say you're a manipulative little slut who uses sex to get what she wants."

Her eyes shot open, and before he realized what she was doing, she jerked her legs from his hold, pushed her hands against the floor and shot forward so her legs were around his waist, her chest was plastered to his, and her arms were locked tight around his shoulders.

Her slick and tempting pussy clenched around his length as she lifted and lowered herself on his lap. "I'm not," she breathed against his lips as his hands settled at her hips. "I didn't. I only want you. I've only ever wanted you."

She pressed her mouth to his and kissed him, and as her tongue swept into his mouth and she groaned, he felt her climax claim her, and the feeling was so tight, so right, so seductive, it triggered his.

Grunting, he pushed her to the carpet and gave himself over to her kiss, to her body, to everything she was and the ecstasy she could give him.

When he was spent, when all he could do was twitch and groan, he pulled free of her slick core and pushed up on one hand to gaze down at her sexy, sated features covered in a thin layer of sweat.

His chest grew tight, so tight he knew it was way past time he left.

He braced his hands on the carpet and started to push up. Her legs hooked around his hips, preventing him from pulling free of her body, and then her hands were at his shoulders, pulling him back down to her.

"Uh uh." She tugged him back against all her tantalizing heat and stared up at him with eyes that were a soft, relaxed blue and lacked any of the anger he'd seen there before. "I said I'm not through with you, and I meant it."

His own anger had eased now that he'd released some stress, but he didn't want to do anything to trigger it again. "Sera." He reached up to pry her arms from his neck. "This has run its course."

She tightened her hold. "Not even close."

Frustrated, desperate now to leave, he frowned down at her. "I'm not going to stay here when—"

"I was wrong. I shouldn't have jumped to conclusions. I was just..." She bit her lip, looking sexy and nervous and innocent all at the same time. "I was scared, okay? I fell for you a year and a half ago during my training sessions. I fell hard, and when our sessions were over, you moved on to a new trainee as if I hadn't even existed. That hurt me."

A little of his frustration waned. He braced a hand on the floor near her head. "I didn't have a choice in that."

"I know, I just... It still hurt. And when I heard you in there with the Argonauts, I thought... Well, I thought you were getting ready to move on again. I lashed out because I'm weak."

He frowned. "You're spirited and frustrating and sexy as hell, but you're not weak."

One corner of her mouth curled.

He sighed, liking the way she fit against him way too much. Knowing it was going to be a major problem for him when he left here. "I wasn't saying no to them because I wanted to leave you. I said no because I have no interest in returning to the Underworld, even for just a visit. I spent thousands of years there doing shit work for Hades. As soon as I step in that realm he'll try to find a way to keep me, prophecy or no prophecy, whether I use my cloak of darkness or not. Life on Olympus serving Zeus wasn't a helluva lot better than it was serving Hades, but at least on Olympus I was away from all that misery and death. I can't go back there."

"I know. I'm sorry. I should have realized that. I wasn't thinking. Please forgive me."

He wanted to believe her, but he was still unsure what was truth. He only knew one truth he should have told her before. "For what it's worth, I had to put you behind me at the Siren training compound. I couldn't get emotionally involved with you then. It would have meant the end for both of us. But I didn't forget about you. I never forgot about you."

"You didn't even know who I was when you tackled me in the forest."

"I knew who you were as soon as I saw you. As soon as I touched you. How could I forget the one person in the world who ever made me feel alive?"

Her eyes went all soft and dreamy, and before he realized it he grew hard inside her once more.

"And what about now?" she asked, her words distracting him from how tight and wet she was around him. "We're not in danger anymore and you're free to make your own choices here in Argolea. Do you still want me? Because I want you. I wasn't lying when I said I'm yours. I want only to be yours, Erebus. Now and always."

His heart skipped a beat. But he was still worried. Especially if she would only ever see him as a servant to the gods. "That depends on your friends in the other room. The only thing they want me for is to sacrifice myself for some prophecy I know nothing about. They won't let me stay in this realm now that I've said no."

"Then we'll go somewhere else."

When he looked away, she tugged him down to her, so his chest was pressed up against her gorgeous breasts and her mouth was a breath away from his lips. And around his cock, she clenched her muscles until it was all he could do to keep giving in to the pleasure and thrusting hard and deep all over again.

"I don't care what they want, Erebus. I mean, yes, I want them to be safe. I don't want any other realm to suffer what Atlantis did, and I was willing to help them if I could, but not if it means losing you. They have the key. We brought it to them. Whatever they do with it now is up to them, not us. All I want is you. I want the future we couldn't have before." She clenched even tighter, drawing a groan from his throat. "I love you, Erebus."

His lungs felt as if they'd completely closed off. And for a moment, he didn't breathe. Just stared down into her soft blue eyes, trying to see the lie, the manipulation, the contrary truth she was keeping hidden. But he didn't see any of those things. He saw her. Her innocence when they'd first met on Olympus. He saw the fire inside her when she'd run from him at that half-breed colony. And he saw love. The kind of love he'd always hoped for but never thought was possible.

His mouth was dry as cotton when his lips parted, and the words stuck in his throat. "I..."

She pressed her lips against his. "Say you want the same. Say it, you dirty, dark, sexy god. Say you love me just as much. I know you do. I knew it the moment you pushed me up against the wall and I saw how much I'd hurt you." She kissed him softly again, lifted her hips and flexed around his aching cock. "I'm sorry. I'm so sorry for that. Stay with me. Stay and let me make it up to you. I need you. Not for your powers or what you can do. I need you simply because I love you and want you in my life."

Something in his chest warmed and swelled until it felt like he might crack open wide. Lifting his hands to her face, he drew back from her mouth and brushed the soft locks from her intoxicating eyes. "Oh, Sera. You're the only one who's ever said that to me."

"I'm the only one who's ever going to love you like this." She did that wicked rocking again that made him nearly see stars. "Promise you won't leave me."

He couldn't. Not anymore.

He captured her mouth with a searing kiss he felt everywhere, and when she groaned and kissed him back, the last of his doubt faded into the darkness.

He rolled to his back, tugging her on top of him. Brushing the hair back from her face, he drew his mouth back a fraction of an inch and said, "Since you asked so nicely, I'll stay. But only on one condition."

She grinned down at him. "Anything."

"Show me how much you love me, *agápi*. Make me believe it."

"I can do that." Her lips curled in a wicked smile, and she braced her hands on his chest and began to move. "I can happily spend the rest of my days doing that."

Oh, fuck yes...

She lowered and took his mouth, and as he kissed her back, he knew this time what she said was true. He also knew that he would easily be as happy letting her prove it to him for however long they were together.

He just hoped it was more than a few days. Because now that he'd betrayed Zeus and said no to the Argoleans, they'd soon have to leave this protected realm. And there weren't many places left in the world where he could hide from the Olympians and keep her safe.

CHAPTER TEN

Sera stretched and opened her eyes. The room was still dark, which meant morning hadn't hit yet. Snuggling back into her pillow, she closed her eyes and reached her foot back, searching for Erebus's heat behind her.

Her muscles were sore and exhausted from hours of pleasuring him, and she knew she needed a little longer to rest and recharge her batteries, but she was already thinking up ways to pleasure him all over again. And as soon as he curled up against her back again—the same way he had when he'd wrung the last orgasm from her body and finally let her drift to sleep—she knew she wouldn't be able to stop herself from doing just that.

Her foot passed over the cold sheet, and she moved it farther back, still searching for him. Rolling to her other side, she reached out her hand, but found nothing but cold sheets and an empty bed.

She lifted her head and peered around the dark and silent room. "Erebus?"

No answering voice called out to her. Nothing but silence met her ears.

A knock sounded at the suite's outer door, and she jumped. Pushing up to sitting, she captured the sheet at her breasts and held her breath as she listened, afraid she might have imagined the sound. Another knock echoed through the suite.

She exhaled and threw back the covers. It had to be him. He must have been hungry and gotten up to find something in the kitchen. They'd skipped dinner. Neither had wanted to venture out of their room. She wasn't sure if the outer door automatically locked when it closed, but she guessed it had and that he'd forgotten to take a key.

The knock sounded again.

"Hold on," she called, searching the floor for Erebus's T-shirt. She couldn't find it. Frowning, she grabbed her pajama bottoms and a cotton tank from the bottom dresser drawer and tugged both on as she moved into the living room.

Her stomach rumbled as she moved into the dark entryway. She hoped he was bringing back a feast because she was suddenly ravenous.

"I hope you brought enough to share," she said as she yanked the door open, "because I'm starv—"

Her words died as she looked into Elysia's brown eyes. "Lys, what are you doing here this late? Is everything okay?"

"No, everything's not okay." Dressed in her own pink cotton PJs, her hair pulled back in a messy tail, Elysia glanced past Sera and into the suite. "Is Erebus with you?"

Alarm bells sounded in Sera's mind. "No. I think he went down to the kitchen to get something to eat. Why? What's wrong?"

Elysia's jaw hardened. "What time did he leave?"

Those bells shrilled louder. "I don't know. I was asleep. Why? What's happened?"

Elysia reached for her hand. "A lot. You'd better come with me."

Elysia wouldn't say more than that the queen wanted to see Sera, and Sera's anxiety inched up the closer they drew to the queen's office.

What was going on? Were they kicking her and Erebus out of the realm right now? In the middle of the night? That didn't make sense, but neither did Elysia coming to her room at two a.m. acting cryptic and weird.

The queen's office was filled with more testosterone than Sera could handle. All the Argonauts turned to look at her as she entered, each one decked out not in pajamas like her and Elysia, but in thick leather pants, long-sleeved shirts, boots, and straps and gear she immediately recognized as warrior attire.

"There she is." The leader of the Argonauts stalked up to her and pinned her with a hard glare. "When was the last time you saw your god?"

"Erebus? I-I don't know." She looked from face to face, wondering what was going on. "A few hours ago, I guess. I was asleep when he left."

"So he was with you tonight?" the blond Argonaut to the leader's right asked, his silver eyes focused and expectant. "What time did you fall asleep?"

Why were they asking her these questions? She looked to Elysia at her side for help, suddenly feeling like a prisoner being interrogated.

Elysia patted her shoulder. "It's all right. Just answer them truthfully."

Truthfully...

She glanced back at the blond guardian, the one she was pretty sure was named Zander. "Eleven thirty, I guess. I don't know for sure though. Why? What's happened?"

"I'll tell you what's happened." The queen stepped out from behind the tall Argonaut—Demetrius—and wove through the sea of massive bodies before stopping in front of Sera. "Erebus is gone, and so is the key."

No.

Disbelief churned inside Sera. That couldn't be true. She wouldn't believe it. "He went to the kitchen to get food fo—"

"He's not in the kitchen," the queen said, interrupting her. "He's not anywhere in the castle. Maelea, Gryphon's mate, has the ability to sense energy shifts. We had her use her gift to scan outward from the castle, to see if he's hiding somewhere within the realm. Cerek said he was asking about Kyrenia and any settlements in the Aegis Mountains. But Maelea found no sign of him. He left Argolea, Sera. And it's no coincidence the key is missing now too. There's only one place we can figure he would go. To Olympus. To give the key you stole back to his master Zeus."

Pain slashed through Sera's chest, and her mouth fell open. She couldn't believe it. She didn't *want* to believe it. But even she couldn't deny it looked bad. He'd stormed out of this office only hours ago, seething with anger because the Argoleans were talking about destroying the key. She knew he didn't want to go back to the Underworld. She remembered the rage in his eyes when those Sirens had spotted him in this realm. If he was scared Zeus already knew he was here, if he thought his only chance for survival was to return the key to Zeus, would he do it?

Doubts, questions, fear vibrated in her chest and made her pulse race like wildfire. He'd told her he hated serving the gods. She knew that was true. But he'd also told her about his family, how the Titans had stripped the primordial deities of their human forms and cast them into nothingness, and she knew he'd do anything to prevent that from happening to him.

Voices echoed around her but she couldn't make herself listen to the words. Her head spun with memories of Erebus on Olympus, here in their suite, in that half-breed settlement just before they'd made love.

"If I had known about your past, things would have been different. I never would have let you be hunted. After all you've been through, agápi, *you deserve to be cherished and protected. Because you're special. Precious. You are the epitome of rare and irreplaceable and unique, and I won't ever let anyone hurt you again. I'll do whatever I have to do to keep you safe. I vow this to you here and now."*

Her stomach tightened as the words circled in her head. He hadn't said he loved her tonight, but she'd felt it. She'd felt every ounce of his love, and remembering his words from the half-breed colony, she knew they were true. He'd do anything to keep her safe. Even the very thing he'd told her he wouldn't do.

She glanced over the faces in front of her, over the Argonauts arguing about what they needed to do next. And in the center of her chest, her heart beat hard and fast, not from fear or heartache, but with love.

A love that told her exactly where Erebus had gone, and why he'd taken the key.

* * * *

The fiery river of Phlegethon snapped and sizzled as Erebus drew close under the cloak of darkness he'd cast. The heat was unbearable, the gasses and fumes from the river singeing the hairs on his forearms, the air so oppressive this deep in the Underworld he wanted to gag.

Swiping the sweat from his brow, he moved from sand to blackened rock. He'd told himself he'd never venture into the Underworld again. Vowed nothing and no one could lure him back. Yet here he was, all because of a female. One who'd awed him with her ability to love. One who'd mesmerized him with the strength and light inside her. One who'd made him feel alive...so alive he knew she was worth sacrificing everything for so she could live.

His fingers closed around the medallion in his palm as he stepped around a charred boulder. He knew in his heart this was the right thing to do; he just really hoped like hell those Argonauts were right when they'd said the prophecy wouldn't apply to an immortal. Because he didn't want to get stuck down here. He wanted to get back to Sera, wanted to slide between those sheets, wanted to show her just how much he loved her with his hands and mouth and body.

A chuckle echoed at his back. One that pushed thoughts of Sera from his mind and brought his feet to a stop.

But it was the darkness lifting all around him that shot his adrenaline sky high.

"Well, well, well," a familiar voice said in the eerie red light. "This is a surprise. A very good surprise."

Slowly, Erebus turned and stared into Hades's face. The god was just as tall as Erebus remembered—seven feet of muscle and brawn—and he had the same angular jaw line, the same dark hair, the same soulless black eyes Erebus remembered from over a hundred years ago when Hades had been his master. But then, being immortal, he never changed.

"I would say you're busted, but I think we both already know that, don't we?" Hades nodded at Erebus's closed fist. "You came to use my river, I see."

Erebus was careful not to show any kind of reaction. He knew how Hades fed off emotional outbursts. "Don't try to stop me."

"Oh, I wouldn't dare." Clasping his hands at his back, Hades moved to his right and glanced toward the swirling river of fire. "Destroy it. I've no use for the key to Argolea. I don't need it." His dark eyes sparked. "Because I'm not an Olympian."

Erebus had forgotten that. Although Hades was technically the eldest son of Krónos and Rhea and brother to the Olympians Zeus and Poseidon, he himself was not considered an Olympian—all because Zeus, the ruler of Olympus, had denied Hades a temple within his realm.

"Personally," Hades said while Erebus's thoughts spiraled with options on how to get out of this one, "I'm just thrilled you're back." He laughed, a dark, menacing sound. "I thought I was going to have to find a way to scheme you out from under Zeus's thumb, but here you are. In my realm, all by your own choosing." He lifted his dark brows and nodded toward Phlegethon. "Go on. Destroy it. I'll not try to stop you. I'm tickled you had the balls to screw Zeus over on this." He winked. "Though I'm sure screwing his Sirens was a hell of a lot more fun."

For the first time since he'd been caught, Erebus's pulse raced. Hades didn't know about Sera, did he? He was doing this to keep her safe. He had to be careful not to show emotion or let Hades know what she meant to him. The last thing he wanted was the god-king of the Underworld crossing into Argolea to hurt her.

Without answering, he turned toward the river.

"I just wish I could see Zeus's face when he realizes his precious key is gone for good." Hades chuckled again. "Oh, to be privy to *that* temper tantrum." He sighed. "I guess I'll just have to console myself with the knowledge that my favorite primordial deity is back in my realm, ready to serve me for all eternity."

Erebus's steps stopped feet from the fiery river.

"Let me guess: you didn't realize destroying the key would trap you in the Underworld? That's the best part." Hades snapped his fingers. "See, there's this prophecy Zeus made up when he ordered Hephaestus to forge the key. 'He who destroys the key will be imprisoned in the realm from whence it was destroyed.' That's here. *My* realm."

Erebus glanced over his shoulder. "I'm immortal, though. And I no longer serve you. I serve Zeus."

"Not from where I'm standing, you don't. From where I'm standing it looks like you've gone rogue. I suppose I could turn you over to my brother for punishment, if, that is, you decide not to serve me."

They both knew what kind of punishment Hades was referring to. Erebus's palms began to sweat.

"Regardless," Hades said, blinking away the terrorizing look. "Zeus didn't care if the destroyer of the key was mortal or immortal. And neither do I. Once you throw that key in Phlegethon, consider yourself done with Zeus for good. You'll be mine for all eternity. So get on with it. Throw it in the fire so we can move on to more important things."

Hades's soulless black eyes burned with an unnatural light, and as Erebus looked back at the fiery river, the totality of his life stretched before him.

He'd never fought, not even at the beginning when his family had been dissolved into nothing and he'd been handed over to Krónos. He'd served one god after another, for thousands of years, never challenging their rules, never questioning the things they ordered him to do, no matter how mundane or vile. He hadn't even thought to defy Zeus and the Sirens when they'd taken Sera from him on Olympus and forced him to train yet another faceless recruit in the ways of seduction.

He opened his palm. Stared down at the medallion and the imprint of Heracles. There weren't many things in his life he could be proud of, but this...protecting Sera from Zeus's retaliation and preventing another realm from the destruction her realm had faced...this he could be proud of. *This* was worth the sacrifice. She was worth sacrificing everything for.

His pulse slowed. His fingers curled around the medallion. It was warm not from the power inside it, but from him. From what was inside him.

Closing his eyes, he drew a deep breath and tugged his arm back. Before he could hurl it into the fiery river, a growl echoed at his back, followed by Hades's hissed words.

"No-good meddling Argonauts."

Erebus glanced over his shoulder, his eyes growing wide when he spotted three, four—no, seven Argonauts fanning out around Hades.

"Nice try, Guardians," Hades sneered. "But the god of darkness is mine. And none of you are strong enough to challenge me for him."

"None of them might be," a voice called from the back of the group. "But we are."

Two men—no, not men, gods, Erebus realized—stepped in front of the group. One was older, with dark hair and fine lines fanning out from his eyes. Strength radiated from his strong body and an aura that marked him as a Titan. The Titan Prometheus, Erebus realized with wide eyes.

His gaze strayed to the other god, the one leveling his amber gaze on Hades and smirking. Power emanated from his muscular body as well, but this power was directly linked to Krónos. Even across the distance Erebus could feel that power snapping and sizzling and just waiting to be freed, and in a rush Erebus remembered what Cerek had told him about the other god in Argolea when they'd been on their tour.

"Surprise, *adelfos,*" Nick said.

For a moment, Hades stood completely still, then another growl built in his throat, one that grew in strength and intensity until it was a roar all across the land. He lifted his hands out wide. The ground shook. Rocks split apart, and the dirt cracked opened, shooting steam high in the air.

The shaking knocked Erebus off his feet. The medallion flew from his hand and ricocheted off a boulder. He scrambled up just as a seven-foot, ugly-ass daemon that looked like something straight out of a nightmare, crawled out of the hole and bared razor-sharp fangs at the Argonauts.

"Devour them," Hades cried.

All around the Argonauts, daemons climbed out of the ground and charged.

A massive battle broke out. Weapons clanged and fists slammed into bone. Voices echoed through the eerie red light and over the barren land, and Erebus knew he needed to join them, to fight with the Argonauts, but he had to find the key first. He had to destroy it before one of those daemons decided to keep it or Hades realized he could trade it to Zeus for something more valuable.

He streaked across the ground, kicking up blackened dirt and rocks, searching for the shiny medallion in the dead soil. Motherfucker, why couldn't he find it? It had hit the ground right here. It had to be close. He dropped to his knees, swept his hands through the dirt and rocks, searching. Knew it had to be somewhere—

There! From the corner of his eye he spotted a shiny object catching the firelight from the river. He skidded across the ground and scooped it up. Dirt and grime stuck to his skin, but when he brushed his finger across the surface of the object, the dull image of Heracles shone up at him.

He rushed back to the edge of the fiery river, drew his arm back, ready to throw it into the fires. Just before he could release it, a burning pain stabbed into his thigh and knocked him off his feet.

The medallion flew from his grip and smacked against the dirt. He hit the ground on his butt and grunted from the impact. His hands flew to his leg, and in total disbelief he focused on the arrow sticking out of his thigh, his blood gushing around the wound to stain his jeans a deep shade of red.

Footsteps sounded close. He lifted his head to see who had hit him, and his eyes widened when he saw Sera—*his* Sera, decked out in the same tight black fighting gear she'd worn on Olympus with the Sirens—stalking toward him with a bow in one hand.

"I'm sorry." She knelt at his side and pressed a kiss to his lips. "But I can't let you do this."

Confused, he reached for her, but she moved away before he could grasp her. Her slender fingers scooped the medallion from the ground.

He didn't know what was happening. He didn't know why she was here. He didn't know—

Every thought came to a shuddering stop when she stepped toward Phlegethon and drew her arm back.

"No! Sera!" He struggled to his feet. Tried to go after her. Tried to stop her. The second he put weight on his injured leg, though, his leg buckled and he hit the dirt face first.

He sputtered, coughed, spit the grimy black dirt from his mouth and lifted his head. Then watched in horror as she swept her arm forward and released, sending the medallion flying toward the fiery river.

"No..." Pain sliced through his chest. A blinding, burning pain that drowned out everything else—the sounds of the battle at his back, the burn of the arrow stabbing into his leg, the all-powerful gods wrestling for cosmic power only yards away. All he could see and hear and feel was what she'd just done.

His vision blurred as she drew close. He struggled to his side, pushed himself to sitting, and grabbed hold of her as soon as she knelt close. His dirty hands streaked up into her soft hair, and he pulled her mouth down to his, kissing her again and again, afraid to let go of her. Afraid of what would happen next.

"What did you do? How could you do that?" He pulled her onto his lap, not caring about his leg or what was happening around them. Not caring about anything but her. He kissed her again. "You stupid nymph. Why would you do that? Don't you know what that means?"

Her lips curled against his. "I know exactly what it means."

She drew away, and though he wanted only to pull her back, she pushed to her feet where he couldn't grab her.

"Do you want me to tell him, Hades? Or would you like to be the one to enlighten him?"

Erebus stared up at her gorgeous face, confused by the words she was speaking. To his left, he heard Hades growl, "Scheming Argonauts."

Blinking, Erebus looked across the barren ground toward the Argonauts and the two gods surrounding Hades. All around them, dead daemons littered the ground.

"Enlighten me about what?" Erebus asked, more confused than ever. "What the fuck is going on?"

Sera knelt at his side and placed a warm hand on his shoulder. "The prophecy said '*He* who destroys the key shall be imprisoned in the realm from whence it was destroyed.'

She didn't elaborate, which only frustrated him more. "Yeah? So, we already know that." He reached for her hand. "I'm not letting him keep you."

She smiled and squeezed his fingers. "You don't have to, because he can't keep me. Isn't that right, Hades?"

Her gaze lifted. To Erebus's left, Hades growled low in his throat but didn't make any move to imprison her.

"I don't understand," Erebus said.

Sera ran her fingers over his jaw and grinned. "I am not a he."

Erebus stared into her gentle eyes, still trying to make sense of everything, when one of the Argonauts called out, "Duh. She's a *she*, dude. And a pretty clever one at that."

Holy shit. Hope filled Erebus's chest like sweet, sweet air. "So he can't—"

"Nope." Sera's smile widened. "I told you you were mine, silly god. I meant it."

He sucked in a breath as she leaned down to kiss him, and when their lips met, he felt the love she'd showered on him push aside all the emptiness inside him.

"You are defeated for now, Hades," Nick declared in a loud voice, causing both Erebus and Sera to look toward the god. "Tuck your tail and run back to your lair before Prometheus and I decide to punish you for this little stunt."

A growl echoed, then in a swirl of black smoke, Hades poofed away from Phlegethon.

Drawing Erebus's face back to hers, Sera gently kissed his lips. "Sorry about shooting you in the leg. It was the only way I could stop you from throwing the medallion in the river." Her eyes narrowed. "But running out on me in the middle of the night was not a smart thing to do."

"What can I say? I learned all about running from this really hot nymph I was once assigned to for seduction training."

Her lips curled. "Good answer, *omorfos*."

He tugged her down onto his lap and held her close. "I love you, *agápi*."

"I know. Which is the only reason I'm not going to make you suffer. Beg, moan, cry out in pleasure...absolutely, yes. But no more suffering. Never again."

He smiled, thinking that sounded just about perfect right now.

Someone cleared his throat. From the group to their left, another voice said, "Um, any chance you two can do that back in Argolea, away from torment and death and the ruler of this realm who would be more than happy to come back here and try to kick our asses again?"

Sera smiled.

Erebus chuckled.

Neither looked toward the group.

"What do you say, *agápi*? Want to start forever with me in the blessed realm of the heroes?"

She bit her lip in a nervous, sexy, adorable way. "Your forever and my forever aren't exactly the same. I'm not immortal like you. I may live for hundreds of years, but eventually, my time will come."

His heart squeezed tight because he didn't want to think about that. He searched her eyes, searching for something to say, for a solution he couldn't find.

"Not exactly," someone said before he could come up with anything.

Sera glanced over her shoulder where Nick was walking toward them.

"What do you mean?" Erebus asked, looking toward the god.

"My mate is Argolean," Nick answered, stopping not far away. "Her lifespan is the same as an Atlantean. And Gryphon's Argolean, whereas his mate is immortal. The Fates aren't going to let any of us suffer alone. When the mortal mate's time come, the choice to stay or go with them to the other side rests with the immortal mate."

Erebus glanced at Sera then back to Nick. "I don't see a Fate here offering us that option."

"Pretty sure the Fates steer clear of the Underworld." Nick winked. "But trust me, after the sacrifice you both made not just for Argolea but for the entire world, once we get home, I'm fairly certain one will be waiting for you. And if she's not, I'll find her and make sure she offers you the same deal. You deserve it after everything you've done us."

Hope bloomed inside Erebus, and he looked back to Sera. "*Agápi*? What do you think about forever in the realm of the heroes now?"

A wide smile spread across Sera's gorgeous face. "I think it sounds perfect. But only if you'll be my hero."

"Baby, I'm the only hero you'll ever need."

She slid her arms around his neck and lifted her mouth to his. "Damn right you are."

* * * *

Also from 1001 Dark Nights and Elisabeth Naughton, discover Surrender.

ETERNAL GUARDIANS LEXICON

adelfos. Brother

agapi. Term of endearment; my love.

Argolea. Realm established by Zeus for the blessed heroes and their descendants

Argonauts. Eternal guardian warriors who protect Argolea. In every generation, one from the original seven bloodlines (Heracles, Achilles, Jason, Odysseus, Perseus, Theseus, and Bellerophon) is chosen to continue the guardian tradition.

Council of Elders. Lords of Argolea who advise the king

daemons. Beasts who were once human, recruited from the Fields of Asphodel (purgatory) by Atalanta to join her army.

Fates. Three goddesses who control the thread of life for all mortals from birth until death

Isles of the Blessed. Heaven

Misos. Half-human/half-Argolean race that lives hidden among humans

Olympians. Current ruling gods of the Greek pantheon, led by Zeus; meddle in human life

omorfos. Handsome

oraios. Beautiful

Orb of Krónos. Four-chambered disk that, when filled with the four classic elements—earth, wind, fire, and water—has the power to release the Titans from Tartarus parazonium. Ancient Greek sword all Argonauts carry.

Siren Order. Zeus's elite band of personal warriors. Commanded by Athena

skata. Swearword

Tartarus. Realm of the Underworld similar to hell

therillium. Invisibility ore, sought after by all the gods

Titans. The ruling gods before the Olympians

Titanomachy. The war between the Olympians and the Titans, which resulted in Krónos being cast into Tartarus and the Olympians becoming the ruling gods.

Sign up for the 1001 Dark Nights Newsletter
and be entered to win a Tiffany Key necklace.

There's a contest every month!

Go to www.1001DarkNights.com to subscribe.

As a bonus, all subscribers will receive a free copy of
Discovery Bundle Three
Featuring stories by
Sidney Bristol, Darcy Burke, T. Gephart
Stacey Kennedy, Adriana Locke
JB Salsbury, and Erika Wilde

ABOUT ELISABETH NAUGHTON

Before topping multiple bestseller lists--including those of the New York Times, USA Today, and the Wall Street Journal--Elisabeth Naughton taught middle school science. A voracious reader, she soon discovered she had a knack for creating stories with a chemistry of their own. The spark turned into a flame, and Naughton now writes full-time. Besides topping bestseller lists, her books have been nominated for some of the industry's most prestigious awards, such as the RITA® and Golden Heart Awards from Romance Writers of America, the Australian Romance Reader Awards, and the Golden Leaf Award. When not dreaming up new stories, Naughton can be found spending time with her husband and three children in their western Oregon home. Learn more at www.ElisabethNaughton.com.

DISCOVER MORE ELISABETH NAUGHTON

SURRENDER
A House of Sin Novella
By Elisabeth Naughton

Coming June 12, 2018

From New York Times and USA Today bestselling author Elisabeth Naughton comes a new story in her House of Sin series…

The leaders of my House want her dead.

The men I've secretly aligned myself with want her punished for screwing up their coup.

I've been sent by both to deal with her, but one look at the feisty redhead and I've got plans of my own.

Before I carry out anyone else's orders, she's going to give me what I want. And only when I'm satisfied will I decide if she lives or dies.

Depending, of course, on just how easily she surrenders...

Every 1001 Dark Nights novella is a standalone story. For new readers, it's an introduction to an author's world. And for fans, it's a bonus book in the author's series. We hope you'll enjoy each one as much as we do.

DISCOVER 1001 DARK NIGHTS COLLECTION FIVE

Go to www.1001DarkNights.com for more information

BLAZE ERUPTING by Rebecca Zanetti
Scorpius Syndrome/A Brigade Novella

ROUGH RIDE by Kristen Ashley
A Chaos Novella

HAWKYN by Larissa Ione
A Demonica Underworld Novella

RIDE DIRTY by Laura Kaye
A Raven Riders Novella

ROME'S CHANCE by Joanna Wylde
A Reapers MC Novella

THE MARRIAGE ARRANGEMENT by Jennifer Probst
A Marriage to a Billionaire Novella

SURRENDER by Elisabeth Naughton
A House of Sin Novella

INKED NIGHT by Carrie Ann Ryan
A Montgomery Ink Novella

ENVY by Rachel Van Dyken
An Eagle Elite Novella

PROTECTED by Lexi Blake
A Masters and Mercenaries Novella

THE PRINCE by Jennifer L. Armentrout
A Wicked Novella

PLEASE ME by J. Kenner
A Stark Ever After Novella

WOUND TIGHT by Lorelei James
A Rough Riders/Blacktop Cowboys Novella®

STRONG by Kylie Scott
A Stage Dive Novella

DRAGON NIGHT by Donna Grant
A Dark Kings Novella

TEMPTING BROOKE by Kristen Proby
A Big Sky Novella

HAUNTED BE THE HOLIDAYS by Heather Graham
A Krewe of Hunters Novella

CONTROL by K. Bromberg
An Everyday Heroes Novella

HUNKY HEARTBREAKER by Kendall Ryan
A Whiskey Kisses Novella

THE DARKEST CAPTIVE by Gena Showalter
A Lords of the Underworld Novella

DISCOVER 1001 DARK NIGHTS COLLECTION ONE

Go to www.1001DarkNights.com for more information

FOREVER WICKED by Shayla Black
CRIMSON TWILIGHT by Heather Graham
CAPTURED IN SURRENDER by Liliana Hart
SILENT BITE: A SCANGUARDS WEDDING by Tina Folsom
DUNGEON GAMES by Lexi Blake
AZAGOTH by Larissa Ione
NEED YOU NOW by Lisa Renee Jones
SHOW ME, BABY by Cherise Sinclair
ROPED IN by Lorelei James
TEMPTED BY MIDNIGHT by Lara Adrian
THE FLAME by Christopher Rice
CARESS OF DARKNESS by Julie Kenner

Also from 1001 Dark Nights:

TAME ME by J. Kenner

DISCOVER 1001 DARK NIGHTS COLLECTION TWO

Go to www.1001DarkNights.com for more information

WICKED WOLF by Carrie Ann Ryan
WHEN IRISH EYES ARE HAUNTING by Heather Graham
EASY WITH YOU by Kristen Proby
MASTER OF FREEDOM by Cherise Sinclair
CARESS OF PLEASURE by Julie Kenner
ADORED by Lexi Blake
HADES by Larissa Ione
RAVAGED by Elisabeth Naughton
DREAM OF YOU by Jennifer L. Armentrout
STRIPPED DOWN by Lorelei James
RAGE/KILLIAN by Alexandra Ivy/Laura Wright
DRAGON KING by Donna Grant
PURE WICKED by Shayla Black
HARD AS STEEL by Laura Kaye
STROKE OF MIDNIGHT by Lara Adrian
ALL HALLOWS EVE by Heather Graham
KISS THE FLAME by Christopher Rice
DARING HER LOVE by Melissa Foster
TEASED by Rebecca Zanetti
THE PROMISE OF SURRENDER by Liliana Hart

Also from 1001 Dark Nights:

THE SURRENDER GATE By Christopher Rice
SERVICING THE TARGET By Cherise Sinclair

DISCOVER 1001 DARK NIGHTS COLLECTION THREE

Go to www.1001DarkNights.com for more information

HIDDEN INK by Carrie Ann Ryan
BLOOD ON THE BAYOU by Heather Graham
SEARCHING FOR MINE by Jennifer Probst
DANCE OF DESIRE by Christopher Rice
ROUGH RHYTHM by Tessa Bailey
DEVOTED by Lexi Blake
Z by Larissa Ione
FALLING UNDER YOU by Laurelin Paige
EASY FOR KEEPS by Kristen Proby
UNCHAINED by Elisabeth Naughton
HARD TO SERVE by Laura Kaye
DRAGON FEVER by Donna Grant
KAYDEN/SIMON by Alexandra Ivy/Laura Wright
STRUNG UP by Lorelei James
MIDNIGHT UNTAMED by Lara Adrian
TRICKED by Rebecca Zanetti
DIRTY WICKED by Shayla Black
THE ONLY ONE by Lauren Blakely
SWEET SURRENDER by Liliana Hart

DISCOVER 1001 DARK NIGHTS COLLECTION FOUR

Go to www.1001DarkNights.com for more information

ROCK CHICK REAWAKENING by Kristen Ashley
ADORING INK by Carrie Ann Ryan
SWEET RIVALRY by K. Bromberg
SHADE'S LADY by Joanna Wylde
RAZR by Larissa Ione
ARRANGED by Lexi Blake
TANGLED by Rebecca Zanetti
HOLD ME by J. Kenner
SOMEHOW, SOME WAY by Jennifer Probst
TOO CLOSE TO CALL by Tessa Bailey
HUNTED by Elisabeth Naughton
EYES ON YOU by Laura Kaye
BLADE by Alexandra Ivy/Laura Wright
DRAGON BURN by Donna Grant
TRIPPED OUT by Lorelei James
STUD FINDER by Lauren Blakely
MIDNIGHT UNLEASHED by Lara Adrian
HALLOW BE THE HAUNT by Heather Graham
PRINCE ROMAN by CD Reiss
THE BED MATE by Kendall Ryan
DIRTY FILTHY FIX by Laurelin Paige
NO RESERVATIONS by Kristen Proby
DAWN OF SURRENDER by Liliana Hart

Also from 1001 Dark Nights:

TEMPT ME by J. Kenner

ON BEHALF OF 1001 DARK NIGHTS,

Liz Berry and M.J. Rose would like to thank ~

Steve Berry
Doug Scofield
Kim Guidroz
Jillian Stein
InkSlinger PR
Dan Slater
Asha Hossain
Chris Graham
Fedora Chen
Kasi Alexander
Jessica Johns
Dylan Stockton
Richard Blake
BookTrib After Dark
and Simon Lipskar

CPSIA information can be obtained
at www.ICGtesting.com
Printed in the USA
LVOW11s2310080418
572690LV00006B/541/P

9 781948 050456